Jude Deveraux

Twin of Fire

POCKET BOOKS
New York   London   Toronto   Sydney

This book is a work of historical fiction. Names, characters, places and incidents relating to non-historical figures are either the product of the author's imagination or are used fictitiously. Any resemblance of such non-historical incidents, places or figures to actual events or locales or persons, living or dead, is entirely coincidental.

An Original Publication of POCKET BOOKS

POCKET BOOKS, a division of Simon & Schuster, Inc.
1230 Avenue of the Americas, New York, NY 10020

Copyright © 1985 by Deveraux Inc.
Front cover illustration by Shasti O'Leary-Soudant

ISBN: 13: 978-0-671-72299-9

First Pocket Books printing August 1985

18 17 16 15 14 13 12 11 10 9

POCKET and colophon are registered trademarks of Simon & Schuster, Inc.

For information regarding special discounts for bulk purchases, please contact Simon & Schuster Special Sales at 1-800-456-6798 or business@simonandschuster.com

Printed in the U.S.A.

Critical acclaim for Jude Deveraux's marvelous companion novels
TWIN OF ICE
and
TWIN OF FIRE

"A new innovation from a versatile author."
—*Affaire de Coeur*

"Sophisticated and ambitious. . . . No reader could finish *Twin of Ice* without wanting to pick up the sequel."
—*Chicago Sun-Times*

"A delightful . . . rollicking story."
—*Denver Rocky Mountain News*

. . . and her sparkling new bestseller

THE SUMMERHOUSE

"Deveraux is at the top of her game here as she uses the time-travel motif that was so popular in *A Knight in Shining Armor*, successfully updating it with a female buddy twist that will make fans smile."
—*Booklist*

"Entertaining summer reading."
—*The Port St. Lucie News* (FL)

"Leslie, Madison, and Ellie wiggle quickly into readers' hearts as their tales are unfolded. . . . [A] wonderful, heart-warming tale of friendship and love."
—America Online Romance Fiction Forum

Books by Jude Deveraux

THANK YOU

I'd like to thank the two editors I had on these books, Kate Duffy and Linda Marrow. They read rewrite after rewrite, some of them in my microscopic handwriting, and they listened to me for hours on end. My characters didn't sneeze that they didn't discuss it with me and they never once lost patience.

Thank you to all the Colorado librarians. Heaven is peopled with Colorado librarians.

I'd like to thank Dr. Tom Dilday and Dr. Curtis Boyd for talking to me about repairing broken bodies. And Annette Swanberg for going out of her way to take me to the Huntington house for one more look.

And I'd like to thank Glenna Boyd for taking me for walks in beautiful places, then listening to me for hours blabbing about dynamite and four-horse-team versus six-horse-team wagons and The Sisterhood. I will try to look at the scenery in the future.

I'd also like to thank Ron Busch, who believed that I could make it and brought me into the family of the best publishing house in the world.

AUTHOR'S NOTE

Until I started researching my novels, I had the idea that, until after WWI, men and women were content with their roles in life. I thought women sweetly submitted to their husbands and husbands were happy with their docile women.

But when I delved into the medieval period, I was shocked to find out that, even in the fourteenth century, women were writing very modern sounding books on the oppression of women by men. And as for the men, there's a joke that made the rounds long before Shakespeare used it that said a prize would be given to any man who could command his wife to follow him and she would obey with no questions asked or excuses as to why she couldn't go. As the story goes, the prize is still waiting to be handed out.

If I was shocked in my medieval research, there's no word to describe what I discovered while looking into the nineteenth century. I have read a great deal of twentieth century feminist writings, but nothing today is more militant than that written by nineteenth century women. They were fighting exactly the same battles: for equal pay, against rape and wife beating, to make laws so men could not kidnap their children from their ex-wives, and for hundreds of other reforms. The big difference seemed to be that for every book a woman wrote about sexual equality, a man wrote a book stating that if women didn't get back into the kitchen, they were going to destroy the world. Now, a hundred years later, it looks as though women are still fighting, while men have almost given up. Too bad, because, as I think it's obvious from my writing, I just love a good rousing argument.

Twin of Fire

Prologue

Philadelphia, Pennsylvania
April 1892

"Surprise!" eleven people shouted as Blair Chandler entered the dining room of her Uncle Henry's house. She was a pretty young woman, with dark brown hair highlighted with red glints, wide-set blue-green eyes, a straight, aristocratic nose and a small, perfectly shaped mouth.

Blair paused for a moment, blinking back tears of happiness, as she looked at the people in front of her. There were her aunt and uncle, Alan beside them, watching her with love in his eyes, and surrounding him were her fellow medical students—one woman and seven men. As they beamed at her with pleasure, standing behind the table heaped with gifts, she couldn't seem to remember the past few years of struggle to graduate and earn her medical degree.

Aunt Flo, with the grace of a young girl, hurried forward. "Don't just stand there, dear. Everyone is dying to see your gifts."

"This one first," Uncle Henry said, holding out a large package.

Blair thought she knew what was in the box, but she was afraid to hope. When she tore away the wrapping and saw the leather case with the clean, new medical instruments, she sat down heavily in the chair behind her, unable to speak. All she

1

could do was run a finger over the brass plate on the bag. It read: Dr. B. Chandler, M.D.

Alan broke the awkward silence. "Is this the woman who put the rotten eggs in the surgeon instructor's wardrobe? Is this the woman who stood up to the entire Philadelphia Board of Hospitals?" Bending, he put his lips close to her ear. "Is this the woman who placed first in the exams at St. Joseph's and became the first woman to intern on their staff?"

It was a moment before Blair could react. "Me?" she whispered, looking up at him, her mouth open in disbelief.

"You won your internship," Aunt Flo said, her face beaming. "You're to start in July, just as soon as you return from your sister's wedding."

Blair was looking from one person to the other. She had tried her best for St. Joseph's, had even hired a tutor to help her prepare for the tests, but she'd been told that this city hospital, as opposed to a women's clinic, did not accept female physicians.

She turned to her Uncle Henry. "You've had a hand in this, haven't you?"

Henry swelled his big barrel chest with pride. "I merely made a wager that if my niece didn't score higher than anyone ever had on their test, they didn't have to give her a position. In fact, I told them you'd even consider giving up medicine and staying home to take care of Alan. I don't think they could resist the chance to see a lady doctor brought to her senses."

For a moment, Blair felt a little weak. She'd had no idea that so much had been riding on that treacherous three-day test.

"You made it," Alan laughed. "Although I'm not sure I like being the consolation prize." He put his hand on her shoulder. "Congratulations, sweetheart. I know how much you wanted this."

Aunt Flo handed her a letter that gave confirmation that she had indeed been accepted at St. Joseph's Hospital for internship. Blair clutched the paper to her breast and looked at the people around her. Right now, she thought, my entire life is stretching before me—and it is perfect. I have family, friends; I am going to be allowed to train at one of the finest hospitals in the U.S.; and I have Alan, the man I love.

She rubbed her cheek against Alan's hand as she looked at the shiny medical instruments. She was going to realize her lifelong dream of becoming a doctor and marry this kind, loving man.

All that remained was for her to return to Chandler, Colorado, and attend the marriage of her twin sister. Blair was looking forward to seeing her again after all these years, and to the two of them sharing their happiness about the men they'd chosen, about the lives they'd chosen for themselves.

And while she was in Chandler, Alan was going to visit and meet her mother and sister. They would formally announce their engagement then, the wedding to be held after both she and Alan finished their internships.

Blair smiled up at her friends, wanting to share her happiness with everyone. Just another month, and all that she'd worked for would begin.

Chapter 1

Chandler, Colorado
May 1892

Blair Chandler was standing quietly in the ornate front parlor of the Chandler house, amid heavy, dark, carved furniture dressed with little lace doilies. It didn't matter that her mother had remarried many years ago and her new husband, Duncan Gates, had ended up paying for the house, the townspeople still thought of it as having belonged to William Houston Chandler—the man who'd designed it, had it built, and died before he could make the first payment.

Blair kept her eyes downcast, covering their blue-green light that was flashing now in anger. She'd been in her stepfather's house for a week, and all the coarse-looking little man did was yell at her.

To all the world, she looked to be a respectful young woman, standing there in her proper white blouse and dark cord skirt, most of the voluptuousness of her hourglass figure concealed in folds of cloth. And her face held such a quiet, gentle prettiness that no one would have guessed the spirit beneath. But anyone who was around Blair for long knew that she could hold her own in an argument.

Which was why Duncan Gates didn't lose a minute in telling her how to become a "proper" lady. And his idea of what a lady was did not include a young woman who had been trained to be a doctor and was especially good at gunshot wounds. He couldn't appreciate the fact that Blair's sewing ability worked just as well on a perforated intestine as it did on a sampler.

He ranted and raved, as he'd done for a week, and Blair took it until she could stand no more, then she began to give him back some of his own. Unfortunately, that was usually when Blair's mother or sister stepped in and prevented further words from being spoken. It hadn't taken Blair long to learn that Mr. Gates ruled his household, and the women in it, with an iron fist. He was allowed to say what he pleased, but no woman was allowed to thwart him in any way.

"I'm hoping that you will come to your senses and give up this medicine nonsense," Gates was shouting at her now. "A lady belongs in the home and, as Dr. Clark has proven, when a woman uses her brain, her female functions suffer."

Blair gave a great sigh, barely glancing at the worn pamphlet that Mr. Gates held aloft. Dr. Clark's booklet had sold hundreds of thousands of copies and had done an enormous amount of damage to the furthering of education for women. "Dr. Clark did not prove anything," she said tiredly. "He said he'd examined a flat-chested fourteen-year-old female student and, from that one examination, he concluded that if women used their brains, their reproductive systems would suffer. I don't consider that conclusive evidence at all."

Mr. Gates's face began to turn red. "I'll not have language like that in my house. You may think that because you call yourself a doctor you have a right to indecent behavior, but not in my house."

The man was beginning to pass what Blair could tolerate. "Since when is this *your* house? My father—."

At that moment, Blair's sister, Houston, stepped into the room and put herself between them, giving Blair a look of anguish. "Isn't it time for dinner? Perhaps we should go in," Houston said in that cool, reserved voice of hers—a voice that Blair was beginning to hate.

Blair took her place at the big mahogany table and all

through dinner answered Mr. Gates's nasty-tempered questions, but her mind was on her sister.

Blair had looked forward to returning to Chandler, to seeing her sister and mother, to again seeing her childhood playmates. It had been five years since she'd been back and, the last time, she'd been seventeen, preparing to enter medical school and bursting with enthusiasm about her new studies. Perhaps she'd been too wrapped up in her own thoughts to really see the atmosphere in which her mother and sister were living.

But, this time, she'd felt the oppression as soon as she got off the train. Houston had met her, and Blair was sure that she'd never in her life seen a more perfect specimen of a rigid, frigid, unbending woman. She looked like a perfectly formed woman who just happened to be made out of ice.

There were no exuberant huggings at the train station, nor were there exchanges of gossip as they were driven back to the Chandler house. Blair tried to talk to her sister, but she only received that cool, remote stare. Even the name of Leander, Houston's fiancé, brought no warmth to Houston's demeanor.

Half of the short trip was made in silence, Blair clutching her new surgical bag, afraid to let it out of her hands, while they drove through Chandler.

The town had changed a great deal in the five years since Blair had seen it. There was a feeling of newness about the place, that things were building and growing. The western town was so different from cities and towns in the East, where traditions were already established.

The buildings, with their false fronts, a style someone had called Western Victorian, were either new or under construction. Chandler had been merely a pretty piece of land with a magnificent amount of surface coal when William Chandler had arrived. There'd been no railroad, no town center, no name for the few stores that were serving the scattered ranchers in the area. Bill Chandler soon remedied that.

When they pulled into the drive of the Chandler house—or mansion, as the townspeople liked to call it—Blair smiled up at the ornate three-story building with pleasure. Her mother's garden was green and lush and she could smell the roses.

There were steps from the street up to the house now because the hill in the street had been levelled for the new horse-drawn trolley cars, but it hadn't changed much otherwise. She walked across the deep porch that wrapped around the house and went through one of the two front doors.

It didn't take Blair ten minutes inside the Chandler house to see what had taken all the spirit out of Houston.

Standing inside the doorway was a man with a solidness that any self-respecting boulder would envy—and the look on his face matched the shape of him.

Blair had been twelve years old when she'd left Chandler to go to Pennsylvania to live with her aunt and uncle so she could study medicine. And in the intervening years, she'd forgotten just what her stepfather was like. Even as Blair smiled at him and offered him her hand, he started telling her what a bad woman she was and that she wouldn't be allowed to practice her witchcraft doctoring under his roof.

Bewildered, Blair had looked at her mother in disbelief. Opal Gates was thinner, her movements slower than Blair remembered, and before Blair could reply to Mr. Gates's remarks, Opal stepped forward, hugged her daughter briefly, and led her upstairs.

For three days, Blair said very little. She became a bystander who watched. And what she saw frightened her.

The sister she remembered, the one who laughed and played, the one who used to delight in the twin game of trading places with her sister, and causing trouble, was gone—or buried so deep that no one could find her now.

The Houston who used to organize games, the Houston who was always so creative, Houston the actress, was now supplanted by a steel-backed woman who owned more dresses than the rest of the town put together. It seemed that all of Houston's creativity had been rechannelled into the choosing of one stunning dress after another.

On her second day in Chandler, Blair found out from a friend something that gave her hope that her sister's life wasn't completely without purpose. Every Wednesday, Houston dressed as a fat old woman and drove a four-horse wagon loaded with food into the coal camps that surrounded Chandler. This was quite dangerous since the camps were

7

locked and guarded to prevent the infiltration of unionists. If Houston had been caught delivering illegal goods to the miners' wives—goods not bought at the company store—she could be prosecuted, that is, if the guards didn't shoot her first.

But on the third day, Blair gave up the little hope she'd found, because on the third day she re-met Leander Westfield.

When the Westfields had moved to Chandler, the twins had been six-year-olds, and Blair had been confined to her room with a broken arm and so had missed meeting the twelve-year-old Leander and his five-year-old sister. But Blair'd heard all about him from Houston. Disobeying her mother, Houston had slipped into Blair's room to tell her that she'd met the man she was going to marry.

Blair had sat there and listened with wide-eyed attention. Houston had always known what she wanted, always seemed like an adult.

"He's just the sort of man I like. He's quiet, intelligent, very handsome, and he plans to be a doctor. I shall find out what a doctor's wife needs to know."

If possible, Blair's eyes had opened wider. "Has he asked you to marry him?" she'd whispered.

"No," Houston had answered, pulling off her still-clean white gloves—if Blair'd had on those gloves for even thirty minutes, they'd have been soiled black. "Men as young as Leander don't think of marriage, but we women have to. I have made up my mind. I shall marry Leander Westfield as soon as he finishes medical school. This is subject to your approval, of course. I couldn't marry someone you didn't like."

Blair had been honored that Houston had given her this power, and she'd taken her responsibility seriously. She'd been a little disappointed when she'd met Leander and found that he wasn't a man at all but just a tall, slim, good-looking boy who rarely said anything. Blair had always liked the boys who ran and threw rocks and taught her how to whistle with two fingers in her mouth. After a few initial unpleasant encounters with him, she had begun to see what people liked about Lee after Jimmy Summers had fallen out of a tree and broken his leg. None of the other children had known what to do and just stood back and watched Jimmy cry in pain, but Lee had taken over and sent someone for the doctor and someone else for Mrs. Summers. Blair had been quite impressed with him and, as she'd turned toward Houston, Houston had nodded her head once, as if to say that this episode had reaffirmed her decision to become Mrs. Leander Westfield.

Blair was willing to admit that Leander did have a few good qualities about him, but she'd never really liked him. He was too sure of himself, too smug . . . too perfect. Of course, she had never told Houston she didn't like him and, too, she had thought maybe he'd change, become more human as he grew older. He didn't.

A few days earlier, Lee had come to pick up Houston to take her to an afternoon tea and, since Opal was out and Mr. Gates at work, Blair had a chance to talk to Lee while Houston finished dressing—it usually took her an eternity to get fastened into one of those lace and silk concoctions she always wore.

Blair thought that they'd have a common ground for conversation since they were both doctors, and that he'd no longer antagonize her as he had at one time.

"I'll be interning at St. Joseph's Hospital in Philadelphia next month," she began, when they were seated in the front parlor. "It's supposed to be an excellent hospital."

Leander just looked at her with that piercing look of his that he'd had since he was a child. It was impossible to tell what he was thinking.

"I wonder," she continued, "do you think it would be possible for me to make rounds with you at the Chandler Infirmary? Maybe you could give me some pointers that I could use when I start training next month."

Lee took an infuriatingly long time to answer. "I don't think that would be advisable," was all he said at last.

"I thought that between doctors . . ."

"I'm not sure the Board of Directors would consider a woman a fully qualified doctor. I might be able to get you into the women's hospital."

In school, they'd been warned that they would be treated

like this at times. "It may surprise you to know that I plan to specialize in abdominal surgery. Not all female doctors want to become glorified midwives."

Leander arched one brow and looked her up and down in an annoying way that made Blair wonder if all the men in Chandler believed that women were idiots who shouldn't be let out of the house.

Still, she was determined not to judge him. After all, they were adults now and childhood animosities should be put aside. If he was the man Houston wanted, then she should have him—Blair didn't have to live with him.

But days later, after she'd spent time with her sister, she began to question the idea of a marriage between Leander and Houston, because, if anything, Houston was even more rigid when Lee was present. The two of them rarely spoke to each other, nor was there any of the putting of heads together and giggling as there was between most engaged couples. They were certainly not like she and Alan, Blair thought.

And tonight, at dinner, things seemed to come to a head. Blair was tired from the constant harassment of Gates, and she was sick at seeing her sister in this horrible atmosphere of oppression. When Gates kept after Blair, she exploded and told him that he had ruined Houston's life, but he wasn't going to ruin hers, too.

Blair regretted having said that as soon as it was out and she meant to apologize, but just then his royal highness, Leander Westfield, entered and everyone looked up at him as if a demigod had come into the room. Blair had a vision of Houston as a virgin sacrifice to be given to this cold, unfeeling man. And when Leander dared to call Houston his bride, as if he already owned her, Blair could stand no more and ran from the table in tears.

She had no idea how long she had been crying before her mother came to her, held her in her arms and cradled her like a child.

"Tell me what's wrong," Opal whispered, stroking her daughter's hair. "Are you so very homesick? I know Mr. Gates hasn't made your visit pleasant, but he means well. He wants you to have a home and children and he's afraid that, if you're a doctor, no man will have you. You won't have to stay with us much longer, then you can go back to Henry and Flo and start work at the hospital."

Her mother's words made Blair cry harder. "It's not me," she sobbed. "I can leave. I can get out of here. It's Houston. She's so miserable and it's all my fault. I went off and left her to that awful man and now she's so very unhappy."

"Blair," Opal said firmly, "Mr. Gates is my husband and, whatever else he is, I respect him and I cannot allow you to speak that way about him."

Blair raised tear-stained eyes to her mother. "I don't mean him. He's here now, but Houston can get away from him. I mean that Leander."

"Lee?" Opal asked, incredulous. "But Leander is a darling boy. Why, every young lady in Chandler was dying to be asked for even a dance with him, and now Houston is going to marry him. You can't mean you're worried about Houston marrying Lee?"

Blair moved away from her mother. "I have *always* been the only one to see what he's like! Have you ever really looked at Houston when he's around? She freezes! She sits there as if she's afraid of the world and of him in particular. Houston used to laugh and have a good time, but now she doesn't even smile. Oh, mother, right now I wish that I'd never left. If I'd stayed here, I could have prevented Houston from agreeing to marry that man." She ran back to her mother and buried her face in her lap.

Opal smiled down at her daughter, pleased by her caring concern. "No, you shouldn't have stayed here," she said softly. "You would have become like Houston and believed that the only thing a woman can do is to make a home for her husband, and then the world would have lost a fine doctor. Look at me." She lifted Blair's face.

"We can't really know what Houston and Lee are like when they're alone. No one can know what's in another's personal life. I imagine you have a few secrets of your own."

Immediately, Blair thought of Alan and her cheeks pinked. But now was not the time to talk of him. He'd be here in a few days, and then maybe she'd have someone who agreed with her.

"But I can see the way they are," Blair persisted. "They

11

never talk, never touch, I never see either one of them look at the other with love." Blair stood. "And, the truth is, I never have been able to stand that pompous, upright, shining citizen, Leander Westfield. He's one of those spoiled rich kids who's been handed everything on a silver platter. He has never known disappointment or hardship or struggle or ever heard the word no. When I was in school, the neighboring male medical school allowed the top five women from my female college to attend some classes. The men were quite polite until we women began to score better on the tests than they did—and then we were asked to leave before the end of the term. Leander reminds me of all those smug young men who couldn't stand the competition."

"But, dear, do you really think that's fair? Just because Lee reminds you of others doesn't mean that he's actually like them."

"I've tried several times to talk to him about medicine and all he does is stare at me. What if Houston decides she wants to do something with her life besides match his socks? He'll come down harder on her than Gates ever has on me, and it won't be temporary, either. Houston won't be able to get away."

Opal was beginning to frown. "Have you talked to Houston? I'm sure that she can explain to you why she loves Leander. Perhaps in private they're different. I do think she loves him. And no matter what you say, Leander is a good man."

"So is Duncan Gates," Blair said under her breath. But she was learning that "good" men could kill a woman's soul.

Chapter 2

Blair tried her best to talk to Houston, tried to reason with her, but Houston just got a tight look on her face and said that she loved Leander. Blair wanted to cry in frustration, but as she followed her sister downstairs, she began to concoct a plan. They were going into town today, Blair to pick up a medical journal Alan was sending in care of the Chandler Chronicle office and Houston to do some shopping, and they were going with Lee.

So far, she'd been polite to Leander, but what if she forced him to show his true colors? What if she made him show what an unmoveable, hardheaded tyrant he really was? If she could prove that Lee was as oppressive and narrow-minded as Duncan Gates, then maybe Houston would reconsider spending her life with him.

Of course, Blair could be wrong about Lee. And if she was, if Lee was a considerate, open-minded man—like Alan—then Blair would sing the loudest at Houston's wedding.

As soon as they reached the first floor, there was Leander waiting.

She was mute as she followed the two of them out the door. They never looked at each other and certainly never touched.

13

Houston just walked slowly, probably because her corset was so tight she couldn't breathe, Blair thought, and allowed Lee to help her into his old, black carriage.

"Do you think a woman can be anything besides a wife and mother?" Blair asked Lee, when he started to help her into the carriage. She kept Houston in her corner vision, to make sure her sister heard Lee's answer.

"You don't like children?" he asked, surprised.

"I like children very much," she answered quickly.

"Then I guess it's men you don't like."

"Of course I like men—at least some men. You aren't answering my question. Do you think a woman can be anything besides a wife and mother?"

"I guess that depends on the woman. My sister can make a damson plum conserve that will make your mouth cry with joy," he said, eyes sparkling and, before Blair could reply, gave her a wink, grabbed her by the waist and half tossed her into the carriage.

Blair had to calm her temper before she could speak again. It was quite obvious that he wasn't going to take her seriously. At least he has a sense of humor, she admitted reluctantly.

They drove down the streets of Chandler and Blair tried to keep her mind on the sights. The old stone opera house's doors had been repainted, and there looked to be at least three new hotels in town.

The streets were full of people and wagons: cowboys just in from remote ranches, well-dressed Easterners wanting to capitalize on Chandler's prosperity, a few men from the coal fields, and residents of the town who waved and nodded to the twins and Leander. Shouts of, "Welcome back, Blair-Houston," followed them down the streets.

Blair glanced at her sister and saw that she was looking toward the west, at the most monstrously big house she'd ever seen. It was a white house, perched on a high hill, the top of which had been flattened by one Mr. Kane Taggert in order to build the oversized hulk that loomed over the entire town.

Blair knew that she couldn't be fair about the house, because for years all her mother and Houston had written her

14

about was that house. They had ignored births, deaths, marriages, accidents—nothing that went on in Chandler was considered important if it didn't relate to that house.

And when it had been completed, and the owner of the house had invited no one to see the inside of it, the despair in the letters Blair'd received was almost humorous.

"The whole town still trying to get inside the place?" Blair asked, as she tried to reorganize her thoughts. If Leander never took her questions seriously, never gave her a straight answer, how was she going to prove anything to Houston?

Houston was talking about that monstrous house in an odd, dreamy voice, rather as if she thought of it as a fairy castle, a place where dreams came true.

"I'm not so sure all the things people say about him are rumors," Leander was saying, referring to Houston's mention of Taggert. "Jacob Fenton said—."

"Fenton!" Blair exploded. "Fenton is a conniving, thieving man who uses entire lives of people just so he can get what he wants." Fenton owned most of the coal mines around Chandler and kept the people locked inside the camps as if they were prisoners.

"I don't think you can blame Fenton alone," Lee said. "He has stockholders; he has contracts to fulfill. There are others involved."

Blair couldn't believe what she was hearing and, as they paused to let a horse-drawn trolley pass, she glanced at Houston and was glad she was hearing this. Leander was defending the coal barons, and Blair knew how deeply Houston cared about the miners.

"You've never had to work in a coal mine," Blair said. "You have no idea what it means to struggle daily just to live."

"And I take it you do."

"More than you do," she spat. "You got to study medicine at Harvard. Harvard doesn't allow women."

"So, we're back to that," he said tiredly. "Tell me, does every male doctor get blamed for a few, or have you singled me out particularly?"

"You're the only one marrying my sister."

He turned to look at her, eyebrows raised in surprise. "I had no idea you were jealous. Cheer up, Blair, you'll eventually be able to find your own man."

Blair clenched her fists at her sides, looked straight ahead, and tried to remember her original purpose in even speaking to this man who had such an overinflated sense of his own worth. She hoped Houston appreciated what she was doing for her!

Blair took a deep breath. "What do you think of women as doctors?"

"I like women."

"Ah ha! You like women as long as they're in their place and not in your hospital."

"I believe you said that, not me."

"You said that I wasn't a 'real' doctor and couldn't make rounds with you."

"I said that I thought the Hospital Board wouldn't accept you. You get their permission and I'll show you all the bloody dressings you want to see."

"Isn't your father on the board?"

"I don't control him any more now than I did when I was five—maybe less so."

"I'm sure he's just like you and doesn't believe that women should be doctors."

"As far as I remember, I haven't made a statement as to my personal beliefs concerning women in medicine."

Blair felt as if she were about to scream. "You're talking in circles. What *do* you think about women in medicine?"

"I think that would depend on my patient. If I had a patient who said he'd rather die than be treated by a woman, I wouldn't let a female doctor near the man. But if I had a patient who begged me to find a lady physician, I guess I'd scour the earth if I had to."

Blair could think of nothing else to say. So far, Leander had managed to turn around every word she'd said.

"That's Houston's dream house," Leander said when the trolley car had passed, making an obvious attempt to change the subject. "If Houston didn't have me, I think she'd have joined the line of women fighting for Taggert and that house of his."

"I *would* like to see the inside," Houston said in a faraway voice, then asked Lee to let her off at Wilson's Mercantile.

When Houston had gone, Blair felt no need to even speak to Leander, and he didn't seem to feel that it was necessary to make conversation, either. It was on the tip of her tongue to ask him more questions about the hospital, but she didn't want more of his clever little retorts.

He let her out at the Chandler Chronicle office and she stopped to talk to some of the people she'd known all her life, all of whom called her Blair-Houston because they couldn't tell the twins apart. She hadn't heard the name in years and wondered how Houston felt about always being a part of a whole, never quite her own person.

She picked up her new medical journal at the newspaper office and started down Third Street on the wide wooden boardwalk toward Farrell's Hardware, where she was to meet Houston and Leander.

Lee was there alone, leaning against the railing, the carriage drawn by that big black and white spotted horse of his nearby. There was no sign of Houston, and Blair thought of waiting in the shoe shop across the street until her sister showed up. But Lee saw her and shouted loud enough for the entire town to hear, "Planning to turn tail and run?"

Blair straightened her spine, crossed the dusty street and went to meet him.

He was grinning at her in a smirking way that made her wish she were a man and could challenge him to a duel.

"I don't think that what you're thinking is very ladylike. What would Mr. Gates say?"

"Nothing that he hasn't already said to me, I'm sure."

Lee's expression changed instantly. "Houston told me he was being pretty rough on you. If there's anything that I can do to help, let me know."

For a moment, Blair was bewildered, both at his change in attitude and at his offer of help. She thought he despised her. Before she could speak, Houston appeared, her face flushed and distracted looking.

"I'm glad you showed up now because you just saved your sister from a fate worse than death. She was about to have to say something pleasant to me."

17

"I beg your pardon," Houston said.

Lee took her elbow and escorted her to the carriage. "I said that you'd better get home now so you can start getting ready for the governor's reception tonight."

He helped Houston into the carriage, then reached for Blair.

With a glance at her sister, Blair knew that she had to try again to show her what Leander was really like.

"No doubt you're a believer in Dr. Clark's theory concerning the overuse of a woman's brain, too," she said loudly.

Leander, his hands on her waist, gave her a blank look for a moment, then began to smile. After a lusty look up and down, he said, "Blair, I don't think you have anything to worry about. It looks to me like all your brains are going to the right places."

Blair sat in the carriage, listening to Leander's chuckling, and thought that surely no other sister had endured what she was going through for hers.

As they were leaving town, two big, beefy men, driving a wagon that was so dilapidated that no respectable farmer would have had it, yelled at Leander to halt. The dark man, a fearsome, bearded, dirty-looking brute, addressed Houston in an aggressive way that Blair had never seen her allow in a man before. If there was one thing that Houston knew how to do, it was to stop men who were too forward.

Houston nodded politely to him and he bellowed at the horses and left in a cloud of dust.

"What in the world was that about?" Leander asked. "I didn't know you knew Taggert."

Before Houston could answer, Blair said, *"That* was the man who built that house? No wonder he doesn't ask anyone to it. He knows they'd turn him down. By the way, how could he tell us apart?"

"Our clothes," Houston answered quickly. "I saw him in the mercantile store."

"As for no one accepting his invitation," Lee said, "I think that Houston might risk plague or anything else for that matter to see that house."

Blair leaned forward, across her sister. "Did you receive letters about that house?"

"If I could sell the words by the pound, I'd be a million-aire."

"Like him," Blair answered, looking up at the house that dominated the west end of town. "He can keep his millions, and he can keep his dinosaur of a house."

"I think we've agreed again," Lee said, acting surprised. "Do you think this'll become a habit?"

"I doubt it," Blair snapped, but her heart wasn't in the remark. Maybe she'd been wrong about him.

But twenty minutes later, she was just as worried about her sister's future as ever. She'd left Lee and Houston in her mother's garden alone, then remembered that her journal was still in Lee's buggy. Hurrying downstairs to catch Lee before he left, she was a witness to a little drama between the couple.

Leander, reaching behind Houston's head to shoo a bee away, made her stiffen. Even from where Blair stood, she could see the way her sister drew away from being touched by Lee.

"You don't have to worry," he said in a deadly voice. "I won't touch you."

"It's just until after we're married," she whispered, but Lee didn't reply before he stormed past Blair and drove away very fast in the carriage.

Leander stormed into his father's house and slammed the door behind him, rattling the stained glass. He took the stairs two at a time and at the landing turned left and headed for his room, the room that he was to give up as soon as he married Houston and moved into the house he'd bought for her.

He nearly ran over his father, but didn't apologize or slow down.

Reed Westfield, glancing up at his son as he passed, saw the look of anger on his face and followed him to his room. Leander was already throwing clothes into a valise when Reed arrived.

Reed stood in the doorway for a moment and watched his son. Even though they looked nothing alike, Reed being short, stocky, and having a face with all the delicacy of a bulldog, they had much the same temperament. It took a great deal to rouse the Westfield ire.

"Is it an emergency patient that needs your attention?" Reed asked, as he watched his son throw clothes at the case on the bed, and, in his rage, miss half the time.

"No, it's women," Lee managed to say through clenched teeth.

Reed tried to hide a smile, coughed to cover it. In his legal practice, he'd learned to hide his own reaction to whatever his clients said. "Have a spat with Houston?"

Leander turned to his father with a face full of fury. "I've *never* had a spat or a fight or an argument or any disagreement whatsoever with Houston. Houston is utterly, totally perfect, without flaw."

"Ah, then it's that sister of hers. Someone mentioned that she was badgering you today. You won't have to live with your sister-in-law, you know."

Lee paused in his packing. "Blair? What's she got to do with anything? She's the most enjoyment I've had with a woman since I got engaged. It's Houston who's driving me to drink. Or, more correctly, she's the one forcing me to leave Chandler."

"Hold on just a minute," Reed said, taking his son's wrist. "Before you jump on a train and leave all your patients to die, why don't you sit down and talk to me and tell me what's made you so mad?"

Lee sat in a chair as if he weighed a ton, and it was several minutes before he could speak. "Do you remember why I asked Houston to marry me in the first place? Right now, I can't seem to remember a single reason that made me do it."

Reed took a seat across from his son. "Let me see—if I remember correctly, it was pure, clean, old-fashioned lust. When you returned from Vienna and the last of your medical studies, you joined the legion of men, young and old, following the luscious Miss Houston Chandler around town, begging her to attend whatever you could think of, anything, just so you could be near her. I believe I remember your rhapsodizing about her beauty and telling me how every man in Chandler had asked her to marry him. And I also remember the night you asked her yourself and she accepted you. I think you walked around in a daze for a week."

He paused for a moment. "Does that answer your question? Have you decided now that you *aren't* lusting after the lovely Miss Houston?"

Leander gave his father a serious look. "I've decided now that that shape of hers, that walk of hers that has grown men fainting in her wake, is all show. The woman is a block of ice. She is completely frigid, without any emotion at all. I cannot marry someone like her and spend the rest of my life trying to live with a woman who has no feelings at all."

"Is that all that's wrong?" Reed asked, obviously relieved. "Good women are supposed to be like that. You wait, after you're married, she'll warm up. Your mother was very cool to me before we were married. She broke her parasol over my head one evening when I got too fresh. But later, after we were married . . . well, things got better—much better. You take the word of someone who's more experienced in these matters. Houston is a good girl and she's had to live with that bigot Gates all these years. Of course she's nervous and frightened."

Leander listened to his father's words carefully. He'd never planned to spend his life in Chandler. Instead, he'd planned to intern in a big city, work on the staff of a big hospital and eventually have his own practice and make a lot of money. He had lasted but six months before he decided to come home where he was needed, where he would have more important cases than a rich woman's hysteria.

All the time he'd been away from Chandler, Houston had written him letters, gossipy letters about what went on in the town and later about her finishing school. He'd always looked forward to the letters and looked forward to once again seeing the little girl who'd written them.

The night he'd returned home, his father threw a party of welcome and the "little girl" walked into the room. Houston had grown into a woman with a figure that made Lee's palms sweat, and as he was gaping, an old friend had punched him on the arm.

"It's no use trying. There isn't a single man in town who

hasn't asked for her hand in marriage—or for anything else she'll part with—but she'll have none of us. I think she's waiting for a prince or a president."

Lee had grinned smugly. "Maybe you boys don't know how to ask. I learned a few tricks while I was in Paris."

And so he had become a contestant in the local race to see who could get Miss Chandler to marry him. He still didn't understand what had happened. He had taken her out to a few parties, and at about the third one, he'd asked her to marry him, saying something to the effect of, "I don't imagine you'd want to marry me, would you?" He had expected her to refuse; then he could laugh with the men at his club, saying that he'd tried, too, but alas, he also had failed.

He had been shocked when Houston had accepted his proposal immediately and asked if the twentieth of May would be a date that suited him, all in the same breath. The next morning, he had seen his picture in the paper as being engaged to Houston, and the article further stated that the happy couple was choosing her ring that morning. After that, he'd never had a moment to think about what he'd done when he'd proposed. If he wasn't at the hospital, he was at a tailor's shop or agreeing with Houston about what color the draperies should be in the house he'd suddenly found himself buying.

And now, just weeks before the wedding, he was having second thoughts. Every time he touched Houston, she moved away from him as if he were repulsive. Of course he knew Duncan Gates, knew how the man never missed an opportunity to put a woman in her "place." His father had written a few years ago that Gates had tried to bar women from the new ice-cream parlor that had opened in town. His reasoning was that it would encourage women to be lazy, to gossip, and to flirt. All of which, Reed had written, had proven true— and the men were delighted.

Leander took a long, thin cigar from his pocket and lit it. "I've not had much experience with 'good' girls. Before you married Mother, did you worry that she might not change?"

"Worried about it night and day. I even told my father that I refused to marry her, that I wouldn't spend my life with a woman made of stone."

"But you changed your mind. Why?"

Reed made an apologetic little smile. "Well, I . . . I mean I . . ." He turned his head away, in what looked to be embarrassment. "If she were here today, I think she'd want me to tell you. The truth is, son, I seduced her. I gave her too much champagne and sweet-talked her for hours and seduced her."

He turned back abruptly. "But I'm not advising you to do that. I'm advising you to learn from what I did. You can get into an awful lot of trouble that way. To this day, I think you came about two weeks earlier than was proper."

Leander was studying the tip of his cigar. "I like your advice and I think I'll take it."

"I'm not sure I should have told you this. Houston is a lovely girl and . . ." He stopped and studied his son for a moment. "I trust your judgment. You do what you think is best. Will you be here for dinner?"

"No," Lee said softly, as if in deep thought. "I'm taking Houston to the governor's reception tonight."

Reed started to say something but closed his mouth and left the room. He might have reconsidered saying what he thought if he'd known that later his son called a saloon to order four bottles of French champagne to be sent to his new house, then asked the housekeeper to prepare a dinner that began with oysters and ended with chocolate.

Chapter 3

Blair sat in her room on the top floor of the Chandler house and tried to concentrate on an article about peritonitis, but, instead, her eyes kept moving to the window where she could see her sister cutting roses in the garden below. Blair could see that Houston was humming, smelling the roses and, in general, enjoying herself.

For the life of her, Blair couldn't understand Houston. She'd just had an argument with her fiancé, he'd stormed away in anger, yet Houston wasn't in the least upset.

And then there was that episode in town with that man Taggert. Blair had never seen Houston so responsive to a man to whom she hadn't been formally introduced. Houston was a stickler for rules and etiquette, yet she'd greeted that ill-clad, hairy man as if they were old friends.

Blair put her journal down and went to the garden.

"All right," Blair said as soon as she reached her sister. "I want to know what's going on."

"I have no idea what you're talking about." Houston looked as innocent as a baby.

"Kane Taggert," Blair answered, trying to read her sister's face.

24

"I saw him in Wilson's Mercantile and later he said good morning to us."

Blair studied Houston and saw that there was an unnatural flush in her cheeks, as if she were very excited about something. "You're not telling me everything."

"I probably shouldn't have involved myself, but Mr. Taggert looked as if he were getting angry and I wanted to prevent a quarrel. Unfortunately, it was at Mary Alice's expense." Houston then told a story about Mary Alice Pendergast's baiting of Taggert, of referring to him as a coal miner, of turning her nose up at him. And Houston had taken Taggert's side.

Blair was stunned that Houston would involve herself in something that wasn't any of her business, but worse, Blair didn't like the look of Taggert. He looked capable of doing anything to anybody. And, too, she'd heard many references to the man and his cronies, men like Vanderbilt, Jay Gould, Rockefeller. "I don't like your getting mixed up with him."

"You sound like Leander."

"For once, he's right!" Blair snapped.

"Perhaps we should mark this day in the family Bible. Blair, after tonight, I swear I'll never even mention Mr. Taggert's name."

"Tonight?" Blair had a feeling that what she should do right now was run, not walk, to the nearest place of safety. When they were children, Houston had been able to involve her in several projects with unhappy endings—all of which Blair had been blamed for. No one could believe that sweet, demure Houston was capable of disobedience.

"Look at this. A messenger brought it. He's invited me to dinner at his house." Houston pulled a note from inside her sleeve and handed it to Blair.

"So? You're supposed to go somewhere with Leander tonight, aren't you?"

"Blair, you don't seem to realize what a stir that house has caused in this town. *Everyone* has tried to get an invitation to see the inside of it. People have come from all over the state to see it, but no one has ever been invited in. Once, it was even put to Mr. Taggert that an English duke who was passing through should be allowed to stay in the house, but Mr.

Taggert wouldn't even listen to the committee. And now *I've* been invited."

"But you have to go somewhere else," Blair persisted. "The governor will be there. Surely he's more important than the inside of any old house."

Houston got an odd look on her face, the same one she'd had that morning when she'd gazed up at that hulking house. "You couldn't understand what it was like. Year after year we watched the train unload its goods. Mr. Gates said the owner didn't build a spur line to the house site because he wanted everyone to see everything going all the way through town. There were crates of goods from all over the world. Oh, Blair, I know they must have been filled with furniture. And tapestries! Tapestries from Brussels."

"Houston, you cannot be in two places at once. You promised to go to the reception and you must go," she said flatly, hoping to end the matter. Of the two men, Leander was definitely the lesser evil.

"When we were children, we could be in two places at once," Houston said, as if it were the simplest statement in the world.

Blair was sure her breath stopped. "You want us to trade places? You want *me* to spend an evening with Leander, pretending I like him, while you go see some lecherous man's house?"

"What do you know about Kane to call him lecherous?"

"Kane, is it? I thought you didn't now him?"

"Don't change the subject. Blair, please trade places with me. Just for one night. I'd go another night but I'm afraid Mr. Gates would forbid it, and I'm not sure Leander would want me to go either, and I'll never get another opportunity like this. Just one last fling before I get married."

"You make marriage sound like death. Besides, Leander would know I wasn't you in a minute."

"Not if you behaved yourself. You know that we're both good actresses. Look at how I pretend to be an old woman every Wednesday. All you have to do is be quiet and not start an argument with Lee, and refrain from talking about medicine and walk like a lady instead of looking like you're running to a fire."

Blair's mind was reeling. Ever since she'd returned to Chandler she had been frantically worried about her sister, afraid that all her spirit had been suppressed. This was the first sign of life Houston'd shown in a week. It was like when they were children, getting into scrapes, pretending to be each other, and laughing hilariously together later.

But what about Leander? All he had to do was start teasing Blair about being a lady doctor and . . .

Her head came up. Leander never teased Houston, and for one night she'd *be* Houston. And, too, this would be her chance to reassure herself that Leander really was the wonderful man both Opal and Houston said he was. She would be able to satisfy herself that, when they were alone, Lee and Houston were right for each other, that they were in love.

"Please, please, Blair. I hardly ever ask you for anything."

"Except to spend weeks in the house of our stepfather whom you know I detest. To spend weeks in the company of that self-congratulating man I think you intend to marry. To—," Blair said, but she was smiling. She could return to Pennsylvania in peace if she were sure her sister was going to be happy.

"Oh, Blair, please. I really do want to see this house."

"It's just his house you're interested in, not Taggert?"

"For Heaven's sake! I've been to hundreds of dinner parties and I haven't yet been swept off my feet by the host. Besides, there'll be other people there."

"After the wedding, would you mind if I told Leander he spent an evening with me? Just to see the look on his face would be worth everything."

"Of course you may. Lee has a very good sense of humor, and I'm sure he'll enjoy the joke."

"I somehow doubt that, but at least I'll enjoy it."

"Let's go get ready. I want to wear something befitting that house, and you'll get to wear the blue satin Worth gown."

"I should wear my knickerbockers, but that would give it away, wouldn't it?"

Blair followed Houston into the house, pleased by the entire arrangement. It wouldn't be easy to impersonate Houston and that slow, lazy walk of hers, but Blair considered it a challenge and looked forward to it.

Blair started having second thoughts about the whole affair when she felt Houston tightening the corset strings. Houston didn't have any qualms about enduring a little pain for the sake of beauty, but Blair kept thinking about how her internal organs were being reorganized by the whalebone instrument of torture. But when she put the dress on and saw herself with the exaggerated hourglass figure like Houston's, she wasn't displeased at all.

Houston watched her sister in the mirror. "Now you look like a woman." She glanced down at the skirt and blouse she wore, feeling the lightly tied corset underneath. "And I feel as light as a feather."

They paused for a moment and studied each other in the mirror. "No one will know one of us from the other," Houston said.

"Not until we speak," Blair answered, turning away.

"You don't have any problems. At least as me, you can get away with not speaking."

"And does that mean that I talk too much?" Blair shot back at her.

"It means that if Blair were quiet, we'd never get out of the house because Mother'd call a doctor."

"Leander?" Blair asked, and they both laughed.

Later, as they were both dressed and ready to go out for the evening, Blair supposedly to spend the evening with her friend, Tia Mankin, she got to see something that few people ever saw: she saw herself as others saw her.

At first, she was so busy concentrating on trying to be Houston, imitating her walk, the way she entered a room, the way she looked at people as if from far away, that she didn't see the way Houston was mimicking her.

Mr. Gates walked into the room and said very politely that both young women looked lovely. Houston, as Blair, leaned her head back and used her superior height to look down at the man. "I am a doctor and being a doctor is more important than being pretty. I want more out of life than just being a wife and mother."

Blair opened her mouth to protest that she never sounded like that and that she'd never attack a man who hadn't attacked first, but as she looked at the faces around her, she saw that no one thought what Houston had said was out of character.

She almost felt sorry for Mr. Gates when the little man's face blew up like a fish's and his skin turned red. Before she knew what she was doing, she stepped between her sister and the angry man. "It's such a nice night," she said loudly. "Blair, why don't you and I sit in the garden until Leander comes?"

When Houston turned around, she had a look of anger and hostility on her face such as Blair had never seen before. Do I really look like that? she wondered. Do I really start most of the arguments with Mr. Gates?

She wanted to ask Houston those questions, but before they could get outside, Leander arrived to pick them up.

Blair stood back and watched Houston pretending to be her and, almost immediately, she wanted to protect him. He was courteous, smiling, polite and oh, so very good-looking. She'd never noticed before that Leander was enough to stop a heart or two. He was a serious-looking man with green eyes, a long thin nose and full lips. Black hair, overly long, scraped the collar of his coat. But what Blair was interested in wasn't his surface good looks, but the expression in his eyes. It was as if those eyes hid secrets that he told no one.

"Houston?" he asked, bringing her back to reality. "Are you all right?"

"Of course," she said briskly, trying to imitate her sister's coolness.

As Leander put his hands on her waist and lifted her into the carriage, she smiled at him and he smiled back, quickly, briefly, but it warmed her and she was glad to have this time with him.

They were no more than in the carriage when Houston started on Leander.

"How do you keep peritonitis from spreading?" she asked in a hostile voice that made Blair look at her in wonder. What was she so angry about? And where had she learned about peritonitis?

"Sew both layers of the intestine together and pray," Lee said quite sensibly, and correctly.

"Have you heard of asepsis here in Chandler yet?"

29

With her breath drawn in, Blair looked up at Lee to see how he'd take this question. Blair thought it was downright insulting, and she wouldn't blame Lee if he gave Houston a piece of his mind. But Lee only glanced at Blair, winked quickly, and told Houston that the doctors in Chandler did indeed wash their hands before surgery.

Blair couldn't help smiling up at him, and she felt that the two of them were in this together. Houston kept on baiting Lee as Blair leaned back in the seat and watched the stars, not bothering to listen to her sister's ranting.

When at last they came to Tia's house, she was very glad. And when Houston was gone and Blair and Lee were alone, she breathed a deep sigh.

"It's rather like the aftermath of a bad rainstorm," she said, looking up at Lee and half dreading his comments about her other self.

"She doesn't mean anything. All doctors are like that when they leave medical school. You're very aware of the responsibility of your profession."

"And it changes later?"

"It does, but I'm not sure how to explain it. I guess you come to learn your limitations and aren't so sure that you can save the world single-handedly."

Blair relaxed against the back of the carriage and thought how kind of him it was that he didn't say anything bad about Houston's attacking him. And he'd called her a doctor.

It felt quite natural when she slipped her arm through his and didn't move to the other side of the buggy now that her sister was gone. She didn't notice the odd way that Leander looked at her, but Blair was quite pleased with the evening.

Chapter 4

Chandler, Colorado, was at the base of the Rocky Mountains with an altitude of seven thousand feet and, as a result, the air was always thin, clear and cool. The summers were pleasant during the day, and when the sun went down, the mountain air made shawls necessary.

Blair sat next to Lee and took deep breaths, inhaling the crisp fragrance of the mountains. She hadn't realized she'd missed it as much as she had.

They had not driven half a mile when a man rode up in a flurry of dust, his horse panting, and yelled at Leander. "Westfield! Somebody needs help. There's a woman down on River Street that just tried to kill herself."

Blair had never seen the man before, and she didn't think she wanted to again. He looked like a cartoon of a gambler, with his coal black hair and his little mustache and, worse, the way he smirked as he stared at her.

He took off his straight-brimmed hat and tipped it to her. "I could understand that maybe you're too busy to come, Doc."

Blair glanced at Lee and saw that he was hesitating, and she

31

knew that it as on her account. "I'll go with you, Lee. Maybe I can be of some help."

The man, a gambler or not, said, "River Street ain't no place for a lady. Maybe I should watch out for her while you go to the suicide."

That settled Lee as nothing else had. He cracked the whip over the horse's head and yelled, "Hang on," to Blair all in one breath.

Blair slammed against the back of the carriage seat and grabbed the roof support as Lee went flying. She closed her eyes in terror twice, as Lee narrowly missed three other carriages. The people saw him coming and started getting out of his way long before he reached them. She heard several shouts of encouragement and guessed that the sight of Lee tearing through the streets was a familiar one.

He halted the horse in the northeast corner of town, across the Tijeras River and between two railroad tracks—a place Blair had never seen or been curious about. In one motion, he tied the horse, grabbed his bag, leaped to the ground, and ordered Blair to remain in the buggy.

After a quick glance at the leering face of the gambler, she followed Lee into the house with the red lights on the outside. Lee went up the stairs as if he knew where he was going, but Blair couldn't help looking around.

Everything seemed to be red. The walls were red, the carpets were red, the furniture was upholstered in red with red fringe. And what wasn't red was made of very dark wood.

At the head of the stairs, she saw a tight group of women in various stages of undress and, just as she reached them, they began backing away from the door.

"I need help, I told you," Blair heard Lee shouting as she pushed her way through the crowd.

Lee glanced up at her. "I told you to stay in the car." On the bed in front of him was a pale, thin young woman, actually little more than a girl, writhing in pain that Blair guessed was from swallowing an alcohol-based disinfectant.

"Carbolic?" Blair asked, and as she saw Lee removing a stomach pump from his bag, she knew what had to be done.

Blair didn't lose a moment going to work. With a voice of authority, she ordered three women, one wearing only her corset and a thin black wrapper, to hold the girl's arms and legs, and another one to fetch towels. When a tall, well-dressed woman who looked as though she knew how to give orders came into the room, Blair sent her after two raincoats, and when the coats were there, Blair watched Lee until he had a free hand, then she slipped it into the sleeve of one oiled, waterproof garment. She then put the other raincoat on over her sister's dress.

Lee talked to the girl, soothing her even as he pushed the pump down her throat, and when the carbolic came up, it came with all the contents of her stomach, splattering everyone in the room.

Gagging, sick, weak, covered in filth, the girl clung to Lee, and he held her, while Blair quietly organized the cleaning.

"Nothing is that bad," Lee said, holding the girl as she began to cry. "Here, I want you to drink this," he said, giving her water and two tablets.

He didn't release her until she began to relax and at last fall asleep. Gently, he laid her on the bed and looked up at the tall woman Blair had sent after the raincoats. "Clean her up and send her to the Infirmary tomorrow. I want to talk to her."

The woman nodded silently, looking up at Lee with big, worshipful eyes. She turned to Blair. "I hope you appreciate this man, honey, ain't many like him. He—." The woman stopped at a look from Lee.

"We have to go." With surprise, he glanced down at the raincoat he wore and then looked across the patient's bed at Blair.

"I learned it from my doctor-sister," she said in answer to his silent question and suddenly worried about how Lee would react to her help with the girl.

But as Lee packed his instruments, took her arm and led her outside, he made no mention of her expertise. The people around them mumbled thanks and looked at both Lee and Blair with dull eyes, and Blair thought the young women were thinking that any one of them could have been the girl on that bed.

"Do you come here often?" she asked Lee on the way down the stairs.

"About once a week a doctor is here for one reason or another. I guess I've been here as often as any of them."

At the carriage, Lee paused in front of Blair and she was sure he'd say that he knew who she was. "I really appreciated your going with me on the case and that I didn't have to leave you somewhere first. It meant more to me than you'll know."

She gave a smile of relief. "You were very good with the woman, fast, as careful as possible."

With a slight smile, he touched the hair at her temple. "You're sounding like Blair again, but whatever the reason, I thank you for the compliment."

When Blair was in medical school, she had had a teacher who warned them that the curse of young female doctors was that they tended to fall in love with whichever man was the best surgeon. The instructor had said that all a new female intern had to do was see a doctor remove an ovarian cyst that was difficult, and she'd soon be swooning over him.

At this moment, Blair thought that Lee was one of the best-looking men she'd ever seen. He'd handled the technical side of the case quite well, but, more, his compassion was such as she'd never seen matched. When he moved toward her to kiss her, she realized that she wanted him to kiss her as herself, as Blair, rather than as Houston.

She turned her face away.

Leander dropped his hand from her face instantly, and the anger in his eyes was frightening. He turned away, every movement showing his anger.

Blair felt a moment of panic. Right now, she was Houston and not Blair, and of course she would kiss the man she loved.

Blair caught his arm. He stopped and looked at her, his eyes blazing with fury, and it took a great deal of courage not to step back. Boldly, she put her arms around his neck and touched her lips to his.

He stood there as if he were made of stone, not moving, not responding to her advances.

For a moment, it occurred to Blair that Dr. Leander Westfield was certainly a spoiled man if he reacted so severely to his fiancée's refusing him a single kiss. As he continued to show no reaction, she thought of this as a challenge, like getting through the first year of medical school.

She stood on tiptoe and began to show a little passion to this unyielding man.

She wasn't prepared for his reaction—nothing that had ever happened to her in her lifetime had prepared her for his reaction.

He caught her head in his hand, twisted her head around and applied his mouth to hers with a passion that made her breath disappear. And Blair reacted in kind. She pressed her body against his and only clung harder when he pushed his knee between her legs and thrust his tongue into her mouth.

"Excuse me," came a voice with laughter in it, and it was several moments before Lee pulled away.

Blair stood there with her eyes closed and was glad of the support of the carriage behind her or she probably would have fallen. She was vaguely aware that it was the dreadful gambler-man who was there, and that he was smirking at them even while he spoke to Lee, but she didn't really care. Perhaps Houston's reputation was ruined forever, but the last thing Blair was thinking about was her sister.

"Ready?" she heard Lee saying softly in her ear when the man was gone. She could feel the warmth of his body so near hers.

"For what?" she murmured, then opened her eyes.

"Houston, we don't have to go to the reception," Lee said.

Blair stood up straighter and remembered who she was and where she was and that she was with her sister's fiancé. "Yes, of course we do," she said shyly, not meeting his eyes and ignoring the fact that his hands lingered much too long on her waist as he helped her into the carriage.

Once seated, she kept her eyes on the road ahead. So *this* is why Houston loves him, she thought. And to think that she'd worried that they were too cool to each other in private.

She glanced at him once as he turned to her, and his eyes were alive, sparkling—and hungry.

She gave him a weak smile and told herself to think of Alan. Alan. Alan!

Blair managed to get herself under control somewhat, but,

still, her senses were reeling, so that she wasn't aware that Lee had driven them across the river and into the deep recesses of Fenton Park. Midnight Lane spread before them as Lee halted the horse next to the park bandstand and moved to help her out of the carriage.

"Why are we stopping?"

"I have the smell of carbolic in my nose and I thought the fresh air would help get rid of it."

He smiled at her as he lifted her from the carriage, and she had to turn away from him or she knew she'd be in his arms again. "You really were very good with the girl tonight."

"You said that," he answered, releasing her as he took a cigar from his pocket and lit it. "Why did you go with me tonight? You never have before."

Blair caught her breath. She had to think fast. "I guess I was worried about this afternoon. You seemed awfully angry," she said, hoping it sounded plausible.

He cocked his head to one side and looked at her through a cloud of smoke and moonlight. "You've never seemed to worry about *that,* either."

What in the world had she stepped into? Blair wondered. And why hadn't Houston warned her about whatever Lee was talking about?

"Of course I worry, Lee," she said, turning away, her hand on the bandstand. "I always worry when you're upset with me. I won't let it happen again."

He was silent for so long that she turned to look at him. He was watching her with the same hungry eyes she'd seen before.

"Lee, you're making me blush. Shouldn't we go to the reception?" Blast Houston! she thought. Once again she'd allowed her sister to talk her into doing something that was going to get her, Blair, into trouble. She hoped seeing that oversized house was worth this.

Slowly, Lee's hand reached out to touch her arm. She backed away and came up against the wooden bandstand.

He threw his cigar down and advanced a step toward her.

Blair gave him a little smile, grabbed her skirts and ran up the stairs to the center of the bandstand. "We used to have the loveliest concerts here," she said, backing up, as she watched him moving toward her. "I remember wearing pink and white and . . ."

Her voice trailed off as he stood before her and she could back no further. As she looked up at him, feeling the warmth of his body near hers, he held out his arms to her and she went to him.

There was no music except the sounds of the night, but Blair was sure she heard violins as Lee waltzed her about the bandstand. Closing her eyes, her skirts over her arm, she followed him as if in a trance, giving no thought to any moment but this one. And when he pulled her close and kept waltzing, his legs pressed against her own, she gave herself over to feelings such as she'd never experienced before.

She wasn't aware of time passing as he held her, nor did she remember that she was supposed to be her sister or that this man who held her so intimately was a stranger. She was only aware of the present, there was no past, no future.

When he began to kiss her neck, her cheek, her temple, she leaned into him, slipped her arms around his neck and kept dancing slowly, seductively.

"You said you could be different," he whispered, but Blair didn't hear any words. "Come, kiss me once more before we have to leave."

Only some of the words reached her brain. She didn't want to leave, wanted this moment never to end, and when he kissed her again, it weakened her more than before, and Lee had to hold her against him or her knees would have given way.

He pulled back and for a moment she couldn't move, her eyes closed, her head back.

When she did look at him, he was grinning—an expression of delight on his face such as she'd never seen before. She smiled, too.

"Come on, sweetheart," he laughed, sweeping her into his arms. "I want to show you to the world."

Once Lee'd put her in the carriage, Blair's mind began to work again. This evening was not going as she'd planned. She'd wanted to find out if her sister was marrying the right man and, instead of making a scientific study, every time Leander touched her, her knees turned to jelly.

"This is utterly ridiculous."

"What is?" Lee asked from beside her in the carriage.

"That . . . that I should have acquired this raging headache all of a sudden. I think I ought to go home."

"Here, let me look."

"No," Blair said, leaning away from him.

His long, strong fingers took hold of her chin as he moved his face closer to hers. "I don't see any signs of pain," he whispered, "except maybe this little vein right here," he said, kissing her forehead at her hairline. "Does that help any?"

"Please," she whispered, trying to turn away. "Please don't."

After a slow, lingering caress, he took the reins to the horse and drove them out of the park.

Blair put her hand to her breast and her pounding heart. At least they would be in a public place, she thought, and then he'd take her home, and she'd once again be able to be herself—and keep this dangerous man in his place, which was in her sister's arms, not hers.

Later, someone told Blair that there had indeed been a reception for the governor, and that she had attended and met him, and had managed to speak in a coherent manner, but she couldn't remember any of it. She had seemed to always be in Leander's arms for those few hours, dancing across a floor of glass and seeing nothing but his eyes, drowning in the green depths of them.

She remembered several people telling her that they'd never seen her looking lovelier or seen Lee so happy. There were a thousand questions about the wedding and Blair knew none of the answers, but it didn't matter because Lee was always there to take her away to the dance floor again.

If they had talked, she remembered nothing of what they had said. She thought only of his arms and his eyes and how he made her feel.

It was when a boy brought a message to say that Lee was needed elsewhere that she came to her senses and realized that this magic night was over. She felt like Cinderella, and now she had to pay the price for her wonderful night.

"You may stay and I'll get someone to take you home," Lee said. "Or you can go with me."

"You," was all she said and he took her to his waiting carriage. They didn't speak on the drive through the quiet streets of Chandler, but Blair knew that she was long past any coherent thoughts.

He reached over, took her hand in his, and when she looked at him, he smiled. For a moment, Blair remembered her sister and knew that she shouldn't be here now, that what she'd seen tonight was too intimate a thing to share, that these smiles and kisses were for Houston, and Blair had no right to intrude on their love. Until this night, she'd had no idea that the twin bond was as strong as it was, that she could spend one evening with the man her sister loved and, through that bond, could react so strongly to this man, could almost feel that it was she who was in love with him.

"Warm enough?" Lee asked and she nodded.

Warm enough, cold enough, drunk enough, sober enough, she thought.

Leander stopped the carriage in front of a house that Blair'd never seen before. "Is your patient here? I thought we were going to the Infirmary."

Lee lifted his arms for her. "I'd like to think that my presence has made you forget the house we chose."

Before Blair could cover her error, he continued.

"I thought maybe we could talk about some of the plans for the wedding. We haven't been able to talk much lately."

"But what about your patient? Shouldn't we—"

He swung her down. "There is no emergency, nor is there a patient. I wanted an excuse to get out of there and I'm afraid I used my profession. You don't mind, do you?"

"I really must get home. It's already late and Mother will probably be waiting up for me."

"I thought your mother was a heavy sleeper and you had trouble waking her?"

"Well, yes, she is, but what with Blair home, she's changing." Blair smiled at his puzzled frown and quickly said that she'd love to talk about the wedding. She swept past him and stopped at the locked door, hoping that he wouldn't ask her too many more questions.

The interior was lovely, feminine without excluding the masculine. Blair was sure that Houston had decorated it. In the parlor, a small fire was burning against the Colorado mountain chill, and in front of it was a low table set with candles, roast duckling, caviar, oysters, chocolate truffles and four silver buckets filled with ice and French champagne. Fat pillows surrounded the table.

Blair took one look at Lee standing there in the firelight and at the food and the champagne and thought, I'm in trouble.

Chapter 5

The way Leander stood there looking at her made Blair feel as if the blood were draining from her body. She'd spent the last week near this man and she'd never noticed that he had any special powers over women, especially not over her. It had to be the twin bond that was making her react this way. Houston was certainly a sly one who managed to conceal all this passion under her cool persona. No one, not even her own sister, had ever guessed what fires lay beneath that haughty-seeming exterior. And how Houston must have laughed to herself at Blair's fears that she and Lee weren't compatible!

Of course, Blair thought, if I were engaged to a man who made me tremble every time he so much as brushed against me, I don't think I'd allow another woman to be alone with him—not even my own sister, or perhaps especially not my own sister.

But even as Blair thought those words, she told herself that she *did* have a man who made her tremble with his every touch. Well, perhaps not with every touch, but with enough touches to make her love him.

As she looked at Lee again, at the way his upper lip curled

and at the burning intensity of his eyes, she knew that if she were honest, she would have to admit that *no* man anywhere had ever made her feel like this before, nor had she had any idea that this kind of passion was possible.

"I think I should go home. I think I forgot to do something," Blair mumbled.

"Such as?" He was advancing on her in slow, steady steps.

"Stay there," she answered, swallowing hard.

Lee took her arm. "You aren't afraid of me, are you? Come over here and sit down. I've never seen you like this. Not that I don't like it, but . . ."

Blair tried to relax, tried to remember that she was supposed to be her sister. If she told Lee now of the trick the twins had been playing on him all evening, he'd be furious—perhaps furious enough to break the engagement. She thought that if she could keep him talking, if they could eat a little, drink very little, then maybe she could get him to take her home. Anything, so long as she didn't allow this man to touch her.

She took a seat on one of the pillows and helped herself to a raw oyster. "I haven't seen you very often as Dr. Westfield," she said, not looking up at him, but she heard the sounds of a bottle of champagne being opened.

"Never, as I remember. Have a strawberry," he said, as he dipped the berry in champagne, ignored her extended hand and put it into her mouth.

He was bringing his mouth to hers when Blair choked on the fruit. Lee handed her a glass which she drank from gratefully. Unfortunately, it was champagne and, almost instantly, she could feel it going to her head.

"Never?" she asked, trying to suppress the lightheaded, dizzy, happy feeling that was beginning to overwhelm her. "That seems like an awfully long time."

"Too long for most things." He took her fingertips and began to nibble them.

She pulled away from his touch. "What's that?" she asked, pointing to a bowl.

"Caviar. It's said to be a wonderful aphrodisiac. Would you like some?"

"No, thank you." She was drawn to the wineglass that

Lee'd refilled. As she sipped it, she said, "How *do* you prevent peritonitis?"

He moved closer to her, spearing her with his hypnotic eyes. "First, you have to examine the patient." He put his hand on her stomach and began to move it around in a slow, easy way. "I feel the skin, the warm, alive skin and then I move lower."

Blair, in one frantic motion, managed to move away, and knocked her glass of champagne over so it ran down the table and onto Lee's hand.

He pulled back with a laugh. "I'll put more wood on the fire."

She thought he seemed awfully pleased with something. "I really think I should go home. It must be awfully late."

"You haven't touched your food." He took a seat on the pillow next to her.

"I'll eat if you'll talk. Tell me how you became a doctor. What made you want to do it?"

He paused in putting choice bits of food on her plate and looked at her speculatively.

"Did I say something wrong?"

"No, but you've never asked me that before."

Blair wanted to shout that that was because she'd never really talked to him before. She took a deep drink of wine to cover her embarrassment, while Lee put chicken in wine sauce on her plate. "Maybe it was seeing you with the girl tonight."

He stretched his long, lean form out beside her, inches away, pants tight around his thighs, wine in hand, looking at the fire. "I wanted to save people. Did you know that Mother died not because she was having a baby at forty-five but because the midwife had just come from another delivery and hadn't washed her hands?"

Blair paused with her fork on the way to her mouth. "No," she said quietly, "I didn't know. It must have hurt when Blair asked about aseptic conditions."

He turned to look at her, smiling. "Blair doesn't bother me at all. Here, have another oyster."

Blair didn't know whether to be glad or offended by his comment that she didn't bother him at all. "You certainly upset her. Did you know that she thinks you're just like Mr. Gates?"

Lee's mouth dropped open a fraction. "What an absurd idea. Why don't you relax here beside me?"

Blair moved toward him before she even considered what she was doing, but she stopped. Maybe it was the champagne that was making her so forward. Of course, that didn't explain how she'd behaved on River Street, or in the park, or at the reception. "No, thank you," she said in a prim little Houston-voice. "I'm quite fine where I am. Do you plan always to work at the Infirmary?"

With a sigh, he looked back at the fire.

"You didn't have to become a doctor to help people, did you?" she persisted. "You could have built a hospital, couldn't you have?"

"Thanks to my rich grandfather who left me a trust, yes, I could have. But I wanted to do something on my own. If I could ever find another doctor who's interested, I'd like to open a women's infirmary, something a great deal more complete than that two-bit clinic that's set up for them now. I'd like a decent place where women like my mother could be treated. But all the doctors say gynecology is treating women whose illnesses are in their heads."

"What about Blair?" she asked, suddenly alert.

"Blair? But she's a wo—." He broke off at the look in her eyes. "Perhaps. When she's finished her training. Let's not start talking about her again. Come over here."

"I really think I should go . . ."

"Houston!" he snapped. "Is this the way it's always going to be? Will you always refuse me?" His voice was showing his growing anger. "If we get married, will you still refuse me then?"

"If?" Blair whispered. "*If* we get married?" What had she done to cause this? Could he be thinking of calling off the wedding after only one evening with Blair? Was Houston so much warmer to Lee than this that he considered her reactions tonight unforgivably cold?

"Sweetheart, let's not argue." He opened his arms to her.

Blair hesitated only a moment before she remembered Houston's caution about not arguing with Lee. Perhaps if she kissed him just a few more times, then he'd be satisfied and take her home to safety.

She went to him, let him hold her, her body full against his and, as he began to kiss her, she forgot about everyone except the two of them.

Leander held her close to him in a way that was almost desperate, almost as if he feared that she'd disappear, and Blair was acutely aware that this could be the only time in her life that she would be near this man who made her feel like this. His mouth held hers in a deathless grip, never letting her go as she clung to him.

When his hands went to her back and his skillful surgeon's fingers began to unfasten the hooks and eyes at the back of her dress, she had no thoughts about stopping him. The dress began to fall away and, as her shoulders became visible, Lee kissed them, ran his hands over her skin until it tingled.

Within moments, the dress was in a heap beside them and the rustle of the pink silk taffeta petticoat between them was a further spur to their growing passion. Leander's long legs moved over the stiff fabric, twisting it and pulling it from her body at the same time.

Blair couldn't move away from his lips and her hands buried themselves in his long, clean hair and she could smell the deep male scent of it.

"Leander," she whispered, as his lips moved own her arm and his hands rid her of two more petticoats. Satin, taffeta, and the softest of cottons surrounded them, cocooning them together in the warm glow of the firelight.

His hands on her body seemed to be everywhere, stroking her, caressing her, removing clothing with infinite care and slowness, sliding each piece of fabric down her skin, exposing more of her to his touch.

With his hand on her leg, running up and down over her silk stocking, his lips on her earlobe, she realized that he was still wearing his clothes and she began tugging at them.

In removing his own clothing, he did not use the care he did with hers, but instead, pulled it off with a force just short of violence.

In medical school, Blair had seen many men nude, and once she had seen Alan with his shirt off, but she had never seen a warm, alive man with dark, sunbrowned skin coming at her with the fire in his eyes that Lee had now. For a moment, she pulled back from him as he moved to draw her back into his arms.

There was caution in his eyes when she withdrew from him, but Blair didn't see it. All she saw was Lee—his skin, his lovely skin, curving around firmly muscled shoulders, tapering down to his flat stomach. With interest, she looked downward, curious as to the difference between a man who was alive and one who was dead—the only way she'd seen a man who was fully nude before today.

"Do I pass inspection?" he asked, and his voice was husky.

Blair didn't answer as she drew him to her and put her arms around that skin that glowed so.

Leander wasted no more time in removing the rest of her clothing, slipping the garters off the hose and even unbuttoning her shoes, all without ceasing his caressing of her, so that by the time Blair was completely bare, she was beginning to feel that her passion was rising to a level that might eventually cause her to burst.

Nothing she had ever felt before prepared her for the feeling of her skin against Lee's. With a gasp of pleasure, she clung to him, slipped her leg between his and tried to get closer to him.

Lee pulled her over on top of him, kissing her, his hands running down her back, over her thighs, and back up her buttocks, lingering by her sides at her breasts.

His mouth never left hers as he rolled her to her back and slowly spread her legs with his own.

In theory, Blair knew how the human species reproduced itself. They'd had special classes for unmarried women at her medical college, but none of the teachers had mentioned the passion involved in the act. She had not guessed that a woman felt this way, that it wasn't an act purely for the purpose of procreation, but it was an act of love and lust.

She was ready for Lee when he entered her, but it still hurt, and she gasped with the pain. He lay still for a moment, his breath hot on her neck, his lips quiet as he waited for some sign from her.

Blair recovered from the first moment of pain and began to

move her hips slowly, her hands on his back and moving downward over his hips. Only Lee's jagged breathing in her ear showed her the supreme effort he was exerting to control himself with her, to hold back so he didn't hurt her.

It was only when she began to move that he followed her lead and very slowly began to make love to her.

There was no pain as Lee made slow, gentle strokes and Blair, awkward at first, moved with him. After a few moments, the slowness left them both and their passion showed itself in a frenzy. They could not get enough as they arched against each other, clinging, clutching, trying the impossible of getting closer until at last they exploded together.

Blair held on to Lee as if she were afraid to let go. Their sweaty bodies stuck together, even their skin melded into one.

"I love you," Leander whispered into her ear. "I'm not sure I did before. I'm not sure I knew you before tonight. I'm not sure either of us is the same person as yesterday, but I do know that I love you and, Houston, I've never loved another woman."

For a moment, Blair couldn't understand why the man in her arms had called her by her sister's name.

Remembrance came to her all too swiftly. With a feeling of sheer horror, she started to pull away from Lee. "I have to go home," she said, and her voice showed all that she felt.

"Houston," Lee said, "it's not the end of the world. We'll be married in two weeks, and then we'll spend all our nights together."

"Let me up! I have to get home."

He looked at her for a long moment, as if he were deciding whether or not to be angry, but at last he smiled. "You can be as shy as you want, sweetheart. Here, let me help you with that."

Blair couldn't even look at him. It had been the most wonderful experience of her life, but it hadn't really belonged to her. She had cheated her sister, cheated the man she was to marry, and lied to this man who . . . who . . .

Under her eyelashes, she looked at Lee as he helped her with her corset strings. If she wasn't careful, she'd be back in his arms and, if he asked her, she'd probably board the next train with him and forget all about her obligations to other people.

"You certainly seem to know your way around a woman's underclothing," she snapped at him.

Lee chuckled as he held the taffeta petticoat for her to step into. "Well enough, I guess. Shall I do your garters for you?"

Snatching her hose out of his hand, she sat on a chair and began to roll them onto her legs, trying her best to ignore him. What in the world had she done? Houston was going to hate her. And what would Lee say when he found that his bride was a virgin—again? And what would Alan say if he knew? How could she explain to him? Would anyone believe her if she said that he'd touched her and after that she'd had no more control over her own body? Maybe all the things that Duncan Gates said about her were true.

"Houston," Lee said, kneeling in front of her. "You look as if you're about to cry." He took her hands in his. "Look at me, sweetheart. I know how you've been raised, and I know you meant to stay a virgin until we were married, but what happened tonight was between us and it was all right. I'll be your husband in very little time, and then we can enjoy each other as often as we want. And if you're worried about the morality of what we did, I'm a doctor and I can tell you that many, many women who enter marriage have spent some time alone with the men they love."

He was making everything worse. The man she loved was not the man she'd just made love to, and the man she was to marry had not taken her virginity.

She stood. "Please take me home," she said, and Leander obeyed her.

Chapter 6

"Good morning," Leander said with uncharacteristic jubilation to his father and sister, Nina, who sat at the breakfast table.

Nina, twenty-one and very pretty, paused with her coffee cup on the way to her mouth. "Then it's true what I heard," she said.

Lee helped himself to an enormous plateful of food from the sideboard.

"Sarah Oakley called first thing this morning and told me that last night at the reception you and Houston couldn't take your eyes—or hands—off each other. She said that she'd never seen two people so in love."

"Did she now?" Lee asked. "And just what was so unusual about that? I *have* asked the beautiful lady to marry me."

"But there have been times when you looked as though you wanted to run away rather than stay with your lovely bride."

Lee smiled at his sister. "When you grow up, baby sister, maybe you'll know a little more about the birds and the bees." As he put his plate down across from her, he reached over and kissed her on the forehead.

Nina nearly choked on her food. "That does it," she said,

looking up at her father. "He's either mad or he's finally fallen in love."

Reed was leaning back in his chair and watching his son with great interest. When Lee looked up at him and winked, his worst fears were confirmed.

"You sure know a lot about women, Dad," Lee grinned and Reed burst out laughing.

"I don't think I want to know what that little exchange was about," Nina said primly as she rose to leave. "I think I'll call Houston and give her my condolences."

"Tell her I'll pick her up at eleven," Lee said with his mouth full. "And I'll bring a picnic basket."

Reed stayed in his chair and lit his pipe, something he rarely did in the morning, and watched his son eat. Usually, Leander ate slowly and carefully, but today he was wolfing food as if there were no tomorrow. He seemed to be lost in a world of his own, a world of happiness and plans for the future.

"I've been thinking about that women's hospital lately," Lee said, as he bit into a two-inch-thick biscuit. "Actually, Houston made me think of it. Maybe it's time that I start looking into building the thing, or maybe I'll buy that old stone warehouse at the end of Archer Avenue. With some work and some money, that place could be just what I need."

"Houston had this idea?" Reed asked.

"Not really, but she helped. I have to get to the hospital, and later I'm to meet Houston. I'll see you." He grabbed an apple and, at the doorway, he paused to look back at his father. "Thanks, Dad," he said, just the way he did when he was a boy, and today he reminded Reed of the boy he'd once been, before he took on the responsibility of planning marriage.

All morning, Lee whistled at the hospital and his cheer was infectious. Before long, the entire hospital was smiling and grumbling less about the work to be done. The young prostitute who'd tried suicide the day before benefited the most from Lee's good humor. He talked to her about the joy of being alive and then got her a position on the nursing staff at the women's clinic, promising to watch over her and to help her in the future.

At ten minutes to eleven, he jumped in his carriage and drove downtown to pick up a basket that he'd had Miss Emily prepare at her tea shop.

"So it's true," Miss Emily said, smiling and making her pink-and-white face crinkle into tiny tissue paper wrinkles. "Nina has been talking about her lovesick brother all morning."

"My sister talks entirely too much," Lee said, but he was smiling. "I don't know what's so unusual about my being happy, because I'm marrying the most beautiful woman in the world. I've got to go," he said, as he rushed out of the shop.

He left his horse and buggy to the care of the Gates's stableboy, Willie, took the steps two at a time and raised his hand to knock.

"You can go in," came a voice from the shadowed side of the deep porch. "They're expecting you."

Leander looked into the shadows and saw Blair there, her face turned away, but he could see that her hair was straggling and her face streaked. He went to her. "Has something happened? Is Houston all right?"

"She's fine!" Blair snapped, starting to rise.

Lee caught her arm. "I want you to come over here and sit down so I can look at you. You don't look well at all."

"Leave me alone!" she half cried, half shouted. "And don't touch me!" She jerked away from him, ran down the stairs and out of sight around the house.

As Lee was standing there in open-mouthed astonishment, Houston came onto the porch, pulling on gloves of white lace.

"Was that Blair shouting? You weren't having another one of your arguments, were you?" she asked.

Lee turned to her with a look of pure joy, his eyes going up and down her, as if he wanted to drink in all of her. "It was Blair," he said in answer to her question.

"Good," Houston said, "I was hoping you'd see her. She's been like that all day. For some reason, I think she's been crying. I thought you might know what was wrong with her. She won't answer any of my questions."

"I'd have to examine her," Lee said, as he helped her into

the carriage, but as soon as he touched her, he couldn't seem to let go, and held onto her waist.

"Lee! People are watching."

"Yes, of course," he grinned, "but we'll soon remedy that."

He didn't trust himself to speak much on the way out of town, only occasionally glancing at Houston, noting the way she sat so far to the side of the carriage, away from him as she always had until last night. He couldn't help smiling to himself to think that this cool young woman was the same one who hadn't been able to resist him last night.

He hadn't slept much, but had lain awake reliving every moment he'd spent with Houston. It wasn't so much the sex, he'd had that with women before and hadn't fallen for them, but it was something about her attitude that had made him feel wonderful, powerful, as if he could do anything.

He drove them to a secret place he'd found once when he'd been called to set the broken leg of a prospector and been caught in a summer storm. It was a secluded place amid enormous rocks, with tall trees swaying overhead, a spring trickling out of the rocks. He'd never brought anyone here before.

He stopped the carriage, jumped out, tied the horse and went to get Houston. As he lifted her in his arms, he let her slide down and pulled her close to him, hugging her so that she couldn't breathe. "I thought about nothing else but you last night," he said. "I could smell your hair on my clothes, I could taste your lips on mine, I could—."

Houston pulled away from him. "You what?" she gasped.

He touched the hair at her temples with the backs of his fingers. "You aren't going to be shy with me today, are you? You aren't going to be the way you were before last night, are you? Houston, you've proven to me that you can be different, so there's no need to go back to being the ice princess. I know what you're really like now, and I can tell you that if I never see that cool woman again, I'll be even happier. Now, come here and kiss me like you did last night."

Houston pushed free of him. "Are you saying that last night I wasn't like I usually am? That I was . . . better?"

Smiling, he advanced on her. "You know you were. You

were like I've never seen you. I didn't know you could be like that. You'll laugh at this but I was beginning to believe that you were incapable of any real passion, that beneath your cool exterior was a heart of ice. But, if you can have a sister like Blair who starts fires at the least provocation, surely some of it had to rub off."

He took her wrist in his hand and pulled her to him, ignoring the way she resisted. He also ignored the way she tried to turn her head away when he put his mouth on hers.

The lips under his were unresponsive, held together rigidly, hard. At first, he was amused that she was trying to keep herself under control and doing such a damn fine job of it, but as the kiss continued, and she still made no response, he pulled away from her in anger.

"You're carrying this game too far," he said. "You can't be wildly passionate one minute and frigid the next. What are you, two people?"

Something in Houston's eyes gave him the first seed of doubt. But of course he was wrong. He took a step backward.

"That's an impossibility, isn't it, Houston?" he said. "Tell me that what I'm thinking is wrong. No one can be two people, can she?"

Houston just stood there and looked at him with stricken eyes.

Lee walked away from her and at last sat down heavily on a rock. "Did you and your sister trade places last night?" he asked softly. "Did I spend the evening with Blair and not with you?"

He barely heard her whispered, "Yes."

"I should have known from the first: how well she handled that suicide and she didn't even know it was the house I'd bought for her—you. I don't think I wanted to see. From the moment she said she wanted to go on the case with me to see if she could be of any help, I was so stupidly pleased that I never questioned anything after that. I should have known when I kissed her . . .

"Damn both of you! I hope to hell you enjoyed making a fool of me."

"Lee," Houston said, her hand on his arm.

He turned on her angrily. "If you know what's good for

you, you won't say a word. I don't know what possessed either of you to play such a dirty little trick, but I can tell you that I don't like being the butt of such a joke. Now that you and your sister have had a good laugh at my expense, I have to decide what to do about last night."

He half shoved her into the carriage and cracked the whip over the horse as they tore back into town. At the Chandler house, he didn't get out but let Houston get herself, and all her yards of skirts, out of the carriage unaided. On the porch, waiting, was Blair, her face red and swollen from crying for hours on end. Leander glared at her with a mixture of anger and some hatred before he yelled at the horse and took off again.

He paused for only moments at his father's house before mounting a big roan stallion and taking off for the mountains at breakneck speed. He didn't know where he was going, but he knew that he had to get away and think.

He climbed with the horse until the animal could go no farther, then dismounted and led the horse, straight up, over rocks, across arroyos, through cacti and mean little under-brush. When at last he came to the top of a ridge, when he could go no higher, he pulled the rifle from the horse's saddle, jammed it against his leg and fired it up into the air, emptying it. Once the air had cleared of screaming birds and gunsmoke, he yelled at the top of his lungs, giving vent to his frustration and anger.

"Damn you, Blair!" he shouted. "Damn you to hell."

The sun was setting as Reed Westfield walked into the library. As he reached for the light switch, he saw the glow of one of his son's cigars.

"Lee?" he asked, as he pushed the button for the lights. "The hospital was calling for you."

Leander didn't look up. "Did they find someone?"

Reed studied his son for a moment. "They found someone. What happened to the man who left here this morning? Don't tell me that Houston regretted what happened last night? Women do that. Your mother—."

Lee looked at his father with bleak eyes. "Spare me more

54

of the advice about women. I don't believe I can stand any more."

Reed sat down. "Tell me what's happened."

Lee flicked the ash off his cigar. "I believe that, as they say, all hell is about to break loose in a few minutes. Last night," he paused to take a breath and calm himself. "Last night, the Chandler twins decided to play a game. They thought it'd be great fun to switch places and see if they could fool poor stupid Leander. They did quite well."

He jammed his cigar into an ashtray and stood, walking to the window. "I was fooled all right, and not because Blair did such a good job of pretending to be her sister. In fact, she did little more than dress like Houston. Blair assisted me in a medical case without my giving her any instruction; she was interested in my life, something Houston's never cared much about; Blair asked me about my dreams and hopes for the future. In other words, she was the perfect woman whom every man dreams about."

He turned back to look at his father. "And she was the perfect lover. I guess every man's vanity wants a woman who can't resist him. He likes to think that he can talk her into anything. So far, all the women I've known have been interested in the money I had in the bank. I've had women who weren't interested in me when they thought I was a lowly, unpaid doctor, but when they learned that my mother was a Candish, their eyes began to sparkle. Blair wasn't like that. She was—."

His voice trailed off as he turned back to face the window.

"Houston isn't interested in your money," Reed said. "She never has been."

"Who knows what Houston wants out of life. I've spent months with her and I don't know anything about her. To me, she's a cold woman who does nothing more than look pretty. But Blair is alive!"

He said the last with such passion that Reed narrowed his eyes. "I don't think I like the sound of that. Houston is the woman you're going to marry. I know Blair is a forward girl, and it's a shame about what happened last night, but I tried to warn you that that kind of thing could get you in trouble. I'm sure Houston will be angry, but if you court her enough and send enough flowers, she'll eventually forgive you."

Lee looked at his father. "And what about Blair? Will she forgive me?"

Reed walked to the big walnut desk that dominated the room and took a pipe from a box. "If she's the kind of girl who'd sleep with her sister's intended, then I imagine she already knows how to get over this sort of thing."

"And just what is that supposed to mean?"

"Exactly what it sounds like. She's been back East all these years, going to school with men, studying things she has no right to know anything about, and trying to be a man. Girls like her know from experience how to recover from affairs of one night's duration."

Leander took minutes to get his emotions under control. "I'm going to forget you said that, but I want you to know that if you ever say anything like that again, I'll walk out the door and never come back. It's none of your business, but Blair was a virgin until last night. And in two weeks' time I mean to make her my wife."

Reed was so flabbergasted that he just stood there opening and closing his mouth like a fish out of water.

Lee took a seat and lit another cigar. "I think I'd better tell you all I know of what's happened. As I said last night, for some reason, the twins decided to trade places so it was Blair I took to the reception. I had already planned to do my best to seduce her and, if I found her unwilling, I was going to break off the engagement. I think I was expecting to have to do that, since I was sure that no one, or at least not me, could break through that coating of ice that surrounds Houston."

He held the cigar out, and a faint smile curved his lips as he remembered last night. "Within five minutes of being alone with her, I was so pleased with Blair that I never thought of questioning who she was or why she was behaving so differently. There was an emergency on River Street and she went with me, unlike Houston who always insisted that I drop her at one of her friends' houses. We went to the reception and later to our house. Altogether, it was the most pleasurable evening of my life."

"So now, you think you have to marry her," Reed said with

heavy-sounding finality. "Couldn't you give it some time? You hardly know her. Marriage is forever. You'll have to spend your life with this woman, and one night's acquaintance isn't enough to base that on. Just because she's feisty in bed doesn't mean—." He stopped at Lee's look.

"All right," Reed continued. "So now, you ask for the young lady's hand in marriage. What happens to Houston? Do you just walk away from her? Women take these things quite hard, you know."

"Since all this was started by the twins, I don't feel too bad. They should have thought of the consequences."

"They could hardly have known that you would choose that night to decide the fate of your future. Before you ask Blair to marry you, why don't you wait a month or so? That'll give both of you some time to think about what you're doing."

"It's too late for that. Besides, I don't think Blair would marry me."

"Don't . . . ?" Reed began. "If she'll sleep with you, why the hell won't she marry you?"

In spite of the anger in his father's voice, Lee began to smile. "I'm not sure she likes me. She thinks I'm a bigot like Gates, and I honestly believe that if I asked her to marry me, she'd laugh in my face."

Reed threw up his hands in despair. "I don't understand any of this."

At that moment, the front door was thrown open, and immediately there was the sound of shouting throughout the house.

Lee rose from his chair. "That will no doubt be the outraged Mr. Duncan Gates. I went to his brewery an hour ago and told him that I had deflowered his stepdaughter and, to make amends, I would marry the wayward girl. He is bringing Blair and the four of us are going to discuss the matter. Don't look so glum, Dad. I mean to have her and I'll use any method I can to get her."

Chapter 7

"I have absolutely no intention of marrying him. None," Blair said for the twentieth time.

"You are soiled, unfit," Duncan raged. "No one else will have you."

Blair tried her best to keep calm and not show the turmoil that was boiling inside her. Gates had been shouting at her and trying to intimidate her for three solid hours. She thought about her Uncle Henry's calmness, how he'd look at what had happened with some humor, and they would sit down and talk about the situation as if they were sane adults. But not Gates. He had the medieval idea that now that she was no longer a virgin, she should be cast down to the dogs—or to Leander, which was about the same thing as far as Blair was concerned.

"May I ask why you don't want to marry my son?" Reed Westfield asked.

Blair could feel animosity coming from the man, like heat waves on the desert. "I have told you that I have been accepted to intern at a major hospital in Pennsylvania and I plan to take the offer. Besides, I don't love your son. He is engaged to my sister and, as soon as possible after their wedding, I will return to Pennsylvania, and no one in this town need ever see me again. I don't know how to make myself more clear than that."

"You've ruined your sister's life!" Gates shouted. "You don't think she can marry him after this?"

"Are you insinuating that Leander was . . . ah, unsoiled, as you put it, before last night?"

Duncan's face turned red.

"Calm down, Duncan," Reed said. "Blair, there must be some way that we can work this out to everyone's satisfaction. Surely, you must have *some* feelings for my son."

Blair looked at Lee, who was standing at the back of the room and appearing to enjoy everything. Not any feelings that she could tell publicly, she thought, and as if Lee could read her mind, he smiled at her in such a way that she blushed and had to look away. "I told you before," she said. "I was pretending to be my sister, and I was acting the way I thought she would act with the man she loved. I don't think I should be punished for being an excellent actress."

Reed lifted one eyebrow. "I don't think any actress carries her role that far."

"And I'll not have Houston's name dragged through the mud by you or anyone else," Duncan shouted. "She wouldn't have done what you've done. She's a good girl."

"And I'm not, is that it?" Blair asked, torn between tears and outrage.

"A decent woman wouldn't—."

"I've heard all I want to hear," Lee said, stepping forward. "Would you leave us now? I want to talk to Blair alone."

Blair wanted to protest that she didn't want to see him alone, but perhaps he wasn't as bad as all of them shouting at her.

"Would you like some sherry?" he asked, when they were alone.

"Please," she answered, taking the glass with shaking hands.

He frowned when he saw her hands. "I had no idea that he was as bad as that. Houston'd told me, but I hadn't imagined half of it."

Blair drank the wine gratefully and hoped it would calm her

nerves. "If you didn't think he was so bad, why did you enlist his help in your preposterous scheme?"

"I wanted all the help I could get. I thought—correctly—that if I went to you on my own, you'd laugh in my face."

"I'm not laughing now."

"All right, then let's get this settled. The invitations are at the printer's, and all that has to be changed is your name for Houston's."

Blair jumped up from her chair. "Of all the stupid ideas I have ever heard, that's the worst. Can't you hear me? I don't *want* to marry you. I don't want to spend another minute in this dreadful town. I want to go home and I want my sister to get her fiancé back. What can I say to you people to make you understand? I want to go home!"

In spite of her good intentions, she collapsed in the chair, put her face in her hands and burst into tears. "He's right," she cried, "I've ruined Houston's life."

Lee knelt before her and very gently pulled her hands down. "Don't you understand that I want to marry *you,* not Houston?"

She looked at him for a moment, felt his warm hands on her wrists and considered the matter, but before she could let herself be persuaded, she got up and went to stand before the window.

"You belong to my sister. Since she was a child, she has planned to marry you. She has a trunkful of linens embroidered with an *L* and an *H* intertwined. She's never wanted to be anything but Mrs. Leander Westfield. She loves you, don't you know that? And what I love is medicine. Medicine has been my life since I was twelve and now I've earned this internship and I want to take it and marry Alan and live happily ever after."

Leander lost the concerned look he was wearing and stood bolt upright. "Alan? And just who the hell is he?"

"Since I've returned to this town, no one has asked me about my life in Pennsylvania. Gates shouts at me that I'm immoral, Mother just sits and sews, Houston spends most of her time ordering new dresses, and you . . . you just stand there giving me orders."

Several emotions went across Lee's face. "Who is Alan?"

"The man to whom I'm engaged. The man I love. The man who is coming to Chandler in two days to meet my family and tell them that he would be honored to marry me."

"*I'm* asking for that honor."

"I'm sure that you fell in love with me after one night." To her surprise, Leander said nothing to this.

He toyed with a letter opener on the desk. "What if I make you want to marry me? What if by the end of two weeks you *want* to walk down that aisle to me?"

"There's not a chance in the world of that happening. Alan will be here soon and, besides, I told you, you belong to Houston."

"I do, do I?" he said and, in one stride, he was across the room to her and had her in his arms.

His kiss was as draining to her senses as it had been last night when she'd pretended to be her sister. She was weak when he released her.

"Now, tell me I don't have a chance." He moved away from her. "Did it ever occur to you that this Alan might not want you after you explain why your name is on the wedding invitation?"

"He's not like that. He's a very understanding man."

"We'll see how understanding he is. You're going to marry me two weeks from now, and you'd better get used to the idea."

Blair somehow managed to remain calm until Mr. Gates took her back to the Chandler house—and then she saw Houston's face. Her sister looked as if nothing in life mattered any more. Blair had been worried about Houston's future, had been so concerned that she'd wanted to go out with Leander just to assure herself that her sister would be all right. And what she'd managed to do was destroy Houston's entire future.

Blair begged her sister to answer, but Houston refused to speak to her, and even when Blair burst into tears, Houston wouldn't relent.

Mr. Gates fairly pushed Blair up to her room on the third floor and locked the door behind her. Even when Opal came to the door and asked to see her daughter, Gates refused to open it.

Blair sat for a long time inside the dark room, her eyes too dry to cry since she'd been crying all day and quite a bit of the night. Now, she had to make a plan to get herself out of this mess. She wasn't going to be forced to stay in this town and marry a man she didn't want to marry, nor was she going to give up her internship at St. Joseph's Hospital.

She sat quietly until she heard no more sounds from inside the house, and then she went to the window. As a child, she'd managed to climb to the ground by using the long, serpentine branches of the old elm tree on the east side of the house. If she jumped, she thought she could make the largest branch of the tree—and if she missed . . . She didn't like to think of that.

Hurriedly, she packed a soft bag with a few clothes and tossed it to the ground, waiting a moment for the sounds of alarm. So far, so good. No one seemed to have heard her. She slipped into a divided skirt and climbed onto the window ledge, holding on with one hand and reaching as far as she could with the other. She could just barely reach the tree branches. She pulled back, knowing that there was no way that she could get to the tree except by jumping. She crouched in the window, and with one big leap, sent herself hurtling through the air, grabbing the tree branch as she went by.

She hung there, suspended in the air, and she could hear the slight cracking of the wood. It took several tries but she managed to get her legs around the branch just before her arms gave out. Using all her strength, while hanging upside down by her hands and ankles, and feeling the bark and sharp places scratch her skin through her clothing and hose, she managed to propel herself to the trunk of the tree. Once there, she took a moment to catch her breath before beginning the descent.

When she was finally on the ground, she looked back at the house with a feeling of triumph. They weren't going to make her stay where she didn't want to.

A sound to her left made her whirl about.

A match was lit and the flame showed Leander's face as he held the match to a cigar. "Need some help with your bag?" he asked, when he looked at her.

"What are you doing here?" she gasped.

"Protecting what I've come to think of as mine," he said, smiling.

"You were standing here while I was fighting for my life at the top of that tree?"

"Not quite the top, and I didn't see that you were in any real danger. Who taught you to climb like that?"

"Certainly not you. You were too busy saving lives to learn how to climb trees when you were a boy."

"What odd ideas you have about me. I can't imagine where you got them. Now, if you've had your nightly exercise, I suggest that we get you back into the house. After you, my lady," he said, making a sweeping bow toward the tree.

"I have no intention of returning to that house. There's a train to Denver in a little while and I will be on it."

"Not if I tell Gates. I'm sure that he'll be after you with a shotgun."

"You wouldn't!"

"Do you forget that I was the one who started this in the first place? I don't plan to let you leave Chandler now or ever."

"I think I'm beginning to hate you."

"You didn't hate me last night," he said softly. "Now, do you want a repeat demonstration of just how much you don't hate me or do I help you back into your boudoir?"

Blair gritted her teeth. He had to sleep sometime and when he did, she'd be ready to escape.

"Stop looking at me as if you'd like to have me on a platter for breakfast and come on." He grabbed the lowest branch of the tree and swung himself up, holding out his hand to her.

Reluctantly, she took his hand and let him pull her up. She did get some satisfaction from the fact that she did very little to help, and he had to pull her dead weight.

When they were at the roof, he helped her into the window, leaned forward and whispered, "How about a good-night kiss?"

Blair, with a little smile, leaned toward him as if she meant to kiss him and, at the last minute, slammed the window down so that Lee had to jump to keep his fingers from getting caught. From behind the glass, she puckered her lips into a kiss before she pulled the shade down to block him from view.

As she was smiling, she heard a crack of wood from outside, a muffled cry, then a heavy thud.

"He's fallen," she gasped, as she threw open the window and stuck her head out. "Lee!" she called as loud as she dared.

To her surprise, he put his head around the window jamb and kissed her quickly and firmly. "I knew you couldn't resist me."

With that, he jumped to the longest branch and was on the ground in record time. "You should have let *me* teach you how to climb trees," he laughed up at her and then sat down under the tree as if he planned to spend all night there.

Blair slammed down the window and went to bed.

Chapter 8

On Sunday morning, Gates told Blair to get dressed for church, and she was to look as much like a lady as she could manage.

Breakfast was a sullen meal, with Houston more rigid than usual, and both she and Opal looked as if they'd been crying most of the night. Duncan's face seemed to be permanently set in the mask of a martyr who was suffering for everyone.

Immediately after the awful meal, Opal said that she didn't feel well enough to attend church and retired to her room. Gates got Blair into a corner and told her that she was killing her mother with her wicked ways.

Church was the worst. The minister seemed to think that what had happened between the twins was a great joke and made the congregation laugh when he said that Lee had changed his mind about which twin he wanted to marry.

After the service, people gathered around them, wanting to know what was going on, but Houston just stood there looking as if she were made of steel. And when Leander tried to talk to her, she answered him with barely concealed anger, so of course he decided to take his fury and frustration out on

Blair. He grabbed her arm and half dragged her to his waiting carriage.

Blair was thrown against the seat of the buggy as Lee took off and headed for the south of town. It wasn't until they were out of town that he slowed down.

Blair straightened her hat. "Did you think that she'd smile at you and say something pleasant?"

He halted the buggy. "I thought she'd be reasonable. It was the two of you who started the whole game. I never meant to publicly humiliate her."

"All you have to do is help me get back to Pennsylvania, and you can go back to Houston on bended knee and I'm sure she'll have you."

He looked at her for quite a while. "No, I won't do that. You and I are going to be married. I brought a picnic basket and I thought we could have lunch." He wrapped the reins around the brake handle, climbed down and went to help Blair down. But as he came around the horse, he paused. "I seem to have a rock in my shoe," he said, and leaned against a tree to remove it.

Blair sat there for a moment and watched him, thinking about her sister's face during the announcement in church; thinking that she didn't want to remain in Chandler or become this man's wife; then she grabbed the reins, flicked them, and yelled to the horse to go while Leander stood there wearing only one shoe. He chased her for a while, but he soon stopped when he stepped on something with his stockinged foot and started limping.

When she was safely out of reach of him, she slowed the horse and returned to Chandler. She had to find a way to escape the town. After this morning's announcement, she couldn't very well board a train without some curiosity being aroused. Being a Chandler in a town named Chandler had drawbacks. Tomorrow, Alan would arrive and perhaps he'd help her. In spite of what she'd told Lee, she had some worries about whether Alan would still want her after what had happened.

The minute Blair saw the Chandler house, she knew something was wrong. Opal was sitting on the porch, and when she saw Blair, she jumped up.

"Do you know where your sister is?"

Blair hurried up the stairs. "Has she run away? Let me change and we'll start looking for her."

"It's worse than that," Opal said, sitting down in the porch swing. "That awful man, Mr. Taggert, came to the church and told everyone that he and Houston were going to be married, that it was to be a double wedding with you and Leander. What is happening to my family? Mr. Gates says that that man Taggert has killed people to get what he has, and I can't help but feel that Houston is taking this man because she lost Leander and she wants to show the town that she can get another husband. And he must be very rich. I'd hate to think that she's marrying the man for his money."

Blair sat down in the swing beside her mother. "This is all my fault."

Opal patted her daughter's knee. "You always were easy to talk into anything. Don't look so surprised, dear, I know my daughters quite well. For all that Houston looks as though butter wouldn't melt in her mouth, I know she was the one who used to talk you into the most daring things. You've always had the very biggest of hearts and always wanted to help people, which is why I'm sure that you'll make a very good doctor."

"If I ever get out of here and can continue my education," Blair said bleakly.

Opal toyed with a clematis vine running up the side of the porch. "I've been thinking about you and Lee. You might not think so at the moment, but he really is a very fine man. I don't think anyone knows him very well. He was always so quiet around Houston, but in the last few days, he's been more animated than I've ever seen him."

"Animated! Is that what you call it? He orders me about, tells me I am going to marry him, says that a woman can't be his partner in the clinic he wants to build and, in general, is a narrow-minded pig of a man."

"And did you think that on Friday night?"

Blair turned her face away to hide a blush. "Perhaps I didn't then, but I'd had a great deal of champagne, and there was moonlight and dancing and things just happened."

"Mmmmm," Opal said noncommittally. "However you saw that night, I don't think Lee saw it the same way."

"I'm not sure I care how he saw it. The problem now is Houston. I have returned to this town and effectively ruined her life, and now she says that she's planning to marry that ugly Midas, Kane Taggert. How are we going to prevent that from happening?"

"Mr. Gates and I are going to talk to her as soon as she returns home and see if we can persuade her to believe that there is another solution to this problem, other than the drastic one she seems set on."

Blair looked out through the greenery surrounding the porch and toward the white corner of the Taggert mansion. "I deeply and sincerely hate that house," she said with feeling. "If Houston hadn't wanted to see it so badly, we wouldn't have changed places, and I wouldn't have spent the night with Leander and, now, if she didn't want that house so much, she wouldn't be considering marrying that barbarian."

"Blair, you should rest this afternoon. Read some of the books you brought, and let us worry about Houston. By the way, where is Lee? Why didn't he bring you home?"

Blair stood. "I think I will rest. I didn't get much sleep last night. And Lee will probably be by in a while to pick up the carriage. Under no circumstances do I want to see him."

Opal hesitated a moment before she agreed. "I'll send Susan up with a tray. You rest, dear, because, if I know this town, tomorrow will be hectic. Just as soon as everyone hears about your marriage to Lee and Houston's to that man, I'm sure . . . Oh my, I don't even like to think about it."

Blair didn't want to either and, gratefully, she went to the sanctity of her room, where she stayed for the rest of the day.

Monday was worse than Blair ever imagined it could be. Breakfast was dreadful. Gates kept yelling, his mouth stuffed with food, that Blair had ruined her sister's life. Since Blair tended to agree with him, it was difficult to defend herself. Opal kept crying, while Houston managed to look faraway, as if she weren't hearing any of it.

After breakfast, people began to arrive in droves—wagonloads of them bearing food and flimsy excuses as to why they were there. It'd been so long since she'd lived in a small town that she was appalled at how nosy the people were. There didn't seem to be anything that they considered none of their business. Paramount was the answer to why Lee was now marrying Blair. And they were very curious about Taggert, asking Houston thousands of questions about him and what his house was like.

At eleven, Blair went into the house, to put away one of the numerous pies that someone had brought, and managed to slip out the back door without anyone seeing her. She practically ran the two miles to the train station and she felt, with every step, that she was getting closer to freedom. When Alan came, he would be able to straighten out the entire mess, and then Houston would be able to marry Leander and Blair could return home.

Impatiently, she waited for the train to pull into the station and when it did, at last, she thought the steam would never clear. But through the mist, she saw him and began to run with the train, following him until he could jump off and take her in his arms.

She didn't care that the people of Chandler watched them, or that they thought that she was engaged to another man— all that mattered was that she was with Alan again.

"What a wonderful welcome," he said, holding her close.

She pulled back to look at him. He was still as handsome as she remembered, still with his blond-haired, blue-eyed wholesome good looks, a few inches taller than she was.

She had started to say something when she saw that his attention was directed to something over her shoulder. She turned quickly—but not quickly enough.

Leander deftly slipped his arm about her waist and managed to pull her to him and away from Alan in one motion. "So, you must be Alan," he said smoothly, with a warm smile. "I've heard so much about you. Of course, there aren't many secrets between lovers, are there, sweetheart?"

"Release me!" she said under her breath while trying to smile at the look of puzzlement on Alan's face. While shoving an elbow in Lee's ribs, she told Alan, "May I introduce my sister's fiancé? This is Leander Westfield. And this is Alan Hunter, my—."

Lee cut her words off by squeezing her ribs with his hand, and even three sharp elbowings in his side didn't make him release her. He extended his hand to Alan. "Excuse Blair, won't you? She's a little excited today at getting to see an old and dear friend. I am *her* intended. She and I are to be married in two weeks, actually less than that now, isn't it, dear? Just a few short days and you will become Mrs. Leander Westfield. I know the anticipation is making you a bit nervous and forgetful, but let's not give your friend the wrong impression." He smiled angelically at Alan.

"This isn't the way it seems," Blair began. "This man is crazy, and he has some very strange ideas." With one big push, she managed to move away from Lee. "Alan, let's go somewhere and talk. I have a great deal to tell you."

Alan looked up at Lee, who was several inches taller than he. "I think we do need to talk." He held his arm out to her. "Shall we go?" He looked over his shoulder at Lee. "You may carry my bags, young man."

Lee successfully pushed himself between the couple. "I would generally take great delight in carrying the bags of a friend of my wife-to-be, but today I have a little problem. Yesterday, I had to walk four miles in new shoes, and my feet are too blistered to endure any extra weight. My doctor has insisted that I put no stress on them. Come along, Blair, we'll meet your little friend at the carriage."

"You beast!" Blair spat up at him as he pulled her toward the carriage. "And just what doctor would prescribe an asinine remedy like that?"

"Dr. Westfield at your service," he said, as he helped her into the carriage.

"That's an unusual horse," Alan said as he threw his bags in the back, referring to the appaloosa that pulled Lee's carriage.

"The only one in this area," Lee said proudly. "Wherever I go, people can see that horse and recognize it, so if they need help, they can find me."

"What kind of help?" Alan asked, as he climbed into the carriage.

"I'm a doctor," Lee answered, as he cracked the whip over

the horse and sent the buggy flying before Alan was fully seated next to Blair.

It was a hair-raising ride that Lee took them on, and the citizens of Chandler, thinking he was on an emergency case, moved out of his way. He halted in front of the house he'd bought for Houston.

"I thought this would be a good place to talk."

Blair's eyes widened. She hadn't seen the house since the night she and Lee'd . . . "I need to talk to Alan, not you, and definitely not *here*."

"The scene of the crime, so to speak? Well, I guess we could go to Miss Emily's Tea Shop. She has a private room."

"Much better, but I'd like to be alone with Alan. Houston and I—." She stopped, since Lee had taken off like lightning again and thrown her and Alan against the back of the buggy.

"And here are our little lovebirds, now. Lee, you should have told us about you and Blair," Miss Emily said. "When Nina told us you were the lovesick young swain, we all thought it was Houston."

"I guess it's true that love is blind," Lee said, winking at the older woman. "Could we have the private dining room? An old friend of my fiancée's has come to visit, and we'd like to talk."

Miss Emily took one look at Alan and smiled. "You have to meet Nina, Leander's sister, such a pretty young lady."

By the time they got into the private dining room, and tea and cakes had been set before them, Blair was grimacing, Alan was still looking puzzled, but Lee was smiling proudly.

"If you don't mind, I'll tell Alan the truth," Blair said, as soon as the door was closed. "My sister, Houston, wanted to go somewhere and—."

"Where?" Lee interrupted.

She glared at him. "If you must know, she had received an invitation to see that monstrous house of Taggert's that night and she wanted to go, and the only way she could was if I posed as her and went to the reception with you. Anyway," she turned back to Alan and her voice lost its anger, "my sister wanted to trade places for the evening, like we used to do when we were children, so we did. Except I didn't know what I was getting myself into because *he,*" she glanced at Lee, "kept getting angry at me, I mean Houston, and I kept trying to get away from him but he wouldn't let me. And then, the next day, he found out we'd traded places, and now he stupidly thinks I want to *marry* him."

Alan was quiet for several moments. "The story seems to be missing a few pieces."

"I'd say about half of it's missing," Lee said. "The truth is, the twins did exchange places, and I don't for the life of me know why I didn't see it right away. I was engaged to Houston, who's a cool little thing, so I should have guessed it wasn't her because when I touched Blair she practically ignited."

"How dare you say such a thing!"

Lee looked completely innocent. "I'm just telling the truth, sweetheart. I took her to my house for a late supper and, well, let's just say that we had the wedding night a couple of weeks early."

"Alan, it wasn't like that. I was Houston and *she* loves him, Heaven only knows why, because *I* don't even like the man. He's bigoted, egotistical and thinks a woman couldn't be a partner in the clinic he wants to open. I just want to go home and work in St. Joseph's and marry you, Alan. You have to believe that."

Alan was frowning as he ran his fork across the tablecloth. "You must have some feeling for him or you wouldn't have—."

"I told you," Blair interrupted, her face showing her anxiety. "I was Houston. Alan, please believe me. I'll leave with you right now."

"Over my dead body," Lee said.

"Ah! at last a pleasurable thought," she said, smiling at him with her eyes narrowed.

Alan interrupted them as he turned to Lee. "Tell me, do you plan to drag her down the aisle by her hair?"

"I have nearly two weeks. By the day of the wedding, she'll be begging to marry me."

"Are you sure of that?" Alan asked.

"Positive," Lee answered.

"Shall we put it to a test? On the twentieth she either leaves with me or marries you."

"Agreed."

"Agreed!?" Blair rose from the table. "I don't think I want either one of you. I'll not be bargained over like a head of cattle."

"Sit down." Lee put his hand on her shoulder and pulled her back into her chair. "You say you're in love with him, yet you can't resist me, so who else do you want to choose from?"

"I don't want to choose at all. I want to marry Alan."

"That's what you say today, but you've only just met me," Lee said smugly. "Of course, it was an impressive first meeting, but—. Here! sit down." He looked back at Alan. "We need some rules set up. First, she has to agree to stay in Chandler until the twentieth. No leaving town. And second, she has to accept my invitations. She can't sequester herself in Gates's house or only go out with you. Anything else is open territory."

"That sounds fair enough to me. What about you, Blair?"

Her first thought was to walk out of the tearoom and leave them both there, but first, she wanted to know the consequences. "What if I don't agree?"

"If you don't agree, and I take that to mean you plan to slip out of town," Lee said, "I'll send Gates after you in Pennsylvania, and after he finishes telling his story, you won't have a medical career. On the other hand, if on the twentieth, you should mistakenly choose Alan, I'll buy your train ticket and I'll somehow pacify Gates."

She considered this for a moment, then looked at Lee. "All right, but I'll give you warning now. I don't want to marry you, and I'm going to make you feel nothing but relief on the twentieth when I leave this bigoted little town with Alan, because I'm going to make your life as miserable as possible between now and then."

Lee turned to Alan. "I love a woman with fire in her veins. May the best man win." He extended his hand and Alan shook it. It was settled.

Chapter 9

The day after Alan arrived, Blair was stretched on her back on a quilt spread across the grass under a tree in Fenton Park. Alan was reading an article to her about the latest advancements in the treatment of diphtheria while she watched the clouds moving overhead, listened to the buzzing of the bees and heard the laughter of the other people in the park on this beautiful day.

"Blair, did you hear me? I was reading Dr. Anderson's report. What do you think?"

"About what?" she asked dreamily, turning onto her stomach. "Oh!" she said, startled. "I guess I wasn't listening. I was thinking about my sister and what happened yesterday."

Alan closed the book. "Care to share your thoughts?"

"That man Taggert sent her a carriage and horse and, along with it, the world's largest diamond. Houston wasn't even ruffled. She just very calmly clutched that ring to her heart, walked out to that carriage and drove away, and she didn't get home until after nine o'clock. By then, Mother was prostrate with grief because her daughter was selling herself, so I had to spend hours trying to quiet her before she could sleep. And this morning, Houston left before daylight—which started Mother crying again."

"And she isn't worried about you?" Alan asked, as he put the medical text down and leaned against the tree.

"I think that both she and Mr. Gates believe that I'm getting a better man than I deserve—or at least Gates thinks that. I'm not sure what Mother thinks. She's too worried about how Houston's life has been ruined."

Alan ran his fingers along the edges of the book. "And you still think that I shouldn't be introduced to your mother and stepfather?"

"Not yet," she said, sitting up. "You can't imagine what Gates is like. If he heard that I'd—." She stopped because the last thing she wanted to do was to remind Alan of why she'd become engaged to Lee in the first place. But she knew that if Gates heard that she'd slept with one man while being engaged to another, her life would be more miserable than it was already. That man never missed a chance to point out to her that she was ruining her sister's life so that Houston thought she had to marry a man for his money, anything so she could save herself from humiliation in front of the entire town—humiliation that was entirely caused by Blair and her immorality. Night and day, that's what she heard from her stepfather.

She gave Alan a weak smile. "Let's not talk about anything unpleasant on this lovely day. Why don't we go for a walk or, better yet, why don't we rent a canoe and go out on the lake? I haven't had any practice on the water since I left the rowing team in the fall."

"I would like that," he said, rising and offering his hand to help her up.

They folded the blanket, took the book, and started toward the small rental shop beside Midnight Lake, where they rented a canoe. There were several couples on the lake and they called out in greeting.

"Good morning, Blair-Houston," they said, looking with interest at Alan, and some of them hinted that they'd like to be introduced, but she didn't oblige. Houston might feel an obligation to satisfy the curiosity of the townspeople, but Blair didn't think she had to.

She leaned back in the canoe while Alan paddled, her face protected from the fierce high-altitude sun of Chandler by a large hat, letting her hand trail in the water; she nearly fell asleep.

"Good morning!" came a voice that made her sit upright. She looked into Leander's face as he rowed alongside them.

"What are you doing here?" she asked, jaw clenched. "Go away."

"According to your mother, I'm out with you. Well, Hunter, you don't look altogether comfortable with that paddle. Maybe it's too much city living."

"Will you get out of here and take your snide remarks with you? We were perfectly peaceful until you came along."

"Careful with your temper, people are beginning to look, and you wouldn't want them to think there was anything wrong in paradise, would you?"

"Paradise? With you? You're nothing but a—."

Leander interrupted her. "Hunter, can you give me a hand? I seem to have caught my foot under this seat and it's beginning to swell."

"Alan, don't do it," Blair warned. "I don't trust him."

But it was too late. Alan, newly out of medical school and very aware of his responsibilities as a healer, could not resist a plea for help. He instantly put the paddle down and leaned over the side to help Lee—and as soon as he was stretched across the water, Lee gave the canoe a shove, and Alan, after a moment of struggle, fell into the lake. Blair instantly leaned over to help Alan, but Lee grabbed her about the waist and hauled her into his boat.

There was laughter surrounding them, and the sound of Alan thrashing in the water as he tried to get back into the canoe, and there was the sound of Blair flailing at Lee to make him let her go. Somehow, he managed to row them the few feet to shore using just one oar, while holding Blair with his other arm and suffering as little physical injury as possible from her flying fists.

Once on shore, he stood before her and grinned like a little boy who'd just done a magnificent feat.

"My hat," Blair said through clenched teeth and Lee, still grinning, went to the little wooden boat to get it.

And when he had his back turned and he was off guard, Blair grabbed a discarded paddle and pushed him in the back with all her might. To her great joy, Leander went face down in the mud at the edge of the lake.

But Blair didn't have time to enjoy her success, because she saw that Alan was still floundering in the water. She thanked heaven for her years on the women's rowing team as she made her way out to Alan in Lee's boat.

"I never learned to swim," he said, as she leaned over to help him over the side. "Just to tread water."

They managed to get him inside the boat, Alan coughing, dripping water and weak, after what, to him, had been a harrowing experience. Blair glanced toward shore and saw Lee standing there covered with mud, and that gave her some satisfaction.

Expertly, she turned the boat and rowed them to the other side of the lake to the rental place.

She took care of the rental while Alan stood to one side and sneezed, then got them a hired carriage to take them back to the Imperial Hotel where he was staying.

Blair was so angry that she didn't even look at Alan all the way through town to the hotel. How dare Leander treat her like that in public—or in private for that matter, she thought. She had made herself perfectly clear that she wanted nothing to do with him, yet he insisted on forcing himself on her.

She followed Alan up the stairs to his room. "If I ever get my hands on that man, I'll kill him. He is the most insufferable creature! Thinking that I could ever possibly want to marry someone like that is just a perfect example of his self-centeredness. Give me your key."

"What? Oh. Here. Blair, do you think you should go into my room with me? I mean, how do you think it will look?"

Blair took the key from him and opened the door. "Could you imagine living with that man? He is like a very large spoiled boy who has to have his own way. Now, he's decided that he wants me, probably because I'm the first woman to ever say no to him, and so he sets out to make my life miserable." She stopped and looked at Alan as he stood dripping on the hotel room floor. "Why are you standing there in those wet clothes? You should get undressed."

"Blair, I don't think you should be here, and I certainly don't plan to undress in front of you."

Blair began to come back to her senses and realized where she was. "You're right, of course. I guess I was too angry to think. Will I see you tomorrow?"

"If I don't die of pneumonia before then," he said with a smile.

She smiled back at him, started to leave, then, on impulse, she turned back and flung her arms around him as she pressed her mouth to his.

He held her tentatively at first, as if he didn't want to get her wet, but as Blair applied more pressure and more passion, he held her closer, turning his head as he became more involved in the kiss.

Blair pulled away. "I have to go," she said softly, as she moved toward the door. "I'll see you tomorrow."

Alan stood still for a while after Blair'd gone, not bothering to change out of his wet clothes. "You *didn't* say no to him, Blair," he whispered, "and when I kiss you you have to go, but he can make you stay all night."

On Thursday morning, Blair burst into the Chandler house, tears running down her face, and ran upstairs to her room. She had to plow through several bouquets of flowers before she could get to the bed. Sweeping aside a half dozen boxes of chocolates, she flung herself on the bed where she spent an hour weeping. Leander Westfield was making her life impossible. Yesterday he'd once again ruined a pleasant afternoon with Alan. She and Alan had gone on a picnic in the country and Lee had shown up, firing a six-gun in the air to frighten the horses, and trying to pull Blair atop his horse. But, again, she'd managed to thwart him by making the horse rear, and she got away.

Alan had stood there watching them, not able to participate since he knew very little about the temperament of horses that weren't attached to a carriage. In fact, Blair'd had a difficult time talking him into taking a ride, rather than renting a buggy as he preferred to do.

When Blair had gotten away from Lee and his rearing

horse, she mounted one of the horses that she and Alan had rented—the other one had run away at the sound of Lee's pistol—and spent some moments persuading Alan to mount behind her.

Blair'd spent a great deal of her childhood on a horse, and she needed all her skill now, as she raced to get away from Lee. As she turned back to look at him once, with Alan holding onto her for dear life, Alan screamed in fear. They were fast approaching a tree, and the horse was going to hit it if he wasn't given room to pass it.

Leander saw the danger at the same time and, in a lightning-fast movement, swerved his horse so hard that the animal unexpectedly reared, throwing Lee into the dust. Because of his action, Blair and Alan were able to get away safely.

Unfortunately, or fortunately from Blair's point of view, Lee's horse kept on going, heading for the safety of his stable.

Alan was clutching both Blair and the saddle as she kept up a brisk pace back to town. "Aren't you going to give him a ride? It's miles back to town."

"It's only about six miles," she answered over her shoulder. "And, besides, he should be used to walking by now."

That had been Wednesday, and compared to today, that had been a day of thanksgiving. Early this morning, Gates had started on Blair because he'd finally heard what had happened at the lake, and how Blair had been seen with another man, and how she'd humiliated Lee before everyone.

Blair didn't want to argue with him, so she said that she was to meet Lee at the hospital this morning. She lied and said that Lee wanted to talk to her about medicine, but the truth was, she was hoping Lee wouldn't be at the hospital, because she certainly didn't want to see him.

Gates insisted that she go with him as he left for work, and when he dropped her off, he waited to see her go through the doors. Like a prisoner, she thought.

The inside of the hospital was familiar to her, and the smell of carbolic, wet wood and soap was like coming home. No one seemed to be around, so she started wandering about the wards, peering inside the rooms, glancing at the patients and wishing that she could get back to Pennsylvania and go to work.

It was on the third floor that she heard something that she identified at once: the sound of someone trying to breathe.

She became Dr. Chandler instantly, running into the room, seeing the older woman choking and beginning to turn blue. Blair didn't waste a second before she began pushing on the woman's chest and then using her own lungs to force air into the woman.

She hadn't applied two breaths before she found herself forcibly pulled away.

Leander pushed so hard that she nearly fell as he began clearing the woman's throat. Within minutes, the patient was breathing evenly again and he turned her over to a nurse.

"You come to my office," he said to Blair, barely looking at her.

What followed for Blair was twenty minutes of a tongue-lashing such as she'd never had before in her life. Lee seemed to think that she was trying to interfere in his work and that she could have killed his patient.

Nothing Blair said made any difference to his rage. He said she should have called for help rather than worked on a patient that she knew nothing about, that the treatment she'd tried might have been the wrong one and she could have done more harm than good.

Blair knew he was right and, even as he spoke, she began to cry.

Leander relented, stopped his tirade, and put his arm around her.

Blair drew away, screaming that she hated him and she never wanted to see him again. She ran down the stairs and hid inside a doorway while he ran past looking for her. When the way was clear, she left the hospital and caught a trolley car home—where she was now, crying and never wanting to see that horrible, hideous man again.

At eleven, she managed to pull herself together enough to

leave the house to meet Alan. She told her mother she was meeting Lee to play tennis and Opal merely nodded, mistakenly trusting her daughter.

Opal was sitting on the back porch, trying to enjoy the spring afternoon and not worry about her daughters, her embroidery in her hands, when she looked up to see Leander standing in the doorway. "Why, Lee, what a pleasant surprise. I thought you and Blair went to play tennis. Did you forget something?"

"Mind if I sit down and join you for a while?"

"Of course not." She looked at him. Rarely was Lee's handsome face marred by a frown, but today he looked as if he were deeply worried about something. "Lee, is there something you'd like to talk about?"

Leander took his time in answering as he withdrew a cigar from his inner coat pocket and motioned to Opal for permission to smoke. "She's out with a man named Alan Hunter, the man she says she's going to marry."

Opal's hands stopped sewing. "Oh, dear, yet another complication. You'd better tell me all of it."

"It seems that she accepted this man's marriage proposal in Pennsylvania and he was to come Monday and meet you and Mr. Gates."

"But by Monday, Blair'd already . . . And the announcement of your marriage had been made, so . . ." She trailed off.

"It was my doing that our engagement was announced. Both Houston and Blair wanted to keep quiet and forget any of it'd ever happened. I'm almost ashamed to admit that I blackmailed Blair into remaining in Chandler and participating in the competition."

"Competition?"

"I met Hunter at the train station on Monday, and I talked him into competing with me for Blair's hand. I have until the twentieth to win her, because on the twentieth she's going to decide whether she wants to marry me or leave town with Hunter."

He turned to Opal. "But I think I'm losing, and I don't

know how to win her. I've never had to court a woman before, so I'm not really sure what has to be done. I've tried flowers, candy, and making a fool of myself in front of the entire town—all the things I thought women liked, but nothing seems to be working. On the twentieth, she's going to leave with Hunter," he repeated, as if it were the most tragic of thoughts and, with a sigh, he told Opal what had been going on in the last few days, told her about the lake incident and then the time with the horses and ended with this morning at the hospital when he had, admittedly, been a little rough on Blair.

Opal was thoughtful for a moment. "You love her a great deal, don't you?" she said with surprise in her voice.

Lee sat up straighter in his chair. "I don't know whether it's love exactly . . ." He glanced at Opal, then seemed as if he realized he was fighting a losing battle. "Well, all right, maybe I am in love with her, so in love that I don't even mind looking like the town idiot—if only I get her."

He quickly began to defend himself. "But I'm not about to go to her looking moony-eyed and tell her that I did an unmanly thing like fall in love with her on the first night I spent with her. It's one thing to have your roses thrown back in your face, but I'm not sure I'd like to have the same thing done to my declarations of undying love."

"I think you may be right. Do you know how this other man is courting her?"

"It's something I clean forgot to ask."

"He must be the 'friend' who keeps sending her medical books. Blair reads one, and an hour later she leaves the house, saying she's meeting you."

"I have a room full of medical books, but I can't imagine sending one to a woman. I guess I have to agree with Mr. Gates when it comes to medicine. I wish she'd give up this absurd idea and settle down and—."

"And what? Be more like Houston? You had a perfect homemaker, yet you fell in love with someone else. Did you ever think that if Blair gave up her medicine she'd not be Blair?"

There was silence between them for a few moments.

"At this point, I'm willing to try anything. So you think I should send her some medical textbooks?"

"Lee," Opal said softly. "Why did you become a doctor? When did you first know that you wanted to dedicate your life to medicine?"

He smiled. "When I was nine and Mother was ill. Old Doc Brenner stayed with her for two days and she lived. I knew then that that's what I wanted to do."

Opal looked out across her garden for a moment. "When my daughters were eleven, I took them to Pennsylvania to visit my doctor brother, Henry, and his wife, Flo. We had no more than arrived when Flo, Houston, and I came down with a fever. It wasn't serious, but it kept us in bed and left the care of Blair to the staff. My brother thought she looked lonely, so he invited her to go on his rounds with him."

Opal paused to smile. "I didn't learn what went on until days later, when Henry was so excited that he could no longer contain himself. It seems that Blair disobeyed Henry when he told her to stay away from the patients he was treating. The first day, Blair helped her uncle in a difficult, messy birth, keeping her head clear, never panicking, even when the woman began to hemorrhage. By the third day, she was assisting him in an emergency appendectomy performed on a kitchen table. Henry said he'd never seen anyone so suited to medicine as Blair was. It took me a while to get over the shock of the thought of my *daughter* being a doctor, but when I talked to Blair about it, there was a light in her eyes that I'd never seen before, and I knew that if at all possible I was going to help her become a doctor."

She paused to sigh. "I hadn't reckoned on Mr. Gates. When we returned to Chandler, all Blair could talk about was becoming a doctor. Mr. Gates said that no girl under his protection was going to do anything so unladylike. I stood back for a year and watched Blair's spirit gradually become smothered. I think the final straw was when Mr. Gates forbade the library to loan Blair any more books on the subject of medicine."

Opal gave a little laugh. "I think that was the only time that

I ever stood up to Mr. Gates. Henry and Flo had no children, and they begged me to let Blair come live with them, promising that Henry would take the responsibility of seeing that Blair received the best education money could buy a woman. I didn't want to see my daughter go, but I knew it was the only way. If she'd stayed here, her spirit would have been broken."

She turned to Lee. "So you see how much medicine means to Blair. It's been her entire life since she was just a girl and now—." She broke off as she pulled an envelope from her pocket. "This came the day before yesterday, from Henry. He sent it to me so I could break the news to Blair as gently as possible. The letter says that even though she qualified to intern at St. Joseph's, even though she placed first in the three-day-long testing, the Philadelphia City Commissioner has vetoed her placement, because he says it's an impropriety to have a lady working so closely with men."

"But that's—," Lee burst out.

"Unfair? No more unfair than your asking her to give up medicine and stay home to see that the maid irons your shirts the way you want them."

Lee looked out at the garden, smoking his cigar, thinking.

"Maybe she'd like to visit a few cases with me in the country. Nothing too difficult, just some routine checks."

"Yes, I do think she'd like that." She put her hand on his arm. "And Lee, I think you'll see a different Blair from the one you've seen up 'til now. Because Blair tends to be a bit outspoken, people sometimes don't see the size of her heart. If you continue to make Mr. Hunter look like a fool in front of her, she'll never forgive you, much less begin to love you. Let her see the Leander this town knows, the one who repeatedly gets out of bed at three o'clock to listen to Mrs. Lechner's complaints of mysterious pains. And the man who saved Mrs. Saunderson's twins last summer. And the man who—."

"All right," Lee laughed. "I'll show her that I'm actually a saint in disguise. Do you think she really *does* know anything about medicine?"

It was Opal's turn to laugh. "Have you ever heard of Dr. Henry Thomas Blair?"

"The pathologist? Of course. Some of his advances in disease detection have been—." He stopped. *"He's* Uncle Henry?"

Opal's eyes twinkled in delight. "The same, and Henry says Blair is good, very good. Give her a chance. You won't be sorry."

Chapter 10

Blair's day was not improved by her tennis game with Alan. During her schooling, her uncle had emphasized the importance of exercise. He said that vigorous physical exercise would help improve her ability to think and to study. Therefore, Blair had joined the rowing team, had learned to play tennis with some of the other students, and, when she could, she'd participated in gymnastics, bicycling, and done a little hiking.

She beat Alan at tennis.

Alan was looking distracted as he walked toward the side of the court. Throughout the game, he'd watched over his shoulder, with an expression on his face that showed that he thought someone was going to appear at any moment.

Blair was very annoyed when the game was finished, because she suspected that Alan's worry about Leander was keeping him from playing well.

"Alan, I almost think you're afraid of him. So far, we've beaten him every time."

"*You* have beaten him. I'm useless in this country. Now, if we could meet in a city, perhaps I'd have a chance."

"Leander has studied all over the world. I'm quite sure he's as at home in a ballroom as on a horse," she said as she cleaned off her racquet.

"A Renaissance man?" Alan said archly, an edge to his voice.

Blair looked up at him. "Alan, you look as if you're angry. You know how I feel about the man."

"Do I? What I know are the facts, that you went out with him once and ended up spending the night with him, yet when I touch you, you seem to have infinite control."

"I don't have to listen to any of this." She turned away.

He caught her arm. "Would you rather that Westfield said it? Would you rather that he were here now with his blazing six-guns and his ability to trick a gullible young medical student?"

She gave him a cool look worthy of her sister. "Release my arm."

He did so immediately, his anger leaving him. "Blair, I'm sorry, I didn't mean what I said. It's just that I'm so tired of looking the fool. I'm tired of staying in my hotel room and of not being allowed to meet your parents. I feel like the one who's unwanted, rather than Westfield."

She felt herself giving in to him. His anger was perfectly understandable. She put her hand to his cheek. "I wanted to leave with you that first day, but you wanted a competition. You agreed to it, and now my future life as a doctor is in jeopardy. I can't leave Chandler with you until the twentieth. But have some faith that I *will* leave with you."

He escorted her to within a block of her house, and when they parted, Blair felt the tension in Alan. He was worried and nothing Blair said seemed to make any difference.

At the house, she went to her room, glad for once that her mother didn't give her an itemized list of the flowers and candy that Leander had had delivered while she was out. Instead, Opal merely greeted her pleasantly and went back to her sewing, while Blair had to practically drag herself up the stairs.

She was determined not to spend the afternoon crying, as she'd spent the morning, so she stretched out on the bed and tried to read a chapter about burn victims in a book that Alan had lent her.

At three, Susan, the upstairs maid, came in with a tray of food. "Mrs. Gates said I was to bring this up to you and to ask if you needed anything else."

"No," Blair said listlessly, pushing the food out of reach.

Susan paused at the door, running her apron along the door frame. "Of course, you heard about yesterday."

"Yesterday?" Blair asked, without much interest. How could Alan think that she was interested in Leander? Hadn't she made it clear to everyone involved that she wanted nothing whatever to do with him?

"I thought maybe since you were asleep when Miss Houston came in last night, and then you left so early this morning, that you might not have heard about Mr. Taggert and the awful mess he made at the garden party yesterday, and how he carried Miss Houston out, and then he came here and I do believe that your mother almost fell in love with him, and he's going to buy her a pink train and—."

Susan had Blair's attention now. "Slow down a minute and tell me everything." She curled her legs on the bed and began to eat the food in front of her.

"Well," Susan said slowly, obviously enjoying being the center of attention. "Yesterday, your sister showed up at Miss Tia Mankin's garden party—the one you were invited to but didn't go to—and standing next to her was this divine man, and at first no one recognized him. Of course, I was only told this because I wasn't really there, but I got to see him later and everything they said was more than true. I never thought that that big dirty man could look so good. Anyway, he came to the party and all the women gathered around him, and then he took food to Miss Houston and spilled it in her lap. Nobody could say a word for a minute, but somebody started to laugh, and the next thing you know, Mr. Taggert picked Miss Houston up and carried her out of the garden and put her in that pretty new buggy he bought her."

Blair had a mouthful of sandwich and tried to wash it down with milk. "Didn't Houston say anything? I can't imagine her allowing a man to do that in public." Truthfully, she couldn't imagine her sister allowing that in private, either.

"I *never* saw anything like that with Dr. Leander, but not

only did Miss Houston allow it, she brought him here and asked your mother to entertain him in the parlor."

"My mother? But she cries every time she hears the name of Taggert."

"Not after yesterday. I don't know what it is about him she likes, other than his looks, because the man scares me to death, but she almost fell in love with him. I helped Miss Houston change clothes, and when we got downstairs, your mother was asking him to call her Opal, and he was asking her what color train car he could buy her."

Susan took the empty tray off the bed. "But something awful must have happened after Miss Houston left with the man, because she came home last night in tears. She tried to hide it from me when I helped her undress, but I could see that she was crying. And today, she hasn't eaten and she's stayed in her room all day." She gave Blair a sly look as she paused at the doorway. "Just like you. This house ain't a happy place today," she said just before she left the room.

Immediately, Blair left her room and went to her sister. Houston was lying on the bed, her eyes red and swollen and looking a picture of misery. The first thought that Blair had was that her sister's unhappiness was her fault. If she hadn't come back to Chandler, Houston would still be engaged to Leander, and she wouldn't be considering marrying a man who spilled food all over her and mauled her in public.

Blair tried to talk to Houston, telling her that if she made it clear that she still wanted Lee, she could probably still have him, and she wouldn't have to sacrifice herself to that man Taggert. But the more Blair talked, the more Houston closed up. She would say nothing except that Leander no longer loved her, and that he wanted Blair in a way that he'd never wanted her.

Blair wanted to tell her sister that if she'd just wait until the twentieth, she could have Lee. She wanted to tell about the blackmail scheme, and about Alan and how much she loved him, but she was afraid that would make Houston feel worse, as if she were the consolation prize. All Houston could seem to talk about was the fact that Lee had rejected her, that he wanted Blair, and that Taggert was making her miserable, although she wouldn't tell Blair exactly what the man had done to her.

And the more Houston talked, the worse Blair felt. She'd gone out with Leander in the first place because she'd been worried that he wasn't good for her sister. She'd been worried because Houston hadn't been upset after Lee had been angry with her. But now, Houston had a totally different kind of man and she spent the entire day in misery. If only she hadn't interfered!

Houston was standing by her bed, trying to stop the flood of tears cascading down her face.

"You may think that you failed with Leander, but you didn't. And you don't have to punish yourself with an overbearing oaf. He can't even handle a plate of food, much less—."

Blair stopped because Houston slapped her across the face.

"He's the man I'm going to marry," Houston said, anger in her voice. "I'll not let you or anyone else denigrate him."

With her hand to her cheek, Blair's eyes began to fill with tears. "What I've done is coming between us," she whispered. "No man anywhere means more than sisters," she said before leaving the room.

The rest of the day was even worse for Blair. If she'd had any doubts as to why Houston was marrying Taggert, they were put to rest just before dinner when a dozen rings were delivered from the man. Houston took one look at them and her face lit up like a gaslight on high. She fairly floated from the room, and Blair wondered if the presents of the carriage and thirteen rings were going to be enough to make up for having to live with a man like Taggert. From the look on Houston's face, it seemed as if she thought so.

Dinner came, and Houston's cheerfulness made Blair feel terrible, but she knew the uselessness of trying to talk to her sister about anything.

When the telephone rang during dinner, Gates told the maid to tell whoever it was that no one was going to talk on the newfangled thing. "Think they have the right to make you talk to them just because they can make that thing ring," he grumbled.

Susan came back into the room and her eyes were on Blair.

"It's very important, the caller said. I'm to say it's a Miss Hunter."

"Hunter," Blair said, her soup halfway to her mouth. "I'd better answer it." Without asking Mr. Gates's permission, she half ran to the telephone.

"I don't know any Hunters," Gates was saying behind her.

"Of course you do," Opal said smoothly. "They moved here from Seattle last year. You met him at the Lechners' last summer."

"Maybe I did. I seem to remember. Here, Houston, have some of this beef. You need fattening up."

"Hello," Blair said tentatively.

Instead of Alan's voice as she expected, she heard Leander. "Blair, please don't hang up. I have an invitation to extend to you."

"And what do you plan to do to Alan this time? You've used guns, horses, you've nearly drowned him. Did you know that we played tennis today? You could have thrown balls at him or hit him with the racquet."

"I know that my conduct hasn't been the best, but I'd like to make it up to you. I'm going to be on call all day tomorrow to handle any emergencies that come up, and I have several patients in the country that I need to see. I thought you might like to go with me."

Blair couldn't speak for a moment. To spend the entire day doing what she was trained for? To not have to loll about, going from one pastime to another, but to learn something?

"Blair, are you there?"

"Yes, of course."

"If you'd rather not, I'll understand. It'll be a long day, and I'm sure you'll be exhausted by the end of it, so——."

"You pick me up whenever you need to. I'll be ready at the crack of dawn, and tomorrow we'll see who gives out first." She hung up the telephone and went back to the table. Tomorrow she'd be a doctor! For the first time in days, she didn't feel the burden of the weight of responsibility for hurting her sister.

* * *

Nina Westfield heard the pounding on the door for some minutes before someone answered it.

A white-faced maid came into the parlor, her hands trembling. "Miss, there's a man out here, he says he's Mr. Alan Hunter, and he says he's come to kill Dr. Leander."

"My goodness. Does he look dangerous?"

"He's just standin' there and bein' calm, but his eyes are wild and . . . he's very handsome. I thought maybe you might be able to talk to him. He doesn't look like the killin' kind to me."

Nina put her book aside. "Show him in, then get Mr. Thompson from next door to come over, and send someone to get my father. Then send someone to keep Lee at the hospital. Invent an illness if you have to, just keep him away from home."

Obediently, the maid left, and in a moment she escorted Mr. Hunter into the parlor.

Nina didn't think he looked like a killer at all, and she extended her hand to him in friendship, ignoring the maid's gasps when she closed the door to the room. When Mr. Thompson showed up a few minutes later, Nina sent him home, saying that it had all been a mistake, and when her father came, she introduced Alan and the three of them sat and talked until late.

Unfortunately, no one thought about Leander, who was trying to help the man who'd been their family butler for sixteen years. The butler was writhing with pains that no one could pinpoint, although Lee kept trying. And every time Lee left the room, the butler called the Westfield house and was told that the dangerous man was still there, so the butler went back and developed a new symptom.

Which was why Leander got only four hours sleep before the first emergency call came in, and since it was four thirty he hesitated to awaken the entire Chandler family, and instead he climbed the tree to get into Blair's bedroom.

Chapter 11

There was only the faintest hint of bluish-gray dawn when Leander climbed the tree and crossed the porch roof to Blair's bedroom. He felt like a schoolboy about to get caught in a prank. Here he was, twenty-seven years old, a doctor; he'd spent years in Europe; had visited some of the grand salons, but now he was climbing a tree and slipping into a girl's bedroom as if he were a naughty boy.

But when he entered the room and saw Blair outlined by the thin sheet, he forgot all inhibitions. The last few days had been miserable. He'd found her and knew that, as he wanted his own soul, he wanted this woman, but he could see her slipping away from him. Something about her made him clumsy, awkward, and everything he did was wrong. He'd tried to impress her, tried to make himself look good compared to that incompetent, weak, frightened little blond mouse she thought she loved. Lee knew Hunter wasn't man enough for her.

For a moment, he stood over her, liking that she was soft and sweet, as she had been the one night when she hadn't been angry with him.

That night had changed his life, and he was determined to have her like that again.

With a smile, and a feeling that he couldn't help himself, he pulled the sheet back and slipped into bed with her, shoes and all. There wasn't time for prolonged lovemaking and now, before she woke, while he could still think, he knew that the third floor of Duncan Gates's house was not the place.

He kissed her temple as he pulled her into his arms and, sleepily, she snuggled closer to him as he kissed her eyes and cheeks. When he touched her lips with his, she slowly came awake, moving her body nearer his, her thigh sliding between his as his hand moved down to draw her gown up and caress her bare flesh.

His kiss deepened, his tongue touching hers, and she responded eagerly, pushing at him as she tried to get closer.

It was Lee's watch fob piercing her stomach through her thin nightgown that made her waken—but not fully.

"I thought you were a dream," she murmured, as her hand caressed his cheek.

"I am," Leander said hoarsely. Never in his life had he been required to use such control. He wanted to take her gown off, to caress all her warm, lovely flesh, to feel her skin against his. He wanted to run his unshaven cheeks against the soft flesh of her stomach and hear her squeal in feigned protest.

Blair suddenly sat straight up. "What are you doing here?" she gasped.

He put his hand over her mouth and pulled her down beside him, where she began kicking her heels and pushing at him. "If you want to go with me, you have to go now, and since it's not daylight yet, I didn't want to bang on your front door and wake the whole house. Will you stop making so much noise? Gates will be in here, and if he sees you like this, he'll probably parade you downtown in sackcloth and ashes." He moved his hand away as she calmed.

"That's preferable to what you have planned," she said in a loud whisper. "Get off me."

Leander didn't move an inch. "If I'd had time, I would have climbed in here without my . . . ah, shoes," he said, rubbing his leg up and down between hers, still holding her quite close.

"You are a vain, lecherous—."

She broke off because he pinned her arms above her head and kissed her, gently at first, deepening until she couldn't breathe, then gentle again. When he pulled away, there were tears in her eyes as she turned her head aside. "Please don't," she whispered. "Please."

"I don't know why I should have any mercy," he said, releasing her hands but keeping her trapped under most of his body. "You've shown me no mercy in the last few days." At the look in her eyes, he moved off her. "If I leave the way I came, down the tree, will you get dressed and meet me out front?"

Her eyes lost the look of a trapped animal. "And we'll go on call?"

"I never saw a woman look forward to blood and gore before."

"It's not that, it's the helping of people that I like. If I can save one life, then my life—."

He kissed her quickly before climbing out of the bed. "You can give me the new doctor speech on the way. Ten minutes, all right?"

Blair could only nod and was out of the bed almost before Lee was out the window. She didn't give a thought to how unusual their behavior was, because nothing in her life had been ordinary since she'd returned to Chandler.

Out of the small closet in her room, beside some of Houston's stored winter clothes, Blair took a garment that she was very proud of. She'd had it made in Philadelphia by the old, established tailoring firm of J. Cantrell and Sons. She'd worked with them for weeks on designing and fitting a suit that would fill all the needs she could imagine in future emergencies as a doctor and yet remain modest. In the tailor's shop, she'd tried wearing it astride a wooden horse, making sure that it was short enough to be safe and long enough to be respectable.

The jacket was cut with perfect military simplicity; the skirt looked full and feminine, but it was actually divided into two so it had the safety and comfort of bloomers. The suit was made of the finest, most closely woven, navy blue serge that money could buy, with several deep pockets that disappeared into the folds of the fabric, a buttoned flap over each pocket so that no precious instruments could be lost. There was a simple red cross on the sleeve to designate the suit's purpose.

Blair tied on a pair of high laced black calfskin shoes—boys' style rather than the fashionably narrow shoes that tortured women's feet into submission—grabbed her new physician's bag, and hurried downstairs to meet Leander.

He was leaning against the carriage smoking one of his thin little cigars, and for a moment, Blair dreaded going anywhere with him. No doubt she'd spend all day fighting his hands moving all over her, and she'd never get to do anything to help with a patient.

He took one quick look at her outfit and seemed to nod in approval before jumping into the carriage and leaving Blair to help herself get in.

As soon as she climbed into Lee's carriage, he started off in the way that Blair was beginning to prepare herself for. She held on for dear life.

"Where is this first case?" she shouted over the sounds of the carriage tearing along the road south out of Chandler.

"I don't usually do these calls anymore, since I work in the hospital most of the time," he shouted back at her. "So some of the cases I haven't seen, but this one I happen to know. It's Joe Gleason, and his wife's sick. I'm sure it's another baby. Somehow, Effie manages to produce one every eight months." He gave her a sideways look. "Ever caught a newborn?"

Blair nodded and smiled. Since she'd lived with her uncle, she'd an advantage that the other students in her college did not have: she'd been able to work with patients rather than just learn theory from books.

After a ride that left Blair's side bruised from slamming against the side of the carriage, Leander halted in front of a little log cabin that was at the foot of the mountains, the bare yard in front of it full of chickens, dogs and an endless number of thin, dirty children—all of whom seemed to be fighting each other for space.

Joe, little, scrawny, mostly toothless, shooed children and animals out of his way with equal disdain. "She's in here, Doc. It ain't like Effie to lay down durin' the day, and now she's been in bed for four days, and this mornin' I couldn't wake her up. I been doctorin' her the best I could, but don't nothin' seem to help."

Blair followed the two men into the house, looking at the wide-eyed children as she listened to the beginning of Joe's tale of what had happened.

"I was choppin' wood and the axe head flew off and hit Effie in the leg. It didn't cut her real bad but she bled a lot and felt dizzy, so she went to bed—in the middle of the day! Like I said, I doctored her the best I could, but now I'm worried about her."

The little room where the woman lay in a motionless heap was dark and foul smelling.

"Open that window and get me a lantern."

"The wagon man said the air weren't good for her."

Leander gave the man a threatening look, and Joe ran to open the window.

As Joe got the lantern, Lee took a seat by the woman's bed and pulled back the covers. On her leg was a filthy, rancid, thick bandage. "Blair, if what's under here is what I think it is, maybe you—."

Blair didn't give him a chance to finish. She was examining the woman's head, lifting her eyelids, taking her pulse, and at last bending to smell her breath. "I think this woman is drunk," she said with wonder, as she looked about the room. On the crude little table next to the bed was an empty bottle labelled *Dr. Monroe's Elixir of Life. Guaranteed to cure whatever ails you.*

She held it aloft. "Have you been giving this to your wife?"

"I paid good money for that," Joe said indignantly. "Dr. Monroe said it'd do her a world of good."

"Is this thing from Dr. Monroe also?" Lee asked, motioning toward the thick bandage.

"It's a cancer plaster. I figured if it could cure cancer, it'd sure cure Effie of a little cut. Is she gonna be all right, Doc?"

Lee didn't bother to answer the man as he began shoving pieces of wood into the old stove that sat in the corner of the room and put a kettle of water on to boil. As they waited for the water to boil and, later, while Lee and Blair were scrubbing their hands, she asked questions.

"Have you given her anything else?" she asked, dreading the man's answer.

"Just a little gunpowder this mornin'. She was havin' a hard time wakin' up, and I thought gunpowder would help perk her up."

"You damn well may have killed her," Lee said, then his face whitened a bit as he started prying away the edges of the filthy bandage from the unconscious woman's leg just above the knee. As he looked at the flesh under the bandage, he grimaced. "Just what I thought. Joe, go boil me some more water. I'll have to clean this up." The little man took one look under the bandage and hurried from the room. Lee, his eyes on Blair's, pulled the filthy fabric back so she could see.

Tiny, squirming maggots covered the swollen, raw cut.

Blair didn't allow herself to react as she took instruments from Lee's bag and handed them to him. She held an enamelled basin while Lee began to carefully pick out the maggots.

"These things are really a blessing in disguise," Lee was saying. "Maggots eat the putrefied part of the wound and keep it clean. If these"—he held one aloft on the point of his tweezers—"weren't here, we'd probably be amputating now. I've even heard that doctors used to put maggots on a wound just so the worms could clean it."

"So maybe it's good that this place is so filthy," Blair said with distaste, looking about the nasty little room.

Lee looked at her speculatively. "I would have thought that this sort of thing would have been too much for you."

"I have a stronger stomach than you think. You ready for the carbolic?"

As Lee cleaned the wound further, Blair was always ready with whatever he needed, always half a step ahead of him. He handed her the needles and thread, and Blair sewed the raw edges of the cut while Lee stood back and watched her every movement. He grunted when she finished sewing and let her apply clean bandages to the wound.

Joe arrived to tell them the water was boiling.

"Then you can use it to boil these rags you call sheets," Lee said. "I don't want any more flies getting under that bandage. Blair, help me get these sheets out from under her. And I want some clean clothes for her, too. Blair, you can change her while Joe and I have a talk."

Blair didn't attempt to bathe the woman, but she was sure that the wound on her leg was the cleanest spot on her body. She managed to insert the woman's big body into one of Joe's night rails while the woman lolled about and grinned sometimes in her drunken stupor. Through the open window, she could see Lee and Joe at the side of the cabin, Lee towering over the little man, yelling at him, punching his chest with his finger and generally scaring the man to death. Blair almost felt sorry for Joe, who'd only been doing the best he knew how for his wife.

"Where's the doc?"

She turned to see a man wearing the chaps and denim shirt of a cowboy standing in the doorway, his face anxious.

"I'm a doctor," Blair said. "Do you need help?"

His deep-set eyes in his thin face looked her up and down. "Ain't that Doc Westfield's rig outside?"

"Frank?" Lee asked from behind them. "Is something wrong?"

The cowboy turned around. "A wagon fell down an arroyo. There were three men on it, and one of 'em's hurt pretty bad."

Lee said, "Get my bag," over his shoulder to Blair as he hurried to the carriage, and it was already moving by the time she got there. Silently, as she tossed the two bags to the floor of the carriage, grabbed the roof support and put her foot on the runner, she thanked Mr. Cantrell for the design of her suit that gave her such mobility.

Lee did grab her upper arm with one hand, as he held the reins with the other, and helped haul her inside as the horse broke into a full gallop. When she was seated, the bags held firmly between her feet, she looked at Lee and he winked at her—a wink with some pride in it.

"This is the Bar S Ranch," Lee shouted, "and Frank is the foreman."

They followed the cowboy, Lee making the buggy go nearly

99

as fast as the lone rider, for about four miles before they saw any buildings. There were four little shacks and a corral precariously pasted onto the side of Ayers Peak.

Lee grabbed his bag, tossed the reins to one of the three cowboys standing nearby and went into the first shack, Blair, bag in hand, on his heels.

There was a man lying on a bunk, his left sleeve soaked with blood. Lee deftly cut the fabric away and a spurt of blood hit his shirt. The encrustation of dried blood on the cowboy's shirt had temporarily sealed the cut artery and kept the man from bleeding to death. Lee pinched the artery with his fingers and held it; there was no time to think about washing.

The cowboys stood over them, barely giving them room, as Blair poured carbolic over her hands and, with a gesture that was as practiced as if they'd been working together for years, Lee released the artery while Blair's smaller fingers took hold. Then Lee disinfected his hands, threaded a needle and, while Blair held the wound open, he sewed. In another few minutes, they had the wound closed.

The cowboys stepped back and their eyes were on Blair.

"I think he'll be all right," Lee said, standing, wiping the blood off his hands with a clean cloth from his bag. "He's lost a lot of blood, but if he pulls through from the shock, I think he'll make it. Who else?"

"Me," said a man on another bunk. "I busted my leg."

Leander slit the man's pant leg, felt the shin bone. "Somebody hold his shoulders. I'll have to pull it into place."

Blair looked about the room as three men moved in front of her to hold the cowboy's shoulders. Leaning against a wall was an enormous man, with arms the size of hams. His big, wide face that looked as if it'd seen many fights, was white with what Blair recognized to be pain, and he was cradling one arm with the other.

She went to him. "Were you in the wagon accident?"

He glanced down at her, then away. "I'll wait for the doc."

She started to turn away. "I'm a doctor, too, but you're right, I'd probably hurt you more than you could stand."

"You?" the man said; then, as Blair faced him, she saw his face turn even paler.

"Sit down," she ordered and he obeyed, sitting on a bench near the wall. As carefully as she could, she removed his shirt and saw what she'd guessed was wrong with him: that big shoulder of his had become dislocated in the fall. "It's going to hurt some."

He arched his eyebrow at her from under a brow beaded with sweat. "It's doin' that now."

All the cowboys were gathered around Lee as he set the broken leg, and one in the back of the watching crowd had a whiskey bottle to his lips. Blair snatched it away from him and handed it to her patient. "This'll help."

Blair wasn't sure she was physically strong enough to do what she knew had to be done, but she also knew she couldn't stand by and wait for Leander to finish while this man suffered. She'd set a dislocation only once before, and that had been for a child.

With a deep breath and a prayer, she began to flex his forearm, then pressed it against the wall of his massive chest. Grabbing a box of canned goods, she stood on it and, with great effort, managed to raise his big arm high in the air and rotate it. She repeated the procedure, trying not to cause him more pain. She was sweating and panting with the exertion of trying to move that big arm inside a joint that was as big as her hips.

Suddenly, the humerus snapped back into place with a loud click and the deed was done.

Blair stepped back off her box, and she and her patient grinned at each other.

"You're a fine doctor," he said, beaming.

Blair turned around and, to her surprise, everyone in the room, including the two other injured men, were watching her. And they stayed there, staring silently while Blair bandaged the man's shoulder with her best basket-weave pattern, making it pretty as well as comfortable and useful.

Leander broke the silence when she'd finished. "If you two are ready to stop congratulating each other, I have more patients to see to." His words were at odds with the sparkle of pride in his eyes.

"Ain't you one of them Chandler twins?" a cowboy asked, walking with them to the buggy.

"Blair," she answered.

"She's a doctor, too," Frank said, and they were all looking at her strangely.

"Thanks, Dr. Westfield *and* Dr. Chandler," the man with the dislocated shoulder said as they climbed into the carriage.

"Might as well get used to calling her Westfield, too," Leander said as he snapped the reins. "She's marrying me next week."

Blair couldn't say a word, since she nearly fell out of the carriage as Leander's horse leaped ahead.

Chapter 12

Leander slowed the horse when they were away from the line shacks.

"My father's housekeeper packed us a lunch. I'll stand while you get it out, and we'll eat on the way to the ranch."

Lee stood in the carriage, like a gladiator in a chariot, and Blair lifted the seat. "What an awful lot of room," she said, surprised, looking at the blankets, a shotgun, boxes of ammunition, extra harness, and tools that were stored under the hinged seat. "I don't believe I've seen a compartment with that much room before."

Leander frowned at her over his shoulder, but she didn't see him. "That's the way it came," he mumbled.

Blair stuck her head farther into the compartment, looking at the sides of it. "I don't believe it is. I think it's been altered, something removed to make the space larger. I wonder why."

"I bought the thing used. Maybe some farmer wanted to carry his pigs back there. Are you going to get the food or are we going to starve to death?"

Blair took a big picnic basket out of the hole and sat back down. "It's big enough to hold a man," she said, as she

103

withdrew a box of fried chicken, a jar of potato salad, and a jar of iced lemonade from the basket.

"Are you going to talk about that all day? What if I tell you some stories about when I was interning in Chicago?" Anything, Leander thought, to get her mind off that space back there. If the coal mine guards were half as observant as Blair, he wouldn't be alive today.

He ate chicken with one hand, held the reins with the other and told her a long story of a young man who'd been brought in by the police one night and, because he was already blue from not breathing, he was pronounced to be as good as dead—but Leander had thought there was hope. He'd tried rhythmical manipulations, but when there was no response, he'd examined the patient and found that his eyes were pinpoints, so Leander had guessed that the man was a victim of "knockout drops": opium.

"Are you going to eat all of that potato salad yourself?" Lee asked and, when Blair started to hand him the jar with the fork in it, he said he couldn't possibly eat it and the chicken and drive the buggy. So, Blair had to move so that she was sitting beside him and could feed the salad to him.

"Go on with your story."

"I realized that the only way to keep the man from going into a coma was to continue artificial respiration until he revived. None of the other doctors would waste his time on a man they considered as good as dead, so they went to bed and the nurses and I took turns trying to save the man."

"I'm sure the nurses *would* help you," she said.

He grinned at her. "I didn't have much trouble with them, if that's what you mean."

She shoved a large forkful of salad into his mouth. "Are you going to brag or are you going to tell the story?"

Leander continued telling of the long night of trying to save the man, of how he'd taken an icy cloth and repeatedly flicked the man on his bare stomach, then there was heart stimulation, and gallons of black coffee. He and the nurses had worked in relays all night, walking him until morning, when they'd thought he was out of danger and they could put him in bed and let him sleep.

Lee had had fewer than two hours sleep that night before he was due back on duty, and when he made morning rounds, he went into this patient's room, ready to be modest in the blaze of this man's praise for working so hard to save his life.

"But what the man said was, 'See, doctor, see, they did not get my watch. It was safe inside my pants, hidden from the thieves that poisoned me.'"

"He didn't even acknowledge that you'd done all that for him?" Blair asked in disbelief.

Leander smiled at her, and in a moment she began to see the humor of the situation. There were times when being a doctor wasn't the glory that one expected, but it was just plain hard work.

They finished the lunch and, as they travelled, Blair got Lee to tell her more stories about his experiences as a doctor, both in America and abroad. In turn, she told him about her Uncle Henry and her schooling, where the teachers had been so rough, saying that the women would be competing with male doctors who expected the women to be ill-trained, so, of course, the women had to be the best. She told him about the gruelling three-day test that she'd had to take to get into St. Joseph's Hospital. "And I won!" she said and went on to tell Leander about the hospital. She wasn't aware of the way that Lee was looking at her as she talked about her future at the hospital.

In the early afternoon, they reached the outskirts of the Winter ranch, and Lee drove them to the big old ranch house to visit the rancher's eight-year-old daughter who was recovering from typhoid.

The little girl was perfectly fine, and Lee and Blair stayed for a cup of milk warm from the cow and an enormous chunk of corn bread.

"That's all the pay we'll probably get," Lee said, as they got back into the carriage. "Doctors don't get rich in the country. It's good you'll have me to support you."

Blair started to say that she had no plans to stay in Chandler or to marry him, but something made her stop. Maybe it was the way he'd hinted that she really was a doctor, and that when—if—they were married, she would still practice medicine. And considering the prejudice and bigotry in this town, that was saying a lot.

They were barely off the rancher's land when a cowboy rode up to them, his horse stopping on its back legs and raising a cloud of dust over them. "We need some help, Doc," the cowboy said.

To Blair's disbelief, Lee did not take off immediately with his usual lightning speed.

"Aren't you from the Lazy J?"

The cowboy nodded.

"I want to take the lady back to Winter's ranch before I go with you."

"But, Doc, the man's been gut shot and he's bleedin'. He needs somebody right away."

Yesterday, Blair would have been furious that Lee wanted to exclude her from a case, but she knew now that he wasn't against her helping him with the patients, so it had to be something else. She put her hand on his arm. "Whatever happens, I'm in this, too. You can't protect me." There was a hint of threat in her voice that said that she'd follow him if he left her behind.

"They ain't shootin' now, Doc," the cowboy said. "The lady'll be safe while you patch Ben up."

Leander glanced at Blair, then skyward. "I hope I don't live to regret this," he said, as he snapped the whip over the horse, and they were off.

Blair grabbed the side of the carriage and said, "Shooting?" But no one heard her.

They left the horse and carriage some distance away and the cowboy led them to the ruins of an adobe house, stuck on a steep hillside, a section of the roof fallen in.

"Where are the others?" Lee asked and looked to where the cowboy pointed through the trees toward another ruin.

Blair wanted to ask questions about what was going on, but Lee put his hand in the small of her back and pushed her forward into the ruin. When her eyes adjusted, she saw a man and a fat, dirty woman sitting on the floor below what was left of a window, rifles across their shoulders, pistols by their sides, spent shells all around them. In the corner were three horses. With her eyes wide as she looked around, she was sure that she was in the midst of something she didn't like.

"Let's sew him up and get out of here," Lee said, bringing her back to the task at hand.

In the darkest part of the shack, on the floor, was a man holding his stomach with his hands, his face white.

"Do you know how to give chloroform?" Lee asked, as he sterilized his hands.

Blair nodded and began to remove bottles and candles from her bag. "Can he hold his liquor?" she asked the people in the room.

"Well, sure," the cowboy said hesitantly, "but we don't have no liquor. You have some?"

Blair was very patient. "I'm trying to figure out how much chloroform to give him, and a man who takes a lot of whiskey to get drunk requires more chloroform to put him under."

The cowboy grinned. "Ben can outdrink anybody. Takes two bottles of whiskey just to make him feel good. I ain't never seen him drunk."

Blair nodded, tried to estimate the weight of the man and began to pour chloroform onto a cone. When he began to go under, he fought the gas, and Blair stretched her body across the top of him while Leander held the man's lower half. Thankfully, he didn't have too much strength left and couldn't do much damage to his wound.

When Lee pulled away the man's pants and they saw the hole the gunshot had made in his stomach, Blair suspected there wasn't much chance for him, but Lee didn't seem to think that way as he cut into the man's abdomen.

A friend of Uncle Henry's, a doctor who specialized in abdominal surgery, had once visited them from New York and he had been there when a little girl was brought in who'd fallen on the broken half of a bottle. Blair had been in the surgery when the man'd removed the glass from the child's stomach and repaired three holes in her intestines. That single operation had so impressed Blair that she'd decided to specialize in abdominal surgery.

But, now, as she watched Leander, threading one needle after another for him, she was awed. The bullet had entered the man at his hipbone and travelled crosswise to leave at the bottom of his buttocks, puncturing his intestines over and over as it made its way through.

Leander's long fingers followed the bullet's pathway, sewing layers of intestines as he went. Blair counted fourteen holes that he sewed together before he reached the man's skin and the exit hole of the bullet.

"He's to eat absolutely nothing for four days," Leander was saying as he sewed the man back together. "On the fifth day he can have liquids. If he disobeys me and sneaks food, he'll be dead within two hours because the food will poison him." He looked up at the cowboy. "Is that clear?"

No one answered Lee because just then about six bullets came whizzing into the ruined shack.

"Damn!" Lee said, cutting off the last stitches with the scissors Blair had handed him. "I thought they'd give us enough time."

"What's going on?" Blair asked.

"These idiots," he said, not bothering to lower his voice, "are having a range war. There's usually one or two going on around Chandler. This one's been on about six months now. We might be here for a while until they decide to take another break."

"Break?"

Lee wiped his hands. "They're quite civilized about it all. When a person's wounded, they cease fire until a doctor can be found and brought into wherever they're holed up. Unfortunately, they feel no such obligation to stop until the doctor's out again. We may be here until morning. Once I was stuck someplace for two days. And now you see why I wanted you to stay at Winter's ranch."

Blair began cleaning and putting the instruments back into the two medical bags. "So now we just wait?"

"Now we wait."

Lee led her behind a low adobe wall that had once been a room partition. He sat down in the farthest corner and motioned for Blair to sit next to him, but she wouldn't. She felt that she should stay as far away from him as possible and so leaned against the opposite wall. When a bullet hit the wall two feet from her head, she practically leaped into Leander's open arms and buried her face against his chest.

"I'd never have guessed that I could like a range war," he murmured and began to kiss her neck.

"Don't start that again," Blair said, even as she turned her head so he could reach her lips.

It didn't take Lee long to realize that he couldn't continue this pursuit, not here and now with so many people present and bullets flying around them. "All right. I'll stop," he said and smiled at the look on Blair's face.

She didn't move away from him but stayed in his arms, since his nearness made her feel very safe and the sounds of the bullets seem farther away. "Tell me where you learned to sew up intestines like that."

"So, you want more sweet talk. Well, let's see, the first time . . ."

Blair seemed insatiable. For hours they sat snuggled together, Blair asking endless questions about how Leander had learned things, what cases he'd had in the past, what was his most difficult case, his funniest, why he'd become a doctor in the first place, on and on, until, to give himself a break, he began to ask her questions.

The sun went down, there was a lull in the shooting now and then, but for the most part it kept on all night. Lee tried to get Blair to sleep, but she refused.

"I see you're watching him," she said, nodding toward the man who'd been shot. "You have no intention of sleeping nor do I. What do you think his chances of living are?"

"It all depends on infection, and that's controlled by God. All I can do is sew him up."

The sky began to grow light and Leander said he needed to check his patient, who was beginning to stir.

Blair stood to stretch, and the next minute a sound reached her that made her forget everything except her profession. It was the sound of a bullet connecting with flesh.

Blair moved away from Lee and ran around the corner of the low wall just in time to see what had happened. The man who had not spoken had been shot in the chin and the woman had grabbed a handful of fresh horse manure and was about to apply it to the open wound.

Blair didn't think about the bullets flying over her head as she launched herself from a standing position and leaped on top of the big woman.

Startled, angry, the woman began to fight Blair and Blair had to protect herself from the woman's fists—but, under no circumstances was she going to allow that woman to put horse manure on an open wound.

Blair was so set on her purpose that she wasn't even aware when she and the woman went rolling out the wide opening where the door used to be.

One minute, Blair was trying to remove the woman's hand from her hair, and the next minute, there was the thunder of rifle fire directly above them.

Both women stopped their fighting and looked up to see Leander standing between them and the shack across the way, a rifle at his hip, blazing as fast as he could cock it and fire.

"Get the hell inside," he yelled at the women, and the next minute, he let out a stream of profanity directed at the men in the other shack, telling them that he was Dr. Westfield, and that he knew who they were, and if they ever came to him for help, he'd let them bleed to death.

The firing ceased.

When Leander walked back into the shack, Blair was cleaning the chin of the injured man.

"If you ever do anything like that again, so help me—." He broke off as he couldn't seem to find a threat bad enough.

He stood over Blair very quietly as she sewed the man's chin and bandaged it, and when she had put on the last bit of adhesive plaster, he grabbed her arm and pulled her upright.

"We're getting out of here this minute. They can all shoot each other for all I care. I'll not risk you for any of them."

Blair barely had time to grab her bag before Lee pulled her out of the cabin.

"Your union man came last night," Reed greeted his son as soon as Lee walked into the house.

As Leander rubbed a sore place on his back where a wooden plank had gouged it all night, he looked up at his father in alarm. "You didn't let anyone see him, did you?"

Reed gave his son a withering look. "All he's done is eat and sleep, which looks to be something that you haven't done in days. I hope you didn't keep Blair out all night. Gates is after your hide as it is."

Lee wanted nothing more than to eat and take a nap before he had to be at the hospital, but it didn't look as if he were going to have time. "Is he ready to go?"

Reed was quiet for a moment, watching his son, feeling that this might be the last time he ever saw him alive. He always felt this way before Lee left to take one of the unionists into the mine camps. "He's ready," was all Reed said at last.

Wearily, Lee went to the stables and sent the stableboy on an errand while he hitched a horse to his carriage. His appaloosa was too tired after being out all night, so Lee took one of his father's horses. Watching to see that no one could see them, he went to the door to get the man waiting beside his father. Lee only glanced at the young man, but he had the same light in his eyes that all the unionists had: a light of fire, an intensity that burned with such heat that you knew there was no need to talk to the men about the danger that they faced, because these men wouldn't care. What they were doing, the cause they were fighting for, was more important than their lives.

Leander had removed most of the implements of his profession from the compartment in the back of his carriage —the big space that Blair had been so curious about—and now the man slipped inside. There was no talking, because all three men were too aware of the possibilities of what could happen today. The coal-camp guards would shoot to kill first, then ask questions of the dead men.

Reed handed Lee a papier-mâché cast that slipped into grooves in the sides of the compartment above the level of the man, a cast that at quick glance looked like a pile of blankets, a shotgun, rope, and a saw—things that any man might have in his carriage. On top, Lee put his medical bag.

For a moment, Reed touched his son's shoulder, then Lee was in the carriage and off.

Leander drove as quickly as he could without causing the hidden man too much pain. Two weeks ago, he and his father had had another discussion about what Lee was doing, Reed saying that Lee shouldn't risk his life to get these unionists into the camps, that even if he were caught and somehow managed to live, no court in the country would uphold what he was doing.

As Lee drove closer to the road that turned off to the coal camps, he went slower, watching about him as best he could to see that no one was near who shouldn't be. With a smile, Lee remembered when he'd defended the man who owned the coal mines around Chandler, Jacob Fenton, to Blair. He'd made excuses for Fenton and said that the man had to answer to stockholders, that he wasn't fully responsible for the miners' plight. Lee often said things like that to throw people off the track. It wouldn't do for them to find out how deeply he felt about the mistreatment of the miners.

Coal miners were given two choices: they either obeyed the company rules or they were out of work. It was as simple as that. But the rules were not for men, they were for prisoners!

Everything to do with the mines was owned by the company. The men were paid in currency that could be exchanged only at the company stores, and a man could be fired if he were found to have bought something at a store in town. Not that the men were allowed out of the camps to go into town. The mine owners argued that the coal camps were towns, and that the miners and their families didn't need anything from the surrounding town. And the owners said that the guards at the gates, who allowed no one in or out, were keeping out unscrupulous thieves and fast-talking men; the guards were "protecting" the miners.

But the truth was, the guards were there to keep out agitators. They were there to keep away all possibility of union organizers coming into the camps and talking to the miners.

The owners couldn't abide the possibility of a strike, and they had the legal right to post armed guards at the entrances and to search the vehicles that went in or out.

There were very few carriages that were allowed inside: some old women in town brought in fresh vegetables, a couple of repairmen were allowed in now and then, the mine inspectors, and there was a company doctor who made rounds, a man who was so poor a doctor that he couldn't support himself in private practice. The company paid him mostly in whiskey and, in gratitude, he ignored most of what he saw, declaring the company not at fault in every accident case, so that no benefits were due the widow and orphaned children.

A year ago Lee had gone to Fenton and asked permission to go into the camps—at no expense to the mine owner—to examine the health of the miners. Fenton had hesitated, but then he'd given permission.

What Lee had seen had horrified him. The poverty was such that he could barely stand it. The men struggled all day under the earth to make a living, and at the end of the week they could barely feed their families. They were paid by the amount of coal they brought out, but a third of their time was spent on what the miners called "dead work," work for which they received no pay. They themselves had to pay for the timbers that they used for shoring the mines, because the owner said that safety was the miners' responsibility, not his.

After the first days in the coal camps, Lee'd gone home and not been able to say much for days. He looked at the rich little town of Chandler, saw his sister come home from The Famous with fifteen yards of expensive cashmere, and he thought of the children he'd seen standing in the snow with no shoes on. He remembered the men standing in line for their pay and hearing the paymaster tell them what they were being charged for for that week.

And the more he thought, the more he was sure that he had to do something. He had no idea what he could do until he began to see articles in the newspaper about the organization of unions in the East. Aloud, he wondered to his father whether unionists could be persuaded to come to Colorado.

Reed, as soon as he realized what his son was thinking about, tried to dissuade him, but Lee kept going to the camps, and the more he saw, the more he knew what he had to do. He took the train to Kentucky and there met his first union organizers and talked to them about what was happening in Colorado. He learned about the early unsuccessful attempts at unionization in Colorado, and he was warned that his involvement could get him killed.

Leander remembered holding an emaciated little three-year-old girl in his arms as she died from pneumonia, and he agreed to help however he could.

So far, he'd managed to bring three unionists into the camps, and the owners were aware that they'd been there and that someone was helping the miners, so they were more and more on guard.

Last year, a big coal miner by the name of Rafe Taggert had begun to hint that he was the one to blame, that he was the one who was bringing the organizers into the camps. For some reason, the man believed that neither the guards nor the owner would harm him, that no "accidents" would be arranged to get him out of the way. There were rumors that Taggert's brother was once married to Fenton's sister, but no one was sure. Since coal miners had to move around a great deal as one mine after another closed, not many people had been in this area long enough to remember something that may or may not have happened over thirty years ago.

But whatever the reason, the suspicion was on Rafe Taggert, and no one had so far suspected the handsome young doctor who so kindly offered his time to help the miners.

As Lee pulled into the gate area of the Empress Mine, he did his best to act nonchalant and exchange banter with the guards. No one checked him and he drove to the far end of the camp to let the man hide in the trees until Lee could go from house to house to start getting a meeting together. Only three men would meet with the organizer at a time. The young man would stay there all day and into the night, risking his life every minute. And Lee would go from house to house looking at the children and telling the men where to meet the organizer and, with each telling, he was putting his life in peril, because he already knew that one of these men was an informer.

Chapter 13

Blair woke on Sunday morning feeling wonderful. She stretched long and hard, listened to the birds outside her window and thought that it must be the best of days. Her mind was full of all the things that she and Lee had done the day before. She remembered the way he'd repaired the man's intestines, his long fingers expert, knowing what he was supposed to do.

She wished Alan could have seen him operating.

Suddenly, she sat upright. Alan! She'd completely forgotten that she was to meet him at four o'clock yesterday. She'd been so worried about Houston, about how her sister had made a fool of herself over those rings, and then the call from Lee had come, and she'd sensed he was just asking her to go with him out of a sense of duty. She had never dreamed that she'd be away all night.

Susan came to tell her that the family would be leaving for church soon after breakfast and that Mr. Gates had requested that she go with them. Blair hopped out of bed and hurriedly dressed. Perhaps Alan would be at church and she could explain that she'd been away working.

Alan was there, three pews ahead of them, and no matter

what Blair did, he wouldn't look around after his initial glance. To make her feel worse, he was sitting next to Mr. Westfield and Nina. After church, Blair managed to get near him for a few minutes in the little yard outside the building.

"So, you were out with Westfield," Alan began the moment they were alone. His eyes were angry.

Blair stiffened in spite of her good intentions to be humble. "I believe you were the one to agree to a competition, not me, and part of the arrangement was that I not refuse Leander's invitations."

"All night?" He managed to look down his nose at her even though they were nearly the same height.

Blair at once felt defensive. "We were working, and we got caught in the midst of a range war and Leander says that—."

"Spare me his words of wisdom. I have to go now. I have other plans."

"Other plans? But I thought maybe this afternoon—."

"I'll call you tomorrow. That is, if you think you'll be home." With that, he turned on his heel and left her standing there.

Nina Westfield came by to tell her that Lee had to work at the hospital the rest of the day. Blair climbed into the carriage with her mother and stepfather and was only vaguely aware that Houston wasn't with them.

At home, Opal was fussing about the dining room, arranging flowers on the table, setting it with the best tall silver candelabra.

"Are you expecting company?" Blair asked idly.

"Yes, dear, *he's* coming."

"Who is?"

"Houston's Kane. Oh, Blair, he is such a lovely man. I just know you're going to love him."

Minutes later, the door opened and Houston came in leading her big millionaire by the arm, as if he were a prize piece of game that she'd just bagged. Blair had first seen him earlier in church, and she admitted that he was good-looking —not as handsome as Leander, or even Alan—but more than presentable, if you liked that overly muscular type.

"If you'll sit here, Mr. Taggert, next to Houston and across from Blair," Opal was saying.

For a moment, everyone just sat there looking at their plates or about the room, no one saying anything.

"I hope that you like roast beef," Mr. Gates said as he began to carve the big piece of meat.

"I'm sure to like it better'n what I usually get, that is, until Houston here hired me a cook."

"And who did you hire, Houston?" Opal said, with a bit of ice in her voice, reminding her daughter that lately she'd been leaving the house, and been gone for hours, with no one knowing where she was.

"Mrs. Murchison, while the Conrads are in Europe. Sir, Mr. Taggert might have some suggestions for investments," she said to Mr. Gates.

From then on, Blair thought, there was no stopping the man. He was like an elephant in the midst of a flock of chickens. When Mr. Gates asked him about railroad stock, Taggert raised his fist and bellowed that railroads were dying, that the whole country was covered with railroads and there was no more decent money to be made in them—"only a few hundred thousand or so." His fist came down on the table and everything—including the people—jumped.

Compared to Taggert's temper and loudness, Gates was a kitten. Taggert brooked no disagreement whatever; he was right about everything, and he talked in terms of millions of dollars as if they were grains of sand.

And if his bellowing and arrogance weren't enough, his manners were appalling. He cut his slice of roast with the side of his fork, and when it went sliding across the table toward Blair, he didn't even pause in telling Gates how to run the brewery as he pulled the meat back onto his plate and kept on eating. Ignoring the three vegetables that were served, he piled about two pounds of mashed potatoes onto his plate and emptied the gravy boat on top of the white mountain. Before he was finished, he'd eaten one half of the ten-pound roast. He knocked over Houston's teacup, but she just smiled at him and motioned for the maid to bring a cloth. He drank six glasses of iced tea before Blair saw Susan secretly pouring his glass from a separate pitcher. Blair then realized that Houston had arranged for Taggert to drink dark beer with ice in it. He talked with his mouth full and twice had food on his chin.

Houston, as if he were a child, touched his hand, then his napkin, which was still folded beside his plate.

After a while, Blair stopped trying to eat. She didn't like food flying toward her or the silverware jumping or the way that loud, overbearing man monopolized the conversation. Conversation ha! He might as well have been giving a speech.

The worst part was the way Houston, her mother and Gates hung on his every word. You would have thought his words were gold. And perhaps they were, Blair thought with disgust. She'd never thought much about money, but perhaps money was all-important to other people. It certainly seemed to be so important to Houston that she was willing to subject herself to this awful, hideous man for the rest of her life.

Blair grabbed the candelabra before it fell over, as Taggert reached for more gravy. Cook must have made it in a wheelbarrow, she thought.

Just then, Taggert paused long enough in his proposal of allowing Gates to buy in on a land sale to glance at Blair. Suddenly, he stopped talking altogether and pushed back his chair.

"Honey, we better be goin' if you wanta get to the park while it's still light."

Heaven help, Blair thought, that he should have manners enough to ask if anyone else was finished eating. He was ready to leave, and he autocratically demanded that Houston leave with him. Dutifully, Houston followed him.

"Why, Lee," Opal said with a smile, twisting her neck around to look up at him, making the little oak rocker creak. "I didn't hear you come in." She took a closer look at him. "You look happier than you did a few days ago. Has something happened?" There was a hint of an I-told-you-so look on Opal's face.

Lee gave her a quick peck on the cheek before sitting down in the chair next to her on the back porch. He was tossing a big red apple back and forth in his hands. "Maybe it's not that I want your daughter, it's that I want you for a mother-in-law."

Opal kept on sewing. "So, today, you think there's a

chance that you'll get my daughter. If I remember correctly, the last time we talked, you were sure you could never win her. Has anything changed?"

"Changed? Only the entire world." He bit into his apple with gusto. "I'm going to win. I'm not only going to win, but it's going to be by a landslide. That poor kid Hunter doesn't have a chance."

"I take it you've found the key to Blair's heart, and it isn't flowers and candy."

Leander smiled, as much to himself as to her. "I'm going to court her with what she really likes: gunshot wounds, blood poisonings, respiratory infections, amputations, and whatever else I can find for her. She'll probably love spring roundup around here."

Opal looked horrified. "It sounds dreadful. Must it be so drastic?"

"As far as I can tell, the worse the going is, the better she likes it. As long as somebody's there to make sure she doesn't get in over her head, she'll be fine."

"And you'll be the one to take care of her?"

Leander rose. "For the rest of her life. I believe that's the sound of my loved one now. You'll see, in less than a week, she'll be running down the aisle to me."

"Lee?"

He paused.

"And what about St. Joseph's?"

He winked at her. "I will do my best to never let her find out. I want her to turn them down. Who are they to say that she can't work for *them?*"

"She's a good doctor, isn't she?" Opal beamed with pride.

"Not bad," Lee said, chuckling, walking back into the house. "Not bad for a woman."

Blair met Leander in the parlor. Yesterday had turned out to be awful. Alan had not called, she'd heard nothing from Lee, and all day, she'd worried about Houston and that awful man she was selling herself to. So it was with some trepidation that she met Lee now. Was he going to be the doctor Lee or the one who insulted her at every turn?

"You wanted to see me?" she asked cautiously.

Leander wore an expression that she'd never seen before, one of almost shyness. "I came to talk to you, that is, if you don't mind listening to me."

"Of course not," she said. "Why should I mind talking with you?" She sat down on a red brocade chair.

Leander had his hat in hand, threatening to twist it into shreds, and when Blair motioned for him to sit, he merely shook his head no.

"It's not easy to say what I've come to say. It's not easy to admit defeat, especially in something that has come to mean so much to me as the winning of you for my wife."

Blair started to say something, but he put his hand up. "No, let me say what I must without interruptions. It's hard for me, but it has to be said because it's all that I can think about."

He walked to the window, still twisting his hat in his hands. She'd never seen him nervous before.

"Saturday, the day we spent together as doctors, was a monumental day in my life. Until that day, I would have wagered anything that I owned that a woman couldn't be a good doctor, but you proved me wrong. On that day, you showed me that a woman can not only be a good doctor, but might even become better than most men."

"Thank you," Blair said, and a small thrill of pleasure ran through her at his words.

He turned back to face her. "And that's why I'm giving up the race."

"The race?"

"The competition, then, whatever you call it. I realized yesterday, while I was working alone in the hospital, that I had changed after the day we spent together. You see, I've always worked alone, but on that day when we worked together . . . Well, it was like everything that I'd imagined and more. We fit together so well, so rhythmically, almost like lovers." He stopped and looked at her. "I meant that allegorically, of course."

"Of course," she mumbled. "I'm not sure that I understand any of this."

"Don't you see? I may have lost a wife, but what I've gained is a *colleague!* I might treat a woman with little or no respect, might trick her to show that her friend is such a Willie boy that he can't row, swim or even ride a horse, but I could never, never do that to a fellow doctor whom I've learned to respect and even admire."

Blair was silent for a moment. There was something wrong in what he was saying about Alan, but his words of praise were too sweet to cause her to quibble over details. "Are you saying that you no longer want to marry me?"

"I'm saying that I respect you, and you've said that you want to marry Alan Hunter, and I now know that I cannot stand in your way. You and I are equals in the medical profession, and I cannot further humiliate a fellow doctor in the manner that I have in the past few days. Therefore, you are no longer held captive here. You may leave with the man you love at any time, and I can assure you that I'll do everything in my power to keep Gates from letting anyone know about your loss of . . . of chastity."

Blair stood. "I'm not sure that I understand. I'm free to go? You aren't blackmailing me any longer, and you won't cause Alan further embarrassment? And you're doing all this because you believe that I'm a good doctor?"

"That's exactly right. It took me a while to come to my senses, but I have. What kind of marriage could we have if it was based purely on lust? Of course, we do have a mutual attraction to one another, and perhaps that one night was extraordinary, but that isn't a basis for marriage. What you and Alan have is real, that you can spend time together and talk, that you have mutual interests, and I'm sure that you have the same . . . ah, reactions to his touch that you have to mine. Maybe you two have made love several times in the last few days, for all I know."

"I beg your pardon!"

Leander hung his head again. "I'm sorry. I didn't mean to insult you again. I always seem to put my foot in my mouth around you. Now, you'll never listen to what else I have to say."

"I'll listen," she said. "Tell me the rest of it." She was

feeling strangely let down. Of course, the fact that he respected her as a doctor was wonderful, but at the same time she wanted something else, and she didn't know what it was.

When he looked back at her, his eyes were glowing intensely. "I know you want to get back to Pennsylvania, and I don't blame you, but working with you was such a joy and a pleasure and, since I know that I'll never have the chance again because I'm sure that you'll never want to come back to Chandler after what's happened in the last few days, I'd really like to ask if I could have the honor of working with you for the next few days. My father has agreed to persuade the board to allow you into the hospital under my care, and you and I can work together until after Houston's wedding. Oh, Blair, I could show you my plans for the women's clinic. I've never shown them to anyone before, and I'd really like to share them. Maybe you'd even help me plan it—if you had time, that is."

Blair walked to the far side of the room. She didn't think that she'd ever enjoyed anything as much as she'd enjoyed that day with Leander, and if they were no longer engaged, perhaps Houston would not feel that she had to marry that man Taggert and—.

"And Alan can work with us. Gosh, if he's half as good as you are . . . Is he?"

Blair came back to the present and realized with a bit of guilt that she hadn't even thought of Alan. "You mean, is he as good as I am? I guess so. Of course he is! Although I don't think he's had the opportunity to work with doctors as I have. I mean, I was very lucky. My Uncle Henry is quite well respected, and ever since I was little more than a child, I've assisted in surgery and helped with emergency cases and had the opportunity to assist many eminent men, but—." She stopped. "Of course, Alan is an excellent doctor," she said firmly.

"I'm sure he is, and I'm sure it'll be a joy working with both of you. By the way, did Alan take that exam for St. Joseph's Hospital?"

"Yes, but he didn't—."

"Didn't what?"

Her mouth was set in a firm line. "They only accepted the six highest scorers."

"I see. Well, perhaps it was a bad day for him. May I come for you tomorrow morning at six? Until then, my library is always open to a fellow colleague." He quickly kissed her hand and then was gone.

Chapter 14

Blair was dressed and ready to leave at five thirty the next morning. She sat on the edge of her bed and puzzled over what to do. Should she wait downstairs or would he come through the window again as he'd done last time?

When the downstairs clock chimed six, she opened her door and thought she heard the front door. She flew down the stairs and got there just as a sleepy Susan was opening the door to Leander.

"Good morning," he said, smiling. "Ready to go?"

She nodded in answer.

"You can't go, Miss Blair-Houston. You haven't had anything to eat and Cook doesn't have breakfast ready yet. You'll have to wait until she gets dressed."

"Have you eaten?" she asked Lee.

"It seems as though I haven't eaten in days," he answered, smiling back at her, and again she was impressed by how good-looking he was, with those green eyes. And for some reason, she was reminded of the night they'd spent together. It was odd that she should think of that now, because she hadn't remembered it in days. Perhaps it was that now he wasn't trying to enrage her.

"Come into the kitchen and I'll fix you some breakfast. Even I know how to fry eggs and bacon. Mr. Gates's meal will probably be late and the entire household'll catch it, but we'll not be here to hear what he has to say."

A half hour later, Lee leaned back from the big oak kitchen table and wiped his mouth. "Blair, I had no idea that you could cook. It seems too much to hope for in a woman, one who can cook, a woman who can be a man's friend, a colleague," his eyes and voice lowered, "a lover." With a sigh, he looked back at her. "I swore to myself that I wasn't going to be a sore loser, that I was going to give up gracefully." He gave her a sweet little-boy smile. "You'll have to forgive me if I forget sometimes."

"Yes, of course," she said nervously and realized that she was once again thinking of that night together. That night, when she'd been free to kiss him, when his hands . . .

"They aren't clean?"

"I beg your pardon?" she said, coming back to the present.

"You were staring at my hands and I wondered if maybe something was wrong with them."

"I . . . Are you ready to go?"

"Whenever you are," he said, rising and pulling back her chair.

Blair smiled at him and thought of that ill-mannered man Houston said she planned to marry and thought that there was no comparison between him and Lee.

On the way to the hospital, he asked her about Alan and she told him that he was to meet them at the infirmary. He did, looking sleepy and a bit sullen at seeing Leander and Blair arriving together.

The day was a hard, long one. It seemed that every patient was Lee's sole responsibility, and the three of them had to do the work of a dozen people. At one o'clock, four men who'd been hurt when the end of a tunnel of the Inexpressible Mine had collapsed were brought in. Two of them were dead, one had a broken leg, but the fourth man was hovering between life and death.

"He's a goner," Alan said, "might as well leave him."

But Blair was looking at the man's eyes, closed now, but she saw that he was struggling to live. She couldn't tell what was hurt inside him, but she thought that maybe he had a chance. By all rights, he should be dead now, yet he wanted to live enough that he was hanging on.

Blair looked at Lee, and for a moment he was reminded of the union organizers' eyes.

"I think there's a chance. Can we open him and see? I think he wants to live," she persisted.

"Blair," Alan said in an exasperated voice, "anyone can see that he can't live more than minutes. His whole insides must be crushed. Let him die with his family."

Blair didn't even look at Alan, but kept her eyes on Lee. "Please," she whispered. "Please."

"Let's get him to the operating room," Leander bellowed.

"No! don't move him. Keep him on that table and we'll carry it."

Blair was right, but so was Alan. His insides were crushed, but not as badly as they'd thought when they'd first opened him. His spleen was ruptured and it was bleeding a lot, but they managed to remove it and clean some of the other wounds.

Because of the internal bleeding, they had to work fast and, without anyone being conscious of what was happening, Alan was pushed out of the way. Leander and Blair, who worked so well together and who had the experience, sewed as fast as Mrs. Krebbs could thread needles. She was Leander's favorite nurse and had been with him since he'd returned to Chandler. Alan, realizing that he couldn't work as fast as Leander and Blair, stepped back and let the three of them repair the man's mashed insides.

When they had sewed him shut, they left the operating room.

"What do you think?" Blair asked Lee.

"Now is when God comes into the matter, but I think that you and I did the best we could." He grinned at her. "You were damned good in there. Wasn't she, Mrs. Krebbs?"

The stout, gray-haired woman grunted. "We'll see if the patient lives," she said as she left the room.

"Not given to compliments, I take it," Blair said, as she scrubbed the blood from her hands.

"Only when you deserve them. I'm still waiting for mine. Of course, I've only been here two years."

As the two of them laughed together, Blair wasn't aware of Alan standing against the wall watching them.

Once out of surgery, they went back to the wards and, late in the day, attended a child who had been scalded. And as the day wore on, Blair and Leander seemed tireless, but Alan followed them feeling more and more as if he were completely unneeded. Twice, he tried to talk to Blair about going home, but she'd hear none of it. She stayed next to Leander's side every minute. By ten that night, Alan was drooping.

"Come into my office," Lee said at eleven. "I have some beer and sandwiches there, and I want to show you something."

Alan sat in a chair and hungrily ate his sandwich while Lee unrolled plans and spread them across his desk. "These are my plans for the women's infirmary, a place where a woman can go for any ailment and get competent treatment. I'd like a training center, too, for women to be taught how to look after their children's health." He stopped and smiled at Blair. "No horse manure or cancer plasters."

She smiled back at him and realized that his face was inches from hers and that he was moving toward her with an expression on his face that she'd seen only once before—*that* night. Before she knew what she was doing, she was leaning toward him in a way that seemed very natural to her, and it seemed perfectly normal that he should kiss her.

But, only a breath away from her lips, he pulled back abruptly and began to roll the plans. "It's late and I'd better get you home. It looks like we've worn Alan out. Besides, it's useless for me to show you these plans. You won't even be here. You'll be in a big city in an established hospital, and you won't have the nuisance of having to build a place from scratch, of having to plan where you'll put the equipment, of whom you'll hire, of planning just what you'll teach and whom you'll treat." He stopped and sighed. "No, in your city hospital, you'll have everything already planned. It won't be hectic like this new clinic will be."

"But that doesn't sound bad. I mean, it might be fun to

decide how you want things. I'd like to have a burn clinic or maybe a special isolation ward or—."

He cut her off. "That's kind of you to say but at a big city hospital, the people pay their bills."

"If a big hospital is so good, then why didn't you stay in one? Why did you leave?" she asked indignantly.

With a show of great reverence, he put the plans back into the safe. "I guess I like feeling needed more than I like security," he said, turning back to her. "There are more than enough doctors in the East, but out here it's a challenge to keep up with all the work. The people here *need* a doctor more than they do there. I feel as if I'm doing some good here, and I didn't there."

"Is that why you think I want to return East? For security? You don't think that I'm up to all the work here?"

"Blair, please, I didn't mean to offend you. You asked me why I didn't want to work at a big, safe, orderly, comfortable hospital in the East, and I told you, that's all. It has nothing to do with you. We're colleagues, remember? I'd never dream of telling you what you should or shouldn't do. In fact, if I remember correctly, I'm the one who's taking obstacles out of your path. I gave up my intention of marrying you so you could return East, marry Alan, and work in your hospital just like you say you want to. What else can I do to support you?"

Blair had no answer for him, but she felt unsettled inside. At this moment, the thought of working in St. Joseph's Hospital seemed selfish, as if she were seeking glory instead of trying to help people as she should be doing.

"Speaking of Alan," Lee was saying, "I think we'd better get him home."

Blair had completely forgotten Alan and now turned to see him slumped forward in his chair, dozing. "Yes, I guess we'd better," she said absently. She was thinking too hard about what Leander had said. Maybe a big hospital was "safe," but the people there got just as sick as they did in the West. Of course, there were more people to treat them there, and here they didn't even have a decent hospital for women. In Philadelphia, they had at least four infirmaries for women and children, and of course there were women doctors in practice there, and everyone knew that women would sometimes suffer a disease for years before they'd let a man examine them.

"Ready?" Lee asked, after he'd wakened Alan.

Blair thought about what Lee'd said all the way home, and she lay awake in bed for a while and thought about it, too. Chandler certainly needed a female doctor, and she could train with Leander and help run that new clinic of his, all at the same time.

"No, no, no!" she said aloud, as she hit the pillow with her fist. "I am *not* going to stay in Chandler! I am going to marry Alan, train at St. Joseph's Hospital, and I am going to set up practice in Philadelphia!"

She settled down to go to sleep but as she drifted off, she thought of the many women in Chandler who had no female doctor to tend to them. She had a restless night.

On Wednesday morning, Lee came to the house to visit her, and Blair found that she was very glad to see him.

"I don't have to be at the hospital until late this afternoon, and I thought you might want to go riding with me. I stopped by the hotel and asked Alan to go with us, but he said he was tired after yesterday and he didn't like to ride anyway. I don't imagine you'd like to go with me alone, would you?"

Before Blair could say a word, Leander continued. "Of course you wouldn't," he said quickly, looking down at his hat in his hands. "You can't go out with me alone, since you're engaged to another man. It's just that the whole town thinks that I'm to marry you in five days, and no other young lady will go out with me." He turned to leave. "I didn't mean to burden you with my problems. My loneliness isn't your concern."

"Lee," she said, grabbing his arm to keep him from leaving the room. "I . . . I did want to discuss that blood poisoning case with you, maybe—."

Leander didn't give her a chance to finish. "That's great of you, Blair, you're a real friend," he said, as his face split into a grin that made Blair's knees weak. The next moment, he had his hand on the small of her back and he half pushed her out the door to the side yard where two saddled horses waited.

"But I can't wear this," she protested, looking down at her long skirt. "I need a divided skirt and—."

"You look fine to me, and so what if you show a little ankle? I'm the only one who'll be there, and I've seen all of you, remember?"

Blair didn't get a chance to say another word before he lifted her and put her on top of the horse, and she was busy trying to arrange her skirts so she had some modesty left. She prayed that Houston wouldn't see her like this. Houston might one day forgive her sister for stealing the man she was to marry, but she'd never, never forgive her for being seen in public wearing the wrong clothes.

Leander grinned back at her and she forgot all about her sister and that she was with a man she shouldn't be with.

He led her far out into the country. They rode side by side for a while, and Blair got him to talk more about the women's infirmary and tell her some of his plans. And she told him some of her ideas. Only once did he say, wistfully, that he wished he had someone to work with him. Cautiously, Blair asked him if he'd consider a woman doctor. Lee said he'd more than consider her, and for the next half hour he did nothing but tell her how they'd work together on this new infirmary if she stayed in Chandler. Before long, Blair was caught up in the fantasy, and she was talking about how they could work together and all the miracles they could accomplish. Together, they'd wipe out all illness in the state of Colorado.

"And then the three of us could move to California and cure that state," Leander laughed.

"Three?" Blair asked blankly.

Lee gave her a look of reproach. "Alan. The man you love, remember? The man you're going to marry. He'll be in on this, too. He'll have to have a part in the new infirmary, too. And he'll help us like he did yesterday."

It was strange, but Blair could barely recall Alan being at the hospital yesterday. She remembered the way he hadn't wanted to help the man who'd been crushed, but had he been in the operating room with them?

"Here we are," Lee was saying, as she followed him into an enclosed place between gigantic rocks. He dismounted and unsaddled his horse. "I never thought I'd be able to bear this place again after what happened here."

Blair stepped back as he unsaddled her horse. "What did happen here?"

He paused with the saddle in his hands. "The worst day of my life. I brought Houston here after the night we'd made love, and I found out that the woman I'd spent the most wonderful night of my life with wasn't the woman I was engaged to."

"Oh," Blair said meekly, wishing she hadn't asked. She stepped back as Leander pulled a blanket from his saddlebags and spread it on the ground, then watered the horses from a little spring nearby and began to spread food on the blanket.

"Have a seat," he said.

Blair was beginning to think that she shouldn't have come out here alone with him. He was easy to resist when he was being obnoxious and tossing Alan into the lake, but the last time they'd been alone and Lee had been this nice, they'd ended up with their clothes off and making love. Blair looked up at Lee standing over her, the sun making a crescent around his head and thought that, under no circumstances whatsoever, must she let him touch her. And she mustn't let the conversation stray to what had happened between them. She must *only* talk about medicine.

They ate what Lee had brought and Blair talked to him about all the worst cases she'd ever seen in her life. She needed to remember the gory details, because Lee had taken off his jacket and stretched out inches away from her. His eyes were closed, and all he had to do was murmur a response now and then to Blair's stories and she suspected he was falling asleep. She couldn't help looking at him as she talked, those long, long legs, and she thought about how they felt next to her own skin. She looked at his chest, broad, strong, his pectorals straining against the thin cotton of his shirt. She remembered how his chest hairs felt against her breasts.

And the more she remembered, the faster she talked, until the words seemed to clog in her mouth and refused to come out. With a sigh of frustration, she stopped talking and looked down at her hands in her lap.

Leander didn't say anything for a long while, and she thought perhaps he was asleep.

"I never met anyone like you," he said softly, and Blair couldn't help but lean slightly forward to hear him. "I never met a woman who could understand how I felt about medicine. All the women I've known raged at me if I was late picking them up for a party because I was sewing some man back together. Nor have I met any woman who was interested in what I did. You are the most generous, and the most loving, person I've ever met."

Blair was too stunned to speak. Sometimes, she thought she had fallen in love with Alan because he was the first young man who hadn't reviled her for the way she was. There were many times when Blair had tried to be like her sister, to be quiet and genteel, to not tell a man, when he said something stupid, that what he'd just said was stupid, but she couldn't seem to help herself. And as a result of her laughter, of her honesty, she had never had very many suitors. In Pennsylvania, men had seen how pretty she was and been interested, but when they'd found out that she was going to be a doctor, they were interested no longer. And if they had stayed around, they'd soon learned that Blair was very smart, and that was death to a woman. All she had to do was beat a man at chess, or do an arithmetic problem in her head faster than he could, and there would no longer be any interest in her. Alan was the first man she'd ever met who wasn't repulsed by her abilities—and Blair had decided that she was in love with him within three weeks of their first meeting.

Now, Leander was saying that he *liked* her. And when she thought of all the things she'd done to him in the last few days, the times she'd left him in the desert to walk back to town, she was astounded that he could stand the sight of her. He was either a remarkable man or he liked punishment.

"I know that you'll be leaving town in a few days, and maybe I'll never see you again, so I want to tell you what that one night we had together meant to me," he said in a voice that was little more than a whisper.

"It was as if you couldn't help yourself that night, as if my simple touch made you come to me. It was so flattering to my

132

vanity. You've called me a vain man, but I'm vain only when I'm with you because you make me feel so good. And to have found the woman of my life . . . a friend, a colleague, a lover without equal, and now to have lost her."

Blair was inching toward him as he spoke.

Lee turned his head away from her. "I want to be fair about what has happened. I want to give you what you want, what will make you happy, but I hope you don't expect me to be at the train station when you leave with Alan. I imagine that on the day you leave with him, I shall get rip-roaring drunk and tell my problems to some red-haired barmaid."

Blair sat upright. "Is that what you like?" she said stiffly.

He looked back at her in surprise. "Is what what I like?"

"Red-haired barmaids?"

"Why, you stupid little—." Instantly, his face was flushed red with anger, as he stood and began to shove the blanket, pulling it out from under her, and food into the saddlebags. "No, I don't like red-haired barmaids. I wish I did. I was fool enough to fall in love with the most pigheaded, blind, idiotic, stubborn woman in the world. I never had any trouble with a woman in my life until I met you, and now all I have is trouble."

He slammed the saddle on the horse. "There are times when I wish I'd never met you."

He turned back to her. "You can saddle your own horse, and you can find your own way back to town. That is, if you're not too blind to see the trail, because you sure are blind about people."

He put one foot in the stirrup and then, on impulse, turned back to her and took her in his arms and kissed her.

Blair had completely forgotten what it was like to kiss Lee, forgotten that overwhelming sensation. She couldn't have told you who she was when he was touching her, because all sensation left her except for the touch of this one man.

"There," he said angrily, drawing back from her, then having to give her a little shake to make her open her eyes. "I've had blind patients who saw more than you do."

He walked away from her and started to mount his horse, then mumbled, "Oh, hell," and saddled her horse for her and put her in the saddle. He led her a chase back into Chandler, and when he stopped before her house, he said, "I expect you at the hospital at eight tomorrow morning."

She barely had time to nod before he left her alone.

Chapter 15

Bleak was the only way to describe Blair's mood when she got home. She wasn't sure what was wrong with Leander, nor did she understand why she was so upset.

Her mother was in the family parlor surrounded by hundreds of boxes. "What's this?" Blair asked absently.

"They're wedding gifts for you and Houston. Would you like to open some of yours now?"

Blair just glanced at the presents and shook her head. The last thing she wanted was to be reminded of the wedding that might or might not take place—not that Leander still wanted to marry her.

She called Alan's hotel and left a message that they were to be at the hospital tomorrow morning at eight, then went upstairs to fill the bathtub.

When she came back downstairs an hour later, Houston was home, a rare thing for her since she always seemed to be out with Taggert, and she was in a flurry of activity as she opened presents and talked to Opal a mile a minute about the plans for the wedding. Houston exclaimed over the gifts from the East, things from Vanderbilts, the Astors, names that

Blair had only heard of, and now Houston was marrying one of their exclusive society.

Listlessly, she sat on one of the sofas.

"Have you seen the dress, Blair?" Houston asked as she turned around, holding a big cut-glass bowl that must have cost someone the earth.

"What dress?"

"Our wedding dress, of course," Houston said patiently. "I'm having yours made just like mine."

Blair felt that she couldn't stand to be in the room with so much enthusiasm. Maybe Houston could be put in a thrill of delight by a few presents, but she couldn't. "Mother, I don't feel too well. I think I'll go to bed and read for a while."

"All right, dear," Opal said, as she dug into yet another box. "I'll send Susan up with a tray. By the way, a young man called and said he wouldn't be at the hospital tomorrow. A Mr. Hunter, I believe," she said.

If anything, Blair began to feel worse. She'd neglected Alan shamefully in the last few days.

The morning came all too soon, and Blair's mood wasn't much improved. At least, the patients at the hospital kept her mind off her own problems—that is, until Leander came. His black mood made hers seem like a beam of sunshine. Within two hours, he managed to yell at her four times, telling her that if she wanted to be a doctor, she had to learn a few things. Blair wanted to yell back at him but, after one look at his face, she wisely said nothing except, "Yes, sir," and tried to do what she could to obey his orders.

At eleven, she was bending over a little girl whose broken arm she'd just set, when Alan came up behind her.

"I thought I'd find you here—with him."

Blair gave the little girl a smile. "Alan, I'm working."

"We're going to have a talk now, in front of the entire hospital or alone."

"All right, then, come with me." She led him down the corridor to Leander's office. She didn't know the hospital very well, and it was the only place she knew where they could be private. She just hoped that Lee wouldn't come back and discover them in there.

"I should have guessed this is where you'd go. His office!

You must feel comfortable in here. No doubt you're in here often enough." To his consternation, Blair collapsed in a chair, put her hands to her face and began to cry.

Alan was on his knees before her in an instant. "I didn't mean to be cross with you."

Blair tried to control her tears, but couldn't. "Everyone is cross with me. I never seem to please anyone. Mr. Gates never leaves me alone. Houston hates me. Leander can barely speak to me, and now you . . ."

"What's Westfield got to be angry about? He's winning hands down."

"Winning?" Blair pulled a handkerchief from her pocket and blew her nose. "He's not even in the competition. He said he could see that I loved you, and so he was no longer going to compete."

Alan stood and leaned against the desk. "Then why are you spending day after day with him? You haven't been two feet from his side for a week."

"He said that he'd like to work with me for the few days left of my stay. He said he'd never worked so well with anyone before. And he extended the invitation to both of us."

"Of all the underhanded—," Alan began, pacing the room. "He is lower than I thought. I never heard of such a sneaky, dirty trick." He looked back at Blair. "He knows you're infatuated with anything to do with medicine, so he uses that to get near you, and of course he'd invite me! The man's had years of experience and training over mine, so he looks great while I look like an idiot."

"That's not true! Leander said he wanted to work with me, and we *do* work well together. It's as if we read each other's minds."

"From what I hear, it's been that way since the first night you went out."

"Now who's being underhanded?"

"No more than he is," Alan shot back. "Blair, I'm tired of looking like a fool. I'm a student doctor competing in an operating room with a man with years of experience. I grew up in a city, but I'm competing in a canoe and on horseback. There's no possible way that I can look good against him."

"But you don't understand. Leander *isn't* competing. He

no longer *wants* to marry me. I'm staying in Chandler until my sister gets married, and then you and I will leave together. I still have hopes that Houston will marry Leander."

He watched her for a moment. "I believe that some part of you actually believes what you're saying. Let me tell you something: Westfield has *not* left the race. The poor man is competing so hard it's a wonder he has any breath left. And if you believe you're not getting married on Monday, why haven't you put a stop to all the wedding plans your sister is making? Do you plan to sit in the front row and watch your sister get married while you're surrounded by two of everything? What are you going to do with all those presents?"

He put his hands on the arms of the chair and leaned his face into hers. "As for Houston marrying your beloved doctor, I don't think you *could* sit there and watch that."

"That'll be enough, Hunter," came Leander's voice from the doorway.

"It's not nearly enough," Alan said, advancing on Leander.

"If it's a fight you want—."

Lee stopped when Blair placed herself between the two men.

"Blair," Alan said, "it's time you made a decision. I will be on the four o'clock train out of this town today. If you're not there, I'll leave alone." With that, he left the room.

Blair stood there alone with Lee for a moment and neither said anything, then Lee put his hand on her arm.

"Blair," he began, but she moved away.

"I think Alan's right. It's time I made my decision and stopped playing childish games." With that she swept past him and walked the two miles to her house.

When she got home, she very calmly took a pen and paper and began to make a list of the pros and cons of leaving with Alan. There were five good, strong reasons that she could come up with of why she should leave with him. They ranged from being able to get out of this bigoted town to allowing Houston to no longer feel pressured to marry her millionaire.

The only reason she could think of for *not* leaving with Alan was that she'd never get to see Leander again. She'd not be able to work with him on that new infirmary of his—of course, if what Alan had said was true, maybe Leander had shown her his plans just as a ruse to win the competition.

She stood. If she didn't get to work on the clinic here, in Pennsylvania, St. Joseph's Hospital was waiting for her.

She glanced down at her uniform and knew that that one garment was the only thing that she'd take with her. She couldn't walk out the door carrying a bag other than her medical bag, or there'd be questions. All she could take was what she was wearing. She crumbled the list in her hand and kept it there. She might need it to remind her why she was doing this.

Downstairs, her mother was arranging gifts, and Houston was out. Blair tried to say a few words to her mother, to say good-bye without saying the exact words, but Opal was too busy counting pieces of silver.

With her chin in the air, Blair went out the door and walked the long way to the train station. As she walked, she looked at the bustling little town with different eyes. Maybe it wasn't as bad as she'd originally thought. It wasn't Philadelphia, but it had its compensations. Three carriages rattled by carrying people who called out to her, "Hello, Blair-Houston," and the double name for once didn't seem so bad.

As she neared the train station, she wondered what would happen after she'd gone; if Houston would marry Lee, if her mother would understand Blair's disappearance, if Gates would hate her more than he did already.

She arrived at the train station at three forty-five and quickly saw that Alan wasn't there yet. She stood on the platform, her medical bag beside her, fiddled with the list in her hand, and thought about how this could be her last few minutes in the town named for her father. After the scandal she'd caused—stealing her sister's fiancé, then running off with another man four days before the wedding—she doubted whether she could come back before she was about ninety years old.

"Ahem," came a voice that she recognized, and she turned abruptly to see Leander sitting on a bench behind her.

"I thought I'd come to say good-bye," he said, and Blair went to stand in front of him. The list fell from her hand and, before she could pick it up, Leander took it and read it.

139

"I see I lost out to Uncle Henry and to your guilt over Houston."

She snatched the list from his hands. "I have done something unforgivable to my sister, and if I can remedy what I've done, I will."

"She didn't look too unhappy to me the last time I saw her. She was looking at Taggert like he hung the moon."

"Houston likes his money."

Lee snorted. "I may not know much about that woman, but I know she isn't in love with money. I think what she likes is a little more, ah . . . personal."

"You're crude."

"Then I guess it's good that you're marrying somebody perfect like Hunter, and not somebody crude like me. Just because I do things to your body that make you cry with pleasure, because we enjoy each other's company, because we work together so well—those aren't reasons to marry me. I hear you even beat Hunter at tennis."

"I'm glad I'm not marrying you. I never wanted to, ever." A sound made her glance down the track and she saw the train.

Leander stood. "I'm damned well not going to wait here to see you make an ass of yourself." He shoved his hands into his pockets. "You're going to be miserable, and you deserve it." He turned on his heel and left.

For a moment, Blair almost ran after him, but she caught herself. She'd made her decision and she was sticking to it. This would be better for everyone concerned.

The train pulled into the station, but Alan still wasn't there. She stood and walked down the platform while two men got off the train and a man and a woman got on.

The conductor started to motion the train forward.

"You have to wait. There's someone supposed to be here."

"If he ain't here, then he's missed the train. All aboard."

With disbelief, Blair watched the train pull out of the station. She sat down on the bench and waited. Perhaps Alan was just late and meant to catch the next train. She sat there for a total of two hours and forty-five minutes, but Alan didn't appear. She asked the ticket manager if a man fitting

Alan's description had bought a ticket. He'd purchased two tickets early that morning—for the four o'clock.

Blair paced the platform for another thirty minutes, then began to walk home.

So this was how it felt to be jilted, she thought. Funny, but she didn't feel bad at all. In fact, the closer she got to home, the lighter she felt. Maybe tomorrow she could work at the hospital with Leander.

When Blair walked into the house it was as quiet as a tomb, and the only light on was in the family parlor. She walked in, and to her surprise, her mother and Leander were sitting there, talking as quietly as if they were at a funeral.

When Opal saw her daughter, she very calmly, very slowly, dropped her embroidery and fainted. Leander stared at Blair so hard his mouth fell open, his cigar dropped out and set the fringe on a little footstool on fire.

Blair was so pleased with their reactions that she stood there grinning at them. The next moment, Susan came into the room and began screaming.

The screaming revived them all. Lee put out the fire, Blair slapped her mother's hands until she recovered, and Susan went off to make tea.

As soon as Opal was sitting upright, Leander grabbed Blair's shoulders, jerked her to her feet and began shaking her. "I hope that damned dress of yours fits because you're marrying me on Monday. You understand that?"

"Leander, you're hurting her," Opal cried.

Lee didn't pause in shaking Blair. "She's *killing* me! You understand, Blair?"

"Yes, Leander," she managed to say.

He pushed her down on the sofa and stormed from the room.

With shaking hands, Opal picked up her sewing from the floor. "I believe I've had enough excitement in the last two weeks to last me a lifetime."

Blair leaned back on the couch and smiled.

Chapter 16

For three days, Leander kept Blair so busy at the hospital that she had no time to think. He came for her early in the morning and returned her late in the evening. He took her to the warehouse on Archer Avenue and told her of his plans to renovate the place into a women's clinic. Right away, Blair had some ideas of her own, and Lee listened quietly and discussed them with her.

"I think we can have it ready in two weeks, since the equipment is already on its way from Denver," Lee said. "I'd planned it as a surprise, a wedding present, but I've had more than my share of surprises lately and can't stand any more."

Before Blair could say a word, he ushered her out of the warehouse and into his buggy and drove her back to the hospital. She was relieved that what Alan had said wasn't true, that Lee hadn't been lying about the clinic just to win the competition.

As the hours accumulated and the wedding grew closer, Blair wondered why Lee had wanted to marry her. He made no attempt to touch her, and they never talked except to discuss a patient. A few times, she caught him watching her, especially when she was working with other doctors, but he always turned away when she looked up.

And every day, Blair came to respect Lee more and more as a doctor. She soon realized that he could have made a great deal of money if he'd stayed in a big city hospital but, instead, he chose to remain in Chandler where he was seldom paid for anything. The hours were long and hard, the sheer amount of work overwhelming, and the rewards, for the most part, intangible.

On Sunday afternoon, the day before the wedding—when Blair was feeling a little queasy from Houston's pre-wedding party the night before—he called her into his office. It was an awkward meeting for both of them. Leander kept staring at her in a way that made her arms break into gooseflesh, and all she could think of was that tomorrow she was going to walk down the aisle to him.

"I've written a letter to St. Joseph's Hospital, telling them that you'll not be accepting their position."

Blair took a deep breath and sat down heavily in a chair. She hadn't thought about having to give up the internship.

Lee leaned forward on the desk. "I was thinking that maybe I've been a bit highhanded." He began to study his nails. "If you want to call tomorrow off, I'd understand."

For a moment, Blair was so bewildered she couldn't say anything. Was he saying that he didn't want to marry her? She stood quickly. "If you're trying to get out of this after all you've done to force me to marry you, I'll—."

She couldn't say any more because Leander had leaped from behind the desk, grabbed her shoulders and kissed her in a hard, intense way that left her speechless.

"I don't want out," he said when he had released her and Blair had managed to get her weak knees under control. "Now, get back to work, doctor. On second thought, go home and rest. If I know your sister, she has three dresses for you to try on, and your mother will have a hundred things for you to do. I'll see you tomorrow afternoon." He grinned broader. "And tomorrow night. Now, get out of here."

Blair couldn't help smiling back at him, and she kept smiling all the way home.

But her smile disappeared as soon as she entered the

Chandler house. Mr. Gates was furious because she had been working at the hospital on a Sunday and not at home helping her sister with the wedding arrangements, especially when poor Houston wasn't feeling well today. Blair was tired, too, and she was nervous about the wedding, and she was close to tears before the odious man got through yelling at her. Opal seemed to understand what her daughter was feeling and quickly got Mr. Gates to go to his study, as she took Blair into the garden to start writing thank-you notes.

Blair was still smarting from Mr. Gates's attack when she sat down with her mother.

"How could you marry a man like him, Mother? How could you subject Houston to him? At least I got away, but Houston's had to stay here all these years."

Opal was silent for a few minutes. "I guess I didn't consider you girls when I fell in love with Mr. Gates."

"Fell in love with him! But I thought that your family forced you to marry him."

"Where in the world did you get such an idea?" Opal asked, aghast.

"I think Houston and I must have decided it on our own. We couldn't see any other reason for your marrying him. Perhaps we liked to think that after our father died, you were too distraught to care whom you married."

Opal gave a little laugh. "You both were so young when William died, and I'm sure that as children you'd remember him as the most wonderful of fathers, always doing things, creating things, making excitement wherever he went."

"He wasn't like that?" Blair asked cautiously, dreading to hear awful things about her adored father.

Opal put her hand on her daughter's arm. "He was all and more than you remember. I'm sure you don't remember half of his spirit, his flamboyance, or his courage or ambition. Both of you girls have inherited much from him." She sighed. "But the truth is that I found William Chandler the most exhausting man on earth. I loved him dearly, but there were days when I had tears of relief in my eyes when he finally left the house. You see, I'd been raised in the belief that a woman's role in life was to sit in the front parlor and direct servants while she embroidered. The most strenuous thing I had planned to undertake was counted cross-stitch. All those little squares to count!"

She leaned back in her chair and smiled. "Then I met your father. For some reason, he decided he wanted me, and I don't really think I had much say in it. He came into my life with his extraordinary handsomeness, and I don't think I ever even considered saying no to him.

"But then we were married, and there was one crisis after another to handle, all of them caused by Bill's lust for life. Even when William produced children, he made twins; one child wasn't enough for him."

She looked down at her hands, and there were tears in her eyes. "I thought I'd die, too, after Bill passed away. I didn't seem to have a reason for living, but then I began to remember things that I had once enjoyed, such as needle-work, and of course I had you girls. Then Mr. Gates came along. He was as different as night and day from Bill, and he liked what Bill used to call my 'busywork.' Mr. Gates had rigid ideas of what a woman should and should not do. He didn't expect me to spend Sunday afternoons climbing mountains with him as Bill used to. No, Mr. Gates wanted to provide a lovely home for me, and I was to stay in that home and tend to my children and give tea parties in the afternoons. As I got to know the man more, I found that he was easy to please, and that the things that came naturally to me quite often were the ones that he expected from me. With your father, I was never quite sure what I was supposed to do."

She looked up at Blair. "So I found I was in love with him. What I wanted to do and his ideas of what I should do matched perfectly. I'm afraid that I didn't really think of you girls, or realize how much like Bill both of you were. I knew you were like your father, and so I arranged for you to live with Henry, but I thought Houston was like me, and she is to some extent. But Houston is also like her father, and it comes out in odd ways, such as her dressing as an old woman and going into the mine camps. Bill would have done something like that."

Blair was silent for a long time as she thought about what her mother had said, and she wondered if she could ever love

Leander. She'd known for sure that she was in love with Alan, but she hadn't been exactly devastated when he'd jilted her. There was too much bound up in what had happened. She couldn't look at Lee without remembering that her sister had loved him so much and for so long, and now Houston was going to have to watch him marry someone else.

Blair didn't sleep much the night before the wedding, and it seemed that all the demons of the night were still there in the morning. The bright sunlight of the day couldn't rid her of her sense of doom.

For the last few days, she'd managed to forget for whole minutes that she was marrying her sister's intended, but then she'd always believed that it would never actually happen. She had thought that somehow she'd get out of marrying Leander, and Houston could have him back.

At ten o'clock, they left for Taggert's house, where the wedding was being held, Opal and the twins riding in Houston's pretty little carriage, one of the many gifts from Taggert, the stableboy behind, driving a big wagon that Houston had borrowed, the wedding dresses hidden inside muslin in the back. They were silent all the way to the house. When Blair asked Houston what she was thinking, Houston said she hoped that the lilies had arrived undamaged.

Blair knew that this was further proof that her sister's major interest in the man she was marrying was his monetary worth.

And once Blair saw Taggert's house, she was sure that Houston had sold herself to the god of money.

The house looked as if it were carved out of a mountain of marble: cool and white and vast. The downstairs was dominated by a big, sweeping, double staircase that curved up two sides of a hallway that was bigger than that in any house Blair'd ever seen.

"We'll come down there," Houston said, pointing toward the stairs. "One of us on each side." Surrounded by a bevy of prettily dressed girlfriends, she sauntered away and started an inspection of the house, while Blair stood where she was.

"It takes a while to get used to," Opal whispered to her daughter. There was a feeling about the place that it wasn't real, that it was out of a fairy tale and that it would disappear as quickly as it had appeared.

"Houston plans to *live* in this?" Blair whispered back.

"It does seem smaller when Kane is here," Opal assured her. "I think we should go upstairs now. There's no telling what Houston has planned for us."

Blair followed her mother up the wide stairs, looking over her shoulder all the time to the floor below. Everywhere she looked, she saw exotic arrangements of flowers and greenery, and on the landing she paused to look out the window to the grounds below. They were beautiful, with a lush lawn and shrubberies.

Opal paused beside her. "That's the service yard. You should see the *garden.*"

Blair didn't say any more as she followed her mother up to the second floor and the private family rooms.

"Houston's put you in here," Opal said, opening the door to a tall-ceilinged room with a white marble fireplace that was carved with swags and flowers. The couches, chairs, and tables in the room should have been in museums.

"This is the sitting room and through here is the bedroom and that's the bath. Each guest room has a sitting room and a bath all its own."

Blair ran her hand along the marble basin in the bathroom and, although she'd never seen any before and couldn't be sure, she thought the fixtures might be gold. "Brass?" she asked her mother.

"He wouldn't have it in his house," Opal said with some pride. "Now, I must go and see if Houston needs any help. You have hours before you need to be ready, so why don't you take a nap?"

Blair started to protest that she couldn't possibly sleep, but then she looked at the enormous marble tub and thought that she'd like to make use of it.

As soon as she was alone, she filled the tub with steamy hot water and climbed into it, the water relaxing her instantly. She stayed in there a long time, until her skin began to wrinkle, and then stepped out and dried with a towel so thick it could have been a pillow. She wrapped herself in a pink cashmere robe and went into the bedroom, where she promptly fell asleep on the big, soft bed.

When she woke, she felt rested and clear-headed, and she remembered her mother's words of there being a garden in the back of the house. Quickly, she dressed in her usual simple skirt and blouse and left the room. Not wanting to use the main staircase, since she could hear muffled voices below, she went down a corridor past closed doors and eventually found a back staircase that led into a maze of kitchen and storage rooms on the first floor. Every inch of these rooms was filled with people scurrying back and forth and creating wonderful smells of food. Blair had a difficult time getting through the crowd. Several people saw her, but no one had time to comment on a bride being in the kitchen two hours before the wedding began. Blair was only concerned that Houston didn't see her. No doubt Houston had a timetable and she would keep to it no matter what happened. Houston would never find time to slip away into the garden.

Behind the house was a lawn that was now covered with enormous tents, and tables with pink linen tablecloths, and hundreds of vases of flowers. Men and women in uniforms were hurrying in and out of the house to put food and condiments on the tables.

Blair hurried past these people, too, and went to what looked to be the garden below. When she first stepped into the edge of the garden, she was unprepared for what she saw. Before her rolled acres of winding paths, appearing and disappearing amid plants such as she'd never seen before. Tentatively, she began to follow a path.

The commotion of the wedding preparations disappeared behind her and, for the first time in days, she felt free to think.

This was her wedding day, but right now she couldn't remember how she had got here. Three weeks ago, she was in Pennsylvania and she had her entire future mapped out. But how different everything had turned out! Alan had run away rather than marry her. Her sister had lost the man she loved and was now marrying one of the richest men in the country —without any love involved.

And everything was Blair's fault. She had come home to see her sister married and had instead managed to make her into a mercenary. Houston might as well have put herself on the auction block and taken the highest bidder.

As Blair strolled about the garden, frowning over her thoughts, she saw Taggert coming down the path. Before she thought about what she was doing, she turned abruptly and went the other way before he saw her. She'd gone no more than a few feet when she saw an extraordinarily tall woman, who looked vaguely familiar, hurrying along the same path as Taggert. Blair couldn't remember where she'd seen her before.

She shrugged her shoulders, dismissing the woman, and kept walking.

Her thoughts were fully occupied with what was going to happen today, and she was trying to puzzle out exactly how it had come about, when she suddenly remembered who the tall woman was.

"That's Pamela Fenton," she said aloud. Houston and Blair had been at the Fenton house often when they were children, to ride Marc's ponies or to attend one of his numerous parties, and his older sister Pam had been nearly grown then and they had been in awe of her. Then she'd left home suddenly, and there had been whispers about what had happened for years afterward.

So she's come back after all these years, and she'll be at the wedding, Blair thought with some pleasure. Idly, she wondered what Pamela had done so long ago to cause the town to gossip about her. There was something about a stableboy, wasn't there?

Blair stopped where she was. The scandal had indeed been about a stableboy in her father's stables. She'd fallen in love with him, and her father had sent her away as a result of that love affair.

And Kane Taggert was that stableboy!

Grabbing her skirts, Blair ran along the path toward where

both Taggert and Pam had gone. She was several feet away when she halted.

She watched in disbelief as Kane Taggert took Pamela Fenton's face in his hands and kissed her with a great deal of passion.

With quick, hot tears in her eyes, Blair fled down the paths toward the house. What had she done to her sister? Houston was going to marry this monstrous man who kissed a woman two hours before he was to marry another.

And it was because of Blair that this was happening.

Chapter 17

Anne Seabury helped Blair into the elaborate wedding dress that Houston had designed. It was an elegantly simple dress of ivory satin, high necked, big sleeved, and as tight as the steel-ribbed corset could make it. Hundreds, maybe even thousands, of tiny seed pearls were sewn about the waist and at the cuffs. And the veil was of handmade lace such as Blair had never seen before.

As she glanced in the mirror, she wished that she was donning this dress under happier circumstances, that she was going to go down that aisle with a smile on her face.

But she knew that was impossible, since she'd already done what she knew she had to do. As soon as she'd seen that monster Taggert kissing another woman, she had returned to the house and sent the man a note. She had told him that she'd be wearing red roses in her hair, and she instructed the maid to tell him that he was to be sure and stand on the left, not the right as was originally planned.

Blair wasn't sure of the legality of what she was doing, since the licenses gave the proper names of which twin was to marry which man, but perhaps she could buy her sister a little time if the minister pronounced Leander and Houston man

151

and wife instead of marrying her to that lecherous man Taggert. She didn't like to think of the consequences if the marriage was legal and she found herself married to Taggert.

She sent pink roses to her sister and asked her to please wear them.

At the head of the stairs, Blair grabbed her sister to her. "I love you more than you know," she whispered before starting the descent, then, with a sigh, said, "Let's get this spectacle over." With every step, Blair felt that she was moving closer to her execution. What if the marriage was legal and she found herself married to that dreadful man and had to live in this mausoleum of a house?

Inside the enormous room that was supposed to be a library, but could have been an indoor baseball field, she saw Taggert next to Leander on a platform that was draped, hung, and piled with roses and greenery.

Blair kept her head high and her eyes straight. She knew that, by now, Houston must have seen what was going on, that she was, after all, going to get to marry the man she loved.

Blair looked ahead at Kane Taggert, and as she walked down the aisle toward him, she saw his brows draw together in a straight line. He knows! she thought. He knows that I'm not Houston.

For a moment, Blair was amazed at this. Right now, she doubted if even her own mother could tell which twin was which, but somehow, this man knew. She glanced at Leander and saw that he was giving Houston a slight smile, a smile of welcome. Of course, Leander was trusting, she thought; he had no reason to suspect anyone of any bad deed since he was incapable of doing anything bad himself. But Taggert, on the other hand, was reputed to have done many bad things to get his money, so he'd be looking for treachery and could therefore tell the twins apart, Blair reasoned.

Blair didn't look at her sister as they took their places on the platform. Leander took Houston's hand in his, while Taggert turned away from both twins and the minister.

"Dearly beloved, we—," the minister began, but Houston cut him off.

"Excuse me, I'm Houston."

Blair looked at her sister in astonishment. Why was Houston ruining what had been so carefully arranged?

Leander gave Blair a hard look. "Shall we exchange places?" he said to Taggert.

Taggert merely shrugged his big shoulders. "Don't matter much to me."

"It matters to me," Leander said and moved to trade places with Taggert.

Lee took Blair's hand in his and nearly squeezed it off—but she felt little pain. Taggert had publicly admitted that Houston didn't matter to him, that he didn't care whether he married her or someone else. Blair had never asked herself why Taggert wanted to marry Houston, and now she wondered if it was because she was the only one who'd have him.

Leander pinched her and she looked up in time to say, "I do."

Before she was aware of what was happening, the ceremony was over, Leander was grabbing her in his arms and preparing to kiss her. To the audience, it must have looked like a kiss of great enthusiasm, but in truth, Lee whispered in her ear with a great deal of vehemence. "I want to see you outside. Now!"

Tripping over the twelve-foot train of her heavy satin dress, Blair tried to keep up with him as he half dragged her down the aisle. People descended on them as soon as they were in the hall, but Leander didn't let go of her hand as he pulled her into a large, panelled room at the end of the corridor.

"Just what was that all about?" Leander began, but didn't let her answer. "Do you hate the idea of living with me so badly that you'd go to such lengths to get out of it? Would you rather have a man you don't even know than me? Anyone but me, is that it?"

"No," she began, "I didn't even think about you. I just thought about Houston. I didn't want her to feel that she had to marry that awful man."

Leander looked at her for a long moment, and when he spoke, his voice was quiet. "Do you mean that you were willing to marry a man you dislike just so your sister could have the man you think she wants?"

"Of course." Blair was a bit bewildered by his question. "What other reason would I have for making the switch?"

"Only that you thought that marriage to anyone would be preferable to marriage to me." He grabbed her arm. "Blair, you're going to settle this right now. You and Houston are going to talk to one another, and I want you to ask her why she wanted to marry Taggert—and I want you to listen to her answer. You understand me? I want you to really listen to her answer."

Ignoring the hundreds of people around them, all of whom were whispering and laughing about the mix-up at the altar, Leander pulled Blair through the crowd as he asked where Houston was. She wasn't difficult to find, as she sat alone in a small room that was littered with papers.

"I think you two have a few things that need to be said to one another," Leander said through his teeth to Blair as he half pushed her into the room and closed the door behind her.

Alone, the twins didn't speak to each other. Houston just sat in a chair, her head down, while Blair hovered near the door.

"I guess we should get out there and cut the cake," Blair said tentatively. "You and Taggert—."

Houston came out of her chair looking as if she had suddenly been turned into a harpy. "You can't even call him by his name, can you?" she said, anger in every word. "You think he has no feelings; you've dismissed him and therefore you think you have a right to do whatever you want to him."

Surprised, Blair stepped back from her sister's anger. "Houston, what I did, I did for you. I want to see you happy."

Houston's fists were clenched at her sides and she advanced on Blair as if she meant to challenge her to a fight. "Happy? How can I be happy when I don't even know where my husband is? Thanks to you, I may never know the meaning of happiness."

"Me? What have I done except try everything in my power to help you? I've tried to help you come to your senses and see that you didn't have to marry that man for his money. Kane Taggert—."

"You really don't know, do you?" Houston interrupted

154

her. "You have humiliated a proud, sensitive man in front of hundreds of people, and you aren't even aware of what you've done."

"I assume you're talking about what happened at the altar? I did it for you, Houston. I know you love Leander and I was willing to take Taggert just to make you happy. I'm so sorry about what I've done to you. I never meant to make you so unhappy. I know I've ruined your life, but I did try to repair what I'd done."

"Me, me, me. That's all you can say. You've ruined my life and all you can talk about is yourself. *You* know I love Leander. *You* know what an awful man Kane is. For the last week or so, you've spent every waking moment with Leander, and the way you talk about him is as if he were a god. Every other word you say is, 'Leander.' I think you did mean well this morning: you wanted to give me the best man."

Houston leaned toward her sister. "Leander may set your body on fire, but he never did anything for me. If you hadn't been so involved with yourself lately, and could think that I do have some brains of my own, you'd have seen that I've fallen in love with a good, kind, thoughtful man—admittedly he's a little rough around the edges, but then, haven't you always complained that my edges are a little too smooth?"

Blair sat down. "You love him? Taggert? You love Kane Taggert? But I don't understand. You've *always* loved Leander. For as long as I can remember, you've loved him."

Some of Houston's anger seemed to leave her and she turned away to look out the window. "True, I decided I wanted him when I was six years old. I think it became a goal to me, like climbing a mountain. I should have set my sights on Mt. Rainier. At least, once I'd climbed it, it would have been done. I never knew what I was going to do with Leander after we were married."

"But you do know what you'll do with Taggert?"

Houston looked back at her sister and smiled. "Oh, yes. I very much know what I'm going to do with him. I am going to make a home for him, a place where he'll be safe, a place where I'll be safe, where I can do whatever I want."

Blair stood and it was her turn to clench her fists. "I guess you couldn't have bothered to take two minutes to tell me this, could you? I have been through Hades in the last weeks. I have worried about you, spent whole days crying about what I've done to my sister, and here you tell me that you're in *love* with this King Midas."

"Don't you say anything against him!" Houston shouted, then calmed. "He's the kindest, gentlest man and very generous. And I happen to love him very much."

"And I have been through agony because I was worried about you. You should have told me!"

Houston idly ran her hand along the edge of the desk that sat in the middle of the room. "I guess I was so jealous of your love match that I didn't want to think about you."

"Love match?!" Blair exploded. "I think I'm Leander's Mt. Rainier. I can't deny that he does things to me physically, but that's all he wants from me. We've spent days together in the operating room, but I feel there's a part of Leander I don't know. He doesn't really let me get close to him. I know so little about him. He decided he wanted me, so he went after me, using every method he could to get me."

"But I see the way you look at him. I never felt inclined to look at him like that."

"That's because you never saw him in an operating room. If you'd seen him in there, you would have—."

"Fainted, most likely," Houston said. "Blair, I am sorry that I didn't talk to you. I probably knew that you were in agony, but what happened *hurt*. I had been engaged to Leander for, it seemed to me, most of my life, yet you walked in and took him in just one night. And Lee was always calling me his ice princess, and I was so worried about being a cold woman."

"And you're no longer worried about that?" Blair asked.

The color in Houston's cheeks heightened. "Not with Kane," she whispered.

"You really do love him?" Blair asked, still not able to comprehend this fact. "You don't mind the food flying everywhere? You don't mind his loudness or the other women?"

Blair could have bitten out her tongue.

"*What* other women?" Houston asked, eyes narrowed. "And Blair, you'd better tell me."

Blair took a deep breath. It would have been all right to tell Houston what she had seen before she'd married the man, but now it was too late.

Houston advanced on her sister. "If you even consider managing my life again as you did today at the altar, I'll never speak to you again. I am an adult, and you know something about *my* husband, and I want to know what it is."

"I saw him in the garden kissing Pamela Fenton just before the wedding," Blair said all in one breath.

Houston whitened a bit, but she seemed to be under control. "But he came to me anyway," she whispered. "He saw her, kissed her, but he married me." A brilliant smile lit her face. "Blair, you have made me the happiest woman alive today. Now, all I have to do is find my husband and tell him that I love him and hope that he will forgive me."

She stopped suddenly. "Oh, Blair, you don't know him at all. He's such a good man, generous in a very natural way, strong in a way that makes people lean on him, but he's . . ." She buried her face in her hands. "But he can't stand embarrassment of any kind, and we've humiliated him in front of the entire town. He'll never forgive me. Never!"

Blair started toward the door. "I'll go to him and explain that it was all my fault, that you had nothing to do with it. Houston, I had no idea you really wanted to marry him. I just couldn't imagine anyone wanting to live with someone like him."

"I don't think you have to worry about that anymore, because I think he just walked out on me."

"But what about the guests? He can't just leave."

"Should he stay and listen to people laughing about how Leander can't decide which twin he wants? Not one person will think that Kane could have his choice of women. Kane thinks I'm still in love with Lee, you think I love Lee, and Mr. Gates thinks I'm marrying Kane for his money. I think Mother is the only person who sees that I'm in love—for the very first time in my life."

"What can I do to make it up to you?" Blair whispered.

"There's nothing you can do. He's gone. He left me money and the house and he walked away. But what do I want with this big, empty house if he's not in it?" She sat down. "Blair, I don't even know where he is. He could be on a train back to New York for all I know."

"More than likely, he's gone to his cabin."

Both women looked up to see Kane's friend, Edan, standing in the doorway. "I didn't mean to eavesdrop, but when I saw what happened at the wedding, I knew he'd be in a rage."

Houston expertly wrapped the train of her wedding dress about her arm. "I'm going to him and explain what happened. I'm going to tell him that my sister is so in love with Leander that she thinks that I am, too." She turned to smile at Blair. "I can't help but resent the fact that you thought that I was low enough to marry a man for his money, but I thank you for the love that made you willing to sacrifice what has come to mean so much to you." Quickly, she kissed her sister's cheek.

Blair clung to her sister for a moment. "Houston, I had no idea you felt this way. As soon as the reception is over, I'll help you pack and—."

Houston pulled away with a little laugh. "No, my dear managing sister, I am leaving this house right now. My husband is more important to me than a few hundred guests. You're going to have to stay here and answer all the questions about where Kane and I've gone."

"But Houston, I don't know anything about receptions of this size."

Houston stopped at the door beside Edan. "I learned how in my 'worthless' education," she said, then smiled. "Blair, it's not all that tragic. Cheer up, maybe there'll be an attack of food poisoning, and you'll know how to handle that. Good luck," she said and was out the door, leaving Blair alone to the horror of having to deal with the enormous, elaborate reception.

"Why did I ever open my big mouth about that school Houston chose?" she mumbled, as she straightened her dress, tried to breathe inside the tight corset, and left the room.

Chapter 18

The reception was worse than Blair had imagined it could be. People were always running out of this or that and, the minute Houston was out of sight, no one seemed to know what to do. And then, there were what seemed to be hundreds of Lee's relatives to meet, all of them asking questions about the unusual exchanging of twins. Opal began spreading the rumor that Houston's husband had taken her away on a white horse (probably one with wings, Blair thought), and all the young ladies were whispering that Kane was the most romantic of men. All Blair could think of was that she was certainly glad that her switch had failed and she wasn't going to have to spend her wedding night with Taggert.

Some man was asking Blair how he should serve what looked to be a hundred-pound wheel of cheese when she looked across the guests to see Leander watching her, and a small blush began to spread over her body. Whatever else she minded about Lee, spending the night with him was not one of them.

He pushed his way through the crowd of people, gave a few curt directions to the man with the cheese, and pulled Blair away with him into the garden, out of sight of the people.

"Thank heavens a man only has to go through this once in his life. Did you know that Mr. Gates is crying?"

She felt good being here with him in the shade, away from the noise and the crowd, and she wished he'd kiss her. "He's probably happy to see the last of me in his house."

"He told me that now he could relax, because now he knew you'd be happy. Now, you were going to do what the Lord made women for. You'd have a good man—that's me—to take care of you, and at last you'd be fulfilled."

He was looking at her in a way that made her feel very warm.

"You think you *will* be fulfilled with me?" he asked in a husky whisper and began to move toward her.

"Dr. Westfield! Telegram!" came the voice of a boy, and the next minute he was standing there, shattering their aloneness.

Leander gave the boy a nickel and told him to help himself to the food as he began to open the telegram, his eyes on Blair. But the next minute, all his attention was on the paper in front of him.

"I'll wring her neck," he said under his breath, his face beginning to turn red with anger.

Blair took the telegram from his hand.

I HAVE JUST MARRIED ALAN HUNTER STOP WOULD YOU TELL FATHER AND BLAIR STOP I WILL RETURN IN THREE WEEKS STOP DO NOT BE TOO ANGRY STOP LOVE NINA

"Of all the underhanded . . . ," Lee began. "Father and I will go after her and—."

Blair cut him off. "And do what? She's already married and, besides, what's wrong with Alan? I thought he'd make a very good husband."

Quickly, the anger left Leander. "I guess he will at that. But why couldn't she have stayed here and been married in public? Why did she have to run away as if she were ashamed of him?"

"Nina and I have been friends all our lives, and I imagine that she was afraid of me. After all, I didn't get to marry the man I had originally planned to marry, so perhaps she thought I'd be angry about how Alan left me at the train station. No doubt he left me for Nina."

Leander leaned against a tree and took a cigar from his pocket. "You seem awfully cool about this. I gave you the chance to back out. You could have gone back to Pennsylvania. You had the chance."

Later in her life, Blair thought that that was the moment she fell in love with Leander. He'd made such a fool of himself to win her, yet here he stood like a sulky little boy, saying that she didn't have to marry him, that he would have let her go.

"And what would you have done if I'd boarded a train? I seem to remember your shaking me and telling me that I *was* going to marry you and that I had no say in the matter," she said softly, as she moved to stand in front of him, her hand touching his collar. Around her was spread yards of the heavenly silk satin, the beading gently flashing colors in the soft light of the garden.

He watched her for a moment, then tossed the cigar to the ground and grabbed her to him in a kiss of great passion, holding her close to him, trying to merge their bodies into one. He pulled her head to his shoulder, almost smothering her as he hugged her in a way that a mother holds a child that has almost been lost. "You *did* choose him, you went to the train to go with him."

Blair tried to untangle herself and the cascading veil from his grasp. She wanted to look at him. "That's behind us now," she said, as she looked into his eyes and thought about the man behind that handsome face. She remembered the many times she'd seen him working to save a life, especially the day they'd brought in an old cowboy who'd been gored by a bull, and when Lee had been unable to save him, and the man had died on the operating table, Blair was sure there'd been tears in Lee's eyes. He'd said he'd known the old man for years, and it would hurt to know that he was gone.

Now, she stood within his grasp, and she knew that she'd married the right man. Alan hadn't really loved her, nor she him. Not if he could one minute demand that she choose, and a few hours later leave her standing at the train station. And she remembered how relieved she'd been when he hadn't shown up.

"A great deal has happened between us," she said, as she ran her hand down his cheek. It was so nice to be able to touch him, as she'd wanted to since their first night together. He was hers from now on, totally and completely hers. "But today marks a new beginning, and I'd like to start with a clean slate. You and I work well together, and we have . . . other things in common," she said, as she moved her hips just slightly against his. "I want this marriage to work. I want us to have children, and I want us to keep in practice together, and I want us to . . . love each other." She said the last hesitantly, because all he'd ever said was that he desired her, and love had never entered the picture.

"Children," he murmured, pulling her even closer. "Especially, let's make children." He began to kiss her as if he were starving.

"Here they are," someone shouted. "Now, stop that. You have a whole lifetime for that. Now, you have to come and join the party. The cake has to be cut."

Reluctantly, Blair pulled away from her husband. Another few minutes of his kisses and she'd be rolling about the grass with him. She'd already proven that she had no control when it came to him.

With a sigh, Lee took her hand in his and led her back to the mass of people gathered on one of Taggert's too smooth, too big lawns.

Immediately after the cake cutting, the guests separated them and several women started asking Blair hundreds of questions about where Houston had gone.

"That man swept my daughter off her feet," Opal said in a demure way that didn't allow for any disbelief. "Both my daughters have married strong men who knew exactly what they wanted and went after it."

Two of the women in Opal's audience looked as if they were about to swoon at the romance of the stories.

"Mother," Blair said, holding out a dish. "Have a slice of ham." She leaned forward so only Opal could hear her. "Now I know where Houston and I get our acting ability."

Opal smiled at the women, took the dish from Blair and gave her a quick wink.

With a laugh, Blair went away, leaving her mother to brag about her new sons-in-law.

At sundown, there was dancing in the library, and of course Leander and Blair had to lead the dancing. Several people asked if it had been she that night at the governor's reception and not Houston. Both Blair and Lee laughed secretly, and he swept her away in his arms again, whirling her about the polished dance floor.

"It's time we left these people and went home. I don't think I can wait much longer to make you mine," Leander whispered in her ear as he held her.

Blair didn't even nod, but tightened the train about her arm and quickly left the room to go upstairs to change into her going-away clothes. Her mother came to help her and Opal was silent until Blair stood ready.

"Leander's a good man and I know you've had some problems, but I think he'll make you a good husband," Opal said.

"I do, too," Blair said, looking radiant in an electric blue suit that Houston had chosen for her sister. "I think he'll make the best of husbands." And I *know* he'll make the best of lovers, she thought, then kissed her mother quickly and ran down the stairs to meet Leander.

Amid showers of rice so heavy that their health was threatened, they left the Taggert mansion for the pretty little house that would be their home.

But once they were away from the crowd, Blair began to feel timid and shy. From now on, her life would be tied to this man whom she knew only in a professional way. What did she know about him personally? What had he done in his life besides study medicine?

At the house, Lee swept her into his arms and carried her over the threshold, took one look at her white face and said, "This isn't the woman who risked her life to keep a man's chin clean, is it? You're not afraid of me, are you?"

When Blair didn't answer, he said, "What you need is some champagne. And we both know where that will lead, don't we?"

He set her on the floor in the entry hall and turned right into the dining room. Blair hadn't really seen the house, and now she went left into the parlor. Behind the parlor was a tiny bedroom for guests. The furniture was heavy and dark, but the room was still pleasant, with blue-and-white striped wallpaper and a border of pale pink roses along the top. She took a seat on a satin-covered sofa.

Leander returned with two glasses of champagne and a bottle chilling in a silver holder on a tray. "I hope you like the place. Houston did it. I don't think I cared much what she did." He sat at the other end of the couch, away from her, seeming to sense her shyness.

"I like it. I don't know much about decorating houses, and Houston's much better at that than I am. I would probably have asked her to do the house anyway. But now she has Taggert's."

"Did you two get that straightened out?"

The champagne was making Blair relax and Lee refilled her glass. "Houston said that she'd fallen in love with Taggert." Blair's face showed her disbelief. "I can't imagine my sister with that loud, overbearing boor. Why she would prefer him over you is . . ." She stopped, looking embarrassed.

Leander was grinning at her. "I thank you for the compliment." He leaned across the couch and began to toy with the curls that were escaping the neat chignon that Houston had fixed that morning, and, slowly, he began to remove the pins from her hair. "Opposites always seem to attract. Look at you and me. Here I am a fine surgeon, and you're going to be a fine wife and mother and put all my socks in their proper place, and you'll see to the house so it's a comfortable place for a man to come home to and—."

Blair nearly choked on the champagne. "Are you saying that you expect me to give up medicine to wait on you?" she sputtered. "Of all the misinformed, *stupid* ideas I have ever heard, that one is the worst." With a great deal of anger, she slammed her glass down on a side table and stood. "I always tried to tell Houston that you were like Gates, but she wouldn't listen. She said you weren't at all like him. I'll tell you one thing, Leander Westfield, if you married me thinking that I'd give up medicine, we might as well call this whole thing off now."

Leander sat on the couch as she stood over him raging, then, halfway through her speech, he slowly rose to stand in front of her. And when she began to wind down, he smiled at her. "I think you have a great deal to learn about me yet. I'm not sure why you're so ready to believe the worst about me, but I hope to prove to you that I'm not what you think. And I plan to spend the rest of my life teaching you. But lessons don't start until tomorrow," he said, as he put his arms around her and pulled her to him.

Blair clung to him, and when his lips touched hers, she felt as if she never wanted to let go. She knew that she knew nothing about him. She didn't know why he'd wanted to marry her, whether he had merely tolerated her working with him so that he could win the competition as Alan had said, or if he had enjoyed that time together as much as she had.

But right now, she didn't care. All she thought about was his arms around her, his body near hers, the heat he was producing that was making her feel wonderful.

"I've waited a long time for this to happen again," he said, wrapping her hair about his wrist, his other hand caressing her neck and cheek. "Go upstairs and get ready. I'm going to be a gentleman tonight, but I'll never be one again, so you might as well take advantage of this once. Stop looking at me like that and go. I'm sure your sister bought you some outrageous—but proper—nightgown for tonight, so go get it on. You have about ten minutes. Maybe."

Blair didn't want to leave him, but she did and she went upstairs, around the narrow, curving stairs and into the bedroom. There were three bedrooms upstairs: the master bedroom, one for guests and one a tiny nursery. Her clothes were hung in the closet, all her shoes beside Leander's, and for a moment she thought she'd never seen anything as intimate as those shoes next to each other.

On the bed was indeed a beautiful robe of white chiffon with swan's-down about the hem and sleeves, a gown of white satin to go under it. Blair shook her head at the extravagance of the things, but the next moment she was dying to get into them. Sometimes, she was frustrated by Houston's seemingly useless life, but this wedding made her admire her sister as nothing else had. The wedding itself had required the planning of a military general and no detail had seemed too small to attract Houston's attention. She'd even remembered to have her sister's clothes moved to her new house during the wedding, so they'd be here when she returned with Leander.

Blair was only half into the robe when Lee came up the stairs and, by the look in his eyes, he didn't seem to care that it was hanging off her shoulder in a very unkempt way. He bounded across the room and had her in his arms in seconds. In fact, his enthusiasm was so great that Blair took a step backward, tripped on the hem of the robe, and fell back onto the bed. Lee went with her and they fell into the feather bed, bits of swan's-down from the robe floating around them.

They started to laugh, and Lee rolled over, his arms still about her, pulling her with him, kissing her, tickling her, making Blair squeal with delight. The lovely robe came off and she was in the thin satin gown, and he was nibbling at her shoulders and growling like a bear, making her laugh harder. His hands went up and down her thighs while she made halfhearted protests about nothing in particular.

The telephone downstairs began to ring before their play turned serious.

"What's that?" Blair asked, lifting her head.

"I don't hear anything," Leander murmured, his face buried in her neck and travelling lower.

"It's the telephone. Lee, you have to answer it. Someone may be ill and need you."

"Anyone who'd disturb a man on his wedding night deserves what he gets."

Blair pushed away from him. "Lee, you don't mean that. When you became a doctor, you did so because you wanted to help people."

"But not tonight, not now." He tried to pull her back into his arms, but she resisted and the damn telephone kept ringing. "Why did I have to marry a doctor?" he mumbled, as he stood and adjusted his clothes while giving Blair looks that made her giggle and look away. "Don't you go away. I'll be right back," he said before he went down the stairs. "Right after I kill whoever it is on the telephone."

As soon as he picked up the receiver, the operator began to talk. "I hate to disturb you tonight of all nights," she began, "but it's your father, and he says it's urgent."

"It'd better be," Lee said. Then she put Reed on the line.

"Lee, I hate to bother you, but it's an emergency. Elijah Smith is about to die of a heart attack if you don't come right away."

Leander drew in his breath. Elijah Smith was their code name for trouble at the mine. Reed often reported to Lee over the telephone while Lee was at the hospital, and they'd worked out a series of messages. Poor Mr. Smith got everything from poison ivy to smallpox, but a heart attack was what they'd agreed to use to signal the worst that could happen: a riot.

Lee rolled his eyes toward the ceiling, toward the room where his bride waited. "How much time do I have?"

"They needed you an hour ago. Lee, don't go; someone else can take the case."

"Yeah, like who?" Lee spat, taking his anger out on his father. There was no one outside the mines who knew what was going on inside them. And Lee felt responsible for any rioting, since he was the man who brought the unionists in. "I'll be there as fast as I can," Lee said before he hung up the telephone.

As he went up the stairs, feeling as if the worst thing in his life had just happened, he suddenly realized that he had to give Blair a reason for leaving. He was no longer a bachelor who answered to no one. He now had a wife who deserved an explanation as to where he was going. At the moment, he was feeling so miserable that he couldn't think of a lie—and heaven forbid that he should tell her the truth! With Blair's total lack of a self-preservation instinct, she'd no doubt insist on going with him. And if he didn't have enough to worry about, he couldn't have her in danger, too.

The best way was to do it quickly and get out of the house.

He had never moved faster in his life, and considering that there were what seemed to be tears fogging his eyes as he looked at Blair lying there in that thin little piece of cloth, every nook and cranny of her delicious body showing, he should have been given an award. He didn't say much at all, except that he had to go and he'd be back as soon as possible. He ran down the stairs and was out the door before Blair could even move.

At his father's house, he was still feeling miserable and thinking that the miners could riot all night as far as he was concerned.

Reed told Lee that an informer had let the guards know about the unionist, and that the stupid man had gone back into the camp without Lee. He'd sneaked down the back side of the mountain and was being very bold when the guards heard about him. Now, the armed guards were searching each house and making threats against innocent people.

Leander would be able to get into the camp, and if he could find the unionist before the guards did, he might be able to save the man's life—and the lives of the miners who were being falsely accused of bringing the man in.

Lee knew that he was the only one who could do this, and he set to readying his carriage.

"If Blair comes to you, don't even hint at where I've gone. If you tell her I'm on a case, she'll want to know where it is, and she'll want to help. Make up something, but, whatever you do, don't tell her the truth. Anything would be better than the truth because she'd tear into the middle of the riot and I'd have to save both her *and* the unionist."

Before Reed could ask what sort of story his son had in mind, Lee was off with a cloud of dust and rocks spewing behind him.

Chapter 19

Blair's mouth didn't close for several minutes after Leander left their house. She couldn't believe that one minute he was there, and the next he was gone.

Her first reaction was anger, but then she smiled. It must have been a serious case that would take Lee away on his wedding night, something that was life and death—and something that was dangerous, she thought, sitting upright. If it weren't serious, no doubt with guns blazing or outlaws terrorizing people, Lee would have taken her with him.

Blair tossed the covers aside and hurriedly dressed in her medical uniform. Leander was going into something dangerous, and he'd need her help.

Downstairs, she picked up the telephone. Mary Catherine was on the switchboard at this time of night. "Mary, where did Lee go?"

"I don't know, Blair-Houston," the young woman answered. "His father called him, and the next thing Leander said was that he was on his way. Not that I listened in, of course. I'd never do that."

"But if you did happen to hear a few words, what would

they have been? And don't forget the time I didn't tell Jimmy Talbot's mother who broke her best cut-glass pitcher."

There was a pause before Mary Catherine answered. "Mr. Westfield said that some man I've never met was having a heart attack. That poor man. It seems that every time Mr. Westfield and Leander talk on the telephone, it's about this Mr. Smith who has one ailment after another. Last month he had at least three diseases and Caroline—she's on the day shift—said that Mr. Smith was ill twice. I don't think he's going to live very long, but then he seems to heal quickly between illnesses. He must be awfully important for Leander to leave you on your wedding night. You must," Mary Catherine paused to let a rude little giggle escape, "miss him very much."

Blair wanted to tell the woman what she thought of her constant eavesdropping, but she merely whispered, "Thank you," and put the receiver down, vowing to never again say anything private on the telephone.

In the stable behind the house, Lee's carriage was gone, and the only horse there was a big, mean-looking stallion that Blair had no intention of trying to ride. The only way to get to her father-in-law's house was to walk. The cool mountain air gave her energy, and she half ran up and down Chandler's steep streets to the Westfield house.

She had to pound on the door to wake up the household and a sleepy, sullen housekeeper came to the door, Reed just behind her.

"Come into the library," Reed said, his face a strange ashen color. He was fully dressed but looking old and tired. Blair was sure that he was up because he was worried about Leander. What in the world had her husband gotten himself into now?

"Where is he?" Blair asked as soon as they were alone in the well-lit library that was filled with the smoke from too many pipes.

Reed just stood there, his face taking on more of a resemblance to a bulldog.

"He's in danger, isn't he?" Blair asked. "I knew he was. If it were an ordinary case, he'd take me with him, but something's wrong with this one." Still, Reed didn't say anything. "The telephone operator said that he often goes to look after a Mr. Smith. I would imagine that I could find out where the man lives, and I can go from house to house and ask if anyone's seen Leander tonight. If I know him, he left in his usual flurry, and I'm sure several people saw him." Blair's face began to have the same look as Reed's—of complete determination. "My husband is going into something dangerous, as he did that day when he knowingly went into a range war, and he's walking into it alone. I believe that I can help. There may be others wounded, and if Lee were hurt," she stumbled over her words, "he would need attention. If you won't help me, I'll find someone who will." She turned away from him to leave.

Reed was bewildered for a moment. She might not be able to find Lee, but she'd certainly manage to stir up a great deal of trouble, and she'd make people aware that *something* was important enough to take him away on his wedding night. And, of course, people would hear about the riot in the mine, and all that had to happen was for one person to put two and two together and connect Leander and the mine riot. He *had* to tell Blair something that would stop her here and now, something so awful that she'd go home and not wake the town searching for Leander. Damn, but why hadn't Lee married Houston? *She'd* never have questioned her husband's whereabouts.

"There's another woman," Reed blurted before he thought about what he was doing. His own wife wouldn't have let anything stop her except the thought of his love going to someone else. Why didn't women ever feel secure that they were loved? Blair should certainly know, since Lee had done so much to prove to her just how much he loved her.

"Woman?" Blair asked, turning back to him. "Why would he go to another woman? Was she ill? Who is Mr. Smith and why is he always ill? Where is my husband?"

"The ah . . . woman tried to kill herself because of Lee's marriage," Reed said and knew that now his relationship with his son was over, because Lee would never forgive him as long as either of them lived.

Blair sat, or rather fell, into a chair. *"That* kind of woman," she whispered.

At least, he had gotten her off Mr. Smith, Reed thought, and at the same time cursed all telephone operators everywhere.

"But what about Houston? He was engaged to her. How could he be in love with someone else?"

"Lee . . . ah, thought this woman was dead." On the table before Reed was a newspaper, and on the front page was an article about a gang of robbers that had been in the Denver area, but were now beginning to move south. The leader of the band was a Frenchwoman. "He met her in Paris, and she was the great love of his life, but he thought she'd been killed. I guess she wasn't, because she came to Chandler to find him."

"When?"

"When what?"

"When did this woman come to Chandler?"

"Oh, months ago," Reed said offhandedly. "I think maybe you'd better let Lee finish this story. I think I've said enough already."

"But if she came months ago, why did Leander continue his engagement to my sister?"

Reed rolled his eyes skyward, and again the newspaper caught his eye. "She, this woman he loved, was . . . involved in something Lee didn't approve of. He had to do something to distract himself."

"And my sister was that distraction, and then later I was." She took a deep breath. "So, he was in love with this woman and thought she'd been killed, so he returned to Chandler and asked Houston to marry him. And then I came along, and one twin was as good as another, and of course his honor made him feel he was obligated to me. That explains why he'd consider marrying a woman he didn't really love. Is that it?"

Reed ran his finger around the inside of his collar, which suddenly felt as if it were choking him. "I guess that'll do as well as any explanation," he said aloud and then muttered, "Now, I have to explain myself to my son."

Blair felt very heavy as she left the house and began to walk home. Reed had sent for his stableboy to drive her home, but Blair had dismissed him. This was her wedding night and supposedly one of the happiest times of her life, and if she couldn't spend it with her husband, she certainly didn't want to spend it with another man. But her happiness had turned into a nightmare.

How Leander must have laughed at her when she told him that she hoped to make their marriage work. He hadn't cared whom he married. Houston was pretty and would make a good doctor's wife, so he asked her to marry him, but then Houston was cool to him, so when Blair jumped into bed with him on their first night out, he decided to marry her instead. Whatever did it matter, when his heart was already given to another woman?

"There she is!" came a man's voice from behind Blair.

It was just growing light, and she saw a small man on horseback and he was pointing toward her. For a moment, Blair felt a little pride that she was already being recognized in the streets as a doctor. She stopped and looked up at the man and the three men behind him.

"Is someone hurt?" she asked. "I don't have my medical kit with me, but if you'll give me a ride to my house, I'll get it and I can go with you."

The cowboy looked shocked for a moment.

"If you'd rather have my husband, I don't know where he is," she said with some bitterness. "I think you'll have to make do with me."

"What's she talkin' about, Cal?" one of the men in the back asked.

Cal put up his hand. "No, I don't want your husband. You'll do just fine. You wanta ride with me?"

Blair took the hand he offered and let him pull her up to mount in front of him. "My house is—," she said, pointing, but he didn't let her finish.

"I know where your house is Miss High and Mighty Chandler. Or I guess it's Miz Taggert now."

"What is this?" Blair said, startled. "I'm not—." But the cowboy put his hand over her mouth and she could say no more.

Leander put a hand to the small of his back and tried to ease it against the jolting of the hard wagon seat. He had to admit that he had an awful case of feeling sorry for himself.

Last night should have been spent in the arms of his new wife, in a soft bed, making love to her, laughing together, getting to know each other. But instead, he'd been climbing down the side of a mountain and then back up it again with a semiconscious man slung over his shoulder.

When he had got to the mine last night, the gates were locked and there was no sign of a guard, but he could hear the sounds of shouting in the camp and some women screaming words of anger. He hid his horse and carriage in the trees and went up the mountain and down the steep side and got into the camp the back way. He ran under cover of the houses and the dark to one of the miner's houses who he knew was likely to take the risk of hiding the unionist.

The miner's wife was there, wringing her hands because the guards were searching every house and the unionist was hidden in the weeds at the back of the outhouse—and he was bleeding and moaning. No one dared go to him because if he were found, it would be death to anyone found with him. If the guards kept up their search and found nothing, and no trace of an infiltrator, they'd not harm the miners, but if he were found . . . The woman put her face in her hands. If the unionist were found there, she and her family'd be thrown out of the camp with no jobs nor any money.

Lee gave her a few words of sympathy but didn't spend much time talking. He went to the weeds at the back and hauled the short, stocky man across his shoulders and began the long, arduous task of trying to sneak him out. The only way out was straight up the side of the mountain, and that's the way Lee went.

He had to pause several times, both to rest and to listen. The sounds below seemed to be quietening. There were always many saloons in a mining camp, and the men too often spent most of their wages on drink. Now, Lee could hear the drunks singing as they staggered home, probably unaware that their houses had been searched—as was the right of the mine owner's representatives.

Lee stopped at the crest of the mountain and tried to see, in the moonlight, the man's wounds. He'd started bleeding again when Lee'd moved him. Lee wrapped the man's wounds as best he could to stop the bleeding, then started across the crest, and then down to where his buggy was hidden.

He couldn't possibly put the man into the cramped little compartment in the back, so he propped him up beside him and drove as carefully as he could.

He took the road north toward Colorado Springs. He couldn't return with the man to Chandler, or there'd be too many innocent questions about who he was and where he'd been hurt. Lee didn't want to risk being found out. He'd never be able to help anyone again if there were any suspicions attached to him.

On the outskirts of town lived a friend of his, a doctor who wasn't inclined to ask too many questions. Lee put the wounded man on the doctor's surgery table and mumbled something about finding the man on the trail. The old doctor looked at Lee and said, "I thought you got married yesterday. You were out lookin' for half-dead men on your weddin' night?"

Before Lee could answer, the old man said, "Don't tell me nothin' I don't want to know. Now, let's have a look at him."

Now, returning to Chandler, it was two o'clock in the afternoon. Lee was past being tired. All he wanted to do was eat, sleep, and see Blair. He'd spent most of the past several hours planning a story to tell her about where he'd been. He thought he'd tell her that he'd been called to a shootout between members of a gang of bank robbers and that he hadn't wanted to risk her coming along and getting hurt. It had a ring of truth, and he thought he could get away with it. He just prayed that she wouldn't ask him why he had to go when there were other doctors in Chandler who could have gone. Also, there would be no account of the shooting incident in the paper.

If worse came to worst, he planned to act hurt that she didn't trust him and that she seemed to want to start their marriage off on the wrong foot.

At home, he was almost relieved when Blair wasn't there. He was too tired to do his best in the telling of a major lie. He stuck some ham between two thick slices of bread and went

175

up to the bedroom. The room was a mess, with Blair's clothes tossed on the bed, the bed unmade. He glanced at the closet, saw right away that her medical uniform was gone and knew that she'd gone to the hospital. He'd have to do some talking, for the men of the board to continue to allow her to work there. Last time, he'd had to promise to take on nearly every shift before they'd let him bring her into the operating room. He'd nearly worked himself into a stupor, but it had been worth it. He'd won Blair in the end.

He ate half the sandwich, crawled onto the bed, hugged Blair's discarded satin nightgown to him and went to sleep.

When he woke, it was eight o'clock, and he knew right away that the house was empty—and instantly, he began to worry. Where was Blair? She should have been home from the hospital by now. As Leander rose, starting to eat the other half of the now-stale sandwich that was lying beside him on the bed, he saw that her medical bag was on the floor of the closet.

For just a moment, his heart stopped beating. She'd never, never leave the house without taking that bag. It was a wonder that she hadn't carried it down the aisle with her when she'd married him.

But now, it was there on the floor.

He threw the sandwich down and went tearing through the house shouting her name. Maybe she'd come back while he was asleep, and the house just *seemed* empty. It took only minutes to find that she was nowhere, inside or out.

He went to the telephone and told the operator to give him the hospital. No one there had seen Blair since the wedding. After enduring some rude jests, saying that Blair'd already realized her mistake and run away from him, Lee put the phone down.

It rang almost instantly.

"Leander," it was the day operator, Caroline, "Mary Catherine said that Blair called your father right after you left last night to go treat your poor Mr. Smith. Maybe he knows where she is."

Lee bit his tongue to keep from telling Caroline to stop eavesdropping, but maybe this time he had reason to be grateful to her. "Thanks," he murmured and went out to saddle his stallion and get to his father's house in record time.

"You told her *what?!*" Leander yelled at his father.

Reed seemed to shrink under his son's anger. "I had to come up with a story fast. And the only thing I could think of, that was guaranteed to keep her from following you, was a story of another woman. From what I've heard of your recent escapades together, I thought fire, war, or union riots just might make her tear into the thick of things."

"You could have come up with another story—*any* other story but that my one true love was here and that I married Blair because I'd lost my real love."

"All right, if you're so smart, you tell me where you were supposed to be that would keep her from following you."

Lee opened his mouth, but closed it again. If Reed had told her of a disaster, no doubt Blair would have come to help. He knew bullets flying toward her didn't stop her. "Now what do I do? Tell her my father is a liar, that there is no other woman?"

"Then where were you on your wedding night? Other than climbing up and down the side of a mountain and hauling a wounded unionist to safety? What will your little wife do next time you're called away?"

Lee groaned. "Probably something really stupid like hiding in the back of my buggy and joining in the fracas. What *am* I going to do?"

"Maybe we should find her first," Reed said. "We'll start looking as discreetly as possible. We don't want the town to realize that she's walked out, or there'll be questions."

"She hasn't walked out," Lee spat. "She's . . ." But he didn't know where she was.

Chapter 20

Leander and his father looked for Blair all night. Lee had an idea that she might walk when she was upset, and so they combed the streets. But she was nowhere to be found.

By morning, they'd decided to pass the story around that she'd gone to a medical emergency without telling anyone where she was going and that Lee was worried about her. At least, this story allowed them to ask questions about her in the open.

There was some teasing about Lee losing his wife on the first day of their marriage, but he managed to weather it well. His one and only concern was for Blair and where she was. She was so headstrong, and they had so little to base their marriage on, that he was afraid that she'd returned to her uncle in Pennsylvania and that he'd never get her to return. He'd gone through hell trying to get her to marry him, and he certainly didn't want to have to go through anything like that again in order to persuade her to live with him.

By afternoon, he was exhausted and he collapsed on their still unmade bed and slept. He'd have to telegraph Dr. Henry Blair tomorrow morning and tell the man to keep Blair there until he could come and get her.

He was wakened by a heavy hand on his shoulder.

"Westfield! Wake up."

Sluggishly, Lee turned over to see Kane Taggert standing over him, the man's face showing anger. In his hand was a piece of paper. "Where's your wife?"

Lee sat up, ran his hand through his hair. "I think she may have left me," he said. It was of no use trying to conceal the truth. Soon, the entire town would know.

"That's what I thought. Look at this."

He thrust a dirty, torn piece of paper into Lee's hands. On it, in primitive block letters, was the message:

WE HAVE YOUR WIFE. LEAVE $50,000 AT TIPPING ROCK TOMORROW. YOU DON'T SHE DIES.

"Houston?" Leander asked. "I'll get my gun and go with you. Do you know who has her? Have you told the sheriff yet?"

"Wait a minute," Kane said, lowering his big form to sit on the bed. "Houston's fine. Me and her've been gone since the weddin'. We just got back this mornin', and this was on my desk with a lot of other mail."

Lee stood as if lightning had struck him. "Then they have Blair. I'll get the sheriff or . . . That man'll never find her. I'll go by myself and—."

"Hold on a minute. We got to think about this. When I got back this mornin', there was a man to see me, a man that'd come down from Denver, and on the way here he was robbed by a new gang that seems to wanta make their headquarters outside Chandler. This little man was real upset, sayin' that all Westerners were outlaws and that they even captured women. It seems he'd heard one of the men that came ridin' up durin' the robbery say that they'd got 'her.' That could mean your wife."

Leander was changing clothes, into denim pants, chaps, a heavy cotton shirt, and a gun on the belt at his hips. Some of his original fury was leaving him and he was beginning to think. "Where was the man held up? I'll start there."

Kane rose and Lee gave only a glance at the man's heavy work clothes. "I figure this is my fight, too. They want my money, and it's my wife they think they got." He looked at Lee out of the corner of his eye. "When I saw this note and realized that it was Blair that they had, I figured this town would have been turned upside down lookin' for her but, as far as I can tell, don't nobody know she's missin'. I think there's some reason you wanta keep quiet about this."

Lee started to tell him that he didn't want her many friends upset, but he didn't. "Yeah," he said, nodding, "there's a reason." He waited, but Taggert said nothing more. "You know how to use a gun? How to ride?"

Kane gave a grunt that sounded somewhat like a bear. "Houston ain't civilized me that much. And don't forget that I grew up here. I know this area, and I have an idea where their hideout is. Twenty miles north of here is a box canyon that's almost hidden from the outside. You could walk past it and not even see it. I got caught in there in a flash flood once."

For a moment, Lee hesitated. He didn't know this man, didn't know if he could be trusted or not. For years, he'd heard stories about the illegal means Kane had used to obtain his money, that nothing else mattered to the man but money. But here he was telling Lee that he was willing to help—and willing to respect Lee's right to keep secret whatever he wanted kept secret.

Lee tied the holster of the gun to his leg. "You got a gun with you?"

"I got enough for a small army outside on my horse, and I also got the fifty grand they want. I'd rather give the money away than risk shootin' around a lady," he said, grinning. "After all, she did wanta marry me a couple of days ago."

At first, Lee didn't remember what he meant, but then exchanged grins with him. "I'm glad it worked out the way it did."

Kane ran his hand over his chin and seemed to be laughing at some private joke. "Me, too. More glad than you know."

Fifteen minutes later, they were saddled, their bags packed with food, and on the trail out of town. Lee had left a message with the operator to tell his father that he'd gone to see about Mrs. Smith. Lee didn't even listen to the operator's murmurs of sympathy about the poor Smith family.

Once outside the town limits, they rode hard, Lee's big horse eating up the miles. Kane's animal was a magnificent beast that carried the two hundred and fifty pounds or so of the man with relative ease. Lee's only thoughts were of Blair, and he hoped she was safe and unharmed.

Blair struggled again against the ropes that held her to the heavy oak chair. Once, she'd managed to escape, so they'd tied her to a chair, and yesterday she'd managed to turn the chair over, but before she could get untangled from it, *that* woman had come into the room and ordered the chair to be nailed to the floor. Blair sat there for hour after hour and watched the woman as she gave orders to her men.

She was called Françoise and she was the leader of the outlaws. She was tall and pretty, slim, with long black hair that she obviously took an inordinate pride in, wore a gun belted about her hips, and was smarter than all the men who rode with her put together.

And Blair knew immediately that this was the woman Leander loved.

Everything fit what Reed had said. She was French, speaking with an accent so heavy that at times her men had difficulty understanding her, and she was involved in something that Lee could not approve of. Blair couldn't help feeling her opinion of Lee fall somewhat because he loved a woman who was capable of such dishonesty.

She sat in that hard chair and watched the woman with unconcealed hostility. Because of her, she'd never have her husband to herself, she'd never be able to erase the past from his mind. Maybe men liked the glamour of being in love with a criminal. Maybe Leander wanted to nurse his broken heart all his life.

The woman stood in front of her for a moment and watched Blair's eyes blazing above the gag. Then she pulled a chair from under an old table and sat across from her.

"Jimmy, remove the cloth," she said to the big bodyguard who was always with her. She said it as, "Jeemy, remove zee cloth."

Once it was gone, she motioned the big man away so that they were alone in the room. "Now, I want to know why you look at me with such hatred. You do not look at the men that way. Is it because I am a woman, and you do not approve of a woman who is so skilled as I am?"

"Skill? Is that what you call it?" Blair asked, flexing her sore jaw. "Just because men are such fools that they can't see through a woman like you, doesn't mean that I am. I know what you are."

"I am so glad that you do, but then I don't believe I have ever lied to anyone."

"You can stop lying to me for one. I know all about you." She lifted her head somewhat and tried to muster what pride she could. "I am Leander's wife."

Blair had to admit that the woman was certainly a good actress. One after another, emotions passed across her face. They ranged from puzzlement to disbelief, and ended with humor.

The woman stood, her back to Blair. "Ah, Leander," she said at last. "Dear Leander."

"There's no need to act so smug," Blair shot at her. "You may think you have him and that he'll always be yours, but I'll make him forget everything that ever happened between the two of you."

When the woman turned back to face Blair, her face was serious. "How could he forget what we had? No one alive could forget something like that. It happens only once in a lifetime. So, he has married you. How long ago?"

"Two days. You should know, since he spent our wedding night with *you*. Tell me, how did you try to kill yourself? You look as if you've recovered well enough. Perhaps it was merely a play for sympathy and not a true attempt at suicide. I can't imagine that you'd be a good loser when it came to someone like Leander."

"No," she said softly. "I didn't want to lose Leander, but I didn't want anyone else to have him, either. Did he tell you why we are no longer together?"

"He didn't tell me a word about you. After finding out what you've become, I'm sure he can barely stand to think of you. Reed told me. But perhaps you don't know Lee's father, since you're not the sort of woman a man can bring home to his family. Lee thought you were dead, and he left Paris thinking you were dead. He returned to Chandler." Blair thought of all the stories he'd told her about his years in Europe, and he'd never even hinted about another woman. But maybe it was too painful a subject for him to talk about.

"I'm going to win him," Blair said. "He's my husband, and neither you nor anyone else is going to take him from me. He'll come for me and you may see him again, but you won't have a chance with him."

"Paris, was it?" the woman said, smiling. "Perhaps this Leander Taggert and I—."

"Taggert? Leander's no Taggert. Houston married Tag—." She stopped. Something was wrong here, but she didn't know what.

Françoise put her face close to Blair's. "What is your name?"

"Dr. Blair Chandler Westfield," she said, frowning.

Immediately, the woman turned on her heel and left the cabin.

Blair slumped back into the chair. She'd been here for nearly two days now, and she'd had very little sleep and even less food, and she was beginning to have trouble fully comprehending what was going on.

After they'd taken her, they'd blindfolded and gagged her and then ridden for what seemed like hours. Most of the time, she'd concentrated on keeping the hands of the cowboy who rode behind her in the saddle from running all over her body. He kept whispering that she "owed" him. For the life of her, Blair couldn't remember having met the man before or having done anything to him.

She moved all over the horse, as far as she could, to get away from him, and when the horse began to grow restless and prance, one of the other men ordered the man in the saddle with her to leave her alone, saying that she belonged to Frankie.

That idea sent a shiver up Blair's spine. Just who was Frankie and what did he want with her? She still had hopes that they needed her medical services but, because they hadn't let her get her bag, she doubted it.

When they'd removed the blindfold, she was standing in front of a rundown little shack, a porch with a fallen post on one end. Around her were six men, all small and stupid-looking like the one who'd taken her. There was a small corral to her right, and a few other outbuildings here and there. And everything was surrounded by high, sheer cliff walls. White rock kept them protected—and hidden—like a fort. At the moment, Blair couldn't even see the entryway into the canyon, but realized it must be small enough that the cabin could block it from view.

But she soon lost interest in her surroundings, because on the porch appeared Frankie, the Frenchwoman who was the love of her husband's life. Hate, anger, and jealousy combined to make Blair speechless as she gaped up at this woman who was the leader of this two-bit band of semimorons.

Someone pushed Blair into the shack: a dirty, dark little place with two rooms, one with a table and a few broken chairs, the other with a bed. Supplies were on the floor in the main room.

For the first twenty-four hours, they'd been fairly lax in their guarding of Blair, but after four attempts to escape,—she'd almost succeeded in one of them—they'd tied her to the chair, and then ended by nailing it to the floor.

Now, her wrists were raw from the rough rope and from pulling on it for long hours, and Frankie had decided that perhaps a little less food would help her stay in place and keep her from again trying to scale the rock wall that protected them.

Blair wasn't sure her mind was functioning properly. It seemed so long since she'd eaten or rested, and there was this horrid woman who was her husband's lover. Part of her said that Leander had to be part of this, part of her said that Frankie had done it on her own, that she wanted to see Leander again. And if Lee saw her again, would he want Blair, or would he this time go with the woman whom Reed had called his one true love? Of course, Leander *had* left her on their wedding night to go to this woman. She had that kind of power over him. So who was to say that Leander wasn't hiding behind the cabin somewhere, that he hadn't arranged everything so that he and Frankie could be together?

There were tears running down Blair's face when Frankie came into the room, with the cowboy who'd abducted Blair in tow by his ear, as if she were his schoolteacher. There were bright red handprints on the boy's face where he'd been slapped.

"She is the one?" Frankie asked the boy. "You are the one who says he knows. Do you know or do you lie to me to settle an old debt?"

"It's her. I swear it is. Her husband tossed me in the dirt, and he's worth millions."

Frankie, in disgust, pushed the boy away. "How stupid I was to send a boy to do a man's job. You see this?" She held up a torn newspaper. "They are identical twins. One is married to a rich man, and one is . . ." She turned to glare at Blair, who was listening with wide-eyed interest. "And one is my dear, beloved Leander's wife."

Blair was much too upset, hungry, tired, and too ready to believe what she thought to be true, to hear the sarcasm in the woman's voice.

"Get out of here," the Frenchwoman shouted at the boy. "Let me think what's to be done."

She might have thought faster if she'd known that at that moment a man was lying on his stomach on the rock above, his rifle aimed and ready, three more rifles at his side. And another man waited at the entrance to the hidden canyon to receive a signal from the man above.

Chapter 21

Blair was sure that her spirits had never been lower in her life. Maybe it was a combination of hunger, thirst, fear, everything combined, but it suddenly seemed that very few people in her life had ever really loved her. Her stepfather had always hated her, and in school, the only man who'd ever been interested in her had ended by jilting her, and now her husband was actually in love with another woman—and always had been. She didn't actually believe that she could get him back. Back? She'd never had him to begin with.

"I need to go to the outhouse," she mumbled to Françoise at dawn, when the woman returned to the shack. Blair had waited as long as possible, because the last time she'd gone, Françoise had sent one of her outlaws to guard Blair, and then she'd caught the man peeping through a knothole.

"I shall go with you this time," the Frenchwoman said as she untied the knots on Blair's wrists.

When Blair stood, she was dizzy and began to sway on her feet. The lack of circulation in her body was making her extremities cold.

"Come on," the woman said, jerking Blair. "You didn't look too tired when you were scaling that wall."

"That might have been what did it," Blair said, as the woman caught her arm and half dragged her from the shack.

The outhouse stood near the entryway into the box canyon, as if someone had planned to keep guard from inside that malodorous place. Blair went inside while Françoise stood outside, a rifle across her shoulder, keeping watch.

Blair had no more than closed the door when she heard a muffled scream. With some curiosity, but also with a feeling of dread that something awful had happened, she leaned forward to look out the convenient knothole. The next moment, the door was rattled and, when it was found to be locked, she was knocked backward by the force of an enormous fist, knuckles wrapped, coming through the weathered boards of the door. Before she could straighten up and look for a weapon to protect herself, the sound of shooting came from outside.

The hand that was coming through the door fumbled for and opened the latch. Blair poised herself to leap at the man who was trying to take her.

When the door was opened, she jumped and landed against the big, hard form of Kane Taggert.

"Stop that!" he ordered when she started beating him with her fists. "Come on, let's get you two out of here. Another minute, and they'll see that you're missin'."

Blair quietened and glanced down at Françoise, tucked under Taggert's left arm as if she were a sack of flour. "Is she hurt?"

"Just a nick on the chin. She'll wake up in a little while. Run for it."

Blair ran through the narrow opening, ducking the bullets that seemed to be coming from everywhere. Behind her was the big body of Kane and she wondered who it was shooting from the cliff above them. She prayed that it wasn't Houston.

Kane tossed Françoise's unconscious body across the saddle of his horse. "I hadn't figured on her. Get up there," he said, as he picked Blair up and dropped her into the saddle behind the inert form of the Frenchwoman. "Tell Westfield that I'll stay here a while and keep 'em busy down there. The three of you head on up to the cabin and I'll meet you there."

With that, he slapped the horse on the rump and started Blair up the hill.

Blair hadn't gone but a few feet when Lee jumped out from the trees and grabbed the horse's reins. The grin he wore threatened to split his face. "I see you're all right," he said, as he put his hand on her leg and caressed it.

"And so is she," Blair said with all the haughtiness she could muster, as she gave him Kane's message. "I'm sure you had Taggert rescue her for yourself."

Leander gave a groan and looked at the woman as if he'd just noticed her. "I hate to ask this, but is she the Frenchwoman who is the leader of the gang that kidnapped you?"

"I'm sure you know who she is as well as anyone. Tell me, did you arrange for me to be taken?"

Lee swung up on his horse. "No, but I may arrange for something lethal to happen to my father. Let's not waste any more time. Taggert says there's a cabin hidden up in the mountains. We'll stay there while he gets the sheriff and a posse. Let's go—and stop giving me death looks!"

Blair tried her best to maneuver the big horse up the mountainside to follow Lee, but it wasn't easy. Françoise began to wake and moan, and when her movements caused the horse to shy, Lee stopped and looked back at the women. With a sigh of exasperation, he glanced at Blair's face, then away. He pulled the Frenchwoman onto his horse in front of him, and told her that if she knew what was good for her, she'd be quiet.

Blair turned her nose up in the air and moved away from them both.

Kane caught up with them by taking a shortcut up a steep bit of rock that the horses couldn't travel and met them before they'd gone very far.

Lee dismounted but stayed close to his horse—and to Françoise. "What's going on?"

"They're after us," Kane said, as he drank from a canteen. "My guess is that they'll stay around until they get her back." He nodded his head toward Françoise. "I don't think they're much without her." Kane looked at the woman who was sitting on the horse with her spine straight. "I think you'd better watch her. She's pretty smart."

"I'll take care of her," Lee said. "I think they'll look for us south, on the way back to Chandler. We'll be safe enough, but you'll have them on your tail. Why the hell did you take her, anyway? She'll be more trouble than she's worth."

Kane stoppered the canteen and shrugged his big shoulders. "I was behind her and, at first, I thought she was some other woman they'd captured. Then she turned around, and I saw that she was carryin' a rifle so I clipped her one on the chin. It occurred to me that she might be useful."

"Makes sense, but I don't relish trying to take care of her until you get back. I wouldn't mind a dozen men, but two women?"

Kane put his hand on Leander's shoulder. "I don't envy you one bit. I'll see you in a few hours, Westfield. Good luck." He helped Blair from his horse and mounted and was down the mountain, out of sight, in minutes.

"Why aren't we going with him?" Blair asked.

"We didn't know how they'd treated you, so it was decided that you and I'd stay higher up on the mountain in a cabin while Taggert went to get the sheriff." Lee's eyes lit up and he took a step toward her. "I thought maybe we'd have some time to ourselves, just the two of us."

Both of them seemed to have forgotten the presence of Françoise, although Lee still firmly held the reins to the horse on which she sat. The terrain around them was much too steep and wild to try to escape.

The Frenchwoman slid off the horse and put herself between Blair and Leander, who were moving toward each other as surely as magnets.

"Oh, Leander, my chérie, my darling," she said, putting her arms around him and plastering her body against his. "You must tell her the truth. We cannot keep what we feel for each other a lie any longer. Tell her that you want only me, and that this was all planned by you. Tell her."

Blair turned on her heel and started down the mountainside.

Leander had the dual problem of trying to untangle himself from the dark woman's grasp and of keeping his jealous wife from running into the outlaws who were looking for them. He couldn't release the Frenchwoman, so he held onto her wrist, and the horse, and started chasing Blair.

"Darling," Françoise said, as Lee pulled her along, "you're hurting me. Let her go. You know she never meant anything to you. She knows the truth."

With every word, Blair blindly hurried faster down the steep slope.

Lee stopped long enough to turn back to Françoise. "I've never hit a woman, but you are tempting me. Blair," he called, "you can't keep running. There are men with guns looking for us."

Françoise sat down on the solid rock that was the mountainside, put her face in her hands and began to cry. "How can you say such things to me? How can you forget our nights in Paris together? What about Venice? And Florence? Remember the moonlight in Florence?"

"I've never been to Florence," Lee said, as he grabbed her by the arm and pulled her up; then, when she wouldn't walk, he tossed her over his shoulder and went skidding down the mountain after Blair, catching her by the back of her skirt. Thanks to the expert tailoring of J. Cantrell and Sons, the fabric held. He kept pulling, as Blair did, and finally, he sat on the rocky surface and pulled her into his lap.

It occurred to him that he was a ridiculous sight, with one woman draped over his shoulder, bottom end up, and another one held on his outstretched leg. When Françoise started to move, he smacked her on her rump. "You stay out of this."

"Whenever you touch me there, I obey you," Françoise said in a purring voice.

Blair started to get up, but Lee held her.

"Blair," he began, but she wouldn't look at him. "I have never seen this woman before today. I did *not* meet her in Paris. I have never been in love with anyone except you, and I married you because I fell in love with you."

"Love?" Blair said, turning to look at him. "You never said that before."

"I have, but you never listened. You were too busy telling me that I was in love with Houston. I didn't love her, and I certainly never loved this . . . this . . ." He looked at the ample rear end that was beginning to strain his shoulder. He shrugged her off, but kept her wrist in his grasp.

Blair was starting to lean toward Lee. Maybe he was telling her the truth. She did so want to believe him.

"You lie very well, Leander," Françoise said. "I never knew that about you. Of course, then, you and I only knew one another one way." She leaned toward him. "But such a way. Ooh là là."

Blair tried to get out of Lee's lap, but he held her firmly, and with one look at his wife's face, he gave a heavy sigh and took the wrists of both women and led them up the mountain.

Blair followed him but only reluctantly. It was a long, hard climb. They had to walk across an area that was covered with fallen trees, repeatedly stepping high up and over. The air was getting thinner as they travelled upward, and it was more difficult to get the oxygen needed to counteract the exertion of the climb.

All the while, Lee kept his hold on Françoise and every time he tried to help Blair, she pushed his hand away.

The cabin was between two steep-sided ridges, hidden so well that they walked past it twice before they saw it, and then they came upon it suddenly, as if it had just appeared out of nowhere.

There wasn't much land in front of the cabin, as the mountainside fell away sharply, but outside was a breathtaking view. The grass was ankle deep and was interspersed with three colors of daisies and clumps of wild roses.

The floor of the forest was soft with hundreds of years' worth of decayed vegetation and so their passage had been silent.

Lee didn't say a word as he motioned for Blair to watch Françoise while he checked the cabin to make sure it was empty. And when he was sure that it was safe, he motioned for the women to enter.

It was an ordinary little cabin: two rooms and a little loft over the door, filthy from years of being invaded by animals and negligent men, but it was obviously a private place, and that was what they wanted.

Blair watched without much interest as Lee tied Françoise to a post in the cabin, giving her freedom to move somewhat and not gagging her.

He had a bandanna in his hand, ready to cover her mouth, but he couldn't seem to bring himself to use it. "I don't think your men will find us here. I'll be outside listening, and if I hear anything, I'll put this on you."

"Chérie, you aren't going to keep up this charade, are you? She knows about us. She told me everything."

"I'll bet she did," Lee said, tightening the ropes. "She told you enough that you can continue this lie. What's in it for you?"

Françoise just looked at him.

When Blair looked up at the two of them, they were staring deeply into one another's eyes.

Lee turned back as if to say something to Blair, but he seemed to change his mind when he saw her expression. He picked up his rifle. "I'll be outside if you need me. There's food in the saddlebags."

With that, he left the women alone.

Slowly, Blair began to remove what food there was in the saddlebags that Lee'd thrown on the old table near the post where Françoise was tied. There was a fireplace in the cabin, but heaven only knew when the chimney had been cleaned last and, besides, they didn't need smoke to advertise their whereabouts.

While Blair put cheese and ham on bread and ate, Françoise talked, never letting up in her declarations of what she and Leander had meant to each other.

"He'll come back to me, you know," Françoise said. "He always does. No matter how hard he's tried to leave me, he couldn't. He'll forgive me for whatever I've done, and this time he'll join me. We'll ride together, love together. We'll—."

Blair grabbed a sandwich and a canteen and left the cabin.

Chapter 22

Lee was some distance from the cabin and so well concealed that Blair didn't see him until he called to her.

"What's happened?" Lee asked, as he took the sandwich from her and managed to caress her wrist at the same time.

"Don't touch me," she said, jerking her arm away as if he'd tried to hurt her.

Lee's expression changed to anger. "I've had about all of this I can take. Why don't you believe me when I say that I've never met her before? Why do you believe her over me, your husband?"

"Because your *father* told me about her. Why shouldn't I believe him?"

"My father lied to you because I told him to!" Lee snapped.

She took a step backward. "Lied? So you admit it? What would take you away on our wedding night? There was no medical emergency. I somehow doubt that your mysterious Mr. Smith actually exists, so where were you?"

Leander didn't answer for a moment, as he turned to look back at the distant forest and eat his sandwich. He wasn't going to compound his problems with another lie. "I can't tell you," he said quietly.

"You won't tell me." She turned away, heading for the cabin.

He caught her arm. "No, I *can't* tell you." His face showed his rising anger. "Damn it, Blair! I've not done anything to deserve your mistrust. I was *not* out with another woman. Lord, but I can barely handle one woman, much less two. Don't you realize that it had to be something important, something dire, to take me away on my wedding night? Why the hell can't you trust me? Why do you believe my father, who was lying on my behalf, and that bitch in there who makes her living by stealing?"

He dropped her arm. "Go on, then. Go ahead and believe her. That's just what she wants. I'm sure she'd like nothing better than to see us at each other's throats. It'd be much easier for her to escape one captor than two. If she keeps on, and you continue believing her, another couple of hours and you'll *help* her escape just to get the two of us apart."

Feeling quite weak, Blair sat down on the grass. "I don't know what to believe. She seems to know so much about you, but then I have no right to expect you to be faithful. You didn't want to marry me in the first place. It was only a competition."

Leander grabbed her upper arm and hauled her to her feet. "Get back to the cabin," he said with teeth clenched, then turned his back to her.

Blair was bewildered by everything. Her head down, her feet dragging, she started back to the cabin. One time Aunt Flo had complained to her husband that Blair knew nothing about life. "If a man told her she'd broken his heart," Aunt Flo said, "Blair'd look in some medical text to find out how to sew it back together. Medicine is not all there is to life."

Blair stopped and turned back toward Lee. "Have you really never been to Florence?" she asked softly, but the sound carried in the silent forest.

He took a moment before he turned to look at her. His face was unyielding. "Never."

Cautiously, Blair took a step toward him. "She's not really

194

your type, is she? I mean, she's too skinny and doesn't have enough on top *or* bottom, does she?"

"Not nearly enough." Still, his face didn't change as he watched her approach.

"And she wouldn't know a hernia from a headache, would she?"

He watched her until she was standing in front of him. "I wouldn't have made a fool of myself in front of the town if I'd loved someone else."

"No, I guess you wouldn't have."

His rifle in one hand, he held out one arm to her and she snuggled against him, her head against his chest. His heart was beating wildly.

"You owe me a wedding night," she whispered.

Suddenly, he grabbed her hair, pulled her head back and kissed her deeply, his tongue touching hers.

When Blair turned her body to his and pressed her knee between his legs, he let her go, gently pushing her away.

"Go back inside," he growled. "I need to keep watch and I have some thinking to do—and I certainly can't think with you near."

Reluctantly, she moved away from him.

"Blair," he said, when she was no longer touching him, "I'm beginning to come up with a plan. I haven't worked it out yet, but don't let her"—he nodded toward the cabin—"know that you know she's lying. Pretend that you believe what she says. I think I can use your anger."

"I'm glad to be useful," she muttered before returning to the cabin.

Jealousy was a new emotion to Blair. Never before had she experienced it. She sat in that dirty little cabin and listened while Françoise recounted her grand passion with Leander. Part of her wanted so badly to believe Lee, but part of her was sure this awful woman was telling the truth. Blair had to sit on her hands or she would have leapt for the woman's throat. She did her best to think of other things.

After a while, Blair got herself under control enough to realize that what Françoise was saying was very general.

"And your sister . . .," Françoise was saying, "ah, her name is . . ."

"Charlotte Houston," Blair said absently, wondering where Lee could have gone on their wedding night if it wasn't to another woman.

"Yes, Charlotte," Françoise was saying. "I had to fight Charlotte for many months, but then when she married Taggert . . . I imagine Lee felt obligated—."

"He must have discussed her with you at length," Blair said, suddenly alert.

"When he could get away. The truth is, I am already married, and we thought my husband would never release me, but he will. You see, I found out that I was going to be free on the night he married you."

"So, he left me to go to you," Blair said. "Of course, now I'm free and you're shackled to the post, but I'm sure it'll work itself out. Excuse me, I think I'll get a breath of air."

When Blair walked out of the cabin, she felt as if she'd lost twenty pounds. She felt light and happy and free. No matter what Lee'd said, there'd been some doubt about his relationship with the Frenchwoman. But now, Blair was sure he'd been telling the truth.

As she stood on the porch and breathed deeply of the clean, cool air, an iridescent hummingbird came up to inspect the red insignia on her shoulder. Blair held very still and watched the little bird hovering about her, smiling at it before it realized that she was nothing edible and flew away. Still smiling, she walked down to where Leander hid in the grasses.

She sat down beside him without saying a word, listening to the wind in the aspens overhead.

"She didn't know Houston's name," she said at last, and when he looked at her with curiosity, she continued. "I haven't always been a part of your life, but Houston has. I don't imagine anyone you've ever known hasn't heard her name, if for no other reason than for the sheer quantity of letters that Houston wrote you."

Lee put his arm around her, chuckling and shaking his head. "You don't believe me, but you do believe her. I guess I'll have to take whatever I can get."

She leaned against him and they just sat there together,

listening to the wind, not saying a word. Blair thought how close she'd come to missing this moment. If she'd had her way, she'd be in Pennsylvania with Alan right now. Alan who was so small, Alan who wasn't even a doctor yet, and would probably never be as good as Leander was, Alan who didn't know which end of a gun to hold, Alan who would have probably gone to the sheriff and would never have rescued his wife on his own.

"Thank you for rescuing me," she said, and she meant for rescuing her from more than just her kidnappers.

Lee moved to look at her, then pushed her away, as if she had turned to poison. "I want you to go sit by that tree," he said, and there seemed to be a quiver in his voice. "I want to talk to you, and I can't do it with you so near me."

Blair was so flattered that she moved to all fours and put her face in front of his. "Maybe you regret leaving on Monday night," she said, her lips almost touching his.

Lee drew back from her. "Go!" he ordered, and there was a threat in his voice. "I can't keep watch and do what I want to do to you at the same time. Now, get over there and be still."

Blair obeyed him, but his words were sending little chills up and down her spine. In a few hours, Taggert would have the sheriff in the mountains and they'd take the outlaws and Lee could hand over Françoise, and then they'd be alone. She thought of their one and only night together, and when she looked up at him through her lashes, she heard him catch his breath.

She was very pleased when he looked away.

"I've had time to come up with a plan that just might work," he said, as he looked out across the forest. "What I want you to do is help the woman to escape. Tonight, I'll say something that could mean I plan to sneak off with Françoise —maybe we could have an argument. I'm sure you could manage that," he said, as he turned to look back at her. "What the hell!" he gasped as he looked at her.

"My stocking was loose," Blair said innocently, as she lifted her slim leg and adjusted the tight black cotton garment, wishing with all her might that she were wearing silk.

Maybe there was something to Houston's wardrobe. No doubt Houston had worn nothing but the sheerest of silks on her honeymoon.

"Blair," Leander said. "You are trying my patience."

"Mmmmm," she said, lowering her leg. "What were you saying about an argument?"

Leander looked away, and Blair saw that his hand was trembling. "I said that I want us to stage an argument, and afterward I want you to let Françoise see you put something in my coffee. Make her think that you're going to make me sleep through the night rather than go to her."

"You wouldn't go to her, would you?"

"I'm saving my energy for later," he said, in such a way, looking at her through his thick lashes, that Blair's heart began to pound.

Lee looked back at the forest. "I want her to escape. I can tie the knots so that she can get away, but it will take her a couple of hours to work free. And while she's working them, I plan to run a little errand."

"While you're supposed to be sleeping?"

"As far as I can tell, she's a cautious woman. She doesn't take too many chances with her life, so I want her to feel safe, that I'm in a drugged sleep and you want her to escape. She didn't even try to escape when we were travelling up here," he said, almost as an afterthought.

"It was too steep. She couldn't have."

"Did you try to escape out of that box canyon?"

Blair smiled at him. "How did you know that?"

"A wild guess, based on your recklessness and disbelief that anything can harm you. Now, are you willing? Do you think you can give a good performance?"

Blair grinned at him. "We're here together now because of my extraordinary acting ability."

He returned her smile. "Go back in now, and listen to Françoise. Make her think that you believe every word she says. Make her think that you're ready to murder me."

Blair stood and looked down at him. "I'm not going to let anything happen to you until I get my wedding night," she said, then when Lee started to rise, she ran back to the cabin, making sure that she raised her skirts high enough to let him see a great deal.

"You can have her for all I care!" Blair shouted at Lee. "You can spend the rest of your life together and I hope you're both hanged," she yelled as she ran from the cabin, leaving Leander and Françoise together.

She kept running up the hill, not pausing to look back until she was out of sight of the cabin. Once she was hidden by the trees, she collapsed on the ground and sat there to catch her breath. Below, she could barely see Lee as he began to look for her.

She smiled as she watched him. She was sure that he'd had no idea just how good an actress she could be and that now he was worried that she'd believed what she'd shouted at him. It had been a good fight, long and loud, with lots of anger. Blair had shouted about Lee's father, about his leaving her on their wedding night, about having taken her away from Alan, about his sister taking the man she'd loved. That one had thrown him. He'd stood there looking at her as if he half believed her.

Now, Blair was out of breath and she wanted to stay away from the cabin long enough to make it look as if she were truly angry. And, too, she wanted to think about where Lee was going tonight. Was this another one of his secret visits? Was their entire life together going to be full of these secret disappearances of his? Would he ever tell her what he was doing that was so private that even his wife couldn't be told the truth?

As Blair watched the cabin, and saw Leander looking for her, she decided that there had to be a way to make him trust her. She didn't want to be so ill informed of his life that some woman who didn't even know him could make her believe that she knew something that his wife didn't.

As she was sitting there, lost in thought, she was oblivious to the sounds that were coming from behind her. When she did hear them, she was almost paralyzed, realizing that it was probably Françoise's gang that had at last found them. Very slowly, she turned to look up the hill.

What she saw more than paralyzed her. Coming down the hill were two big black bears—and they were heading toward her.

No one had ever moved faster. Blair shot up and started running before her feet were firmly on the ground. She was at the cabin before she glanced over her shoulder and saw that the bears weren't behind her. Cautiously, she stopped and looked around. There were only the sounds of the forest and no sign of the bears. Curious, she walked to a tree at the edge of the clearing and looked back up the hill. Ordinarily, she would have run to safety, but part of her remembered that she was in the midst of a game with Leander and she couldn't give it away by running into his arms now.

Very slowly, she crept back up the hill, always checking that the way behind her was clear. If the bears were lurking somewhere, she wanted to know about it so she could tell Lee.

About ten feet from where she had been sitting, and only a few yards from the cabin, was a small cave, and from the tracks around it, Blair thought that it must have been used by generations of bears.

"So that's why the cabin is abandoned," she murmured and started down the hill. It was nearly sunset and she had to pretend to give Lee the drug that was to make him sleep.

Later, she thought that she'd done it all very well, and she doubted if even Lee had seen her put the headache powder in his coffee—but she'd made sure that Françoise had. For a moment, she'd been tempted to put a little ipecac into his drink after she'd seen Lee looking at Françoise when he thought no one was watching him.

Within minutes after Lee had drunk the coffee that had been heated on the tiny fire he'd made behind the cabin, Lee was yawning and saying that he had to sleep. After several minutes of telling Blair how to guard the prisoner, he went into the other room, and they could hear him fall onto the dirty little cot.

Françoise looked at Blair in such a way that Blair wanted to cut the woman loose and challenge her to a fistfight. But, instead, she checked the woman's bindings.

"At least, he won't be spending the night with you," Blair

said. "I'm going to sleep." She looked the Frenchwoman up and down as she was tied to the pole. "I hope you're comfortable."

"And what if I escape? How will you explain that to him?"

"With relish," Blair answered. "What do I care what you do as long as you're away from my husband? Besides, I learned a few things about knots in medical school. You won't get out of those so quickly."

Blair went into the other room, and she thought how Lee had been right, that Françoise was extraordinarily careful of her life. How many prisoners asked permission before trying to escape?

A quick check of the cot and she saw that Lee had already sneaked out of the cabin through the open window. Blair made a pile of blankets that she hoped would look like a body and went out the window after him.

She walked for several minutes, but she heard nothing. He seemed to have disappeared. She was heading east, the cabin at her back, and, she hoped, toward where Lee was going. Of course, he hadn't seen fit to tell her any of his plans, but she guessed this might be the direction he'd be taking, for whatever he planned to do. She hid when she heard a sound behind her.

"All right, come out of there."

She heard the voice, and it sounded like Lee's, but it wasn't the voice he used with her. It had a hard, metallic sound to it—and it was accompanied by the clicking of the hammer of a gun being pulled back. With a sheepish look, Blair stepped out of her hiding place.

Muttering a curse, Lee reholstered his gun. "Why aren't you at the cabin where I left you? Why aren't you guarding that woman?"

"I wanted to know where you were going."

"*Not* to meet another woman. Now, go back to the cabin. I have some unfinished business to attend to, and I don't have much time, and I can't do anything with you around."

"If you're not meeting someone else, then where are you going? I thought we were supposed to wait for—."

"What do I have to do? Tie you up, too?"

"Then I was right. You *are* somehow involved with those

robbers and that woman. Or else you could tell me where you're going. Oh, Leander, how could you?" She started to turn away, but he caught her arm and spun her around.

"All right, I'll tell you! The Inexpressible Mine is less than a mile from here, and I plan to sneak down the back side, break into the explosives shed, steal some dynamite and blow the end of that canyon up. I can't get all of them, but I can trap most of that gang inside the canyon—especially if I use their lady-leader as bait."

Blair blinked several times, then took a step toward him, her eyes glistening. "It'll take less time if you just take me with you." Before he could speak, she continued. "I can help. I can climb. I almost climbed out of the canyon where the robbers held me. Please, please, Leander." She grabbed him and began kissing his neck and face. "I'll obey you and never get in your way, and if anybody gets hurt, I'll thread the needles for you."

Leander knew he was a beaten man. "I didn't know when I was well off with a dull, obedient lady like Houston," he said under his breath, as he started walking at a quick pace.

Blair bit her tongue to keep from telling him that her sister secretly drove a huckster wagon into the mine camps. Instead, she just smiled back at him and began to follow him through the dark forest toward the mine.

Chapter 23

Leander set such a hard pace down the mountainside that Blair almost wished she hadn't gone with him. She could be safe now, asleep, instead of half falling down the dark, steep cliff. Twice, she skidded down on her back, but managed to catch herself before she fell too far. Lee seemed to be saying that since she'd been fool enough to want to come with him, she had to look out for herself.

They finally came out at the bottom of the steep ridge and looked out over the little mining community.

"I guess it's useless to ask you to stay here, isn't it?"

"Entirely," she replied.

"All right, then, stay close to me. Don't get more than two feet from me. I want to know where you are every minute. You understand? And if I tell you to run, that's just what I want you to do. No questions, no arguments. And be as quiet as you can."

Blair nodded in answer to his warnings and began to follow him down into the camp.

It was late and most of the lights were out. Only a few saloons were still open and busy. They ran from the cover of one building to another, and Blair could feel her heart pounding with excitement.

"We'll have to break into the company store first. I'll need a crowbar to get that lock and chain off."

They crept to the back of a large building that was nearly in the center of the town. Three times, they had to duck when people walked by.

"Blair," Lee whispered, "I've got to break this glass. I want you to laugh to cover the sound. Make it a loud laugh, like a pros—like a lady of the evening. No one will pay attention to a familiar sound like that, but they'll come running to the sound of breaking glass."

"Leander," she said stiffly, "I am not as experienced as you are. I have no idea how a lady of the evening laughs."

"Suggestively. Sound like you're trying to get me to go into the woods with you so you can do pleasurable things to my body."

"That should be easy," she said, and meant it.

Lee wrapped his hand in his handkerchief and prepared to smash through the glass in the door. "All right. Now!"

Blair tossed her head back and gave a raucous laugh that filled the air, and when Lee looked back at her, there was admiration in his eyes.

"I'll take you up on that offer as soon as possible," he said, even as he reached inside and opened the door. "Stand over here and be ready to run if someone sees us."

Blair stood to one side of the door and watched Lee as he made his way about the store looking for a crowbar. Behind her were stacks of canned goods, bags of flour, a barrel of crackers. On one shelf were six little barrels of honey. Looking at them, Blair smiled, as they reminded her of the bears.

Suddenly, without having a specific plan, she grabbed a rucksack from a pile on the floor and shoved two barrels of the honey into the bag and put it on her back. By the roll of wrapping paper on the counter was a pencil so, quickly, she tore off a corner and wrote a note.

"What are you doing?" Lee demanded.

"Leaving an IOU, of course. After tomorrow, I'm sure the

entire town will know we blew up part of a mountain, and people will know we had to have stolen the dynamite. Unless you usually carry some in your medical bag. You weren't planning to just take this without saying who did it, were you? Someone else would be blamed."

Lee looked at her for a moment. "Good thinking," he said at last. "There'll be no reason for secrecy tomorrow. But I don't want to be caught tonight. Let's go. Wait a minute. What do you have on your back?"

"Honey," she answered, and she didn't give him time to ask more questions before she left the store ahead of him. He closed the door carefully and, unless you looked for it, you couldn't see the broken glass.

Lee led her through the camp, back to the outskirts, and once it occurred to her that he knew the place awfully well. But then, she'd heard that he sometimes treated injured miners.

They walked over ground that was crunchy from slag, and the slight wind blew coal dust into their eyes. Behind the railroad tracks, behind a fifty-foot-tall mountain of coal dust waste, behind the long rows of ovens where the sulfur was burned from the coal, was the explosives shed.

Rubbing her eyes, Blair stood in the shadows while Lee pried the door off the shed. As quickly as possible, he shoved sticks of dynamite under his shirt and wired the door shut. He wouldn't leave it hanging open for a passerby to help himself to what was inside. Whoever opened it next would still have a difficult time.

"Let's go," he said, and Blair began the steep ascent to the top. At times, the ground was directly in front of her face and she had to pull herself up.

Lee was waiting for her at the top, but he didn't give her time to catch her breath. They nearly ran to the cabin. "I'm going to saddle my horse and leave it in front. I thought you might get out of bed to get something to eat, and you might forget and leave a knife within her reach. I'll be waiting outside to follow her when she goes back to the canyon."

"We," was all Blair said, but the way she looked at him made him sigh.

"All right, but get inside now and wait for me."

"I have to tend to a personal matter first—in the bushes," she said, and she didn't know whether she was blushing from her words or from the fact that she was lying.

Lee didn't even look at her as he saddled his horse. Blair ran up the side of the hill toward the bears' den. Cautiously, she approached the black hole of the cave, listening for any sounds. Holding her breath in fear, she picked up a rock and smashed it against the corked hole in one of the barrels of honey she'd taken from the pack on her back, then listened again for sounds of movement. Still quiet.

Turning the barrel so the honey ran onto the ground, she began to make her way down the mountain toward the cabin, leaving a thick trail in the leaves and grass.

Lee's horse stood ready and saddled in front of the cabin, and Blair managed to remove the cork from the second barrel of honey without any noise before she tied it on the back of the saddle. For a moment, she hesitated about what she was doing, because if Françoise took too long to cut herself loose and the bears smelled the honey first, then the bears could go for the horse before it had a rider. Timing was everything.

She climbed in the cabin window and saw, even in the dark, Lee frowning at her because she'd taken so long. As quickly as she could, she removed her medical uniform. She wanted to look as if she'd just wakened.

Françoise was lying on the floor and Blair could see that there were raw places on her wrists where she'd tried to get out of the bindings. Blair's stomach lurched. She'd taken a vow to relieve suffering, and she hated to be the cause of pain in anyone.

Françoise opened her eyes as Blair walked by.

"I guess I haven't recovered since you tried to starve me," Blair said, as she sliced a piece of cheese from the chunk on the corner of the table. "It won't be long now before the sheriff will be here."

"If he were coming, he's had time. The man who came with Leander has been killed by now."

"Too bad," Blair said nonchalantly. "He's Taggert, the one with the money."

With a fierce yawn, Blair put the knife on the table and

picked up the piece of cheese she'd cut. "I'm going back to bed. Sleep well," she laughed before leaving the room.

As soon as she was out of sight of the woman, she began to dress, slowly and silently, while she placed herself so that she could see Françoise. The outline in the moonlight showed that the woman lost no time in taking the knife from the table and even less time in cutting her bindings. She was out the door in seconds.

"Let's go," Lee said as soon as he heard his horse take a step.

"Let me guess, more walking," Blair said heavily, feeling very tired.

"When we get through with this, you can stay in bed for a week," Lee said. "With me."

"That sounds restful," Blair said sarcastically.

Lee led her down a sheer rock face. She had an idea that if she were to see this place in daylight, she'd refuse to try to climb it. As it was, she didn't seem to have a choice. They had to beat Françoise back to the box canyon.

Lee stopped abruptly and below them lay the canyon. It was quiet around the darkened little cabin, and she wasn't sure there was anyone in there.

"They're waiting for her. I don't think they make a move without her telling them what to do."

"Lee, it's taken Taggert a long time, hasn't it? Do you think he's all right?"

"I don't know. There were many of them against one of him." He moved to the mouth of the canyon and began to place the dynamite. "As soon as we get them sealed in here, I'll ride back to Chandler and get help."

"Ride? On what?"

"Here, hold this," he said, handing her a fuse. "I'll show you later. Now, it's all set. We just have to wait for our lady outlaw."

They sat there in silence for a few minutes. "She should be here by now. I hope she isn't lost."

"Or gone elsewhere," Blair added. "Lee, I think I should tell you something. It's about the honey. I—."

"Quiet! I think I hear something."

It was nearing daylight and in the hazy dawn they could just see the outline of a rider on horseback. The horse was giving the rider a very hard time, and the slim woman was having difficulty controlling it.

"Up there! Now!" Lee ordered Blair, and she began to run to the safety of the higher rocks.

The next minute, all hell broke loose. Françoise began screaming and, in the canyon below, men started running and shooting their guns before they even knew what was wrong. Blair stopped on her way up to look back, and she saw the Frenchwoman on the big stallion, fighting to control the animal, and behind her were two bears, loping along, stopping now and then to lick the rocky ground.

Blair heard a muffled sound from Lee, and the next thing she knew, he was tearing up the hill, his arm catching her about the waist. All the while, he was whistling in an odd way, two short, piercing tones, then repeated.

"Get down," he said and shoved Blair so that she scraped her elbows on the rock. She scooted forward until she could see into the chaos in the canyon below. The horses in the corral were going crazy now that the bears were in the canyon with them, and the people were running around trying to shoot the bears, calm the horses and escape the confusion. Françoise was pulling on the reins of Lee's horse, and screaming and pointing at the entryway, as she tried to get the men to listen to her.

Suddenly, Lee's big horse reared and dumped her onto the ground, then the animal turned and started running toward the entrance, oblivious to the bears that stood in his way.

"He'll get caught in the blast," Lee said, standing to see better into the canyon. There was a great deal of sadness in his voice when he spoke of the inevitability of losing his beloved horse.

The horse kept running and the bears got out of its way.

Less than a minute later, the dynamite exploded, closing the entrance to the canyon and trapping the outlaws inside. Lee was knocked to the ground by the blast, but the dust hadn't settled before he was running down toward the opening. When he was halfway down, his big horse came running to him with rolling, terrified eyes. Lee hugged the animal's head and talked to him to quiet him.

"What the hell were those bears for?" Lee yelled at Blair, who'd followed him down. They could hear the shouts and shots in the canyon below, and the dust hadn't settled yet from the explosion.

"I didn't mention it, because I knew you'd patronize me, but it's been too long," Blair said, almost shouting, not letting him frighten her. "Taggert's been gone more than enough time. I knew the outlaws were going to find us before long, and then we'd be stuck in that cabin with a dozen men shooting at us. They can climb out of that canyon fairly easily, but I thought that maybe, if it were timed right, the bears could delay things. I do hope no one hurts the bears. All they wanted was the honey."

Lee started to say several things to her, but nothing seemed to fit. "I've never seen a woman who didn't have a sense of danger. Don't you realize that you could have been hurt?"

"So could you," she said, with her chin in the air.

He grabbed her by the arm, not yet ready to forgive her. "Now, I'm afraid to leave you here while I go for the sheriff."

He didn't have a chance to say anything else because at that moment, the sheriff and six men came running up the mountainside. They were completely out of breath.

"You all right, Doc?" the sheriff asked, panting, his big chest heaving. For all his gray hair, he was a man in good condition, and he'd made it up to the canyon in very little time. He'd known exactly where the canyon was after Taggert had described it—and he also knew, better than anyone else in town, Leander's propensity for taking things into his own hands. "Taggert said you were in trouble." The next moment, his mouth fell open as he looked over the rim into the canyon below. The people were like toys as they ran around the rock walls and looked for ways to get out. "You do this, Doc?"

"Me and the Missus," Lee said in a drawl that made Blair giggle.

The sheriff pulled back from the edge while the men of the posse kept watching. "Don't let none of 'em escape," he said over his shoulder, as he stood there looking at Blair and Leander. "It looks like you found your match, boy," he said to Lee and there was anger in his voice. "How come you couldn't wait for me to get here? Why'd you have to take the law in your own hands? Somebody could have been hurt by this. Those people down there have killed men. And that Frenchie leader's meaner'n a snake. I've warned you about this sort of thing before. One of these days you ain't gonna come out of one of your do-gooder scrapes alive."

"What's he talking about?" Blair whispered, having never seen the sheriff angry at anyone before. She'd known him all her life, but he was a gentle, quiet man to her.

"What took you so long?" Lee asked, ignoring Blair's question and the sheriff's anger. "We were afraid something had happened to Taggert."

"He got nicked on the head by a bullet and was out for a few hours. That's why it took me so long to get here. We just learned of you capturin' that woman a few hours ago. But it looks like we're too late. She get away?"

"She's down there," Lee said.

"Not for long, she ain't," one of the men of the posse said. "That's a woman climbin' up the side of the canyon."

Blair looked toward the man and, as she did, her peripheral vision caught sight of a movement. She saw one of the sheriff's men, almost hidden by a tree, put his rifle to his shoulder and aim. He's going to shoot her, Blair thought, and she knew that no matter how bad a person was or what he'd done, she couldn't stand by and watch that person be killed. Blair took a flying leap at the man and managed to land close enough that she hit his leg and knocked his aim off. The rifle fired into the air well above Françoise's head.

But Blair hadn't thought about the consequences to herself, and the next moment she was trying to hang onto the cliff edge, her feet dangling over the side.

The sheriff and Lee reacted instantly, each man on his belly, grabbing an arm and pulling her to safety.

"She's the one for you all right," the sheriff said, his voice heavy with disgust, as he helped pull Blair onto the safety of the rocky ledge. "You just be real careful of her and don't let her get hurt."

"I'm doing everything I can to protect her from herself and from me," Lee said solemnly.

Blair sat on the ground at the feet of the two men, dusting

herself off and looking down into the canyon where she'd almost fallen.

"All right, boys," the sheriff said. "Somebody volunteer to stay here and watch 'em while we go get some help. And they all better be *alive* when I get back."

"Sheriff, you mind if you don't mention our names—or Taggert's—in this? And could you send somebody over to the company store of the Inexpressible and claim our IOU for the crowbar and the dynamite?" Lee paused and smiled a moment. "And send the bill to my father. He owes me." He turned, the reins to his horse in one hand, and took Blair's hand in his other.

"Where you off to now?" the sheriff called as they went up the mountain.

"On my honeymoon," Lee called over his shoulder.

"You be careful. That Frenchie escaped, and I don't imagine she has any love for the two of you."

As Lee waved to the sheriff, he whispered to Blair, "Love is just what I have on my mind."

Chapter 24

Blair started walking, but she didn't last long. The combination of little food, less sleep, and even more excitement, at last got to her. When she started to stumble, Lee picked her up and put her on his horse and led the way. Blair nodded off to sleep and the times that she nearly fell from the horse, Lee was there to catch her and put her back on.

They seemed to travel for days and, at one point, Blair was sure that she'd never even seen a bed in her life, much less slept in one.

The sun was hanging low in the sky when they finally stopped and Lee lifted her from the horse. Listlessly, she opened her eyes to look at a large log cabin with a stone foundation.

"Where are we?" she asked, but wasn't really sure that she cared. All she wanted to do was sleep.

"It's my father's hunting cabin. We'll stay here for a few days."

Blair nodded and closed her eyes as Lee carried her inside the cabin. She was vaguely aware that he was taking her up some stairs, but she was too tired to be sure. By the time he placed her on a bed, she was sound asleep.

She awoke to an odd sound outside the window, and as she blinked the sleep out of her eyes, she grew curious as to what the sound was. She tossed the cover back, then gasped when she found herself to be nude. There was a man's shirt on the end of the pine bed and she put it on. Looking down from the window, she saw cows dotting the landscape, and below the window a cow and calf were chomping grass and making the sound that had wakened her.

The cabin was on a slight hill in a clearing in the forest, mountains on all sides, tall trees a few yards from the cabin. The grass was laced with wild rose bushes that were just beginning to bloom.

A sound on the stair behind her made her turn. Lee was just coming up with a tray in his hands, the smell of the food making her mouth water.

"I thought I heard you," he said, smiling at her and looking with interest at her bare legs below the shirt. Blair self-consciously slipped back into the bed and Lee put the tray across her lap.

He removed the cloth that covered the food. "I'm afraid there's no fresh food, but we have everything that's ever been canned or preserved." There was ham and bacon, cheese, peaches, corn muffins, and a tiny dish of wild strawberries.

"It's a feast and I'm starving," she said, and started to eat with gusto.

Lee lounged across the foot of the bed and watched her with a steady intensity that began to make her blush. She was more than aware that now all obstacles to the wedding night were at last removed.

"How long did I sleep?" she asked, mouth full of food.

Lee removed his pocket watch in a slow, easy way that made her pause in her eating. He looked at it, then put it on the little table next to the bed, as if he had no intention of putting it back into his pocket.

"Fourteen hours," he said.

Blair stuffed a corn muffin into her mouth so fast that she nearly choked. "You said that this was your father's cabin. Have you been here often?"

Leander began to unbutton his shirt, taking his time over

213

each button, then slowly pulling it out of his pants. "Since I was a kid," he said.

His eyes on hers were intense and serious—and the way he was looking at her through his lashes was making her nervous. She began to eat faster. "Did you come up here for elk?"

Lee, his eyes never leaving hers, began to unbutton the placket of his trousers.

It didn't take a second glance to show that he was wearing no underwear. Blair's hand began to tremble.

Lee stood and let his trousers slip to the floor.

Blair looked up at him, her eyes on his, her hand halfway to her mouth with a piece of bacon, while he bent toward her and removed the tray and bacon, and set them on the floor.

"You're not Houston now," he said.

For a moment, Blair was afraid of him. She'd fought him every minute for the past few weeks, and she'd felt so guilty about what she'd done to her sister that now she couldn't really believe that it was all right to give in to him.

Lee bent toward her and she moved backward until her head came into contact with the headboard. Part of her wanted to move away, but the other part—the biggest part—would have died before moving.

Very gently, Lee's lips touched hers. He didn't press her or touch her in any other way. There was just this lovely man with this magnificent, nude body bending over her and kissing her.

Blair started sliding down in the bed, or perhaps running down into it would better describe it, rather like butter melting. Lee stayed with her, bending as far as he could until he lost balance and fell on top of her.

From then on, there was no more slowness. Blair opened her mouth to his kiss, and Leander became like a wild man: kissing her with passion, his hands tearing at her hair, running all over her body, ripping the shirt from her. Blair was caught by his passion. For weeks, she'd wanted him, and now he was hers to touch and hold, to help her get rid of this ache that had been caused by holding back for too long.

They clutched each other and rolled on the bed together, their mouths eating at all the bare flesh they could find, hands seeming to multiply, for they were everywhere. Blair had images running through her head of all the times she'd seen Leander and wanted to touch him. She remembered his hands tying delicate knots in surgery, and she'd wanted those hands to touch her. There were times when she'd watched him walk, and she'd thought of his body moving on top of hers. Now, she ran her hands down his back and over his buttocks, so firm and small and beginning to move in a way that made her sure that she was on fire.

He seemed to sense when she was ready, and when he entered her, she gave a little scream and Lee's mouth came down on hers, and she drew on it hungrily.

His movements became rapid and she matched his speed with her own, clinging to him with her hands, mouth, legs. And when he began to move harder and faster, she stiffened, lifting her hips to his, allowing him more access to her body.

And when they finished, Blair again screamed and her body jerked into a spasm of passion as Lee collapsed onto her. Minutes later, Blair relaxed, and for a moment, her body trembled as she clung to him, keeping her legs tight about his waist, determined to never let him go.

They lay together for several minutes before Blair began to relax and released the death hold she had on Lee.

She caressed the damp curls about his neck, running her fingers over the muscles in his shoulders, feeling his skin. He was so new to her, yet, in a way, it was as if they'd always been together. There was so much about him that she didn't know, so much that she wanted to learn.

He raised himself on one elbow and looked at her. "Downstairs I have a hip bath and water heating in the fireplace. Like a bath?"

For a moment, she looked at him, in the light from behind his head, and she realized how precious that head had become to her. Was it just her idea or was he actually the best-looking man in the world?

"Keep looking at me like that and you won't get a bath before next Tuesday."

Lee lifted one eyebrow at Blair's mischievous smile, wrapped her in a blanket and carried her downstairs to the first floor. One end of the cabin was dominated by an enormous stone fireplace flanked by two large windows. The other end contained a kitchen that was littered with dirty dishes, the survivors of Lee's cooking binge. The long walls were stone to about three feet, logs above that, with several windows here and there.

Before the fireplace was a tin tub, taller at one end than the other, now full of cold water that Lee said was from the nearby stream. As Blair stood there, feeling somewhat shy, Lee poured hot water into the tub and then led her toward it. When she still just stood there, he pulled the blanket from her and set her into the water.

The water felt heavenly and she leaned back against the tub and let herself relax. She was aware of Lee standing over her and watching. He'd put on his trousers, but he was shirtless— and stunning: all that dark skin of his stretched over muscles hard from a life spent mostly out-of-doors.

"I married the boy next door," she murmured, smiling.

He knelt at the foot of the tub. "Why did you try to make my life miserable when we were children?"

"I didn't do any such thing," she said, as she began to wash her arms.

"What do you call mud in my face, snowballs flying at me from nowhere, and the time you told Mary Alice Pendergast I was in love with her? Her mother showed my mother love notes that were supposedly from me."

"Because you were taking Houston," she said softly. "She was my *twin*, but suddenly you were there and she seemed to like you more than me."

When Lee didn't say anything, she looked up to see his eyes piercing into hers. He didn't seem to believe her. She hadn't thought of that time when they were children for years. She *had* hated him, hated him from the first moment she saw him. But why? Everyone else seemed to like him, and Houston adored him, but she couldn't stand being near him. She used to leave a room when he entered.

"Maybe . . .," she whispered.

"Maybe what?"

"Maybe I wanted to be your friend."

"But you couldn't, since Houston'd already put her brand

on me?" He lifted her foot from the tub, took the soap and began washing her, his long fingers sliding far, far up her leg.

"You sound as if you weren't involved, but you did ask her to marry you. You must have loved her." Blair watched his hands, *felt* his hands.

He began to soap her toes. "I *guess* I asked her to marry me. Sometimes, I don't seem to remember having said those words to anyone. I think it was a passage of manhood. *Every* man in Chandler asked Houston to marry him."

"Did they?" Blair asked with interest. "Houston never said a word about anything like that. Only Alan asked me to marry him. All the other men were—."

"Fools," he said quickly, washing her foot with great care.

"But I'm so different," she said, and in spite of everything she could do, tears began to form in her eyes. "I've always tried to be like other women, someone like Houston, soft and gentle, but instead I had to become a doctor. And then, I received higher grades than all the other students, male or female, and I could see the men's eyes change when they looked at me. And—."

"You could stand a little work on your suturing," he said, as he dropped her leg and took her right foot into his hands.

"And whenever I beat a man at anything, he—." Her eyes widened. "What?"

"Your stitches, when you're in a hurry, are too big. You need to work on them."

Blair opened her mouth to speak but closed it. She wanted to tell him that her stitches were perfect, but she realized that that wasn't the issue here. He wasn't going to allow her to feel sorry for herself. With a smile, she looked at him. "Will you show me how?"

"I'll show you how to do *anything*," he said, with a look that made her feel very warm, then he resumed washing her. "Those men were fools. No man who's sure of himself would be afraid of any woman. It just took you a while to come home to me."

"Home. Home to my sister's fiancé," she sighed.

Leander was quiet for a moment, washing her hand, soaping it, clasping her fingers with his. "I guess if I had a brother and all the women were after him, and none of them wanted me, I'd be jealous too."

"Jealous! I am not—." She had never thought of it before, but maybe she was jealous of Houston. "She's everything I ever wanted to be. I didn't *want* to be a doctor, I *had* to be one. What I wanted to be was like Houston and keep my gloves clean. She has so many friends. She had you."

He didn't even look up as he began to wash her right arm. "No, she never had me."

Blair kept on talking. "Houston does everything so well. She has an easy way of making friends. People for miles around love her. If Houston'd been leading the Southern troops, they would have won the War Between the States. No one can organize quite the way she can."

"She certainly organized you. Organized you into taking me off her hands."

"You! Oh, no, that just happened. That was entirely my doing. Houston was innocent in that."

"Blair," he said softly, "the night of the governor's reception, I was going to tell Houston the engagement was off."

"Off? I know you said something like that, but you surely didn't mean it."

He paused in washing her. "I don't know Houston at all. I don't think I ever did, but I can see things in you that I think are in Houston, too. Houston just covers whatever she's thinking with those damned white gloves of hers. For some reason, she decided when she was a kid to marry me. I wasn't a person to her, just a goal. Maybe it was like you and medicine, except that your goal was right. I think Houston wanted a reason to back out of our engagement because she had begun to see it wasn't going to work."

"But you didn't see her the night Mr. Gates told her I was to marry you."

"What if you'd studied medicine for years, and then found out the sight of blood made you faint? That carbolic gave you hives?"

"I would have . . . died," she said at last.

"I think I gave Houston hives. We got so we could barely stand each other. We never talked, never laughed, and she curled her lip if I tried to touch her."

"I can't imagine that!" Blair said in genuine horror.

Grinning, he began to wash her upper chest, his hands sliding around her neck and up her cheeks. "Maybe part of her realized that you and I were right for each other, and that's why she sent you out with me."

"But she just wanted to see Taggert's house and—."

"Now, there's a laugh! The lovely Miss Ice Princess Houston Chandler never backed down for any man in her life, but from the first time she set eyes on Taggert, she began to thaw. Remember the time we saw him in town, and he stopped and leered at Houston? I didn't realize it then, but I should have been jealous, that is if I had been in love with Houston as I was supposed to be. But I remember being more curious than anything else."

"Taggert," Blair said. "I can't imagine how any woman could want that awful man."

"He was certainly ready to risk his life to help us," Lee said. His slick, soapy hands were sliding lower down her chest. "Frankie's gang thought you were Houston. They demanded fifty grand for ransom. Taggert not only brought a gun, he brought money."

Blair didn't hear what he was saying because his hands slid over her breasts. She lifted her arms to entwine with his, leaning back against the tub, enjoying the sensation of having him touch her.

He moved to stand before her, then lifted her from the water, her wet skin sticking to his. "I've waited a long time for this," he said.

Leander seemed to be particularly adept at removing his clothing because by the time he'd carried her the three steps to the couch, he was bare. His first passion was spent, and this time he seemed to want to do little more than explore her body. Blair felt as if she were being tortured. He knocked her hands away when she reached for him and only allowed himself the pleasure of touching all of her body with his hands, his mouth, rubbing against her skin with his until she was nearly senseless with desire.

When he moved on top of her, she was clutching at him, but he was infuriatingly slow, refusing to hurry, taking his time with long, slow strokes. By the time he began to move faster, Blair was in a frenzy, feeling that she might explode from wanting him so badly.

When at last the peak came, it was such that she was sure for a moment that she had died. Her body ached and trembled, quivered, as she clung to Lee.

He pulled back, smiling at her. "I knew we'd make a great team."

She was serious as she said, "Is lovemaking the only reason you wanted to marry me?"

His face also turned serious. "That and your suturing."

"You!" she gasped, hitting at his ribs with her fist.

But Lee moved off her. "Come on, get up. Let's take a walk. I have some places to show you."

She wasn't used to seeing him without clothing. The only other nude men she'd ever seen were cadavers stretched out on cold marble slabs. Lee looked more alive than anyone she'd ever seen.

"Oh, no, you don't," he laughed, taking her hand and pulling her off the couch. "Get upstairs and get dressed. There're some old clothes in the chest at the head of the stairs. Get them on." He smacked her firm, bare bottom as she went up the stairs.

Blair opened the chest and began to rummage for clothes, but there was a mirror on the wall and she paused to look at herself in it. Her skin was glowing, her cheeks were rosy and her eyes brilliant. Of course, her hair, usually pulled back tightly so it wouldn't interfere with her work, was now standing out in a wild lion's mane about her head.

Could it be true that Leander loved her? He certainly didn't seem to mind her company, and he'd fought awfully hard to win her. Or did he just want a practicing surgeon-partner and an eager bedmate?

"You've got three minutes," Lee yelled from downstairs.

"What's my punishment if I'm not ready?" she called back.

"Abstinence."

With a laugh, Blair began to dress hurriedly in heavy canvas pants and a flannel shirt. The pants were too short, but she managed to get the upper and lower halves of her body covered. The waist was so big she had to hold it in her hand.

Downstairs, Lee was shoving food into a rucksack.

"Do you have a belt?" she asked.

When he glanced at her, she released the waistband and, with an impish grin, let the pants drop to the floor. She was rewarded by Lee's groan.

He turned away toward the woodpile and picked up a length of rope, then went to her, knelt, and put the rope through the belt loops. As he raised her pants, he kissed her legs all the way up, so that by the time the trousers were in place, Blair was swaying on her feet.

Lee walked to the door. "Come on, let's go." This time he was the one with the impish smile.

Weak-kneed, Blair followed him outside.

Chapter 25

Blair followed Lee as he walked along a narrow elk trail, through scrub oak, across a meadow, as he wound up the side of a mountain. The bark of the aspens had been chewed by the elk, killing many of the trees, and they had to walk across the fallen logs. Everywhere were the droppings of the big animals that had now gone north for the summer.

Lee pointed out a hawk to her and named some of the flowers. He seemed to sense when he was going too fast and slowed for her, holding back scratchy little oak trees to make the way clear.

At the top was a narrow ridge, falling off on both sides, with huge fir trees going down one side, and a vista that showed miles of hazy blue mountains on the other. Lee sat down, leaned against a fallen tree and opened his arms to her. She cuddled next to him gratefully, holding his hand in hers and toying with his fingers.

"What did the sheriff mean when he said we were two of a kind?" she asked.

Lee had his eyes closed, the sun warm on his face. "I got into trouble a couple of times when I was a kid. I guess he's not forgiven me."

Blair sat upright. *"You!? You* got into trouble? But you were always a paragon of virtue, every mother's dream."

Not opening his eyes, but smiling, he pulled her back against him. "You know as little about me as possible. I'm not what you seem to think."

"Then tell me how you got into trouble and why I didn't hear about it. I'm sure that in Chandler it would have made front-page news: Saint Leander Does Something Less Than Perfect."

Lee grinned broader. "You didn't hear of it because my father somehow managed to keep it quiet and, also, because it happened in Colorado Springs. What I did was get myself shot twice."

"Shot?" she gasped. "But I didn't see any scars."

Lee grunted. "You've yet to *look* at me. I get near you and you pounce on me."

"I do no such—." Blair stopped because what he said was true. "How did you get shot?" she asked meekly.

"I went with Dad to Colorado Springs when I was about fourteen. He had to talk to a witness for a client of his, and he was to meet the man at a hotel not far north of the bank. We'd just eaten dinner and were leaving the hotel when suddenly guns started firing and somebody yelled that the bank'd been robbed. I looked down the street and saw half a dozen men with bandannas over their faces riding toward us.

"I guess I didn't think, I just acted. There was a buckboard in the alley, hitched with four horses and loaded with feedbags. I jumped into the seat, yelled at the horses and drove the wagon into the street and blocked the outlaws' exit."

"And they shot you."

"I couldn't very well jump off the wagon. The horses would have run ahead and left the street clear."

"So you just sat there and held the horses," Blair said with some awe.

"I stayed there until the sheriff caught up with the bank robbers."

"And then what?"

He smiled. "And then my dad pulled me off the wagon and carried me to a doctor who gouged one bullet out—the other one went through my arm. He also let me get drunk, and I swear the hangover was worse than the holes in me."

"But, thanks to you, the robbers were caught."

"And spent years in jail. They're out now. You even met one of them."

"When?" she asked.

"The night we went to the reception. Remember when we went to the house on River Street? The suicide case? Remember the man outside? I don't think you liked him very much."

"The gambler," she said, thinking of the way the man'd looked at her.

"Among other things. LeGault spent ten years in prison after that robbery in Colorado Springs."

"Because of you," she said. "He must hate you, since you're the one who caught him."

"Probably," Lee said, without much interest. He opened his eyes and looked at her. "But then, I believe you used to hate me, too."

"Not exactly hate . . .," she began, then smiled. "Where did you go on our wedding night?"

"Want to see my bullet scars?"

She started to say something about his refusal to answer her, but she compressed her mouth into a tight little line and said no more.

He put his fingertip under her chin. "Honeymoons aren't the place for anger, or for sulky looks. How about if I tell you about the time I delivered triplets?"

She didn't say a word to him.

"One of them was breech."

Still nothing.

"And they were a month early, and they were each born an hour apart, and to keep them alive we had to . . . ."

"To what?" she asked after several minutes of silence.

"Oh, nothing. It wasn't very interesting. It was only written about in three journals. Or was it four?" He shrugged. "It doesn't matter."

"Why was it written about?"

"Because our method of saving them was . . . But you

probably wouldn't be interested." With a yawn, he lay back against the log.

Blair leaped on him, her hands clenched into fists. "Tell me, tell me, tell me," she shouted at him while Lee, laughing, began to roll across the grass with her. He stopped when she was on the bottom.

"I'll tell you, but you have to tell me a secret about yourself."

"I don't *have* any secrets," she said, glaring at him, reminded of his refusal to tell her where he'd gone.

"Oh, yes, you do. Who put the snakes in my lunch pail and the grasshoppers in my pencil box?"

She blinked a couple of times. "I'm not sure, but I think it might have been the same person who put the taffy in your shoes, who sewed the sleeves of your jacket closed, who put hot peppers in your sandwiches, who—."

"At my mother's garden party!" he said. "I sat there and ate those sandwiches and thought everyone else's were hot, too, and that I was just a coward because they were about to kill me. How did you manage it?"

"I paid Jimmy Summers a penny to release his muddy dog when I dropped my spoon. The dog ran into the garden, and you, always the rescuer, ran to get rid of the dog. Everybody watched you, so I had plenty of time to doctor the sandwiches on your plate. I thought I'd burst to keep from laughing. You sat there sweating, but you ate every bite."

He loomed over her, shaking his head. "And the dried cow pie in my favorite fishing hat?"

She nodded.

"And the pictures of Miss Ellison on my slate?"

She nodded.

"Did anyone besides me ever catch you?"

"Your father did once. Houston said you were going fishing, so I sneaked over to your house, dumped out the worms you'd just dug and put a garter snake in the can. Unfortunately, your father caught me."

"I would imagine he had a few words to say. He hated any pranks of Nina's."

"He said that I was *never* going to be a lady."

225

"And he was right," Lee said solemnly, beginning to rub about on her. "You aren't a lady at all. You're a flesh and blood woman." He grinned. "Lots of flesh in all the right places."

Her eyes widened. "Are you planning to take my virtue, sir? Oh, please, sir, it's the only thing I have left."

"You don't deserve even that for what you've done, young lady," he said, leering, lowering his voice. "You've been tried and found guilty, and you are to be punished."

"Oh?" she said, arching a brow. "Taffy in my shoes?"

"I was thinking more along the lines of your becoming my love slave for the rest of our lives."

"Isn't that a little severe for a bit of taffy?"

"It's for the hot peppers and the—." His eyes widened. "Did you put the sneezing powder on my crackers? And the soot on my father's binoculars the day I took them to school?"

She nodded, beginning to feel a little guilty about the sheer volume of pranks she'd played on him.

He was looking at her with some awe. "I knew you did some of them but I'd always thought John Lechner did most of them. You know, I saw him four years ago in New York and I remembered all the things I *thought* he'd done to me, and I'm afraid I was barely civil to him."

"You didn't retaliate?"

"About a hundred times. I spent years with bruises from fights with John." He grinned. "And to think: he was innocent. As for the ones I knew you did, what could I do? You were six years younger than me and, besides, just thinking of the whipping my father gave me after that one time I did punch you was enough to make me think twice about striking a girl."

"So now I have to pay for some childhood foolishness," she said with an exaggerated sigh. "Life is hard."

"That's not all that's hard," he said with a one-sided smirk. "It's a good thing I'm a doctor and impossible to shock."

"It wasn't your doctoring that attracted me."

"Oh? And what did attract you to me?"

"Your persistence in trying to get my attention. I withstood it long enough but can stand no more."

"If you insist," she said tiredly.

"I love obedient women," he murmured as he ran his hand under her shirt and began to caress her rib cage, moving his hand up to touch her breasts.

Blair was astonished that she could want him again after only a few hours, but when her fingertips touched his warm skin, it was as if it were the first time. She hadn't thought of the pranks she'd played on him in years. At the time, she'd thought she did them because she hated him, that she was getting even with him for taking Houston away. But now, she wondered if all she'd wanted was his attention.

When he lifted his head and started to unbutton her shirt, she took his face in her hands. "I don't understand what you mean to me," she whispered.

Lee gave her a soft, gentle smile. "Not yet? Well, stay by me and it'll come to you. One thing about you, Blair, you sure can put up one hell of a fight. Do you think you'll come to fight *for* me as strongly as you've fought *against* me?"

"I don't know," she said, confused. She was so torn about this man. He'd been her enemy for most of her life. She'd fought him every way she could. And in spite of what Lee had said, she'd effectively managed to sabotage her sister's wedding. Why? Why had she fallen into bed with a man she swore she hated?

Lee took her hands in his and kissed the palms. "While you're trying to find the answers to life, we're wasting time." He finished unbuttoning her shirt.

They made love slowly, almost delicately, Lee watching her face to see her reactions. He kissed each of her fingertips, lingering over them, and the sensation of feeling the warm, moist interior of his mouth went through all of her. He kissed her breasts, ran his hands all over her skin.

And when he came to her, it was gentle, sweet, prolonged.

Later, he held her very close, tucking her legs between his, wrapping himself around her, trying to enclose her body within his.

Blair lay within the circle of his arms, listening to clicking grasshoppers, the high-pitched whistle of a hummingbird, and the wind. The smell and taste and feel of Lee seemed to fill her. How much she wanted this moment never to end.

227

"When we get home, you'll have to hire somebody to take care of my socks," he said softly.

"Your what?" she asked vaguely, holding onto him as if her life depended on it.

"My socks and my shirts—and I like my boots kept polished. And you'll need somebody to clean the place, make the bed and feed us."

Blair was silent for a moment before she began to understand what he was saying. Since she was a girl, all she'd cared about—or learned anything about—was medicine. She had absolutely no idea how to run a house.

She gave a big sigh. "Think anyone'd like to marry us?"

She could feel Lee chuckle. "We can ask. I met a lady criminal who—." He stopped when Blair put her teeth to his skin and threatened to bite.

"Lee," she said, as she moved back to look at him. "I really, truly don't know anything about running a house. My mother tried to teach me but—."

"You climbed trees."

"Or escaped to somewhere. Aunt Flo tried, but Uncle Henry kept saying that there was time, and then he'd take me into the surgery to help him. I guess there wasn't time. Next year, I was planning to enroll in a course in housewifery so I'd be prepared when I married Alan."

"A course, huh? One where they teach you how to get the toilet clean and how to scrub the floors?"

"Think it would have been that bad?"

"Probably worse."

She put her head back into his shoulder. "I *told* you not to marry me. Now you see why no one else wanted to. Houston's so much better at this than I am. You should have kept her."

"Probably," he said solemnly. "I'd certainly never have to worry about her borrowing my scalpel."

"I never borrow yours," she said indignantly. "I have my own."

"Yes, but Houston does know how to run a house. I imagine her husband's socks will always be clean and in order."

Blair pushed away from him. "If that's what you want, you

can just go to her—or to any other woman for that matter. If you think I'm going to dedicate my life to your underwear, you're mistaken." She sat up and angrily began to pull on her trousers.

"Not even *one* sock?" he asked in a pleading way.

Blair glanced at him and saw that he was laughing at her. "You!" she laughed and fell back into his arms, where he hugged her fiercely. "You didn't tell me about the triplets."

"What triplets?"

"The ones you delivered and that were written about in four journals."

He looked at her as if she'd lost her mind. "I've never delivered triplets in my life."

"But you said . . . Oh, you!" she gasped, laughing.

He ran his hand up her trousered legs and over her bare back. "How about walking down to the river? We can eat there."

"And talk about the clinic," she said, as she stood and put on her shirt. "When do you think the equipment will arrive? And you never did tell me exactly what you ordered. Lee, if you don't want to work there all the time, I thought I might write a friend of mine, Dr. Louise Bleeker. She's quite good and Chandler is growing by leaps and bounds, so I'm sure we could use another doctor."

"Actually, I was thinking of hiring Mrs. Krebbs to help in the clinic."

Blair paused in buttoning her shirt. "Mrs. Krebbs! Do you know what she's *like?* One day, a little boy came to the hospital with a chicken bone caught in his throat and dear Mrs. Krebbs suggested I wait for a *real* doctor to arrive."

"And she's still alive today?" he asked, wide-eyed.

She squinted up at him. "Are you teasing me again?"

"I never tease women who look like you do." He looked down at her gaping shirt that was unbuttoned to just above her navel. "Come on," he said before she could answer. "If we're going to talk business, let's at least walk while we do it."

Chapter 26

Leander and Blair, holding hands, ran up the hill to the cabin. They stopped now and then to kiss, and Lee began to tug on Blair's clothes and she on his until, when they reached the rise just before the cabin, they were both unbuttoned to the waist.

But the fun stopped when they looked up the hill toward the cabin, for there on the front porch stood Reed Westfield.

Lee's face instantly turned somber, as he put himself between Blair and the cabin and began to button her shirt. "Listen to me," he said gently. "I think I'll have to go away again. I don't imagine my father'd come here unless it were an emergency."

"Emergency? I can—." Something in his eyes made her stop and her jaw harden. "Is it *that* kind of emergency? One where I'm to be excluded, where I can't be trusted? The emergency that is for men only?"

He put his hands on her shoulders. "Blair, you have to trust me. I would tell you if I could, but for your own good—."

"For my own good, I should remain ignorant. I understand completely."

"You don't understand anything!" Lee said, his fingers

gripping her tightly. "You're just going to have to trust me. If I could tell you, I would."

She jerked away from him. "I understand perfectly. You *are* just like Mr. Gates. You have rigid ideas of what a woman can and cannot do, and I can't be trusted enough to be told what you're doing when you so mysteriously disappear. Tell me, what do you plan to allow me to do now that we're married? That is, besides manage your household and glee-fully share your bed? May I continue practicing medicine, or am I too incompetent to do that, too?"

Lee rolled his eyes skyward, as if looking for help. "All right, have it your way. You seem to think I'm a monster, so I'll be one. My father is here for an important reason, and I have to leave you now. I can't tell you where I'm going or I would. What I'd like you to do now is to return to Chandler with my father, and I will be home as soon as possible."

Blair didn't say another word as she walked past him, up the hill and toward the cabin. It was difficult for her to even look at Reed. He'd never liked her since she was a child and he'd caught her playing a prank on his precious son. When Lee'd said he wanted to marry Blair, Reed had participated in that dreadful interrogation Gates had subjected her to. And later, Reed had pointblank, directly, lied to her, making up that story about Lee and a Frenchwoman.

So now, as she walked past him and into the cabin, she could be neither warm or even especially cordial. She greeted him coolly and went inside.

Even when she was alone, she wouldn't allow herself to unbend. What had she expected except to be treated this way? Lee said he loved her, but what man wouldn't love a woman who was as enthusiastic a bed partner as she was? And Lee's sense of honor would make him feel obligated to marry her, since she'd been a virgin that first night.

Blair went upstairs to remove the men's clothing she was wearing and put her medical uniform back on. The window was open and through it she could hear voices. When she looked outside, she could see Lee and his father at some distance from the cabin and, from the look of their gestures, they were angry with each other.

Lee was squatting in the grass, chewing on a stem, while

Reed was using every inch of his heavy body to lean over his son in an intimidating way. To Blair, it looked as if Reed were threatening Lee.

In spite of herself, she leaned closer to the window. Some words floated to her, words that Reed was punctuating with a finger pointed at Lee. ". . . danger . . ." ". . . risk your life . . ." ". . . Pinkerton . . ."

She drew back. "Pinkerton?" she whispered, as she fastened the last buttons on her uniform. What did Lee have to do with the Pinkerton Detective Agency?

For a moment, she sat on the bed. She hadn't had much time to think about where Lee'd gone on their wedding night. Reed had lied to her and she'd believed him. She was willing to believe that Lee loved someone else; she was willing to believe that he was running into a den of outlaws to save the leader from blood poisoning. But what if Lee were involved in something else, something . . . She hesitated to even think about what he could be involved in. Maybe he was *helping* the Pinkertons. But the way Reed was warning his son, Blair didn't think so.

Leander was involved in something illegal. She knew it, felt it. And that's why he couldn't tell her what he was doing. He wanted her to remain innocent.

Slowly, with heavy feet, Blair went downstairs and arrived at the door just as Lee was entering. "I have to go," he said, watching her.

Blair looked up at him. What act of criminality was Lee into? And why? Did he need money? She thought of the new medical equipment he'd ordered from Denver. It must have cost a great deal, and everyone knew that a doctor made very little money. Of course, Lee'd inherited money from his mother, but who knew how much that was? Was he doing this so he could open his clinic? So he could help people?

"I know," she said, putting her hand on his arm.

As he looked at her, he seemed to sigh with relief. "You're not angry anymore?"

"No, I don't think I am."

He kissed her in an achingly sweet way. "I'll be back as soon as I can. Dad will take you home now."

Before another word was said, he was on his big stallion and riding down the mountain, out of her sight.

Blair mounted the horse Reed had brought for her, and they started the long trek home in silence. Most of the trail, between pine trees, across tiny streams, was, of necessity, single file. Blair was puzzling over Lee's disappearances, telling herself her conclusion was wrong, and praying that he wasn't in danger.

A few miles outside of Chandler, when the land flattened and the terrain dried, Reed reined his horse to ride beside her.

"I think you and I got off on the wrong foot," Reed said.

"Yes," she answered honestly. "From when I was about eight."

He looked puzzled for a moment. "Ah, yes, the pranks. You know, I wouldn't have known about them except that my wife found out about a few of them. Lee never said a word about them. Helen said they were being executed by a girl. She said boys were smart, but they weren't clever like girls, and these pranks were quite clever. She was very interested after I told her I'd seen you exchanging the fishing worms with a snake. 'Blair Chandler,' she said. 'I might have guessed she was the one. She always has had an extraordinary interest in Lee.' I don't know what she meant by that, but I do know that she laughed a great deal whenever she heard about another prank."

"If Lee didn't tell her, how did she find out?"

"Nina sometimes, Lee's teacher at other times. Once Lee came home from school with a stomachache, and after Helen'd put him to bed, she returned to the kitchen to see Lee's lunch pail slowly moving across the table. She said she nearly died of fright before she could open it enough to see what was inside. It was a horned toad, which she gratefully put in her flower garden."

"No wonder you weren't too happy when Lee said he was going to marry me," Blair said.

Reed was quiet for a moment, moving easily with his horse. "I'll tell you my big worry about you and Lee, and it has nothing to do with the pranks. The truth is, my son works too hard. Even as a boy, he used to take on three jobs at once. For some reason, Lee thinks the world's problems are his responsibility. I was proud when he said he wanted to become a doctor, but I was worried, too. I was afraid he'd do just what he's done—take on too much. He works in the hospital, and he manages the place even though Dr. Webster has the title of administrator. Lee also takes the case of anybody in town. Four nights a week he runs off on calls. And he still visits people in the country."

"And you were afraid I'd be more of a burden to him?" Blair whispered.

"Well, you have to admit that excitement does happen around you. I wanted Lee to marry someone as different from him as possible, someone like Houston who's so like Opal, someone who'd stay home and sew and make a home. It's not that I've ever had anything against you, but just look at what's happened in the last few weeks since you returned to Chandler."

"I see what you mean," Blair said, as one picture of excitement after another passed through her mind. "I don't think Lee's had much rest, has he?"

"He nearly killed himself while trying to impress you with what a good doctor he was." He paused and smiled at her. "But somewhere along the way, I began to see how much he wanted you."

"Yes, I believe he does," she murmured, wondering if the wanting of her was leading him into doing whatever he was doing in secret.

She and Reed rode into Chandler in silence, the last few miles in starlight. He left her at the house she shared with Leander, and Blair went inside with a heavy heart. Was he in debt for this place, too?

She took a quick bath and wearily climbed into the empty bed. It seemed that she was destined to spend every night in this house alone.

At six the next morning, she was awakened by the telephone ringing. Groggily, she made her way downstairs.

The operator, Caroline, said, "Blair-Houston, four freight wagons from Denver have just arrived and the drivers are waiting for Leander at the old warehouse on Archer Avenue."

"He can't go, but I'll be there in fifteen minutes."

"But it's the doctor equipment and Leander needs to tell them where it goes."

"According to my diploma, *I* am a doctor," Blair said icily.

"I'm sure I didn't mean anything. I was just passing the message along." She hesitated. "Why can't Leander go?"

Nosy woman! Blair thought. She wasn't about to tell her Lee was on another of his mysterious missions. "Because I exhausted him," she said, and hung up the phone with a smile. *That* should give them something to gossip about.

Blair tore up the stairs and minutes later she was running down the street while still pinning her hair up. By the time she got to the top of Archer Avenue, she saw the men lounging against the wagons and looking impatient.

"Hello, I'm Dr. Westfield."

One burly man, mouth full of tobacco juice, looked her up and down for a moment, while the other men peered around the wagon frames—as if they were trying not to show interest in a freak of nature. The first man spat a big wad of juice.

"Where do you want this unloaded?"

"Inside," she said, pointing to the warehouse.

Immediately, there were problems. She had no key, nor had she any idea where Lee kept a key to the place. The men just stood there looking at her skeptically, as if this were what they would have expected from a woman who called herself a doctor.

"It's too bad we can't get in," she said sadly, "because my stepfather owns the Chandler Brewery, and he promised a barrel of beer, as thanks, to the men who helped me with the new equipment. But I guess—."

The sound of breaking glass cut her words off.

"Sorry, ma'am," said one of the men. "I guess I leaned against the window too hard. But it looks like maybe somebody little could get through here."

A moment later, Blair was inside and unbolting the heavy front door for them. With the sunlight coming in, she could see the place: cobwebs hanging down, the floor littered, the ceiling with at least three leaks. "Over there," she said absently, pointing to a corner that at least looked dry, if not clean. While the men unloaded, she walked through the one vast room and tried to imagine how it would be arranged for the clinic.

The men brought in oak tables, cabinets with little drawers, tall cabinets with glass doors, big sinks, small boxes of instruments, cases of bandages and cotton, everything for a fully equipped infirmary.

"Seem to be enough?"

She turned to Lee, standing there, surveying the crates and furniture.

He was watching her with eyes narrowed, a lit cigar between his lips. His clothes were dirty and he looked tired.

"More than enough," she said, and wondered how much it had cost him. "You look exhausted. You should go home and sleep. I'm going to get some women in here to clean this place."

With a smile, he tossed her a key. "This is to spare the rest of the windows. Come home soon," he said with a wink and then was gone.

For a moment, Blair felt tears come to her eyes. Whatever he was doing, he was doing so he could help other people, of that she was sure. Whatever this equipment had cost him, he was willing to do *anything* to pay the price.

When the men had finished unloading, they gave her a ride back to her house and she called her mother, explaining about the beer. Opal said that Mr. Gates was so pleased that Blair was at last married to a decent man that she was sure he'd give the men a barrel of beer.

After calling her mother, Blair called Houston. Houston would know whom to get to clean the warehouse. Sure enough, by ten o'clock, the place was full of women with cloths about their heads, brooms flying, huge pails of water full of big mops and scrub rags, working.

By eleven, Blair had talked to Mr. Hitchman, who'd built the Chandler house, and arranged for his two sons to start the remodelling according to Leander's plans.

At two, Lee came back and, through the noise and dust, she told him what she'd arranged.

Protesting that she couldn't possibly leave, she allowed him to pull her out to his carriage and drive her into town to Miss Emily's Tea Shop.

Miss Emily took one look at Blair and sent her to the back with an order to wash all of her body that was possible because all of it was dirty. When Blair returned, Lee was waiting behind a table loaded with little chicken sandwiches and cakes iced with strawberry frosting.

Blair, ravenous, began stuffing herself and talking all at once. ". . . and we can use the tall cabinet, the one with the countertop, in the surgery, and I thought that big sink could go—."

"Slow down a minute. All the work doesn't have to be done in a day."

"I don't think it can be. It's just that this town needs a place for women. Years ago, Mother took me to see the Women's Infirmary here. Is it still as bad?"

"Worse than you can imagine," Lee said seriously, then took her hand and kissed it. "So, what are you dallying for? Let's get out of here and go to work. By the way, I called your sister and she's hiring a maid and a housekeeper for us."

"Two?" Blair asked. "Can we afford two?"

He gave her a very puzzled look. "If you don't eat all of Miss Emily's merchandise." He looked aghast when she immediately put down the sandwich she'd picked up.

"What's brought this on? Blair, I'm not as rich as Taggert, but I can certainly afford a couple of maids."

She stood. "Let's go, shall we? I have a plumber coming later."

Still wearing a look of puzzlement, Lee followed her out of the teashop.

Chapter 27

Françoise slammed the glass down on the table and saw, with disgust, that the glass was too heavy, too crude, to break. "It's all her fault," she muttered.

Behind her, a man spoke, causing her to jump. She turned to look up at LeGault, tall, thin, dark—slimy. He had a habit of entering and leaving rooms without a sound. He toyed with his little mustache. "Blaming her again?"

Françoise didn't bother to answer him as she stood and walked toward the window. The shades were drawn and the heavy plush curtains closed. No one must see her, for she was in hiding. She'd been inside this room for over a week now. The men in her band were either in prison or in a hospital. The bears that woman had enticed into the canyon had caused men and animals to panic to the point where one man was trampled by sharp horses' hoofs. Two men had been shot, and another's leg had been mauled by an angry bear. By the time the sheriff's men got the canyon mouth open, the outlaws were crying to be taken into custody.

And all because of one woman.

"I am still blaming her," Françoise said with anger. Mostly what she hated was being played for a fool. That idiot band of men who followed her hadn't had sense enough to find her, yet she'd been holed up practically under their noses.

In the last week, she'd had time to go over every detail of what had happened, and she now saw how that woman had used her. She saw the way Blair had pretended to be angry with her handsome husband, had pretended to drug him, then had "forgotten" the knife so Françoise could get away.

"I don't guess you've considered the doc's involvement in this," LeGault said with a smirk. "Only the woman is guilty, right?"

"She was the instigator." Françoise shrugged. "She is the one I would like to see repaid."

"And I'd like to see Westfield repaid," LeGault said.

"And what has he done to you?"

LeGault rubbed his wrists. He was careful to keep the scars covered—scars made by the iron manacles he'd worn in the prison where Westfield had put him. "Let's just say that I have reason enough to want to see him get some of what he's given me." He paused. "Tonight, the messenger arrives with news. I hope he'll know the day of the shipment."

"No more than I do," Françoise said with feeling. "After this job is done, I'm heading east, to Texas."

"And leave your dear, devoted gang behind?" LeGault said tauntingly.

"Idiots! It will do them good to rot in jail for a few years. About tonight: do you think I could go with you? I'll do anything to get out of here for a while."

"Anything?"

"Anything that will not ruin our partnership," she said with a smile, thinking she'd rather walk into a pit of rattlesnakes than sleep with LeGault. "It will be night and no one will see me. I need air and this waiting is making me miserable."

"Sure. Why not? I have to meet the man in the middle of nowhere, up behind the Little Pamela mine. But if someone recognizes you, don't expect me to stay by you. No one's after me, and I plan to keep it that way."

"Don't worry about me tonight. You have to worry about how to get the boxes we steal out of Chandler, while I hide and you stay in plain sight."

"Don't worry about that. I'll come up with something," he said at the door. "I'll come back for you at midnight."

Hours later, they rode out of town, avoiding the lights on the houses, even the lights on the carriages. Françoise kept her hat down over her face and, in her thick coat and big pants, she didn't look at all like a female.

They met their messenger, and the news was pleasing to them. Smiling, they started down the mountainside to where their horses were hidden.

"Quiet! I hear something," LeGault said, as he jumped for cover behind a boulder.

Françoise hid, too, just as they saw two men emerge from the trees, the moonlight clearly outlining them. One, a short, stocky man, seemed nervous, while the other, tall, slim, the moonlight glinting off a revolver at his side, was calm and watchful. He paused while the short man climbed into a carriage that was well concealed behind a clump of piñon. Still watching, he struck a match and lit a cigar.

"Westfield!" Frankie gasped and LeGault shushed her.

They watched as the tall man, Leander, drove away—but there was no other man in the carriage with him.

"Where did he go?" Françoise asked when the carriage was gone, as she turned around to lean against the rock.

"Hidden," LeGault said thoughtfully. "Now, why would our righteous, do-gooder doctor be hiding a man in his buggy in the middle of the night?"

"Isn't that a coal mine down there?"

"Sure, but what does that matter? Think he's plannin' to steal a couple tons of coal?"

"He and that bitch of his stole dynamite from somewhere, probably from the coal mine."

LeGault played with the tip of his mustache. "He's awfully familiar with coal mines."

"You can stay here all night with your puzzle, but it's too cold for me. We have much planning to do yet, and not much time to do it in."

LeGault didn't say a word as he followed Françoise back to the horses. "This woman Westfield married," he said, hands on the pommel, "she's a Chandler, isn't she?"

"Like the town name, yes."

"Very much like the town name. The most respectable, unsuspected name in the town."

"What are you thinking?"

"You saw Westfield and his bride together. What would you guess she'd be likely to do for him?"

"Do?" Françoise thought of the way the woman'd looked at the doctor, as if he might disappear at any moment—and if he did start to fade, she was going to grab onto his coattails. "I believe she'd do anything—everything—for that man."

LeGault gave a smile that showed perfect, even white teeth. "I don't know what we saw here tonight, but I'm going to find out. And when I do, I'll see how we can use it. We need a way to move that shipment out of Chandler."

Françoise began to smile also. "And who better to do it than a Chandler?"

Leander and Blair worked on the clinic for three days, along with several crews of workers, before they got it ready. On the evening of the third day, Lee climbed a ladder and nailed up the big sign: Westfield Infirmary for Women.

When he stepped down from the ladder, he saw Blair grinning up at the sign with the expression of a child who has tasted ice cream for the first time. "Come inside," he said. "I have a celebration planned for us." When Blair didn't move, he caught her hand and pulled her inside.

Under an oak lid, inside a galvanized sink, were two bottles of champagne in ice.

Blair backed away. "Lee, you know what happens to me when I drink champagne."

"I'm not likely to forget," he said, as he popped the cork and grabbed a crystal glass, filled it and handed it to her.

Blair took a cautious sip, looked at him over the rim, then drained the glass and held it out for a refill.

"Not upset about St. Joseph's? Don't wish you could intern there?"

She kept her eyes on the wine Lee was pouring into her extended glass. "And miss working with the man I love? Hey!" she said, as Lee kept filling and the glass overflowed. She looked up to see him watching her with hot eyes.

"For how long?" he whispered.

Blair tried to be nonchalant. The words had come out unexpectedly. "Maybe forever. Maybe I've loved you since I first met you. Maybe I tried everything I could to hate you, probably because Houston claimed you first, but nothing seems to have worked. No matter what I did to you, you always came out on top."

Lee was standing a foot away from her, but the heat in his eyes was drawing her closer. "So I passed your tests, did I? Rather like Hercules and his tasks."

"It wasn't quite that bad."

"No? People are still asking me if I'd like to go rowing. And, of course, there was that last-minute switch at the altar, and everyone wants to know if I know which twin I *did* marry."

"But there are no more snakes in your lunch pail," she said solemnly.

Leander put his wineglass, then hers, down on the edge of the sink and stepped toward her. "You have a lot to make up to me."

"I shall always keep your scalpels sharp," she said, stepping back.

Leander just stood there, not saying a word, as he watched her. It was nearly dark outside and very dim in the surgery of the hospital. With his eyes locked on hers, Lee began to remove his clothing, inch by inch exposing warm, dark skin, long muscles playing, moving.

Blair stood transfixed where she was, her eyes hypnotized by him, watching his fingers on buttons, watching him as he exposed himself bit by delicious bit. His legs were long and thick-thighed, big muscles about his knees, calves strong and heavy. Her breath deepened and her throat dried as she saw him standing before her nude, his desire for her rampant.

Still watching her, he sat down on a long, low bench, his legs apart, his body ready for her.

"Come to me," he whispered in a voice that came from somewhere inside him.

Blair didn't bother to remove any outer clothing but released the drawstring of her pantalets and stepped out of them as she walked. Her full cord skirt covered them as she straddled him, slipping down on his manhood easily. She wrapped her leather encased feet about his calves for a moment, pulling herself down, closer and closer to him, feeling him against her skin.

Then, on tiptoe, she began to move up and down, slowly at first, watching. His face was expressionless, devoid of lines, angelic almost, as the pleasure began to dissolve over him. A moment later, she arched against him, bringing her knees up to the bench. Lee's hands slid under the skirt, began to move up and down her thighs, clutching her, helping her to move.

Lee's eyes closed for a second, opened, then he leaned his head back and slid downward. Blair moved her hands from his shoulders to his neck and began to move harder and faster, her thighs straining, tightening, as Lee caught her buttocks in his hands and helped her move.

She arched once, hard, backbreakingly hard, holding onto Lee as her body tightened and froze for a moment in a final ecstasy.

Lee held her, even though she almost fought him, not allowing her to fall, himself shuddering with the grip of his passion.

For a moment, Blair didn't know where she was, as she came out of her powerful arch and clung to Lee.

After a moment, he pulled back and smiled at her. "It's nice to have mutual interests."

"Hello. Is anyone here?"

"It's your father," Blair said in horror.

Lee lifted her off him. "Go out there and stall him while I get dressed."

"But I can't—," she began, thinking that he'd know from the look of her what she'd been doing.

"Go!" Lee commanded and gave her a small shove toward the doorway.

"There you are," Reed greeted her, then took one look at Blair's flushed face and began to smile. "I guess Lee's here, too."

"Yes," she said, and her voice cracked. "He'll . . . a, be out in a minute. Could I offer you some refreshment?" She stopped as she remembered that the only thing they had was champagne.

Reed's eyes sparkled. "Come outside. I have something I want to show you."

With a glance over her shoulder, she saw that Lee wasn't ready yet, so she followed Reed outside. Standing in front of the clinic was a pretty little carriage, black exterior, black leather seats, a black box in the back to hold supplies. Blair touched the brass rail that held up the canopy. "It's lovely." She thought it was odd that Reed would buy such a carriage for himself, as it had a decidedly feminine air about it.

"Look at the front of it," Reed said, his ugly little bulldog face still beaming at her.

She looked up to see Leander coming out of the door, and he seemed to be as puzzled by the carriage as she was.

Blair bent over to see that there was a brass nameplate just under the single seat. Dr. Blair Chandler Westfield, it read.

It took Blair a moment to understand. "For me? The carriage is for me?"

"I can't have my new daughter running about the streets of Chandler on foot, and I know this son of mine won't let that old buggy of his out of his sight, so I thought you'd better have one of your own. Do you like it?"

Blair stood back for a moment and looked at the buggy. It seemed that this was what she needed to finish establishing that she was really a doctor. "Yes," she cried. "Oh, yes!" And the next moment, she ran to hug Reed and kiss his cheek, and before he could get embarrassed, she was climbing into the carriage and looking at every nook and cranny. She opened the box in the back. "It's not nearly as big as yours, Lee. Maybe we can have it enlarged. I'm sure that I'll need to carry lots of things."

"Such as rifles, maybe? Look, if you think I'm going to allow you to run around the country all alone in your new carriage, you're deeply mistaken. Dad, I wish you'd asked me about this. Giving her freedom is like letting a self-destructive tornado loose. She'll run off on one case after another and end up getting herself killed."

"And I guess you're so much better," she said, looking down at him from the seat. "You walk into range wars. At least, I went into the thing not knowing what it was."

"That's worse," Lee said. "All someone has to say is that

he needs help, and you're off. You have no sense of taking care of yourself. Look at what happened with the gang that kidnapped you. You jumped on the horse with the man and didn't even ask where he was taking you."

"Wait a minute," Reed said, and there was laughter in his voice. "I guess I didn't think of any of that. Maybe I learned with you, Lee, that I couldn't stop you from doing whatever you wanted to do. Maybe Blair's like you."

"She has no sense about what's safe for her to do," Lee said sullenly.

"And you do?" Reed's eyes bored into his son's.

Blair watched them, and she was further convinced that Lee was doing something dangerous, but she was sure that it was something that would eventually help other people.

Reed glanced at the brown horse that was hitched to the buggy. "I've sent for an appaloosa like Lee's, but the horse hasn't come yet. I thought you'd want to be recognized like Lee is."

"They're going to recognize her because *I* will be beside her," Lee said with determination.

Blair didn't answer that, but merely gave him a little smile with lifted eyebrows that made her think he was going to jump into the seat with her—and she didn't like to think what he was going to do to her.

Reed let out a loud laugh and hit his son roughly on the shoulder. "I hope she leads you a chase as hard as the one you led your mother and me. Maybe you'll understand some of what we went through." He put his hand up to help Blair down. "Did I ever tell you about the time Lee exchanged the rat poison in the attic for bread crumbs? We had every rat in my wife's hometown in our house before we found out what was going on."

"No, you didn't," she said, looking up at Lee's back as they entered the clinic. "And I certainly would like to hear more."

Chapter 28

Blair and Leander had been married only a couple of weeks when the Westfield Clinic was officially opened. Of course, she hadn't finished her internship, but both she and Lee knew it was only a formality. Blair'd had years of practice in hospitals.

The day the clinic opened, Blair was so nervous she spilled her coffee and dropped her corn muffin on the dining room floor. Guiltily, she grabbed the muffin and glanced toward the door to the kitchen.

Lee put his hand over hers. "She doesn't bite, you know."

"Maybe she won't bite you, but I'm not so sure about me." Days ago, the housekeeper-cook Houston'd hired had come to their house and Blair found her to be a formidable woman: a tiny body with stiff steel-gray hair, hard black eyes, and a little slash of a mouth. Mrs. Shainess barely came up to Blair's shoulder, but whenever she entered the room, Blair stiffened. The little woman made Blair feel clumsy and unsure of herself. The first day she'd arrived, she'd gone through Blair's small wardrobe, saying tersely that she was looking for garments that needed repairing or cleaning. She'd sighed as she'd handled Blair's few pieces of clothing, and for hours later, the house smelled of chemicals as the woman cleaned those clothes.

That night, when Blair and Lee returned from the hospital, Mrs. Shainess drew him aside for a private discussion. Afterward, with a smile, Lee told Blair that Mrs. Shainess did not think she had a wardrobe befitting a lady and that Blair was to see Houston's dressmaker tomorrow.

Blair tried to protest, but Lee would not listen. She was worried enough as it was that Lee was in debt without her adding to his expenses. So, the next day, when she went to the dressmaker's, she planned to order very, very little, but she found that Lee had already called and ordered twice as much as Blair thought she'd ever need. Still, she couldn't help being pleased by the beautiful clothing, and she drove home quickly in her new carriage, planning to thank him in the best way she knew how.

But when she entered the drawing room, Lee was engrossed in a letter he held—and when Blair came into the room, he crumpled it, struck a match to it and burned it in the fireplace.

Blair didn't ask him about the letter because she didn't want to hear him tell her again that she wouldn't understand. All her enthusiasm about the new clothes left her, and she spent the evening trying to come up with rational explanations for Lee's actions: he was helping someone; he needed money; he was a criminal; he was a Pinkerton agent.

At night, they made love slowly and Blair clung to Lee. She was getting to the point that she didn't care *what* he was doing. He could secretly own all the gambling houses on River Street and she wasn't sure it would matter to her.

On the first day that the Westfield Clinic was officially open, Lee was called away to help at the Windlass Mine, where the end of a tunnel had collapsed. Blair wanted to go with him, but he sent her off to the clinic to help the needy patients.

When she opened the door at eight that morning, Lee's nurse, Mrs. Krebbs, and three patients were already waiting. Mrs. Krebbs, as cool as ever, nodded slightly to Blair and went to the surgery to check the supplies and instruments.

"This way," Blair said, guiding her first patient into the examining room.

"Where's the doctor?" the woman asked, clutching her handbag to her bosom, as if someone meant to steal it.

"I am a doctor. Now, if you'll have a seat and tell me what's wrong, I'll—."

"I want a *real* doctor," the woman said, backing against the door.

"I assure you that I am a certified doctor. If you'll just tell me—."

"I ain't stayin' here. I thought this was gonna be a real hospital with real doctors."

Before Blair could say another word, the woman was out of the door and hurrying toward the street. Blair kept her anger under control as she ushered in the next patient.

The second woman flatly said that Blair couldn't possibly know what was wrong with her because her illness wasn't pregnancy. Blair had difficulty understanding this until she realized the woman thought Blair was a midwife. The woman left before Blair could explain. The third woman left after she found out that the handsome Dr. Westfield, who she'd met last summer in Denver, wasn't going to examine her.

For hours after the third patient left, no one came to the clinic, and Blair had visions of the telephone catching fire from all the scorching gossip that was passing across its wires. At four o'clock, a salesman touting a pink liquid made for "female problems" came by. Blair was polite but ushered him out quickly. She went back to straightening towels that were already straight.

"They want a man," Mrs. Krebbs said. "They want a trained doctor like Dr. Leander."

"I *am* a trained doctor," Blair said through her teeth.

Mrs. Krebbs sniffed, put her nose in the air and went into another room.

Blair locked the door at six o'clock and went home.

At home, she didn't tell Lee about her lack of patients. He'd gone to so much trouble and expense to start the clinic that she didn't want to bother him. Besides, he was worried enough as it was.

She filled the tub for him, then prepared to leave as he undressed.

"Don't go. Stay and talk to me."

She felt a little shy at first as he stripped and got into the tub. Somehow, this was more intimate than making love.

Lee leaned back in the tub, a faraway look in his eyes, and began to tell her of what he'd been through that day. He told of pulling two bodies out of the mine rubble, of having to amputate a man's foot while in the pit. She didn't interrupt him and he went on to describe the feeling of being inside the mine: the weight of the surrounding walls, the lack of fresh air, the total darkness, no room to stand, no room to move.

"I don't know how they do it, how they can walk into that day after day. At any moment, a roof may fall on them. Each day, they face a thousand ways to die."

She had his foot out of the water and was washing it. "Houston says that for the men to join together in a union is the only way they'll accomplish anything."

"And how would Houston know that?" Lee snapped.

"She lives here," Blair said, surprised. "She hears things. She said that someone is bringing union activists into the camps, and there's going to be a revolution before long. And—."

Lee snatched the cloth from her. "I hope you don't listen to gossip like that. Nobody—neither the miners nor the owners —wants a war on his hands. I'm sure things can be handled peacefully."

"I hope so. I had no idea you cared so much for the miners."

"If you'd seen what I saw today, you'd care, too."

"I wanted to go with you. Maybe next time . . ."

Lee leaned forward and kissed her forehead. "I don't mean to snap. I wouldn't want you up there and, besides, you have all your many patients in the clinic to heal. I wonder what our pretty little housekeeper has for supper tonight?"

Blair smiled at him. "I hope you don't think I had courage enough to ask. I'll go down in the deepest mine with you and face falling roofs, but deliver me from Mrs. Shainess's kitchen."

"Falling roofs—that reminds me. How are you and Mrs. Krebbs doing?"

Blair groaned, and as Lee dressed, she launched into a soliloquy about Mrs. Krebbs. "She may be an angel in the operating room, but elsewhere she is a witch."

By the time Lee was ready to go downstairs to dinner, he was smiling again and gently arguing about whether Mrs. Krebbs's good qualities outweighed her bad.

That night, they snuggled against each other and fell asleep together.

The second day the clinic was open was worse: no one came. And when Blair got home, Lee received one of his cryptic phone calls and was out the door and didn't return until midnight. He crawled into bed beside her, dirty, exhausted, and she experienced male snoring for the first time. She gently touched his shoulder a couple of times and had no effect on him, so, with one big shove, she pushed him onto his stomach and he quietened.

On the third day, as Blair sat at her too-neat desk, she heard the outside doorbell jangle, and when she went into the waiting room, she saw her childhood friend, Tia Mankin. Tia was suffering from a persistent dry cough.

Blair listened to her complaints, prescribed a mild cough syrup, and was smiling broadly when the next patient arrived, another childhood friend. As the day wore on, and one friend after another came in with a vague complaint, she wasn't sure whether to laugh or cry. She was glad that these young women still considered themselves her friends, but part of her was feeling frustrated at the lack of real patients.

In the late afternoon, Houston drove up to the clinic in her pretty little carriage and told Blair she thought she was expecting, and would Blair please examine her to see if she was? Houston wasn't pregnant, and after the exam, Blair showed her around the clinic. Mrs. Krebbs had already gone home and the twins were alone.

"Blair, I've always admired you so much. You're so brave."

"Me? Brave? I'm not brave in the least."

"But, look at all this. It's happened because you knew what you wanted and then went out and got it. You wanted to be a doctor, and you let nothing stand in your way. I used to have dreams, too, but I was too cowardly to pursue them."

"What dreams? I mean, besides Leander?"

Houston waved her hand. "I think I chose Lee because he was such a respectable dream. Mother and Mr. Gates approved so heartily of him, and in turn I got their approval." She stopped and smiled. "I think there was a part of me that enjoyed all those tricks you played on Lee."

"You knew about them?"

"Most of them. After a while, I began watching for them. I was the one who suggested to Lee that John Lechner was the culprit."

"John was always a bully, and I'm sure he deserved whatever he got from Lee. Houston, I had no idea you thought of yourself as a coward. I so badly wanted to be perfect like you."

"Perfect! No, I was just frightened, afraid of disappointing Mother, of enraging Mr. Gates, of not living up to what the town expected of a Chandler."

"While I seemed to make everyone angry without even trying. You have so many friends, so many people love you."

"Of course they do," Houston said with some anger in her voice. "They'd 'love' you, too, if you did as much for people as I do. Someone will say, 'Let's have a social,' then someone else will say, 'We'll get Blair-Houston to do all the work.' I was too cowardly to ever say no. I have organized socials that I didn't even attend. How I dreamed of telling them no. I used to imagine packing a bag and climbing down the tree outside your bedroom and just running away. But I was much too cowardly. You said I had a useless life and it has been."

"I was jealous," Blair whispered.

"Jealous? Of what? Surely not of me."

"I didn't realize I was until Lee made me see it. I've won awards, scored high on tests, had many honors, but I know I've always been lonely. It hurt when Mr. Gates said he didn't want me, but he did want you. It hurt when you wrote me of all the men you danced with one evening after another. I'd be studying a chapter on the correct way to amputate a leg, and I'd stop and reread one of your letters. Men have never liked me as they have you, and sometimes I thought I'd give up

251

medicine if I could be a normal woman, one who smelled of perfume and not carbolic."

"And how many times I've wished I could do something important besides choose the colors of my next dress," Houston sighed. "Men only liked me because they thought I was, as Leander once said, pliable. They liked the idea of a woman they could browbeat. To most of the men, I was a human dog, someone to fetch their slippers for them. They wanted to marry me because they knew what they were getting: no surprises from Houston Chandler."

"Do you think that's why Lee asked you to marry him?"

"Sometimes, I'm not sure he *did* ask me. We saw each other a few times after he returned, and I guess I so expected to marry him that, when the word marriage came up, I said yes. The next morning, Mr. Gates asked if it was time yet for the announcement in the paper. I nodded, and the next thing I knew the house was full of people wishing me a lifetime of happiness."

"I know about the citizens of Chandler and their curiosity. But you loved Lee all those years."

"I guess so, but the truth is, we never seemed to have much to say to each other. You and Lee talked more than he and I did."

Blair was quiet for a long while. It seemed ironic that all these years she'd envied her sister, and at the same time her sister was envying her.

"Houston, you said you used to have dreams that you were afraid to pursue. What were they?"

"Nothing much. Nothing like you and medicine. But I did think I might be able to write—not a novel or anything grand, but I thought I'd like to write articles for ladies' magazines. Maybe about how to clean silk charmeuse or how to make a really good facial mud."

"But Mr. Gates would hate that, wouldn't he?"

"He said those women who wrote were probably adulteresses who'd been thrown out by their husbands and had to support themselves."

Blair's eyes widened. "He doesn't mince words, does he?"

"No, and I let him bully me for years."

Blair ran her finger along a cabinet top. "And your husband doesn't bully you? I know you said you loved him, but now it's . . . I mean, it's after the ceremony and you've lived with him." No matter how many times Houston said she loved the man, Blair would never be able to believe her. Yesterday, she'd seen Taggert in front of the Chandler National Bank. The bank president, half Taggert's size, was looking up at the big man and talking as fast as he could. Taggert had just seemed bored as he looked over the man's head at some place down the street, then he'd taken out a big gold pocket watch, looked at it, then down at the little bank officer. "No," Blair'd heard him say before he walked away. He was impervious to the man's entreaties to stay and listen.

And that's how Blair thought of him: impervious. How could Houston love a man like him?

When Blair looked up, Houston was smiling. "I love him more every day. What about you and Lee? At the wedding, you said you didn't believe he loved you."

Blair thought of this morning, of their exuberant coupling that had tumbled them out of bed, and of later when Mrs. Shainess had nearly slammed breakfast on the table. When the woman's back was turned, Lee had rolled his eyes in such a way that Blair had started giggling. "Lee's all right," she said at last and made Houston laugh.

Houston began to pull on her gloves. "I'm glad everything worked out as it did. I'd better go. Kane and the rest of my family will be needing me." She paused a moment. "What a lovely word. I may not have a medical degree, but I am *needed.*"

"*I* need you," Blair said. "Was it you or Mother who organized all my 'patients'?"

Houston's eyes widened. "I have no idea what you mean. I merely came here because I was hoping I was expecting. I plan to come back at least once a month, or any other time I'm not feeling well."

"I think you should visit your husband more often, not me, if you want a baby."

"Like I hear you're exhausting Lee every night and morning?"

"I what?" Blair began, then remembered her telephone boast. Of course it was all over town.

"By the way, how is Mrs. Shainess working out?"

"Dreadful. She doesn't approve of me."

"That's nonsense. She's bragging to everyone about her lady-doctor." She kissed Blair's cheek. "I must go. I'll call you tomorrow."

Chapter 29

The next morning, early, Blair looked up from her desk to see Nina Westfield, now Hunter, standing before her.

"Hello," Nina said softly, her eyes half pleading. "Wait," she said, when Blair started to rise. "Before you say anything, let me do some explaining. I just got off the train and came directly here. I haven't seen Dad or Lee, but if you say you can't bear the sight of me, I'll leave on the next train and you'll never have to see me again."

"And miss thanking you every day for the rest of my life?" Blair asked, eyes sparkling.

"Thanking . . . ?" Nina said, then realized what Blair meant and, the next minute, she was pulling her sister-in-law out of the chair, hugging her and crying on her neck. "Oh, Blair, I've been so worried that I haven't really enjoyed what I've done. Alan kept saying that you loved Lee but just didn't know it. He said you and Lee were much more suited to one another than you and he were. But I wasn't *sure*. To me, Lee's a brother. I couldn't imagine choosing to live with him. I mean—." She pulled away, blowing her nose and sniffling.

Blair was smiling at her. "I'd offer you tea, but we don't have any. How about a cup of cod liver oil?"

That made Nina smile, as she sat down heavily in an oak chair. "I think this may be the happiest moment of my life. I was so afraid you'd be angry, that the whole town would be angry with me."

"But no one in town knew Alan and I were engaged. They thought Lee and I were to be married."

"But you wanted Alan," Nina persisted. "I know you did. I know you went to meet him at the train."

Blair's curiosity was peaked. "I want to hear the whole story."

Nina looked down at her hands. "I really hate to tell you everything." She looked up, tears beginning to form again. "Oh, Blair, I was so unutterably devious and underhanded. I did everything I could to get Alan. You never had a chance."

"If I shoot you, I promise I'll sew the wound myself."

"You can joke, but you won't after you hear about the things I did." She blew her nose again, and, while looking at her hands, she began. "I met Alan the night he decided to kill Lee."

"What? Leander? He was going to *kill* Leander?"

Nina shrugged. "He was just angry, and I understood so well how he felt. Lee has such a highhanded way about him. When I was little, he used to decide what was good for me and what was bad. It used to make me so angry that I wanted to strangle him."

"I know the feeling," Blair said. "He hasn't changed a great deal."

"When I saw Alan, I knew he wasn't going to kill anyone, he was just enjoying the idea. I invited him into the parlor, and it was quite easy to get him to talk and tell me what was going on. He told me he was in love with you, but I knew that Lee'd already made up his mind that you were going to marry him, so I didn't think Alan had much of a chance. I knew Lee'd win."

"How could you possibly know that?"

Nina looked surprised. "I've lived with Lee all my life. He wins. He always wins. If he decides to play baseball, his team will win. If he enters a fencing tournament, he'll win. Dad says he's even forced dying patients to live. So, of course, I knew he'd win in this competition, whether the prize wanted to be won or not. But anyway"—she ignored Blair's look of astonishment—"I knew how Alan felt, and we started commiserating with one another, comparing examples of Lee's domineering ways. Then Dad came home, and I introduced Alan and we sat up late talking about medicine and life in Chandler compared to life in the Northeast. It was a very pleasant evening."

Nina paused a moment. "After that, Alan began to seek me out whenever Lee did something especially devious, like pushing Alan out of the operating room, making Alan look like an incompetent. He's going to be a very good doctor; he just has a lot of training to do yet."

"I think he will, too," Blair said softly. "So you and Alan fell in love."

"*I* did. I think he did, too, but he wasn't aware of it. I don't mean any disrespect, but I think that after Alan saw you here, he was a little afraid of you. He said that in Pennsylvania the two of you had had a very sedate courtship, holding hands in the park, studying together, but when he came here . . ." Nina's eyes brightened. "Really, Blair, jumping on and off horses like a circus performer, blithely pulling a man's intestines out onto a table so you could reach something underneath, beating him at tennis—no wonder he turned to someone else."

"Lee didn't turn away," Blair said defensively.

"Exactly my point! You and Lee are just alike, always tearing from one thing to another. You exhaust us mere mortals. Anyway, I don't think it occurred to Alan that you and he *shouldn't* get married. After he told you to meet him at the train, he came to me and told me what he'd done. By then, I knew I was in love with him and I didn't think you were, but you were too stubborn to admit that you weren't, or maybe all of you were too obsessed with winning your nasty little competition to look at the issues."

Nina took a deep breath. "So I decided to take matters into my own hands. I thought that if my brother could play some devious tricks to get what he wanted, I could, too. At three thirty, before he was to meet the four o'clock train, I asked Alan to come to the kitchen with me. I heated some molasses, not hot, but just so it was warm and runny; then, while he sat there playing with those blasted train tickets, I 'tripped' and spilled about a quart of it all over him. I must admit I did a good job. I managed to get it in his hair and all the way down to his shoes."

Blair couldn't speak for a moment. "But I stayed at the station for hours," she managed to whisper.

"I . . . ah . . ." Nina stood. "Blair, if my mother were alive, I'd never be able to face her again." She looked back at Blair, her pretty face flaming red, squared her shoulders defiantly and said in one breath, "He went to the bathroom, handed his clothes out to me, but I dropped his watch, it rolled inside the bathroom, I ran after it, the door slammed behind me and the outer key fell out."

Blair thought about this a moment, then began to smile. "You locked yourself inside the bathroom with a naked man?"

Nina set her jaw, put her chin in the air and gave a curt nod.

Blair didn't say a word but went to a side cabinet and withdrew a bottle of whiskey and two glasses. She poured an ounce in each glass and handed one to Nina. "To The Sisterhood," she said and downed the whiskey.

Nina, with a big grin, downed hers also. "You really aren't angry? I mean, you don't mind being married to Lee?"

"I think I might be able to stand the torture. Now, sit down and tell me what your plans are and how is Alan? Are you happy with him?"

Once Nina started, she couldn't stop. She didn't like Pennsylvania much and she said she'd almost persuaded Alan to return to Chandler when he finished interning. "I'm afraid his feelings for you and Lee aren't the friendliest, but I have hopes of working on him. I came back to see if I could persuade you to forgive me and to bear Dad and Lee's wrath."

"I don't think Lee—," Blair began, but Nina cut her off.

"Oh, yes, he will. Wait until you've known him as long as I have. He's a lamb when he's pleased, but when one of the women under his care does something he doesn't approve of, then look out! And Blair," she toyed with her parasol, "I need someone to take over the miners' pamphlets."

Blair's senses were immediately alert. "You mean the paper that may incite the miners to riot, to go on strike?"

"It's merely to inform them of their rights, to point out that if the miners united, they could accomplish a great deal. Houston and the others who drive the huckster wagons are taking them to the mines where they deliver vegetables, but that's only four mines. There are thirteen others. We need someone who has access to *all* the mines."

"You know those places are locked up. Even Leander's buggy is checked—. Nina! you can't think of trying to get Lee to deliver the papers?"

"Not on your life! If he even knew I was aware that there were coal mines, he'd lock me away. But I did think that, with you being a doctor and having the Westfield name, you could maybe see some of the women of the camps."

"Me?" Blair gasped, then stood. This bore thinking about. If she were caught with those papers in her carriage, she'd be shot immediately. But then she thought of the poverty of the mine camps, the way the people had to forfeit all American rights in order to earn a living.

"Nina, I don't know," she whispered. "This is a serious decision."

"It's a serious problem. And Blair, you're home again. You aren't just another body in a big city anymore. You're a part of Chandler, Colorado." She stood. "You think about it. I'm going home to see Dad now, and maybe Lee and you can come over later for supper. I have only two weeks before I have to return to Alan. I wouldn't have asked you, but I don't know anyone else who has access to the mines. Just let me know what you decide soon."

"All right, I will," Blair said absently, her mind completely taken with the idea of delivering seditious news into a camp guarded by men with guns.

All afternoon, as she wandered about the empty clinic, and as she tried to read a medical journal Lee had lent her, she considered the possibilities of what she was being asked to do. Nina had hit on something about Blair: she didn't really consider herself a part of Chandler. When she'd left the town, in her mind she'd left for good. She'd never planned to return, but now she had to face it: she was either a part of the community or she wasn't. She could stay in her clean clinic and occasionally patch broken bodies, or she could help prevent bodies from being broken.

And what if her own body were broken?

Her thoughts went round and round, and she never seemed able to reach a conclusion.

She and Lee ate dinner with his father and sister, and when Nina pulled her aside to question her, Blair said she hadn't decided yet. Nina smiled and said she understood—which made Blair feel even worse.

The next morning, Blair's head ached. The empty infirmary echoed with her steps, and Mrs. Krebbs said she had some shopping to do and left. At nine o'clock, the doorbell jangled and Blair hurried to what she hoped was a patient.

A woman and a little girl, about eight, stood there.

"May I help you?"

"You the lady-doctor?"

"I am a doctor. Would you like to come into my office?"

"Sure. Course." She told the girl to sit and wait while she followed Blair.

"What seems to be your problem?"

The woman sat down. "I ain't strong like I used to be, and I find I need help now and then. Not a lot of help, just a little."

"We all need help at times. What kind of help do you need?"

"I might as well come out and say it. Some of my girls, you know, on River Street, have been sold dirty opium. I thought maybe, with you bein' a doctor, you could get us some pure stuff from San Francisco. I figure you doctors got ways to check it to make sure it ain't bad, and maybe you could afford to buy it in large quantities and sell it. I can find you all the buyers you need and—."

"Please leave my office," Blair said quite calmly.

The woman stood. "Well, ain't you Miss High and Mighty? Too good for the likes of us, are you? Did you know the whole town is laughin' at you? You callin' yourself a doctor and just sittin' here in this empty place and won't nobody come to you. And ain't nobody *gonna* come, either."

Blair walked to the door, held it open for her.

With her nose in the air, the woman grabbed the child's

hand and left, slamming the outer door behind her, the bell falling with a thud to the floor.

Without a trace of anger, Blair sat down at her desk and picked up a piece of paper. It was a household account of expenses Mrs. Shainess had given her that morning. Blair was supposed to add the twenty-two figures and check that Mrs. Shainess's total was correct.

She was looking at the paper when suddenly her eyes blurred, and the next thing she knew, she had her head on the desk and she was crying. She cried softly, tears that fought their way up from her stomach, before she lifted her head to search for a handkerchief.

She gasped when she saw Kane Taggert sitting in the chair across from her. "Do you enjoy spying on people?"

"Haven't done it enough to know," he said, looking at her with concern.

She floundered through desk drawers for a moment before snatching the big handkerchief Kane offered.

"It's clean. Houston won't let me out the door without an inspection."

She didn't answer his attempt at levity, but just turned away from him and blew her nose.

He reached across the desk and picked up the paper of accounts. "This what was makin' you cry?" He barely glanced at it. "It's seven cents off," he said, as he put the paper down. "Seven cents make you cry?"

"If you must know, I got my feelings hurt, that's what. Plain, old-fashioned, got my feelings hurt."

"Care to tell me about it?"

"Why? So you can laugh at me, too? I know your kind. You'd never go to a woman doctor, either. You'd be like all the men and most of the women! You'd never trust a woman to cut you open."

His face was serious. "I ain't never been to any doctor, so I don't know who I'd want cuttin' on me. I guess, if I hurt enough, I'd let anybody work on me. Is that why you were cryin'? Cause nobody is here?"

Blair put her hands down on the desk, her anger, and energy, leaving her. "Lee once told me that all doctors were idealistic, at first. I guess I was worse than most. I thought the townspeople'd be thrilled to have a clinic for women. They are—if Leander is here running it. They see me and they start asking for a 'real' doctor. My mother has been here for three ailments in two days, and a few women I've known all my life have come. And, now, to add to my grief, the Chandler Hospital Board has suddenly decided that they really don't have enough work for another doctor."

Kane sat there and watched her for a while. He didn't know much about his sister-in-law, but he did know she usually had the energy of two people, and now she sat there with a long face and eyes with no light in them.

"Yesterday," he began, "I was in the stable without a shirt on—don't tell Houston—and I rubbed up against the back wall and got a lotta splinters in my back. I can't reach 'em to dig 'em out." He watched as she lifted her head. "It ain't much, but it's all I can offer."

Slowly, Blair began to smile. "All right, come into the surgery and I'll have a look."

The splinters weren't very big, or in too deep, but Blair treated them with great care.

As Kane lay on his stomach on the long table, he said, "How'd your doorbell fall off? Somebody mad at you?"

That's all it took for Blair to tell him about the woman wanting opium, how she'd said everyone was laughing at her. "And Lee's worked so hard for this clinic, and it's been his dream for years, and now he's always on one case after another in the mines, and I have charge of this place and I'm failing him."

"Looks to me like the sick people are failin' you. It's their loss."

She smiled at the back of his head. "It's nice to hear you say that, but you wouldn't have come unless . . . Why *did* you come?"

"Houston's rearrangin' my office."

He said it with such fatality that Blair laughed.

"It ain't funny. She puts the silliest little chairs everywhere, and she likes lace. If I get back and my office is painted pink, I'll . . ."

"What will you do?"

He moved his head to look up at her. "Cry."

She smiled at him. "She paints it pink and I'll come over tomorrow and we'll repaint it. How's that for a deal?"

"The best I've had all day."

"All done," she said a minute later and began to clean her instruments, as he put his shirt and coat back on. She turned to look at him. "Thank you," she said. "You've made me feel much better. I know I've been unkind to you in the past, and I apologize."

Kane shrugged his big shoulders. "You and Houston are twin sisters, so you've got to be somethin' alike, and if you're half as good at doctorin' as she is at runnin' things, you must be the best. And I have a feelin' things are gonna change for you. Pretty soon, ladies are gonna be beatin' down your door with all kinds of diseases. You'll see. You just stay here and clean up this place real good, and tomorrow I bet there'll be some patients here."

She couldn't help grinning at him. "Thank you. You've done a world of good for me." On impulse, she stood on tiptoe and kissed his cheek.

He smiled at her. "You know, for a minute there, you looked just like Houston."

Blair laughed. "I think that may be the highest compliment I've ever received. I guess I do have some work to do. If that shoulder bothers you, let me know."

"I'll bring every broken bone to you, Dr. Westfield, and all my pink walls," he said as he left the clinic.

Blair began to whistle as she started clearing her desk of paperwork, and immediately realized that she didn't know whether the account list was seven cents over or under and had to add it herself. The rest of the day, she felt better than she had in days.

Once, she stopped and thought how kind Kane had been in trying to cheer her, after the way she'd treated him. Perhaps there *was* reason for Houston to love him.

At home, in his dark panelled office, Kane turned to his assistant, Edan Nylund. "Last week, after I bought the Chandler National Bank, didn't they send us some papers?"

"About a twenty-pound stack," Edan said, pointing, but not looking up, as Kane took the papers and thumbed through them.

"Where'd Houston go?"

He had Edan's interest now. "To her dressmaker's, I believe."

"Good," Kane said. "Then we've got the rest of the day, maybe the rest of the week." He strode out of the room, papers in hand.

Edan's curiosity got the better of him and he found Kane in the library, using the telephone. Since the system only connected one house in Chandler to another, and Kane's business dealings were usually out of state, Edan'd never seen Kane use the instrument before.

"You heard me," Kane was saying to the person on the other end. "The mortgage on that ranch of yours is due next week, and I have every right to call it in. That's right. You get an interest-free ninety-day extension if your wife shows up at the Westfield Infirmary tomorrow and is treated by Dr. Blair. She's about to have a baby? Good! She drops it in the office in my sister-in-law's lap and I'll give you a hundred and eighty days. Damn right, you can send your daughters. Yeah, all right. Another thirty days per daughter that shows up tomorrow with somethin' wrong with her. But if Blair gets wind of this, I foreclose. You understand me?

"Damn!" he said to Edan, as he put down the receiver. "This is gonna cost me. Look in there and see who else has a loan due or's been turned down for an extension, and then I want you to see how much whoever owns the Chandler Hospital will sell it for. We'll see if their board of directors will refuse to hire the owner's sister-in-law."

By the next morning, Blair's good mood was gone, and she had to nearly drag herself to work. Another long day with little to do, she thought, walking the distance rather than driving her new carriage. But when she was half a block from the clinic, Mrs. Krebbs came running.

"Where have you been? The place is overrun with patients."

For a moment, Blair couldn't move, but then she ran to the door. The waiting room was a mess: children screaming, mothers trying to quiet them, and one woman groaning with what looked to be labor pains.

Fifteen minutes later, Blair was cutting the umbilical cord of a newborn girl.

"180," the mother murmured. "Her name is Mary 180 Stevenson."

Blair didn't have time to ask any questions before the next patient was brought in.

The next afternoon, a woman brought a little boy to the clinic, an undersized eight-year-old who looked six, a boy who'd already spent two years inside a coal mine. He died in Blair's arms, his frail little body having been crushed by coal falling from a train car.

Blair called Nina, said, "I'll do it," and hung up.

Chapter 30

Blair drove her carriage down the road, away from the Inexpressible Mine and back toward Chandler. Nina had lost no time in arranging for her to take the pamphlets to the mine, perhaps because she was afraid Blair would change her mind. So this morning, Blair had called Dr. Weaver, a young man she'd met at the Chandler Infirmary, and asked him to look after the clinic because she'd been called to a mine emergency. The man'd been happy to oblige.

At the Westfield house, Nina'd done her best to hide the pamphlets under a makeshift piece of wood that was to serve as a false bottom in the back compartment of Blair's new carriage. Throughout Nina's instructions, Blair was so scared that she could barely speak.

At the mine entrance, the guards had teased her, saying that Dr. Westfield had certainly changed since his last visit, but they let her in. She had to ask some coal-dust-covered children how to find the house of the woman who was to help her, and she found the woman, lying on the bed faking illness, to be as nervous as she was. The woman hid the pamphlets under a floorboard and Blair left the camp as quickly as she could manage.

The guards, sensing she was nervous and, with the normal vanity of men, thought it was their presence that was making her so, teased her more as she left.

She was a mile from the mine before she began to shake, and within twenty minutes, she was shaking so badly her hands couldn't hold the reins. She pulled off the road to hide among some rocks, stepped down from the buggy, and when her knees gave way, she sat down on the ground and began to cry tears of relief that it was over.

Her shoulders were still shaking when suddenly two strong hands caught her and pulled her upright.

She looked into Leander's eyes blazing with fury.

"Damn you," he said, before he crushed her against him.

Blair didn't ask questions about how he knew what she'd done—she was too grateful that he was there. She clung to him, and even though he was already nearly crushing her ribs, she wanted him to hold her tighter.

"I was so afraid," she said into his shoulder, standing on tiptoe to bury her face in the soft skin of his neck. "I was so frightened." Tears poured down her face, ran into her mouth.

Lee just held her close to him and stroked her hair, never saying a word while she cried.

It took a while before her tears stopped and her body quit shaking. When she had the courage to release her death grip on Lee, she pulled away and began searching her pockets for a handkerchief. Lee handed her his, and after she'd blown her nose and mopped up her face, she glanced up at him. What she saw made her step backward.

"Lee, I . . . ," she began, taking another step back, until she halted against a boulder.

His eyes were on fire. The teasing, smiling, tolerant Lee that she'd always seen was nowhere near this enraged man.

"I don't want to hear a word," he managed to choke out. "Not a word. I want you to swear you'll never do this again."

"But I—."

"Swear it!" he said, advancing on her and catching her forearm in his hand.

"Lee, please, you're hurting me." She wanted to calm him down, to make him see the need of what she'd done. "How did you know? It was secret."

"I'm in the mine camps every day," he said, glaring at her. "I hear what goes on. Damn you, Blair, when I heard you were to deliver those papers, I couldn't believe it at first." He nodded toward the wet handkerchief that was crumpled in her hand. "At least, you did realize the danger you were in. Do you know what those men would have done to you? Do you have any idea? You might have begged them to kill you after they got through. And they have the law on their side."

"I know, Lee," she said with passion. "They have every legal right to do whatever they want to do. And that's why *someone* has to inform the miners of their rights."

"But not *you!*" Lee bellowed into her face.

She blinked from the blast and curved her backbone against the rock. "I have access to the mines. I have a carriage. I am the logical one to do it."

Lee's face turned so red she thought he might explode as he lifted his hands toward her throat, but caught himself and moved away. As he turned his back to her, she saw his upper body rise and fall with his deep breaths. When he turned back, he appeared to have controlled himself somewhat.

"Now, I want you to listen to me and listen very carefully. I know that what you did was for a very good cause, and I know that the miners need to be informed. I even appreciate the fact that you're willing to risk your life to help others, but I cannot allow you to do this. Am I making myself clear?"

"If I don't, who will?"

"What the hell do I care?" he yelled, then took another couple of deep breaths. "Blair, you are the person I care about. To me, you are more important than all the miners in the world. I want you to swear that you'll not do anything like this again."

Blair looked at her hands. She had been more afraid this morning than she'd ever been before in her life. Yet, some part of her felt that today she'd done the most important thing in her life. "Yesterday, a little boy died in my arms," she whispered. "He'd been crushed in—."

Lee grabbed her shoulders. "You don't have to tell me a thing. Do you know how many children have died in *my* arms? How many arms and legs I've cut off men trapped under beams and rocks? You've never been inside a mine. If you had to go inside . . . It's worse than you think it is."

"Then, something has to be done," she said stubbornly.

He dropped his hands, started to speak, but closed his mouth, then tried again. "All right, let me try another tactic. You're not cut out for this. A few minutes ago, you were a mess. You don't have the personality that it takes to do something like this. You're very courageous when it comes to saving lives, but when you're involved in something that could lead to a war and the loss of lives, you fall apart."

"But it needs to be done," she pleaded.

"Yes, maybe it does, but it has to be done by someone other than you. What you feel shows on your face too easily."

"But how will the miners be told? Who else has access to the mines besides you and me?"

"Not *us*," Lee exploded again. *"Me! I* have access to the mines, not you. I don't know why you were allowed past the guards. I don't want you up here. I don't want you going down into the mines. Last year, I was trapped underground for six hours after a timber gave way. I can't allow the possibility of something like that happening to you."

"Allow?" she asked, and found her fear leaving her. "What else aren't you going to 'allow'?"

He arched an eyebrow at her. "You can take what I've said anyway you want, but the end result is the same: you cannot go into the mines again."

"I guess it's all right for you to sneak off to wherever you go in the middle of the night, but I'm to be the docile little wife and stay at home."

"That's absurd. I've never thwarted you in any way before. You wanted a women's clinic, I gave it to you. And now you can stay there."

"And let you go to the mines, is that it? I guess I'm too much of a coward to go into the mines. You think I'd be afraid of the dark?"

Lee didn't say anything for a moment, and when he did speak, his voice was little more than a whisper. "You're not a coward, Blair, I am. You're not afraid to do something that terrifies you, but I'm too terrified of losing you to ever let you do it again. You may not like the way I say it, but in the end it's all the same: you have to stay out of the mine camps."

Blair seemed to feel every emotion she'd ever experienced go through her at once. She was angered at Lee's highhandedness. Just as Nina had said, his forbidding her to do something infuriated her. But she also thought about what he'd said, that she just plain wasn't any good at the job. Houston went into the camps, but even if her wagon were searched, the guards'd only find tea and children's shoes. It wasn't the same as what Blair had carried. And Lee had said he was worried about what damage the pamphlets could cause. She'd read one of the things and it was full of vicious hatred, the kind of angry words that made men act first and consider what they'd done later.

She looked up at Lee as he watched her. "I . . . I didn't mean to scare you so badly," she stuttered. "I—." She didn't say any more, as Lee held out his arms to her and she ran to him.

"Do I have your promise?" he asked, burying his face in her hair.

Blair started to say that she couldn't give it, but then she thought that maybe there was a different way to get the information into the mines, a more subtle way, one that wasn't likely to get anyone shot.

"I promise that I will never again carry unionist papers into a mine camp."

He pulled her head back to look at her. "And what if someone calls me to a mine disaster, and you answer the telephone?"

"Why, Lee, I'll have to—."

His hand tightened on the back of her head. "You know something, I really like this town, and I'd hate to have to move, but it may become imperative to leave and go to, say, some place in east Texas where there aren't any people to speak of. Some place where my wife *can't* get into trouble." He narrowed his eyes. "And I'll ask Mrs. Shainess and Mrs. Krebbs to live with us."

"Cruel and inhuman punishment. All right, I'll stay out of the mines unless you're with me. But if you ever need me—."

He kissed her to silence. "If I ever need you, I want to

know where you are—*always*. Every minute of every day. Understand me?"

"There are many times I don't know where you are. I think that in all fairness—."

He kissed her again. "When I left the hospital, they were unloading two wagons of injured cowboys, a stampede, I believe. I really ought to—."

She pushed away from him. "What are we standing here for? Let's go!"

"That's my girl," Lee said, as he followed her back to her carriage and his horse.

"Open the gate!"

Pamela Fenton Younger sat atop her horse before the gate to the Little Pamela mine, glaring down at the two guards.

Both guards stared up at her. There was something quite intimidating about a six-foot-tall woman atop a seventeen-hand-high black stallion that was prancing so high its ironclad hoofs showed. Even though they were separated from the animal by a heavy wooden gate, the men stepped back when the horse jerked its head and did a half turn.

"Did you hear me? Open the gate."

"Now, wait a minute—," one of the guards began.

The other guard punched him in the ribs. "Sure thing, Miss Fenton," he said, as he pulled aside the gate for her, then jumped back as she went charging through.

"The mine owner's daughter," the guard was explaining behind her.

Pamela rode directly to the entrance of the mine shaft, the horse's hoofs kicking up a cloud of coal dust. "I want to see Rafferty Taggert," she said, holding the horse on a tight rein, its eyes rolling wildly. "Where is he?"

"On shift," someone said. "Tunnel number six."

"Then bring him up. I want to see him."

"Now, see here—," a man said, stepping forward.

Another man, older, pushed his way toward the nervous horse. "Good mornin', Miss Fenton. Taggert's below, but I'm sure that, for you, someone can bring him up."

"Do that," she said, with a hard pull on the reins to further assert her dominance over the big animal. With a curled lip, she looked about the coal camp, at the dirt, the poverty. When she was a child, her father had insisted she accompany him to this place, to show her where their wealth came from. Pam had looked at everything and said, "I think we're poor."

The place still disgusted her. "Saddle a horse for him and have it waiting. I'll meet him by the bend in Fisherman's Creek." She had to wait while the stallion made a full turn before she could look at the mine supervisor. "And if he's docked even a penny, you'll hear about it." With that, she let the horse have its head and tore back through the camp, cinders flying behind her.

She didn't have to wait long for Rafe. The name of Fenton might have evil connotations for some people but those who worked for Fenton Coal and Iron jumped when a Fenton spoke.

Rafe sat on a mangy horse much too small for his big body. His face and clothes were black with coal dust, but the whites of his eyes showed his anger. "Whatever you want takes first place, doesn't it? Princess Fenton gets whatever she demands," he said as he dismounted, looking her squarely in the eyes.

"I don't like that place."

"Nobody does, it's just that some of us have to earn a livin'."

"I didn't come to fight you. I have something important to tell you. Here." She handed him a bar of soap and a wash cloth. "Don't look so surprised. I've seen coal dust before."

With one more glare at her, he took the soap and cloth, knelt by the stream and began to lather his face and hands. "All right, tell me why you want me."

Pam sat down on a flat rock, stretching her long legs toward him. Her tall, hard, black hat made her seem even taller than she was, but the little black veil gave her face a look of mystery and femininity.

"When I was seven years old, my father lost the duplicate key to his private desk drawer. I found it and put it in my treasure box. When I was twelve, I discovered what the key opened."

"And you've been spying ever since."

"I keep myself informed."

He waited, but she said nothing else. When he turned, his face clean, she handed him a towel. "So what have you found out?"

"My father hired Pinkerton men months ago to find out who's bringing unionists into the coal camps."

Rafe took his time drying his forearms. They were muscled from years of wielding a sledgehammer. "So, what have your Pinkertons found?"

"Not *my* Pinkertons, my *father's*." She picked a flower of Queen Anne's lace from beside her and toyed with it. "First of all, they found that four young women of Chandler, all from prominent families, are disguising themselves as old women and bringing illegal goods into the camp. Illegal being anything that my father doesn't make a profit on." She looked up at him. "One of the women is your nephew's new wife."

"Houston? That fragile little . . ." He drifted off. "Does Kane know?"

"I doubt it, but then I'd have no way of knowing, would I?" She watched him intently. When both she and Kane had been quite young, they'd had an affair that they'd thought was their secret love, but in truth had been the hottest gossip of the town. When she'd met Kane's Uncle Rafe, weeks ago at the twins' wedding, he'd seemed to her to have all the characteristics of Kane that she'd liked, but Rafe also had a gentle side that she'd never seen in the younger man. For days after the wedding, she'd hoped he'd call her or send her a note, but he'd made no effort to contact her. The damned Taggert pride! she'd cursed. And it made her wonder why a man like Rafe worked in a coal mine. There had to be a reason why. He wasn't married, wasn't under the burden of a family to support.

"Why do you stay here?" she asked. "Why do you put up with that?" She nodded toward the road that led up to the mine.

Rafe took a rock in his hand and tossed it, looking out over the little stream. "My brothers were here and Sherwin was dying. He had a wife and daughter to feed and wouldn't take help from me or anyone else."

"Taggert pride," she murmured.

"I went to your father and agreed to work if he'd give my salary to Sherwin. Your father likes to have Taggerts grovelling for his money."

She ignored his last remark. "That way, Sherwin kept his pride and you got to help your brother. What did you get out of it besides a permanent cramp in your back from four-foot-tall ceilings?"

He looked up at her. "It's only for a few years—or was. My brother and his daughter have gone to live with Kane and Houston."

"But you stay."

Rafe looked back at the stream and didn't answer.

"The Pinkerton report said there were three suspects who could be bringing the unionists in. One was a man named Jeffery Smith, the second was Dr. Leander Westfield and the last was you."

Rafe didn't look at her or speak, but his hand clutched and unclutched a rock.

"You don't have anything to say?"

"Are the Pinkertons working as miners?"

"I doubt if they wear uniforms," she said sarcastically.

He stood. "If that's all you have to say, I need to get back to work. I guess you don't know which men are the Pinks?"

"Not even my father knows," she said, standing beside him. "Rafe, you can't go on doing this. You don't have to stay here. I can get you a better job if you want—any kind of job."

He gave her a look from narrowed eyes. "Call it Taggert pride," he said, as he started for his borrowed horse.

"Rafe!" she caught his arm. "I didn't mean—." She stopped and dropped her arm. "I wanted to warn you. Maybe you don't like the way I did it, and maybe you don't like my father's name, but I wanted to give you a chance to decide what you want to do. My father can be a ruthless man when he wants something."

He didn't move or speak, and when she looked up at him, he was looking at her in a way that made her heart jump into her throat. Without conscious thought, she stepped forward into his arms.

His kiss was slow and gentle and she felt as if she'd been looking for this man all her life.

"Meet me here tonight," he whispered. "Midnight. Wear something easy to get out of." With that, he mounted his horse and was gone.

Chapter 31

After the horror of the morning, and then seven hours of mending the young men who'd been hurt in the stampede, Blair was exhausted. She was so tired that she didn't even get angry when Lee received one of his calls that made him ride out without telling anyone where he was going.

At dusk, she started the drive home, stopping off at the telegraph office to send her friend, Dr. Louise Bleeker, a message:

NEED YOU STOP HAVE MORE WORK THAN I CAN HANDLE STOP COME IMMEDIATELY STOP PLEASE BLAIR

At home, ignoring Mrs. Shainess's protests, Blair refused to eat any supper and fell onto the bed, fully clothed, at eight o'clock.

She was awakened by the sound of someone struggling with the bedroom door.

"Lee?" she called, and there was no answer. She got up from the bed, went to the door and opened it. Leander stood there with his shirt dirty, torn, bloody. "What's happened?" she asked, instantly alert. "Who's been hurt?"

"I have," Lee said hoarsely and staggered into the room.

Blair felt her stomach fly into her throat and, for a moment, she just stood there and watched as he staggered toward the bed.

"You're going to have to help me," he said, as he started to pull off his shirt. "I don't think it's bad, but it's bleeding a lot." ·

Blair recovered herself in a rush. She took her medical bag from the closet floor, removed scissors and began to cut away Lee's shirt. She propped his arm on her shoulder and looked at the wounds. There were two long bloody furrows close together on his right side, tearing the skin away from his side, in one place exposing the ribs. She'd seen enough bullet wounds to recognize them as such. Since he'd bled a great deal, she didn't think there would be an infection.

Her mouth was dry when she spoke. "It needs cleaning," she said, as she began to remove instruments and disinfectant. Her hands were shaking badly.

"Blair," Lee said, and the only sign he gave that he was in pain was the sound of his ragged breathing. "You're going to have to help me more than this. I think the men who shot at me suspect who I am. I think they may come here to arrest me."

Blair was so intent on his wound that she didn't quite understand what he was saying. It was the first time she'd ever worked on someone she loved—and she hoped she'd never have to do it again. She was beginning to sweat and her hair was plastering itself to her forehead.

Lee put his hand under her chin to make her look at him. "Are you listening to me? I think there will be some men here in a few minutes, and I want them to think that I've been here all night. I don't want them to think that I've been shot at."

"And hit," she managed to rasp out, as she finished cleaning the wounds and began to bandage him. "Who are these men?"

"I . . . I'd rather not say."

She was worried and afraid because he was hurt, but part of her was becoming angry that he'd ask for her help, but not tell her what she was helping him do. "They're Pinkerton men, aren't they?"

At least, she had the satisfaction of seeing the look of total surprise on Lee's face. "You may think I don't know anything, but I know more than you think." She put the last of the bandages around his ribs. "If you move about much, it'll start bleeding again." Without another word, she went to the closet and withdrew the gown and robe that she'd worn on her wedding night, then hurriedly stripped and dressed in it. Lee sat on the bed and watched her, obviously not sure what she was going to do next.

"We'll see how much time we have," she said as she pitched him a clean shirt. "Can you get into that by yourself? I need to hang upside down."

Lee, in too much pain, too shocked at what Blair had already said to him, did not question her, but tried his best to stuff his injured body into the shirt, while Blair hung herself head down across the bed.

They both froze when the pounding on the door downstairs started.

Blair stood. "Take your time. I'll keep them occupied for as long as I can." Quickly, she glanced into the mirror and ruffled her hair in a becoming way. "How do I look?" she asked, as she turned back to him. Her face was flushed from hanging upside down, and her hair was down about her shoulders in a pretty disarray. She looked for all the world like a woman who had just been made love to.

Blair was surprisingly calm when she reached the front door to the house. When she opened it, there were three big, mean-looking men standing there and they rushed past her into the house.

"Where is he?" one of the men demanded.

"I can go with you," Blair said. "I'll just get my bag."

"We don't want you," said the second man. "We want the doctor."

Blair stood on the second step, so that she was above eye level with the men. "You will get what there is," she said angrily. "I have had about all I can take of this town. Whether you believe it or not, *I* am a doctor just as my husband is, and if you need help, I can give it. Leander is very tired and he needs his rest, and I assure you that I can sew a wound quite as well as he can. Now that that is settled, I'll get my bag." She turned to go up the stairs.

"Wait a minute, lady, we ain't here for no doctorin'. We're here to take your husband to jail."

"Whatever for?" she asked, turning back to them.

"For bein' where he ain't supposed to be, that's what."

Blair took a step down toward them. "And when was this?" she asked softly.

"About an hour ago."

Slowly, with great show, Blair began to tuck her hair into some semblance of order. Most of the time, she wasn't concerned with how she looked, but right now, she wanted to look as seductive as she could. She let the gown fall a little bit off one shoulder, and she began to smile at the men. "Sirs, one hour ago my husband was with me."

"You got any proof of that?" one of the men asked. The other two were looking at her with their mouths slightly open.

"Absolutely none." She smiled graciously. "Of course, I am giving the word of a Chandler in a town named for my father. Perhaps, if you'd like to challenge what I say . . ." She blinked innocently as the men looked up at her.

"I don't think they'd like to do that, dear," said Lee from behind her. His face was flushed and he looked tired—but then, so would a man who'd just made vigorous love to his wife. "I believe I heard you say that I was somewhere else an hour ago." He moved to stand beside Blair and, to the men below, she must have looked as if she were leaning against him, but in truth she was supporting him.

For a few moments, there was silence in the dark little house, and Blair and Lee held their breaths as the men paused, glaring up at them. Finally, the man who was the leader gave a sigh. "You may think you've tricked us, Westfield, but you haven't. We'll get you yet." He looked at Blair. "You wanta keep him alive, you better keep him at home."

Neither Blair nor Lee said a word as the men left the house, slamming the door behind them. Blair ran down the stairs to lock the door, and as she turned back, she saw that Lee was growing paler. She hurried up the stairs and helped him to bed.

Blair didn't sleep anymore that night. After she got Lee to bed, she sat by him, watching his every breath as if he might stop breathing if she weren't there to protect him. Whenever she thought of how close those bullets had come to his heart, she began shaking again, and she clutched his hand harder.

He slept fitfully, a couple of times opening his eyes and smiling at her, then sleeping again.

Blair's emotions ranged from terror that he'd come so close to death, to a realization of how much she loved him, to fury that he was doing something that could possibly get him killed.

When the early morning light filtered into the room, Lee awoke at last and tried to sit up. Blair opened the curtains.

"How do you feel?" she asked.

"Stiff, sore, raw, hungry."

She tried to smile at him, but her lips wouldn't work properly. Every muscle in her body ached from having been held rigid all night. "I'll bring you some breakfast."

She gathered up the bloody rags and Lee's shirt to take downstairs with her. One good thing about a doctor's house was that no one would notice a trash barrel full of blood-soaked rags.

It was too early yet for Mrs. Shainess, so Blair fried half a dozen eggs for the two of them, cut inch-thick slices of bread and filled big mugs full of cool milk. She carried the big tray upstairs, and when she found Lee already out of bed and half dressed, she said nothing but began to set the little table by the window.

Lee painfully sat in the chair and began to eat while Blair sat across from him and moved her food about on her plate.

"All right," Lee said. "Tell me what's on your mind."

Blair took a drink of milk. "I have no idea what you mean."

He took her hand. "Look at you. You're shaking as badly today as you were yesterday."

She jerked her hand away. "I guess you're planning to go to the hospital today."

"I have to show up. I have to pretend that nothing's happened. I can't let people know where I was last night."

"Not *anyone*," she spat at him as her fist came down on the table, and the next moment she was on her feet. "Look at you, you can barely sit up, much less stand in surgery all day. And what about your patients? Can you wield a scalpel accurately? Where were you last night? What is worth risking your life for?"

"I can't tell you that," he said, as he turned back to his eggs. "I would, but I can't."

Tears began to close her throat. "Yesterday, you were furious with me because I'd risked my life. You ordered me to stop risking it, but now the tables are turned, and I'm not allowed the same rights. Same! I'm not even allowed to *know* what I may lose my husband for. I'm just to be a good girl and stay home and wait and, if he comes home bleeding, I'm to patch him. I'm allowed to flirt with Pinkerton men in the middle of the night, but I don't know why. I'm allowed to watch you suffering, but for what I don't know. Tell me, Lee, do you shoot back on these forays? Are you in a kill or be killed situation? Do you murder as many people as you repair?"

Lee kept his head down, eating deliberately and slowly. "Blair, I've told you all I can. You're going to have to trust me."

For a moment, she turned away, trying to control her tears. "That's what a good little wife would do, wouldn't she? Sit at home and wait and ask no questions. Well, I'm not a good little girl! I've always been defiant. I've always been a participator and not an observer. And right now, I want to know what I'm participating in."

"Damn it, Blair," Lee shouted, then closed his eyes against the pain at his side. He looked back at her. "Maybe for once you should be an observer. I've told you what I can. I don't want you involved any more than you are."

"So, I'm to stay innocent, is that right? At your trial, I can honestly say that I know nothing, that even when my husband came home with two bullet wounds, I remained innocent."

"Something to that effect," Lee mumbled, then put down his fork and looked at her. "You say you love me, maybe that you've loved me for years; well, now's the test. If you do love me, you'll have to trust me. For once in your life, you're going to have to put aside your defiance and your participation. I need you now, not as a colleague or an equal, but as a wife."

Blair stood looking at him for a long time. "I think you're right, Lee," she said softly. "I think that maybe until now I never realized what a wife was supposed to be." Her voice lowered. "But I'm going to try to learn. I will trust you, and I won't ask you again where you went. But if you want to tell me, I'll be here to listen."

Much of the pain began to leave Lee's face as he leaned his left hand on the table and raised himself. Blair went to help him.

"Lee," she said. "Why don't you go to the clinic today? You won't have any surgery to do, Mrs. Krebbs will be there to help you, and it will be easier. Besides, a Pinkerton man will look conspicuous amid all the women."

"That's a good idea," he said, kissing her forehead. "That's the kind of talk I like."

"Just trying to be a good wife. Here, let me help you dress."

"What about you? Shouldn't you be getting dressed?"

"To tell you the truth, I think I'm a little tired today. After the dreadful experience of yesterday morning, and then last night, not to mention today, I think I'd like to stay home and pamper myself."

"Why, yes, of course," Lee said. She made sense, but he'd never heard Blair say such a thing before. "You stay home and rest. I'll take care of the clinic."

She smiled up at him through her lashes. "You are the kindest of husbands."

Five minutes after Lee left the house, Blair was on the telephone to her sister. "Houston, where can I buy a twenty-pound box of bath salts? And where can I get a manicurist and an hourly supply of chocolates, and where can I buy silk yarns? Don't laugh at me. I'm going to become the epitome of the perfect wife by this evening. I'm going to give my dear husband what he *thinks* he wants. Now, are you going to giggle all day or answer my questions?"

Chapter 32

When Leander got home at six, he found Blair stretched out on the couch in the parlor, a box of chocolates on the floor beside a litter of magazines. Blair, seemingly unaware of his entry, was sucking on a piece of candy and avidly reading a novel. As he walked toward her, he could see the word "seduction" in the title of the book.

"This is something new," Lee said, smiling down at her.

Blair slowly moved her head to look up at him, a slight smile on her lips. "Hello, dear. Did you have a pleasant day?"

"It wasn't until now," he said, eyes alight as he bent toward her. But Blair turned away just as his mouth came near hers, and his kiss landed on her cheek.

She put the entire piece of chocolate into her mouth, and from the difficulty she was having chewing, it must have been a caramel. "Would you be a dear and go get me some more lemonade while I finish this chapter? And then, you'd better dress for dinner. Mrs. Shainess and I have arranged something special."

He stood, taking the empty glass she handed him. "Since when have you and the housekeeper done things together?"

"She's really a very good woman, if one knows how to talk to her. Now, Leander, please go. I am perishing from thirst, and you wouldn't want to keep a lady waiting, would you?"

With a puzzled look, he backed away. "Sure, I'll be right back."

When he had gone, Blair finished chewing her candy, smiling to herself as she continued reading her book. She hoped the heroine would break a chair over the "sardonic" hero's head and tell him to go drown himself.

"Why, Lee," she said when he reappeared with her lemonade, "you haven't changed for dinner yet."

"I've been too busy fetching lemonade for you so you won't perish," he snapped.

Instantly, Blair's eyes filled with tears, and she applied a lace-edged handkerchief to the corners. "I'm so sorry I imposed on you, Leander. I just thought that since you were up and I . . . Oh, Lee, I've been working so hard today and—."

Lee winced as he knelt beside her, taking her hand in his as he pushed three magazines aside to get to her. "I'm sorry I was cross. But it's nothing to cry about."

Blair sniffed delicately. "I don't know what's wrong with me lately. Everything seems to upset me."

Lee kissed her hand, stroked it. "It's probably nothing. All women get this way sometimes."

He had his head down and didn't see Blair's eyes flash fire. "You're probably right. I'm sure it's just female problems, the vapors or something."

"Probably," he said, smiling, as he stroked her forehead. "You just rest while I change. A nice dinner will make you feel better."

"You're so wise," Blair murmured. "I have the very wisest of husbands."

He stood, smiling down at her, then, with a wink, he left the room.

When Blair heard him go up the stairs, she jumped off the couch and stood with her back to the fireplace, her hands on her hips and glared toward the direction of their bedroom.

"Of all the vain, imperious—," she said aloud. " 'All

women get that way sometimes'! He's worse than I thought."
Her anger made her begin to pace. "I'm going to give you
'women problems,' Leander," she said. "You wait and see if I
don't. I'm going to be more of what you think a woman is
than you ever dreamed."

By the time Lee had bathed and dressed for dinner, Blair
had managed to calm herself so that she could smile at him
again. He was very solicitous, holding her chair for her,
carving the meat and serving her. Blair was quiet and calm,
not saying much, but smiling demurely as she cut her meat
into tiny little pieces.

"Something interesting came into the clinic today," Lee
was saying. "The woman thinks she's pregnant, but I think
it's a cyst. I'd like you to look at her tomorrow."

"Oh, Lee, I can't. Houston made me another appointment
with her dressmaker, and then Nina and I have a luncheon
engagement, and in the afternoon I need to be back here to
supervise the house. I really have no time at all."

"Oh, well, I guess it can wait until later in the week. So,
you won't be at the Women's Infirmary again tomorrow?"

"I don't see how I can be." She looked up at him through
her lashes. "It takes more time than I thought being a wife.
There seem to be so many things that need to be done. And
now that I'm going to be a part of Chandler again, I really do
think I should help with the charity work. There's the Ladies
Aid Society and the Christian Mission and—."

"The Westfield Infirmary," he added. "It seems that what
you're doing there is more than enough to help the town."

"Well, of course," she said stiffly, "if you insist, I'll go to
the clinic tomorrow. I'll cancel the dressmaker, and I'm sure
the other wives can get along without me. They'll have to
understand that you want me to work outside the home. I'm
sure I can make them understand the concept of a woman
having to help pay for the food on the table."

"Pay for—!" Lee gasped. "Since when have I made you
pay for anything in this house? When did I ever fail in my
duties of supporting you? You don't have to work tomorrow
or ever. I thought you *wanted* to work!"

Blair looked close to tears again. "I did; I do. But I had no

285

idea being a wife took so much time. Today, I had to plan meals, that new maid was utterly impossible, and when the ribbons for my new dress arrived, they were the wrong color! I just want to look nice for you, Lee. I want to make a nice home for you and be the best, the prettiest wife any man ever had. I want you to be proud of me, and it's so difficult when I'm at the infirmary all day. I didn't know—."

"All right," Lee interrupted, throwing his napkin on the table. "I didn't mean to yell at you. I just misunderstood what you meant. You don't have to go to the infirmary tomorrow or ever." He caught her hand and began caressing her fingertips.

She pulled away from him and began folding her napkin. "This morning, John Silverman called and asked me to tell you that there was an important meeting tonight at your club. He didn't explain, and I didn't ask what it was about."

"I know what it's about, and they can do without me. I really did have a couple of patients I wanted to talk to you about. There's a man at the hospital who has an infected hand. I thought you might look at him. I'd value another opinion."

"Mine?" Blair fluttered her lashes. "You flatter me, Lee. I haven't even finished my medical training yet. What could I tell you that you, with all your experience, don't already know?"

"But in the past—."

"In the past, I wasn't someone's *wife*. I didn't know what my full responsibilities were. Lee, I really think you should go to your club. I'd feel dreadful if I knew I'd kept you away from your friends. Besides, I really would like to finish my novel."

"Oh," Lee said bleakly. "I guess I could go."

"Yes, dear, you should," she said, rising. "I wouldn't ever want it said that I interfered in your life. A wife should support her husband in whatever he does and not hinder him."

Lee pushed his chair back and started to rise. His side

ached, and he wanted to stay home and read the newspaper, but then it was true that he hadn't visited his club since he'd been married. Maybe Blair was right and he should go. He could sit down there as well as at home, and maybe he could find out what they'd heard about the shooting at the mine last night.

"All right," he said. "I'll go, but I won't stay long. Maybe we can talk when I get back."

"One of a wife's duties is to listen to her husband," Blair said, smiling. "Now, you go along, dear, to your club. I have a little sewing to do, then an early night." She kissed his forehead. "I'll see you in the morning." She swept from the room before Lee could say a word.

Upstairs, she watched him from the guest room window. He moved awkwardly, and she knew his side hurt, but she didn't feel much guilt about sending him away alone. He certainly deserved to be taught a lesson.

When the carriage was out of sight, Blair went downstairs and called Nina.

"Let's go riding tomorrow," Blair said, "or I may go crazy from lack of exercise. Do you think your father can get me into the hospital to see a patient tomorrow? In secret? Without anyone knowing I was there?"

Nina was silent a moment. "I'm sure he can, and, Blair, welcome home."

"It's good to be home," she said, smiling. "I'll meet you at nine at the fork of the Tijeras." She heard Nina hang up the phone, then said sharply, "And, Mary Catherine, if one word of this leaks out, I'll know who did it."

"I resent that, Blair-Houston," the telephone operator said. "I do not eaves—." She realized what she was saying and pulled the plug on the line.

Blair went to the kitchen, where she fixed herself a roast beef sandwich. At dinner, she'd had such a ladylike portion that now she was starving.

By the time Lee came home, she was already in bed and pretending to sleep. And when he began to caress her hip and raise her nightgown, she pleaded tiredness, told him she had a splitting headache. As he turned away, Blair had second thoughts about what she was doing. Was she hurting herself more than him?

"It's osteomyelitis," Blair said to Reed, as she carefully put the man's hand down. "Next time you hit someone in the mouth, find someone who brushes his teeth," she told the patient.

"I believe that was Lee's thought, too," Reed said. "But he wanted another opinion."

She closed her medical bag and moved toward the door. "I'm flattered he chose me to ask. But it's agreed that you won't tell him I was here?"

Reed frowned, his ugly face moving into deep round furrows. "I've agreed, but I don't like it."

"As you've agreed to help Lee with whatever he does that brings him home with bullet wounds?"

"Lee was shot?" Reed gasped.

"A few inches to the left and the bullet would have pierced his heart."

"I didn't know. He didn't tell—."

"It seems that he doesn't tell anyone much about himself. Where does he go that makes him come home bloody?"

Reed looked at his daughter-in-law, saw the fire burning in her eyes, and knew he couldn't tell her about Lee's trips into the mines. Not only did he owe respect to his son's wishes, but he didn't trust Blair's save-the-world personality. It was just like her to do something foolish—maybe as foolish as what Lee was doing. "I can't tell you," he said at last.

Blair merely nodded and left the room. Outside, a saddled horse was waiting for her, and she rode hard and fast to reach the south fork of the Tijeras River where she was to meet Nina.

Nina looked up at Blair, then at the horse, both sweaty, both panting. "My brother caused you to run like this?"

Blair dismounted. "He is the most infuriating, close-mouthed, secretive, impossible man alive."

"I agree, but what's he done specifically?"

Blair began to unsaddle her horse to let the poor animal rest. "Did you know that your father calls him, day or night, wherever he is, then Lee disappears for hours and refuses to tell anyone where he's gone? Two days ago, he came home with two bullet wounds in his side and Pinkertons chasing him all the way to the front door. *They* were the ones who shot at him. What is he *doing?*" she yelled, as she dropped the saddle to the ground.

Nina's eyes were wide. "I have no idea. Has this been going on for long?"

"I don't know. I'm considered too stupid to know. I'm just allowed to sew up his wounds, not to question where he got them. Oh, Nina, what am I supposed to do? I can't just stand by and watch him leave and not know if he'll ever come back."

"Pinkertons shot at him? Then what he's doing must be . . ."

"Illegal?" Blair asked. "At least, on the far side of the law. And you know something, part of me doesn't even *care.* All I want is his safety. I'm not sure it'd matter to me if he were robbing banks in his spare time."

"Robbing—?" Nina sat down on a rock. "Blair, I really have no idea what he's doing. Dad and Lee always protected me from any unpleasantness. And Mother and I always protected them from what unpleasantness we saw. Maybe Mother and I were too involved in what we were secretly doing to think that our men had any secrets."

With a sigh, Blair sat down by her sister-in-law. "Lee found out about my taking the pamphlets into the mine."

"I'm glad to see your head's still on your shoulders. First time you'd seen his temper?"

"And the last, I hope. I tried to tell him that I was just as upset by his disappearances as he was by mine, but he wouldn't listen to me."

"He has a head made of marble," Nina said resignedly. "Now, what are we going to do? No one else has access to the mines, and if Lee found out so easily, I'd be afraid to send the pamphlets with Houston or the other wagon drivers."

"Yesterday, I had time to think, and something Houston said gave me an idea. She said she'd always wanted to write for a ladies' magazine. What if we started a magazine and, out of a sense of charity, we gave copies to the ladies of the coal mines? We could submit preview copies to the mining board for approval, and I'm sure they'd let us distribute it, since it'd be full of utterly innocuous articles."

"On the latest hair styles?" Nina asked, eyes beginning to light up.

"Our most militant plea will be to stop the South American slaughter of hummingbirds for feathers on ladies' hats."

"And not one word about organizing a union?"

"Not one word anyone can *see.*"

Nina smiled. "I think I'm going to like your explanation. Oh, Alan, please finish school so we can come home. *How* will we include our information?"

"Code. I read of a code used during the American Revolution. It was a series of numbers and letters that referred to a specific page in a specific book. The numbers referred to letters and, with a little counting, you could figure out the message. I would imagine that every house has a Bible."

Nina stood, her hands clenched in excitement. "We could put a psalm reference in the first page of the magazine and then . . . How do we disguise the numbers? Won't the mining committee be suspicious of a page of numbers in a ladies' magazine? After all, we ladies don't understand mathematics."

Blair gave her a cat-that-swallowed-the-cream smile. "Crochet patterns," she said. "We'll have pages of crochet patterns full of numbers. We'll put in a 'to make the left sleeve' now and then, but the entire thing will be in code, telling the miners what's going on across the country with the unions."

Nina closed her eyes and put her head back for a moment. "It is absolutely brilliant, Blair, and, more important, I think it'll work. You're at the clinic all the time, so I'll go to the library and study this code and—."

"I won't be at the infirmary for a few days," Blair said, unsmiling.

"But the last I heard, you had so many patients, they were waiting on the street."

Blair looked away toward the river. "I did," she said softly, then abruptly stood. "I could strangle your brother sometimes!" she said passionately. "I'm trying to teach him a lesson, but he may be too pigheaded to learn. He thinks he's my father! He gives me presents—a women's infirmary—he gives me orders, he supervises everything I do and, when I dare ask about him, he acts scandalized, as if I were a child asking her father how much money he earns. I know so little about Leander. He doesn't share one single thing about himself with me, but I can't even step out the door without his knowing about it. I don't want another father, I'm perfectly content with the one I had. But how do I teach him I'm not a little girl?"

"I never made any progress," Nina said. "It's a wonder my father doesn't still buy me dolls for my birthday. You said you were trying to teach Lee a lesson. How?"

"I, ah . . ." Blair looked away. "He keeps telling me he wants a lady, so I've been trying to be one."

Nina thought for a moment. "You mean as in bubble baths and being helpless and crying over broken dishes?"

Blair turned back with a grin. "And spending too much and eating chocolates and having headaches at night."

Nina began to laugh. "I warn you that it may take Lee ten years to realize he's being taught a lesson. You ought to exaggerate what you do. Too bad you can't faint at the sight of a hangnail."

Blair sighed. "So far, except for the headache, he's liked what I've done. He doesn't mind if I just stay home all day and give directions to Mrs. Shainess."

"But you're going crazy, right?"

"Not anymore." Blair smiled. "This afternoon, I'll start working out a code for the unionist material. At least, that'll give me something to do. If I continue staying home, my mother might start sending me baskets of berries to can."

"I have a damson plum recipe that—."

"Will make your mouth cry with joy," Blair finished. "I've heard of it," she said, as she put the saddle back on the horse. "I'm not yet reduced to collecting recipes, but if I look at another fabric swatch, I may actually faint. I'll call you tomorrow and tell you how I'm doing on our crochet patterns. I'd like to get them done before we start on the rest of the magazine, and before we let anyone know of our plans. We'll print them and show the others what we're talking about. When do you have to return to Philadelphia?"

"Another ten days. It's going to seem like an eternity before Alan finishes school."

"I want you to meet my aunt and uncle in Pennsylvania. I'll give you their address and write them about you. And I have a few friends there. You won't be entirely alone."

"Thank you. Maybe they'll help make the time pass faster. Good luck with Lee," she called, as Blair mounted and rode away.

Chapter 33

After four days of being the perfect lady, Blair didn't know whether she was going to be able to stand the strain. Concerning herself with little more than the mundane duties of running a household was making her tired and cross. And the worst part of it was trying to teach a man a lesson when he didn't even know he was in school. He'd had four days of seeing his wife as a semi-invalid, no sex, and all Blair had heard from him was a mumbled, "Guess the honeymoon's over."

During the day, she worked on the code until she was nearly blind, counting words and making notes and translating Nina's pamphlet into a bizarre combination of words and numbers.

By the morning of the fifth day, she was sure that she couldn't last much longer. She left the house with the intention of going shopping and purchasing something frivolous that she could show Lee but, instead, she ended up in Mr. Pendergast's bookstore looking for anything she could find about medicine.

She wasn't even aware of anyone near her until the man spoke.

"He's to deliver the goods on Thursday night."

Blair looked up to see the man Lee had called LeGault standing near her. She had to control a shudder that threatened to shake her. If the man were lying on a cot, bleeding, she wouldn't mind touching him, but, alive and well, she couldn't bear to stand even this close to him. With a slight, cool nod to him, she moved away.

She was looking over a copy of *She* by H. Rider Haggard when her head came up. What had he said to her?

She looked around the store until she saw him about to leave. "Sir," she called, and was aware of the curious looks she received from the store owner and the two women customers in the back. "I found the book you said you were looking for."

LeGault smiled at her. "Thank you so much," he said loudly before moving toward her.

Blair knew that now she had to think as fast as she'd ever thought in her life. She didn't want this man to know that she knew nothing about what he was referring to. And, at the same time, she wanted to find out all that she could.

"He's to deliver them the same place as last time?" she asked.

"Exactly." He was examining the book as if fascinated by it. "There'll be no problems, will there?"

"None." She hesitated. "Except that this time, I'll be making the delivery."

LeGault put the book back on the shelf. "It's not what I was looking for after all," he said loudly. "Good day to you, ma'am." He tipped his hat and left the store.

Blair waited for as long as she dared, then left behind him. Since it seemed that anything that one of the Chandler twins did was news, she could almost feel the eyes of the people in the bookstore watching her as she left. Taking her time to pull her gloves on securely, she could see, out of the corner of her eye, LeGault heading east on Second Street toward Parkers' Ladies Wear. Blair went north, behind the Denver Hotel, across Lead, behind the Raskin Building and came out again on Second—away from the prying eyes of the customers of Mr. Pendergast's bookstore.

LeGault was sauntering down the street, cane over his arm, looking for all the world like a man window-shopping without a care in the world. Blair crossed the street and went to look in the window of the Parker store.

She didn't feel that she had time for small talk with the man. "I know all about everything."

"I thought you did, or I wouldn't have mentioned it to you in the first place." He was looking straight ahead into the window. "But it's not a place for a woman."

"I don't imagine it's a place for a man, either."

He looked at her. "Imagine? I thought you knew."

"I do. I also know that this is the last time my husband will be doing this. He hasn't recovered from his wounds last time, and so I must take his place. After that, you'll have to do what you must by yourself. Neither of us will be involved again."

He seemed to be thinking about her words. "All right then. Thursday night at ten. Meet us at the usual place."

He started to turn away.

"Where should I leave my carriage? I don't want it recognized."

He turned back. "I'm beginning to doubt the wisdom of this. Are you sure you can handle this? That you know what's involved?"

Blair thought it was better to keep her mouth shut, so she just nodded.

"We'll need your carriage, so park it behind the Aztec Saloon on Bell Lane. Wait there, and someone will meet you and give you the trunk. Don't fail me. If you don't show up, it'll be your husband that catches it."

"I understand," she whispered.

For the two days until Thursday, Blair was utterly stupid. She couldn't seem to remember anything, do whatever she was supposed to do, or think of anything besides what she was to do on Thursday night. On that night, she would find out what it was that her husband was doing in secret. She'd told Nina that she didn't care if he were a criminal or not, that she loved him just the same. But soon the moment of truth would come. She was sure that Lee was involved in something illegal, and now she was going to participate in order to keep Lee out of it. She was hoping that what she did would make him stop whatever he was doing.

On Thursday night, she dressed in her medical uniform. Lee was called to the hospital to sew up three gunslingers who had shot it out near the New Mexico border, so Blair was alone. She was frightened and nervous as she went down the stairs to the stable where her carriage awaited her.

Only once before had she been to the part of town where she was to wait for LeGault, and that was the night she'd been with Lee when he ran to save the prostitute who'd tried to commit suicide. Ignoring catcalls at the sight of a woman alone in this area, she pulled in behind the Aztec Saloon and waited.

Kane Taggert woke slowly, feeling that something was wrong but not knowing what it was. The bed was vibrating and he was cold. Startled, he turned to Houston. She was shivering violently, and although she was huddled under covers, she was very cold to touch. He gathered her in his arms and, to his consternation, she still seemed to be sleeping.

"Houston, honey," he said with gentleness but some urgency. "Wake up."

The moment Houston woke, she began to shiver even more as Kane held her.

"My sister is in danger. My sister is in danger," she repeated. "My sister—."

"All right," Kane said, getting out of bed. "You just stay here, I'll call her house and see what's goin' on."

Kane took the stairs down two at a time and ran into the library. There was no answer to the ringing at the Westfield house. The operator said she thought Leander'd been called to the hospital, that there'd been a shooting in the country and he was needed. Kane put a call through to the hospital. The nurse who answered was reluctant to summon Leander to the telephone.

"I don't care what he's doin', it ain't as important as this. Tell him his wife's life is in danger."

Leander was on the phone in under a minute. "Where's Blair?"

"I don't know. Houston's upstairs shiverin' so bad she's about to break the bed and she's colder'n a corpse. She keeps sayin' Blair's in danger. I don't know nothin' else, but I thought you should know. She wasn't like this when Blair was taken by that Frenchwoman, so maybe she's really in danger this time."

"I'll find out," Lee said and put down the receiver to break the connection, then picked it up again. "Mary Catherine," he said to the operator, "I want you to find my wife. Call whomever you have to, but find her as soon as possible. And don't let anyone know you're looking for her."

"I'm not sure I should after what she said to me last week. She accused me of *eavesdropping*."

"You find her, Mary Catherine, and I'll see that she delivers all your children for free—and your sister's. And I'll remove those warts off your right hand."

"Give me an hour," the operator said and pulled the plug.

Lee was sure it was the longest hour of his life. He went back to surgery and was glad to see that Mrs. Krebbs had sewn the wounded gunslinger back together. She had a few things to say to him about leaving the operating room, but he didn't listen. All he could think of was that he was going to kill Blair when he got his hands around her neck. No wonder she'd been so docile lately: she'd probably been planning something that was putting her life in danger.

He went back to the big entry hall of the hospital where the telephone was and smoked one cigar after another, until some of the nurses began to complain about the smoke. He growled so fiercely at the lot of them that they retreated timidly. He paced by the telephone, and when a proud new father started to pick it up, Lee threatened his life and his descendants if he so much as touched the thing. Every two or three minutes, he picked up the receiver to ask Mary Catherine what she'd heard. After the fifth such questioning, she told him she couldn't find out anything if he kept taking her time.

He managed to stay off the phone for an entire five minutes

297

before he reached for it again. It rang as his hand touched it. "Where is she?" he demanded.

"We should have been able to guess. Someone—and I am not at liberty to say who for fear this person's reputation would be damaged forever—said they saw her down past the railroad tracks, pulling in behind the Aztec Saloon. Not that I know where that is, because I've certainly never been there, and Blair shouldn't have been there—."

"Mary Catherine, I love you," Lee said as he dropped the telephone on the nurse's desk and ran out the door.

His appaloosa was trained to move quickly, and the town was used to getting out of the way for Lee's carriage, but tonight, Lee outdid himself as he tore through the streets and across the Tijeras bridge to the part of town that Blair should not have been in. He kept thinking that maybe someone had come to his house wanting help, and Blair'd stupidly gone with the person, but, for some reason, Lee was sure that she was into something more than just a medical case.

At the Aztec Saloon, he left his horse to stand, untied, as it had been trained to do, and went inside. One of the benefits of being a doctor was that he was well known, and that if someone didn't owe him a favor now, they probably would very soon.

"I want to talk to you," Lee said to the big man behind the bar.

Ignoring a customer's request for more beer, the man walked out from behind the bar and nodded to Lee to follow him into a back room.

"Wait a minute!" a cowboy shouted as he was unbuckling his pants. A woman, dirty, bored-looking, lay on a filthy mattress.

"Get out," the bartender ordered. "And you, too, Bess."

Tiredly, the woman got up and started toward the door. "I thought I got lucky this time, and you was comin' to me," she said as she smiled at Lee and ran her fingertips across his jaw before leaving the room.

When they were alone, Lee turned to the bartender. "I heard my wife was waiting behind here tonight. I figure you have to know something about why."

298

The man ran his hand over a three-day growth of beard, then toyed with one of his many chins. "I don't like gettin' mixed up with somethin' like this. LeGault and that woman of his—."

"What's that piece of slime got to do with this?" Lee asked.

"He was the one she was waitin' for."

Lee turned away for a moment. He had hoped that he was wrong and Blair was only repairing somebody, but if she was meeting LeGault . . . "You don't have a choice in this," he said to the fat man. "I don't want to use blackmail or bring the sheriff into this, but I mean to use any method I can to find my wife."

"The sheriff's already in this, and he's after LeGault and that woman. Course they'll look innocent, 'cause that feisty little wife of yours is doin' all their dirty work."

Lee leaned toward the man. "You'd better tell me all of it and fast."

"It's none of my business what they do. I just sell them a little whiskey and mind my own business. All right, don't get so riled up, I'll tell you. LeGault rented a room from me so he could hide a woman in it. I don't know who she was and I only saw her once. Talked funny. A foreigner."

"French?" Lee asked.

"Yeah, maybe. She was a looker, anyway."

"So, LeGault was planning something with Frankie," Lee said thoughtfully. "What else do you know?"

"I happened to overhear them sayin' somethin' about gettin' the goods out of town, and that they was lookin' for somebody nobody would suspect. They talked about this a lot."

Lee turned around and slammed his fist into the wooden wall. The pain did him good. "So they found somebody stupid enough to be suckered in. Where did they go, and what did they want taken out of town?"

"I don't know. I guess you could ask LeGault. He's sittin' in a bar down the street. I told him to get out of here, since I didn't want no ladies in here 'cause they do nothin' but cause trouble."

Lee didn't say a word before he left the room and was soon

on the street again. He slammed into three bars before he found LeGault. He didn't speak to the man but walked straight toward him, grabbed him by the shirt front and hauled him out of the chair.

"You want to come with me peacefully or dripping blood?"

The cards dropped from the gambler's hands and he moved his feet to regain his balance. He gave Lee a quick nod as Lee began to shove him out the back door. No one followed them into the alley, whether because they didn't care, or because they didn't want to anger a doctor, wasn't clear.

Leander was so angry that he could barely speak. "Where is she?"

"It's too late for that now. You should have been here a couple of hours ago."

Lee grabbed the man's shirt front and slammed him against the back wall of the saloon. "I've never killed a man in my life, and I took an oath to save lives, but so help me, LeGault, if you don't answer me right now, I'll break your scrawny little neck."

"By now, she's in the hands of the sheriff, no doubt under arrest for stealing a million dollars' worth of securities."

Lee was so astonished that he released the man and took a step backward. "Where? How?" he managed to whisper.

"I told you I'd get back at you for all those years I spent in jail. She was easy. She thinks she's saving your life, but instead, she's taking stolen goods out of town, and the sheriff has been informed of what she's doing, and by now she's in his custody. I hope you like seeing her in jail."

As Lee raised his hand to strike LeGault, the man began to sneer. "I wouldn't try it if I were you. I have a pistol aimed at your belly. Now, why don't you be a good boy and go visit that pretty wife of yours in her cell? I'm sure it'll be the first of many such visits."

Lee didn't want to waste time on the man, and he didn't think he'd have the courage to shoot him, so he backed out of the alley—he didn't want to give LeGault a clear view of his back.

Lee ran down the street to where his buggy waited and, on second thought, he confiscated a big black gelding that stood tied to the hitching post, vaulted into the saddle and took off southeast out of town. The only place that could have a million dollars' worth of securities was the train station.

He came to a rise and, in the moonlight, he could see a buggy to his right and what could be a posse of men to his left. It looked as if Blair were riding into the men who meant to arrest her—and he was half a mile away.

Chapter 34

Leander kicked the horse, started yelling, fired his pistol, grabbed a rifle from the scabbard on the horse and began firing it, all at the same time. The poor horse, terrified of the strange rider and all the noise and gunpowder, bolted forward, tearing across the moonlit countryside at breakneck speed. Lee wanted to draw attention to himself, to get the posse's mind off his wife.

He succeeded.

When a few "stray" bullets landed a foot away from the lead horse of the posse, all the men halted, trying to control their horses, and giving Lee the precious minutes he needed to reach Blair before they did.

As it was, they all met at the same time. One glance at the sheriff's solemn face and Lee knew that what LeGault had said was true—they'd come to see if one of the Chandlers had indeed been involved in a robbery.

"Damn you!" Lee yelled at Blair as he pulled back on the horse's reins and dismounted, slapping the horse's rump to head it back toward the lights of town. "I can't trust you out of my sight for a minute." He climbed into the buggy, grabbed the reins from her and looked up at the sheriff. "Let a woman have her own carriage, and it's no telling how much trouble she'll get into. And this is the worst. Always doing things for other people, never taking into account her own safety."

The sheriff studied Lee for a long moment, a moment so long that Lee began to sweat.

"Boy, you oughta take care of your wife," the sheriff said solemnly. "Or somebody else might."

"Yes, sir," Lee said. "I'll have her taken care of by morning."

"Six hours, Leander. I'll give you six hours, and then I might be that somebody."

"Yes, sir," Lee said, and felt like crying, he was so grateful. "It won't take me that long, sir." He snapped the reins and moved the buggy off the road, heading it back toward the freight office.

Once they were on the road, Blair spoke for the first time. "So you did come, after all. How did you find out the delivery was tonight?"

Lee didn't look at her. "If you know what's good for you, you'll keep your mouth shut. Your silence may stop me from blistering your rear end and keeping you tied inside the house for the rest of your life."

"Me? Me!" she gasped, holding onto the side of the carriage. "I was just filling in for you. I hoped that if I took over for you once, you'd see the misery you put me through."

"Took over for *me!*" He turned toward her, and his eyes were blazing with rage. "Do you think *I* was stealing securities? That *I* was working with LeGault?"

"What else could you be doing? You don't make any money as a doctor, but you can afford all the medical equipment and the house and the expenses for me, and you come home with bullet wounds and . . ." She stopped as Lee halted the buggy fairly close to the dark freight office.

He jumped down. "Get down and let's see what LeGault planted on you."

As Blair moved, Lee opened the compartment in the back of the buggy and withdrew a small wooden chest and opened it, withdrawing large pieces of floridly engraved paper. He held them up to one of the two carriage lanterns. "Not only

303

were you stealing, but these belong to Taggert and the Chandler National Bank. You could have bankrupted half the town."

Blair took a moment to realize what he was saying, and when it hit her, she sat down on the running board of the carriage. "Oh, Lee, I had no idea. I just thought—."

He grabbed her shoulders and pulled her up. "We don't have time for remorse now. We have to see what LeGault did inside there. Get your bag." He unhooked a lantern from the carriage and began to run, Blair on his heels, her heavy medical bag in her hand.

There was only one entrance into the dark freight office, and as they entered, they saw the big, empty safe standing open, a body before it. Since neither the electric lines nor the telephone lines extended this far out of town, they had to keep the lantern lit.

Lee reached the man first. "It's Ted Hinkel. He's alive, but he's been hit on the head pretty hard."

Blair reached into her bag and withdrew the smelling salts. "If you weren't working with LeGault, where were you?"

Lee gave a big sigh as he took the salts. "I thought I could save you from yourself, but I guess I can't. I didn't tell you what I was doing, because I feared that you'd do some fool thing like this. The truth is, for some time now I've been sneaking unionists into the coal camps."

"Unionists?" she said blankly. "But LeGault—."

"How could you believe I'd have anything to do with a criminal like him? You yourself said that he hated me. I guess he found out about the unionists, figured I'd never tell you what I was doing and used what he knew to make you work for him. If you got the securities out of town, great; if you didn't, even better; he'd have repaid me for sending him to prison."

"But the money . . .," Blair began as she moved the lantern closer to Ted's head. She was unable to comprehend what Lee was saying.

Lee was frowning at the inert young man as he tried to revive him. "How did somebody like me fall for somebody like you? I was raised to believe that how much money a man made was his business and his alone. My mother was from a very rich family, and I'm certainly not one of the richest men in America like Taggert, but I have more than enough. I even *told* you that."

"Yes, but the clinic cost so much."

Lee gritted his teeth and moved Ted upright. "If we ever get out of this, I'll show you my assets. I could afford twenty clinics."

"Oh," Blair said, and handed him carbolic and a cloth to clean the wound on Ted's head. "So I've just stolen . . . How much *have* I stolen?"

"One million dollars."

The bottle of carbolic dropped from her hand, but Lee caught it. "How did you know, and why was the sheriff there, and what was the talk of six hours about?"

"Houston sensed you were in danger and Mary Catherine found out where you'd last been seen. LeGault turned you in to the sheriff, and the sheriff's given me six hours to get the securities back before anyone knows they were stolen. Come on, Ted, wake up!"

Blair put her face in her hands. "Oh, Lee, I've made a mess of everything."

He barely glanced at her, as his concern was with the young man now. "That you have, sweetheart."

"Do you think I'll go to jail?"

"Not if we can get the securities back."

"And how do you plan to do that? Say, 'By the way, Ted, I found this outside'?"

"No, I . . ." His eyes lit. "He's coming to. Give me your underdrawers."

"Lee! Now's not the time—."

"I have some rope, and I'll use your drawers as a sling and lower the chest down the chimney. You have to convince Ted he saved it and the crooks never even got away with it."

Without another word, Blair stood, dropped her drawers, handed them to Lee, then sat and took Ted's head in her lap as Lee went outside.

"Ted! What happened?" she said, holding the salts under his nose.

"The station was robbed," he said, sitting up, his hand to his head. "I have to call Mr.—."

"You have to sit down," she said, helping him to stand, then almost pushing him into a chair. "I have to look at that cut."

"But I have to tell—."

"Here!" Blair put a stinging antiseptic on the cut, and the new pain weakened the young man enough that he leaned back in the chair. "Tell me what happened," she said.

"Two men came in and held a gun to my head. One of them, the little one, knew the combination to the safe."

Out of the corner of her eye, Blair could see something white appearing in the fireplace. "Turn this way toward the light. What happened then?"

"I just stood there while the little one opened the safe and took out a chest. I don't know what was in it. Then, somebody hit me on the head, and the next thing I knew, I woke up and you were here. Blair-Houston, I have to call—."

"That couldn't be *all* of the story. You must have put up a great struggle."

"But I didn't, I—."

"Ted, I want you to lie down on the floor for a minute or ___ ___ried about that cut. You've lost a lot of blood. ___ ___tch out behind that cabinet. I need to ___ my instruments."

Blair ran to the fireplace, grabbed the white drawers and the rope off the chest and stuffed them into her medical case. "I think you'll be all right now, Ted. Why don't you come in here and get your gun, and I'll drive you to the sheriff's?"

Ted, with his hand to his head, walked haltingly around the cabinet, then stood staring in disbelief. "That's it."

"What do you mean?"

"The chest they stole. There it is. How long has it been here?"

"It was here when I came in. Do you mean the robbers didn't take it, after all? Gee, Ted, I know you said you put up a struggle, but you were being modest. Do you mean you prevented them from stealing the chest?"

"I . . . I don't know. I thought—."

"There's the evidence. You *must* have saved it. Ted, you're a hero."

"I'm not so sure. I seem to remember—."

"With a crack like that on your head, you're sure to be fuzzy, but the evidence is right here before us. Why don't we lock it in the safe, and I'll ride to the nearest telephone and get the sheriff out here? And the newspaper. They'll want to hear about *this.*"

"I . . . I guess so." He straightened his shoulders. "Sure, why not?"

Blair put the chest in the safe, locked the door, helped Ted to a chair, then ran outside. Lee grabbed her hand and they ran to the buggy together. It was only a mile to the nearest telephone, and Lee suspected the sheriff had been waiting.

Lee put down the receiver, thanked the bartender for the use and went outside to where Blair waited for him in the buggy.

"Is it really over?" she asked, leaning back.

"The sheriff said LeGault and a very small man—who I suspect is Françoise—got on the train for Denver an hour ago. I don't think we'll see them for a while."

"And all along it was unionists," she murmured. "You know, Lee, I have some ideas about the unions in the coal mines, too. Maybe together we could—."

"Over my dead body!" he said, snapping the reins.

"What am *I* supposed to do? Stay home and darn your socks?"

"You're not bad at darning socks, and I *like* knowing where you are."

"Like you've known for the last couple of weeks?"

"Yeah, I rather like a wife who—."

"Let me tell you, doctor, if you think I'm going to read one more book about a simpering heroine or plan one more dinner, you're out of your mind. Saturday morning, I'm going back to *my* clinic and see to *my* patients."

"Saturday? What about today? Why don't I just drop you off there and you can go right to work?"

"Because I'm spending today in bed with my husband. I have a lot of lost time to make up for."

Lee gave her a quick, startled look, then grinned. "Hijah!" he yelled to the horse. "School's out and Teacher wants to play."

It was Blair's turn to look startled. "You *did* know!"

But Lee only grinned and winked at her.